Praise for *Honor Bound: Book 2*

"…with the same action-packed punch of the first book, this new installment is certain to keep readers turning the pages. …Ryals takes the time to dig into what [the] recovery process must look like… Beyond being likeable, Ryals' cast is also diverse. …a promising series that deserves a powerful conclusion…"

Reader Views Annual Literary Awards

"Gritty, dark; it'll keep you gripped to the very last page."

The Wishing Shelf Book Awards

HONOR

BOUND

Book II

ATHENA RYALS

Fourth Printing, 2025

ISBN 978-1-7346805-1-5

This book is a work of fiction. Any references to historical events, real people, or real places are used fictitiously. Other names, characters, places and events are products of the author's imagination, and any resemblances to actual events or places or persons, living or dead, is entirely coincidental.

Edited by Kylie R. Bean

Cover art by www.ebookorprint.com

Author photo by Lucy Schultz Photography

www.athenaryals.com

I find myself thanking, once again:

Dotty, for being this story's first cheerleader. My friend, I am so glad you are the first person I reached out to at the beginning of this journey. Your gentleness, creativity, and strength are things I am so happy to have in my life.

Bristol, for caring about these characters so much. Your passion for these characters and the world they inhabit inspire me every day.

Sable, for helping me craft this story into what it became. You are in invaluable friend, artist, and brainstorming partner, and I am so glad to know you.

Katie Lewis, for being willing to let me share this story when it was still a secret. I am so incredibly proud of your own achievements, and I'm so grateful for the role you've played in mine.

I now thank:

Katie Faulk, for your kindness, support, and some of the best lines I've ever read in fiction. I admire and love you so much. I love being able to create with you, and I'm grateful for the opportunity to live in your fictional worlds, as well.

Nafio, for your unending support. You have been absolutely irreplaceable with your theories, suggestions, and the best ideas to come out of the story.

Caroline L., for believing in the direction of this story. Getting to talk and explore with you all the possibilities has been so wonderful.

Lucky, for making me absolutely cry with laughter with your reactions to the story. Your art of the characters and your understanding of who they are to each other are things I treasure.

Linnea, for encouraging me to explore the possibilities for where the story could go. You are incorrigible and I am so glad to have had you with me on this.

There are so many others. I cannot express how grateful I am to the people who found this story and helped me make it what it is now.

Chapter 1

Gavin's stomach burned with an almost unbearable anticipation. *I've never had two to play off each other before. And Vera... god, I want to break Vera.* His hand tightened on the collar around Tori's neck and he dragged her higher. She choked and thrashed weakly against his grip, kicking against the carpet in his father's office.

Vera took a lurching step forward. *Christ*, that burning in her eyes, that desperation to protect Tori, to help her... The things Gavin could do with *that*. He imagined how Vera would look when he hurt Tori, *really* hurt her. His mouth watered. Tori writhed against his hold on her collar.

"Ah, ah, ah." His father's voice was low. "No." Vera shuddered. Her muscles locked. "Good girl." Gavin could see her straining forward, towards Tori. "No, you're going to come back and stay with me."

"And I figured, why don't I stay with my dad for a while and bring Tori?" A laugh bubbled out of Gavin's chest. "Let you actually be together, considering how cute you two are. And considering how much we can teach Tori about how to hurt you. She wants to so badly, you know." He'd seen it. That spark of shame in her eyes, the way she shut down when he asked her about it. Tori's struggles were growing weaker.

"Tori..." Vera's voice was hollow, tortured. Gavin let the collar go. Tori slumped to the floor at his feet.

"And you're going to be so good for us," his father crooned softly. He cradled Vera's face. The hopeless terror in her eyes made Gavin's stomach clench. "Because if you don't... I'm going to make you kill Tori."

Gavin's heart sank. *I want to be the one to do it. I want to kill her.* But the abject torment that would rip through Vera's body if he forced her to pull the trigger... If he broke and broke and *broke* her until she did it herself... Gavin's mouth went dry.

His father spoke again. "You were together for a few months, yes? You love her?" Vera's eyes were fixed on Tori as she nodded. "Hm. Then you're going to behave for me, aren't you?" Vera nodded again.

Gavin laughed mirthlessly. He buzzed with pleasure. "Wish I'd known this trick with you before, Vera. Coulda saved myself a lot of overhead. And a lot of hospital bills." He kicked Tori in the back. Tori screamed raggedly through the gag in her mouth.

Vera's body jerked like she'd felt the blow, too. Gavin watched as she spiraled into herself, collapsing, *breaking*, giving herself over to hopelessness. Tears streamed down her face as she looked down at Tori, her chest heaving with sobs. Gavin felt a flutter in his chest at the sight of her.

The pain in Vera's eyes dropped away. *She's under. She's ours.* A grin spread across his face. Vera stepped towards his father and pressed her body against his. She turned her face in to his neck, nuzzling gently. *Is this what he made her? Is this what I could make her again?*

"Hm," his father murmured. "I might not even have to break you in again." Vera looked over his father's shoulder as she brushed her lips against his neck. Her gaze dropped to Tori where she huddled on the ground, wailing into the gag. Vera's expression shifted. Hardened.

She raised her arm and fired a single shot.

Gavin flew back, shock wiping his mind blank before he even felt the impact. The breath rushed out of him. He hung in the air for what seemed like an impossible eternity, falling. He hit the floor. The impact shattered him. The pain rushed in. *I can't breathe.*

"NO!" His father's voice was distant, like he was shouting from another room. Gavin's eyes rolled back. He convulsed against the piercing agony in his chest, heaving and choking against the blood he could already feel bubbling in his lungs.

"BAD GIRL."

He tried to push out a breath, push out a single word. *Help.* This pain wasn't like anything he'd felt before, not even when Isaac had beaten him. This was deeper. More vital.

This was going to kill him.

Gavin's eyes found his father, clutching at Vera's throat, holding her back. He sobbed in terror. He tried to raise a hand to reach out to his father, to beg him to help, to beg him to turn around and hold him and carry him out of that house. His limbs were made of lead, paralyzed by shock and jagged pain. He could only lay there, crumpled on the floor.

Gavin could only watch as Vera lunged at his father, his hand pressed against her throat until the breath whistled out of her. Gavin could only watch in uncomprehending horror as Vera opened her mouth against his father's throat. Could only watch as she sunk her teeth into his flesh and ripped.

His father's scream was inhuman. He sounded like an animal being torn apart. Vera lunged in again, tore at his throat again. Gavin could hear the flesh tear under her teeth. Could hear the wet rip and bubbling sound as his father's trachea was torn open. He could hear the blood pour out onto the carpet. He watched, helpless, as she ripped into him again.

The smell of blood was heavy in the air. Gavin was dizzy with it. Vera was covered in it, great rivulets of blood coursing down her chin and neck, turning the front of her shirt and pants a brilliant, impossible red. *Mine, or his?* She looked like a nightmare. She looked like a monster.

Gavin saw his father, dead on the floor, sprawled only a few feet away from him. His father, the man who had taught him to hurt people, taught him to hurt *her*, was torn open, bleeding, empty. Gavin's throat closed around a tortured sob. His mind twisted around a single, incomprehensible truth. *She killed my father. She tore out his throat with her own teeth.* A shudder coursed through his body as his very being rebelled at the thought.

An agonizing chill settled over his body as he realized something else: *if I move, she's going to kill me, too.*

He trembled on the floor, his breaths coming ragged and harsh. Tears streamed down his face into his hair and onto the carpet. All his thoughts, all the terror in his mind intensified and narrowed down to a single point: *I don't want to die.*

She was speaking. The woman, the *plaything* that had torn out his father's throat, she was talking, her voice pitched high and tense. A wave of sickness passed over him. *Please, please don't kill me, please...* Another voice rose. *Tori.* The one Vera had killed for. Gavin's throat clicked as he swallowed.

Every breath sent an unbearable pain stabbing through his chest. His fingers dug into the carpet. He heard his pulse pounding in his ears. The words swirled through his head, confusing, meaningless. He could only grab one at a time, hold it in place, deduce the meaning, lose it again.

I was wrong about her. He felt like his chest was sinking into the floor. It would drag the rest of him down with it, he was sure. He was *dying.*

His mind drifted, untethered from his body, lost in a sea of unending agony. Every breath, in, out, was pain. Every breath, in, out, was *torture.*

The pain flared and brought him back. He dragged in a desperate inhale. It took all of his strength to lift his head.

He was alone.

He heaved out a sob. His hand moved to his pocket, inch by inch. His fingers closed around his phone. His eyes fell on his father, the grotesque, butchered corpse that had stopped bleeding now.

He cried out as he pulled the phone from his pocket, hands shaking so hard he lost his grip. The phone slid out of his hand and fell to the floor with a dull thud. He sobbed as his fingers closed around it again. He opened the screen. He could barely lift his head.

He left smears of blood on the screen as he went to the recent calls. Scrolled back. Found the number. The screen jerked. He swiped it over and over with his finger and finally, it obeyed. The blood was sticky on his skin. He pressed the call button and his head sank back to the floor. He tried to hold the phone to his ear. It slipped once again from his grip and fell to the carpet beside his face.

It rang once. Twice. Three times. *Please.*

A fourth ring. He whimpered. *Please, please pick up, please...*

A fifth. He sobbed brokenly. *Please, I don't wanna die like this. I don't wanna die...* He glanced at his father, the pool of blood around him creeping away from his body into the surrounding carpet.

A sixth ring. *God no, please, please answer, please don't let me get the answering machine...*

The seventh ring cut off. Relief shot through him like an electric shock.

"Hello, darling." The woman's voice on the other end of the line was warm. Comforting. His heart felt like it would rend itself from his chest.

"Mom," he rasped.

Her tone immediately changed. *"Gavin? What happened? Where are you?"*

He licked his lips, sweat beading on his forehead. "House on 72." He gasped. "Got shot. Please…"

"Oh my god. Oh my god. Gavin. Sweetheart." Her voice grew muffled. *"Patty, get Andrews on the phone. Get the helicopter in the air. 6535 East County Road 72. Gavin's been shot."* Her voice grew louder. *"Honey, where are you shot? Are you…?"* She stifled a small sob. *"Oh my* god.*"*

"In the chest. Once in the chest." Gavin trembled and dissolved into a weak wail. "Mom… I'm scared… *please,* I don't wanna die…"

"I know, sweetheart." Her voice choked. *"We'll get the helicopter to you. It should get there…"* Her voice faded again. *"When?"* It got louder. *"Thirteen minutes, baby. Oh, Gavin… sweetheart…"* Her voice broke. *"Hang on for me, please…"*

"Mom," he sobbed. "Mom." His lips felt numb. His words were clumsy. "She… she killed dad. Dad's dead."

Chapter 2

Gavin choked. Blood bubbled on his lips as he coughed, gasped. He tried to suck more air into his lungs. A dull, heavy weight settled in his chest. *I'm going to die.* His eyes rolled back. *I'm going to die. I'm going to die.* He knew it in his bones.

He rolled onto his side, surprised but relieved to feel his breathing get a little easier. His eyes settled once again on his father and his chest began to heave with sobs.

"Dad..." he whimpered. His father's corpse was splayed on the ground where Vera left it, drained of blood, grotesque and twisted. Gavin rolled himself onto his stomach and tried to drag himself towards his father. As he tried to lift his right arm his chest was shot through with agony. Tears streamed down his face as he pushed himself forward, his left arm shaking under his weight. He shuddered and collapsed to the carpet. He reached out with one hand and brushed his fingers against his father's arm. There was terrible heaviness to it. He gritted his teeth, dragging himself once more, and collapsed on his father's chest. Gavin wailed at the dull, hollow sound.

He convulsed and coughed up blood onto his father's shirt. It mixed in with the red already there until Gavin couldn't tell whose blood was whose. He felt the sticky warmth soaking into his clothes from the ruined carpet. His stomach heaved. His eyes moved slowly from the blood on his father's chest, up his shredded, gaping throat, to his face.

Gavin keened weakly at the dullness of his father's eyes. His face looked vacant, like every person Gavin had killed before. He was a body, empty of everything that had ever made him alive. His father didn't look like he was sleeping. His father looked like he was dead.

Gavin's body rebelled against the thought and he twisted away. He vomited bile streaked with blood. His arms gave out and fell again onto his father's chest.

He could hear his own pulse beating wildly in his ears. He felt like his heart was skipping every other beat, out of control, like it could outrun the shock if it beat fast enough. He pressed his face into his father's shirt, blood staining his cheek. His eyes fluttered shut and he waited to die.

He drifted. He waited for the pain to recede, for his body to get lighter, maybe to start moving towards the light he'd heard so much about. A half-delirious thought floated through his mind. *How many people have I made feel this way?* The thought was gone as soon as he grasped it. He didn't feel lighter, or warmer, or more comfortable. A coldness settled in his bones as darkness clouded his vision. His fingers curled weakly around his father's shirt. *Please, please don't let death feel this way.*

The pounding in his ears grew louder, speeding too fast for him to count. It sounded so far away. He spasmed as agony spiked again. Then, a slower pounding. He heaved out a single, painful laugh. "Come in," he rasped. Someone was knocking on the door of his brain.

Then there were hands on him. The room spun dizzily as someone rolled him onto his back. He felt himself being lifted in someone's arms, his head lolling back against their shoulder, his legs lifted and carried by someone else. He tried to open his eyes. *Am I dead yet?* His tongue felt too big for his mouth. He tried to ask again. *Am I dead yet?*

Light pierced eyes through his closed lids. *There's the light, I guess.* He giggled raggedly. The arms around him tightened.

His breath caught in his chest and he writhed, back arching, mouth gaping as he tried to drag air in. He felt himself being lowered onto something hard, and cold, and the light was gone now. He lurched and felt himself being carried up again. *Death is fucking weird.*

Chapter 3

Fuck.

Gavin's chest was being torn apart with every breath he dragged in. *I could just try not breathing...* The pain burned hotter the longer he forced his ribs to stop moving. He gave up and gasped in a breath, whimpering as it came out. The sheets beneath him were damp with sweat.

His throat felt like it had been scraped raw. He did his best to swallow, the inside of his mouth sticky and dry. *Water.* He realized he had eyes and blinked them open. *I need water. Christ, this hurts.*

Shapes moved in his vision, dark and light and blue... a lot of blue. He squeezed his eyes shut and blinked again. *Where the fuck am I?*

His throat tickled. He coughed, and his chest exploded into agony. A twisted scream punched out of him and he reached for the pain, trying to press on it, push it away, make it *stop. Why, why, why does it hurt so much...?*

He felt a hand on his wrist, cool and strong, pulling it away from his chest. "P-pl..." He croaked. Tears pricked in his eyes, making the shapes so much blurrier before they ran down his cheeks and into the pillow. He could see someone sitting to his left, leaning over him, touching him. He choked on a sob.

"Can you get him something more for the pain? Please..." His mind swirled with confusion. He knew that voice, more familiar than almost any other, scared and strained with tears. The pain gripped him and he cried out.

"Yes, ma'am."

"You're alright, sweetheart. It's o— okay..." He remembered that voice, and memories with it, of being held and cradled when he was good, of that same soft hand wiping away his tears and smoothing his hair when he'd done something well.

"Mom..." he groaned.

"Oh, sweetheart, oh my… my *god*..." A hand touched his cheek. He turned his face into it, whimpering softly. "You're alright, honey, you're safe. My baby…"

Another memory shot through him like a second bullet, thick with the smell of blood and death and fear. "She…" His throat clicked as he swallowed. "Dad's dead. She…" He heaved a dry sob. "She *killed him.*"

"I know, baby…" Her voice broke, and her shape leaned over him as she draped him gently in a hug. "That fucking… *plaything.* I know…" She trailed off into a wail and leaned back.

He could see her now. Her hair was falling into her face, lank and dull, and her makeup was smudged around her red, swollen eyes. Her pale skin was splotchy and raw. Her clothes were wrinkled and unkempt and looked like she'd been sleeping in them. And she was…

She was *crying.* He had never seen her cry before. Her hand pressed against her mouth. She rocked forward with each ragged sob. Tears sprung to his eyes.

"I'm sorry mom, I…" He sighed as whatever he had been given started to take effect. The pain in his chest was drifting further away, just out of reach. He wilted back against the bed, his eyes fluttering shut for a moment. "I'm sorry…"

"Don't you ever say that," she sobbed. "This wasn't your fault… it was *her.*"

Tears rolled down his face and into the pillow. "I couldn't stop her. She shot me first and I just… *lay there.*"

"Gavin, *stop,*" she whispered. "She nearly killed you, honey. It's not your fault." She stared at him, her eyes flicking over the place where the pain still burned faintly, to the IVs in his arms, to the wires connecting him to the monitor behind him. Her face spasmed in pain as her eyes returned to his. "She took your father from us. And she nearly took you from me… twice."

The pain in his chest dulled to a distant ache. He felt warm, like his head wasn't attached to his body all the way. He giggled. "The first time was Isaac," he said with a smile, lifting his hand experimentally from the blanket. It felt like it was floating up of his own accord. His forehead wrinkled.

"She was the one responsible for the explosion too, honey." Her face worked as she looked at him, fighting back tears as he stared, enraptured, at his own hand.

"What did they give me?" he slurred.

"Ketamine." The word was clipped.

"Wow." His head dropped back against the pillow. The pain of his father's death crushed him, but distantly, like he was only remembering the pain. Tears ran freely down his face and into his hair, unbidden. "She killed dad," he whispered. He realized he should probably be alarmed that he felt so disconnected from it.

"She was your father's plaything once. He told me before he left to meet you. I never would have... *imagined*..." She closed her eyes and began to cry again. "He should have killed her. I *wish*..." She sniffled. "I *wish* he'd killed her. I wish he'd ended her wretched little life in our basement fourteen years ago."

"I hurt her once." Gavin's tongue felt loose. "When I was little. Dad took me downstairs and I hurt her. I never knew that was *her*."

"I know." His mother's lips curved up into a pained smile. Her hand went through his hair. "I remember. You were so excited, you couldn't even eat your lunch after." Her eyes crinkled, sending two more tears down her cheeks. "You didn't stop asking about her for weeks. Even after she..." She looked up at the ceiling and drew in a slow inhale. "Even after those *troglodytes* destroyed the house."

"I was excited to hurt her again." The corners of Gavin's mouth turned down.

"And you're going to, sweetheart." His mother smiled as he looked up at her in dizzy surprise. "I'm going to have the entire little troop hunted down and brought back to the house in Fort Meyers. Then you can hurt them all."

"But... mom..." He squinted, doing his best to wrangle his thoughts. They flitted back and forth through his mind, slipping through his fingers every time he tried to pin one down. "I don't wanna see them again."

Her mouth tightened. "What do you mean, sweetheart?"

"I mean…" He swallowed. "They kinda… kicked my ass. Twice. And… I don't know… I can hurt anyone I want. I kinda just want to… stay away from them."

She tilted her head. "Are you scared of them, honey?"

"N-no." His tongue stuck to the roof of his mouth for a second. "I just… don't wanna see them again."

She squeezed his hand. "It's okay, sweetheart. You don't have to worry about any of it. I'm going to find them, and you won't even have to *look* at them until they're all in chains."

"Isaac looks good in chains…" Gavin mumbled.

"Most people do," his mother said with a smile. "You can do anything you want with them. You can hurt them, kill them, make them your playthings… whatever you want. Just…" Her eyes filled with tears and her lips twisted in a snarl. "That little bitch Vera's life is *mine*. I don't care what you do to her, but when it's time for her to die, she's mine." Her lips trembled and she swallowed hard.

"But… I don't…" Gavin shook his head slowly, marveling at the way the room lagged behind.

She squeezed his hand. "We'll talk about it when you haven't had ketamine, baby," she whispered, leaning forward to plant a kiss on his forehead. He aimed a kiss at her cheek as she pulled away. He missed. His forehead wrinkled. *How'd she move so quickly?* Her fingers stroked through his hair as his eyes slid slowly shut.

"Ketamine is good," he sighed.

Chapter 4

Isaac couldn't shake the feeling that someone was watching them. His body coiled with tension beside Gray as he and Finn helped them to the car. His hand was firm on Gray's arm, but he itched to reach for his gun. *There's someone coming someone coming someone coming.* His eyes swept the street, back and forth, blood boiling just under his skin.

This would be the perfect time for the Stormbecks to hit us.

Gray panted raggedly. They stumbled beside Isaac, sweat shimmering on their skin as they pressed a hand to their chest. Finn's mouth flattened into a nervous line.

Doctor Trina followed along behind Isaac. She'd hovered over Gray in the week they'd been at the hospital, spending far more time with them than Isaac thought she could spare. *We saved her son.*

Isaac pulled the door open and helped Gray slowly ease themself inside. They groaned softly, their knees cracking as they folded themself into the back seat. They slumped back as soon as they were inside.

Isaac released Gray's arm and immediately turned to look behind them. *Why aren't they coming for us? We're so fucking vulnerable right here. They've got to be coming. There's no way no one found out we're here.*

Doctor Trina stepped forward and leaned into the car, her hair pulled back into the tight bun she'd worn through the past week. Never seeming rattled. Never seeming overwhelmed. This was the first time Isaac had seen her worried, and that *terrified* him.

"You take care of yourself, Mx. Uriah," Doctor Trina said gently. "No more crazy adventures. No more getting shot by syndicate lunatics. That's an order." Her lips quivered as she forced a smile.

Gray huffed out the smallest laughs, then winced. "No problem," they rasped. Their voice was still hoarse from the intubation, the nurse said. Apparently that was normal. Isaac's head spun.

"Gray…" Dr. Trina said. Isaac swiveled to look at her, the tension in her voice making his muscles clench even more. She wet her lips and paused, her mouth slightly open as she chose her words.

"I know," Gray said softly, staring at the ground. "I almost died."

Doctor Trina blew out a slow breath. "Gray… you saved my son. You saved my Carlos. And for that, I am eternally grateful. But… you are not a young person."

Gray's head dropped back in a silent laugh. "Don't I know it," they whispered.

Doctor Trina's mouth twisted. "Your recovery is going to be hard, Gray. Harder than it would be if it were anyone else in your family." Her gaze moved over each of them in turn, and lingered on Isaac. "You can safely leave, now that the chest tube is out. But… you won't be back to fully functional in… *months*. And you will *never* go back to the way you were before."

"I know," Gray said, pain twisting their voice.

Doctor Trina leaned into the car to take Gray's hand. "Whatever life you're living," she murmured, "Whatever fight you're trying to win…" She blinked tears out of her eyes. "…you won't be able to do it with them anymore."

Gray's lips trembled, and they crumpled into a ragged sob. They leaned forward into their hands and gasped as the movement pulled at their wound.

Tori burst into tears beside Isaac. Vera pulled Tori roughly into her arms, tears shining in her eyes as well.

"I'm sorry," Doctor Trina said softly, taking a step back from the door. "I j-just want you to have, ah, realistic expectations for your recovery. I don't… I don't want to see you getting hurt again. You've done so much for this, um, cause." She wrung her hands, and her lips trembled. She looked around at the others. "All of you have. Thank you so much."

"Of course," Gray whimpered, looking up at Doctor Trina. Their cheeks were stained with tears.

Doctor Trina stepped forward and clasped Gray's hand, her brown skin turning white at the knuckles as she squeezed. "Good luck," she said weakly.

"Thank you," Gray said, meeting her gaze. She wiped her eyes and stepped away. One by one, she took everyone's hand.

"Thank you," she said, to each of them as she turned. Sam. Finn. Ellis. Vera. Tori. Isaac. She turned to Edrissa where she was practically cowering against the side of the car. "And you, Edrissa. You brought them all here and I'm very, very grateful."

Edrissa shivered. Her eyes darted between Doctor Trina's hand and her face. After an awkward beat of silence, Doctor Trina pulled her hand back.

"Well," she said tightly, "You should really go. It's dangerous to stay here."

"Yeah." Isaac nodded, his hand unconsciously inching towards the gun in his waistband. His skin was going to crawl off his body if they didn't get in the cars and leave, right now. *They're coming, they're coming, they're going to catch us and hurt us and take Sam away again...* He swallowed the lump in his throat.

"Right," Gray ground out through their teeth. They gasped in a tortured breath. *"Damn."*

Finn leapt into the seat beside them and immediately felt for the bandages. Ellis walked around to the driver's seat, and Edrissa crept into the front passenger seat, her eyes wide and darting between the others.

Tori and Vera headed to the other car, Sam and Isaac right behind them. Tori and Vera went to the back, and Sam jumped into the front passenger seat. Isaac went to the driver's side.

"The way you all take care of each other," Doctor Trina said, "I know you're all in good hands."

Isaac turned to look at the small caravan. "I know," he said, panic spiking in his chest. He turned his gaze to her and nodded. "Thank you," he said weakly, before he climbed into the driver's seat and started the car.

Ellis pulled away first, merging into the street with a few other cars. They swerved to the side to miss a massive pothole. Isaac's fingers shook on the steering wheel as he pulled away from the hospital. He adjusted his grip on the wheel. "Okay," he whispered to himself. "Okay, okay, okay."

"You good?" Vera said from the back seat. She sounded as frightened as Isaac felt.

"Yeah," Isaac breathed. "Just... tense."

"Yeah," Vera said, and turned around to look behind them.

Isaac glanced in the rear view, following her gaze. There were only a few cars behind them, and none of them seemed to be following them as they changed lanes. They turned onto a different street and kept going. No one followed.

"We should be in front," Isaac muttered. "We know how to throw tails." He forced down a stinging burst of panic. *Hurry up, hurry up, hurry up!* "I mean, we explained it to Ellis, but they might not—"

"If we do get a tail," Vera said steadily, "Then we're best equipped to *handle* it if they get too close. We talked about this, Isaac. We'll make it out. We'll figure it out."

Isaac's left leg bounced as he followed Ellis into another turn. Still no one. His nerves jangled as they slowly made their way out of the city, avoiding potholes that took up the width of the road, and crumbled buildings sending scattered debris too thick to drive over.

"How do people live like this?" Sam breathed.

Isaac lifted an eyebrow. "Like what?"

"They… they fight, and they fight, and they still see their homes destroyed," Sam said, eyes wide as they stared out the window. "I… c-couldn't. I couldn't stand it."

"Some of them can't leave," Tori said from the back seat. "Some of them have nowhere else to go. Some of them choose to stay and fight." Tori cleared her throat. "Just like us."

"We have a home to go back to," Sam murmured. They stiffened and turned to look at Tori. "Tori… oh… Tori, *no*…"

Tori sniffed and held a hand to her mouth. Isaac blinked back tears.

"I know," Tori wept. "W-we can't go back."

"We left all our stuff there," Sam whimpered. "I l-left my backpack and Tori your, your *pictures* and Gray's books and Vera, your, your recipes, and Finn and Ellis's quilt, oh, no, we left *everything*…"

Isaac pulled Sam into a one-sided hug over the center console and squeezed them tight. They latched onto Isaac's shirt and sobbed into his shoulder.

"We have each other," Isaac murmured against the top of their head as he drove. "We're all alive. That's not ever guaranteed but we *have it*."

"I really, really liked that home," Sam whimpered against Isaac's shirt. "I… I loved that home. It was the best home I ever had."

"Mine, too," Isaac said. The words came out choked.

"I always knew I might have to leave in a hurry," Tori said between weak sobs. "I always knew. I always knew, I knew, I *knew*…"

Vera drew her arms tight around Tori. "I'm so sorry, babe," she whispered.

"But we'll…" Sam sniffed loudly and wiped their nose. "We'll, we'll build a new home. We'll get north and we'll, we're gonna find a new house and live there and we'll… we'll make it ours." They sniffed again. "We'll find a new home," they said tremulously. "We'll go on missions but still have a, h-have a *home*."

"Yeah, Sam," Isaac whispered, his chest aching with something he couldn't place. "We will." He squeezed them tight once more. Sam scrubbed their face and looked out the window. They took a deep, quavering breath.

"We're a family," Sam said, almost to themself. "Home is wherever we are."

Tears smarted in Isaac's eyes. He wiped them away and gripped the wheel with both hands. Ellis got onto the highway to take them out of Beringer.

There was still no one behind them.

Chapter 5

Isaac's hands were tight on the wheel as the car bounced down the uneven road. *Even when we aren't running from something, I feel like I'm being chased.* He rolled his neck and consciously relaxed his hands. He couldn't shake the feeling that they were racing against the chance – the inevitability, it seemed – that they wouldn't make it north. That they would be caught. Captured. Tortured. Killed.

"You okay?"

He looked over to see Sam staring at him. Their eyebrows pulled together with concern and they chewed their lip.

"Yeah." He cleared his throat. "Just want to get there. We've got a long way to go."

"Yeah." Sam looked to the car in front of them where Finn, Ellis, Gray, and Edrissa were just visible as silhouettes through the back window.

"We'll make it." Isaac glanced back at Tori as she said it. Her eyes were tense, her lips a thin line. The bruises around her neck were only just starting to turn yellow after a week at the hospital and four days on the road. Vera pressed a kiss against the side of Tori's head, burying her face in her tight curls, and pulled her closer.

They'd been forced to stick to back roads, sometimes staying in one place for hours as they waited for a safe time to move. Just after leaving Beringer, they'd had to hunker down and hide in their cars as a syndicate helicopter circled overhead for most of the day. They still had another two or three days to go, at this rate. Isaac scratched the stubble on his chin that he hadn't bothered to shave at the hospital. *I can't believe we weren't found while Gray was recovering.*

"Do you think we'll make it to the house you told us about by tonight?" Sam turned to Tori.

"We might get there tonight." Tori looked out the window at the unending horizon of brown grass, shimmering almost white with the sun directly overhead. "It might be another eight hours. I don't remember exactly where it is, but I think we're still pretty far away."

"Can we stay there tonight once we get there?" Sam stifled a yawn.

Isaac covered his mouth as he yawned, too. His back ached and his legs had long since cramped. The journey was taking three times as long as it would have if they'd been able to use the highways instead. "If there's no one following us, then yes."

"And if there is?" Sam's throat bobbed as they swallowed.

Isaac blew out a slow breath. "We'll handle it."

Vera wrapped her arms tighter around Tori. Tori folded into her embrace, wincing slightly as Vera's arm pressed against the broken skin of her back.

"Sorry," Vera whispered.

Sam turned back to Isaac. "Do you think it'll just be the syndicates after us? Or... or bounty hunters, too?"

Isaac's jaw clenched. "I don't know."

"Would people... really turn us over to the syndicates?"

"They would if the money was good enough."

"But..." Sam's eyes sparkled with tears. "But we're all on the same *side.*"

"You heard the guards back at the hospital," Isaac said quietly. "There are no more sides. We can't blame people for doing their best to get by."

"I wouldn't give people to the syndicates even if I needed the money," Sam mumbled. They crossed their arms in front of their chest and looked out the window.

Isaac looked over at them, the corner of his mouth turning up in a half-smile. "Not everyone's like you, Sam."

"Interesting that people guarding a hospital would argue there are no sides," Vera snarked.

"Interesting isn't the word I'd use to describe them," Isaac growled, his knuckles going white against the steering wheel.

"What does that mean?" Tori pulled out of Vera's embrace and sat forward.

18

Isaac shot Sam a glance. They had gone very still next to him, staring militantly out the window.

"Isaac?" Vera said tightly.

Sam turned back to Isaac, their eyes downcast. "When we got there they... uh..."

"You don't have to talk about it if you don't want," Isaac murmured. His mouth hardened into a line.

"I... I know." Sam chewed their lip. "Um..." Their voice became very small. "The guards wanted to... um... trade me. For Gray's surgery."

"*Trade...*" Vera's eyes narrowed and her nose wrinkled in revulsion. "Trade, like..."

"Yeah," Isaac spat through clenched teeth. "And you..." He jerked his chin up, eyes fixed on the road. "You were going to give yourself to them."

Sam hung their head. "If it meant Gray got their surgery—"

"Sam, *no.*" Tori whispered. Her hand went over the front seat to rub their shoulder.

Sam turned wide, tear-filled eyes to Isaac. "I knew you would protect me."

"Then why did you—"

"I mean..." They swallowed. "I mean you wouldn't have let them... kill me."

Isaac glanced at Sam, his face twisted in horror. "But you think I'd just... let them...?"

"I just wanted to save Gray," Sam whispered miserably. Vera's hand went to Sam's shoulder, too and she squeezed. They stared at their lap. Their face twisted in shame. "I'm sorry."

Isaac leaned his elbow on the door and pressed his face into his hand. His eyes pricked with tears. "Please don't apologize."

"Sorry." Sam sniffed. They glanced up at Isaac. He felt their eyes on him and his face pulled into a twisted smile. They laughed brokenly. "Sorry."

Isaac licked his lips, working to force down the lump in his throat. "Sam..."

"I know."

"No, you don't." He dashed the tears from his eyes. "I can't protect you. No matter where we go, no matter who we're with, all I can ever think about is how Gavin wants us dead, or worse, and has almost *unlimited resources* to make both those things happen, and no matter *what I do* I can't..." He shook his head bitterly. "I can't keep you safe. Not even from our own... *side*. Because it doesn't matter who's syndicate and who's not anymore. No matter where we go there will be people who want to hurt us, hurt *you* and I... I thought I could stop all that when I went to Gavin. But it turns out that didn't matter."

"Isaac!" Vera's mouth hung open, shocked.

He pushed on, tears burning his cheeks. "None of it matters. Even after all that we've been through you could have been taken, maybe killed, on the steps of a hospital that was supposed to be on our *side*." His hands shook on the wheel. The car jerked slightly.

Sam was quiet for a long moment. "It mattered to me that you went to Gavin in my place," they whispered.

Isaac's eyes snapped to Sam's for a split second and guilt clouded his face. "I'm sorry. That's not what I meant." His hand loosened a little on the wheel and his lip trembled. "I just want to protect you. It's all..." He wiped his nose. "It's all I've ever wanted for you. For you to be safe."

Sam's dark eyes rested on Isaac for a long time. Then, in one motion, they took off their seatbelt and leaned all the way over the center console to tuck themself under his arm. Isaac's breath caught in his chest. He wrapped his arm around them, crushing them against his side. They laid their head against his shoulder and he squeezed them tighter.

"Maybe you can't keep me safe." They shrugged. "Maybe no one can. But... you saved me. Three times." They pressed against his side. "It's more than enough."

His voice wobbled. "Thanks, Sam."

"I mean it." They pulled back and looked at him. "Can't you just... forgive yourself?"

Maybe it was the lack of sleep, or the heavy, metallic dread in his gut, or the weight of the past six months coming down on him all at once. But Isaac looked into Sam's eyes, teary but warm, and he lost control.

He jerked the car onto the shoulder and slammed it into park. He pressed his hands against his face and sobbed. Sam's arms went around him, and he clutched at them, fingers tightening in their shirt as he pulled them firmly against his chest. He heaved forward with each sob, feeling Sam's fingers dig into his back and fist around his shirt.

Isaac heard a door open and close. He looked up to see Vera intercept a very worried-looking Ellis. "We just need to switch out drivers," Isaac heard Vera say faintly through the closed window.

"Is Isaac okay?" Ellis pushed past her, their eyes fixed on him. They pulled the driver's side door open. "Isaac? What's wrong?"

He sniffed. "I'm sorry," he mumbled, scrubbing his face with his sleeve. "It's just been... um..." He blew out a gusty exhale. "I'm just tired I guess."

"Oh. Okay." Ellis's shoulders relaxed. "So everyone's okay?"

"Yeah. Everyone's fine." Isaac pulled away from Sam and ran a hand through his hair. "I guess I *could* take a break from driving."

"I'm up next," said Tori as she climbed out of the car.

"Go tell everyone we're okay or Finn's gonna have a damned aneurism," Vera laughed. They all looked over to see Finn's face plastered against the back window, apparently having crawled into the back of the car to see what was going on, but unwilling to leave Gray's side.

"They've been fussing over Gray's stitches all day," Ellis grumped.

"We can switch if you want..." Vera offered.

Ellis glanced back at the car. Their face pulled into a grudging smile. "No thanks." They turned to walk back to the car. "Next time we pull over you guys can lead for a bit."

"We'll reach the house today, so that works. I can guide us in," Tori called after them. Ellis threw a thumbs up over their shoulder and climbed back into the driver's seat.

Isaac stood up and stretched. "Thanks, Tori," he murmured as she walked to the driver's seat. He climbed into the back. Sam scrambled to join him. Vera laughed and got out, walking over to sit in front with Tori.

Sam moved to Isaac's side as if drawn by a magnet and curled up against him again. His arm went around their shoulder and he pulled them close. Tori put the car in gear and slowly got up to speed behind the other car.

Isaac stared out the opposite window, a few stray tears making their way down his cheeks. He held Sam close. Sam closed their eyes and sighed. They relaxed into his arms and began to snore softly. Isaac smiled.

Chapter 6

Gavin was making a splendid recovery. At least, that's what the surgeon said. He'd been discharged from the hospital days ago and was starting to feel more like a person again.

His mother doted on him endlessly, tending to his every need, waiting on him hand and foot. It wasn't that he minded, but he'd never felt so dependent on someone else since he was a kid.

Maybe that wasn't entirely true. When he'd woken from his medically induced coma after Isaac broke Gavin's nose, cheekbone, and eye socket with just his fist, Gavin needed more help than this. He'd been *cathed,* for Christ's sake. Couldn't even *pee* on his own.

His mother had a husband to dote on when that happened, though. Now she only had him.

The house was a revolving door of relatives and friends passing on their condolences to him and his mother. He'd received them as graciously as he could when he'd still been slightly buzzing from painkillers. He'd withstood their hands on his shoulder, gritted his teeth against their raised eyebrows when he refused to shake hands. Never mind that it sent agony shooting through his chest when he moved, or tried to move, or thought about moving. Never mind he'd been bedbound for the first five days of his recovery, unable to do so much as lift his head without feeling like he'd been shot all over again. Never mind that it was *his father* who'd been murdered, slaughtered in front of his eyes like prey. Never mind the nightmares. They had expectations of him, and he was disappointing them.

His mother swept into the room, her eyes sparkling in a way he hadn't seen since...

He winced. He couldn't go an hour without another crushing realization that something was happening without his father, and that he'd never be there for Gavin again. Gavin sat up slowly, his face twisting as he shuddered against the pain.

23

"Hey mom," he rasped. "What's up?"

"I have a surprise for you." Her lips curved up into a smile that looked almost happy.

"Great." His voice was flat. "What is it?"

"Come with me. I'll show you." She offered her hand to him.

He looked at her hand, then up at her. "Is it okay if you bring it to me? I'm… really hurting right now."

She pursed her lips at him. "No, darling. Come on. It'll make you feel better, I promise."

He hung his head in supplication. "Okay." He took her hand with his left, groaning softly as the pain crescendoed in his chest. He squeezed his eyes shut and stood still for a moment, blowing out a slow breath as he waited for it to fade again. He blinked his eyes open to see her staring expectantly at him. "Okay. Let's go."

She led him through the kitchen out the back door and into the yard. Gavin shivered in the cold air.

This house was small, more like a cottage than anything else. But Gavin had asked specifically to stay here for his recovery. *Out of the way. Away from other people. So I can relax, be by myself.* She led him across the small yard to the work shed with the gardeners' tools they used in the summer to keep the property perfectly, imperfectly manicured to resemble the quaint wilderness-feeling that some cottages in the country had. But it was January, and the gardeners hadn't used it in months. Gavin stared at the ground as they made their way to the door.

His mother turned back to him and clasped her hands under her chin. "I know it's still early in your recovery," she said, gazing at him fondly, "But I really think this will help you feel better. Get you feeling more like… *yourself* again." Before he could ask her what she meant, she pushed the door open and stepped inside.

Gavin's stomach dropped as he realized what exactly she meant by a surprise: in the middle of the floor of the dusty shed, a young man sat tied to a chair, gagged and terrified.

Gavin turned to her with wide eyes. "Mom…"

"I know, I know. Maybe a little early for this. But…" Her hand went to Gavin's cheek and for a moment, her smile fell away to reveal an aching sadness beneath. "It's been… hard… since your father died." She smiled gently and tears ran from the corners of her eyes. "I want you to be reminded that not *everything* has to change."

"But mom, I—"

"This is Peter." She presented the man – maybe a *boy,* he looked like he could be that young – to Gavin with a sweep of her hand. "I wanted to do something for you to help you feel better. You've been so brave, sitting through all these visitors. You've been so brave through the pain." She picked up a knife laid out on the workbench and pressed it into his hand. "Let's do something just for *you.*"

He looked down at the knife, held loosely in his shaking hand. His mouth felt bone dry. He felt the stir of something in him, dark and unsettling and unwelcome. It wasn't the excitement he normally felt when he was about to hurt someone. It wasn't that sweet flutter he got in his stomach when he imagined flaying someone open with a knife.

It was *fear.*

"Mom, I…" He shook his head. "I don't think I can."

She placed her hand gently on his arm. "Sure, you can, sweetheart. I'll help you." She took the knife from his hand. She turned to the boy and held the knife to his throat. He dissolved into sobs behind the gag, thick tears rolling down his cheeks as he whined and sobbed against the blade. For a moment Gavin felt the familiar warmth in him. Immediately on its heels was a creeping dread. He shivered and his lips trembled. He realized his mother was looking at him, waiting for him to step forward. He did, on wobbly legs.

She took the knife away from the boy's throat and drew it down the side of his arm. He whimpered and twisted away from the pain. A slow drop of blood rolled lazily down his arm and dripped with a tiny splatter to the floor.

Gavin's hands shook.

He took another step forward, and he was standing almost between the boy's legs. The boy's eyes were red and raw, like he'd already been crying for hours. Gavin licked his lips. "Where did he come from?"

"Does it matter?" His mother brought the knife to the boy's arm and made another cut, much deeper. The boy screamed, his jaw clenched tight against the gag. A steady stream of red wound down his arm and dribbled onto the floor.

Gavin's voice shook. "N-no." The blood was impossibly red, garish and bright. He hadn't seen anything that color since— He squeezed his eyes shut against the flash of memory. He swallowed hard. *I did this to Sam. I cut them in the same exact place.* He balked at the sudden, unwelcome thought. His eyes flew open and he met the boy's gaze.

"Don't worry about the blood staining, honey." The knife flashed as it went to the boy's arm again, carving into him. Gavin felt dizzy at the boy's scream. *Why do I feel so weird? Usually this makes me feel good.* He experimentally fished around in his mind for the familiar sensation, the warm feeling that spread through his bones at the sound of screams, at the sight of blood. At the sight of a face made haggard with agony. His throat constricted as he tried to swallow.

His mother stepped back and passed the knife to him. He tightened his hand around it, trying to feel the weight, the familiar heft of it. Pain burned deep in his chest. He passed the knife to his left hand. His left wasn't as good, he knew, but… with every movement of his right arm, his muscles locked against the pain that gripped him.

Gavin brought the knife to the boy's other shoulder and drew it across his skin. It split under the knife, opening him up, letting the blood spill out. The boy screamed in agony. For a split second, for just a brief moment of bliss, Gavin felt the familiar sensation inside him again, sharp and warm and so, so good. His heart fluttered. *Maybe I just needed a second to get back into it.* He drew the knife down the boy's chest this time, cutting his shirt and the skin underneath, watching the red stain grow along the edges of the fabric. His own chest ached. He put the feeling away and went to make another cut across the boy's arm. The boy's gaze darted around the room in panic and desperation. His eyes flicked up to Gavin's for a moment, pleading and scared and *delicious.*

The smell of blood hit Gavin.

He staggered backwards, nearly dropping the knife. He stood stock still as memory after memory crashed over him, of his father, his throat hanging open, the blood, his and Gavin's, soaked into the floor, of the mind-numbing terror of lying on the floor of his childhood summer home, bleeding out onto the carpet. A choked sob tore from his throat.

"Gavin, honey?" His mother took a step towards him, her hands held out and stained with blood. "Honey? What's the matter?"

"This used to make me feel good," Gavin whispered, tears threatening in his voice. "Now this just makes me feel scared."

She stared at him, dumbfounded. "What, sweetheart?"

He held the knife out to her. "I'm sorry. I need… maybe I just need more time." He glanced at the boy, whose eyes flicked between him and the knife.

"What, you don't want to try again?"

Gavin shook his head jerkily. "No." He swallowed. "Please."

Hesitantly, she took the knife. "Okay, honey." She walked behind the boy. "Just let me get rid of this." Before Gavin could say anything she drew the knife across the boy's throat, cutting deep.

Gavin screamed and jumped back from the fountain of blood that poured from his neck. The boy paled, shuddered, died. Gavin turned and bolted out the door, barely clearing the threshold before he vomited into the browned, frozen grass. He groaned as he retched, the motion sparking fire in his wound. He heard his mother right behind him, felt her cool hand rubbing unsure circles on his back. Gavin knew his shirt would be stained, now, with the boy's blood. He sank to his knees and sobbed.

Chapter 7

Gavin sat huddled on the couch, his knees pulled up to his chest. His skin still glistened with a thin sheen of sweat and his stomach roiled mercilessly. If he could just keep his mind away from the memories, it was alright. If he could think about anything other than... other than...

He gagged weakly as the memory of blood overwhelmed him again. Lying helpless on the carpet, a hole in his chest, watching his father's throat ripped out by his own plaything. It was burned into his mind, no matter what he did to shut it out.

He did his best to take in a deep breath and blow it out through his lips. His chest ached as his ribs expanded, making his stomach lurch again.

What's wrong with me? His mind shivered at the thought of the young man lying dead in the tool shed. Well, he probably wasn't lying there *now*. The servants had been shooed towards the yard by his mother as she guided him into the house, a worried hand pulling him to the couch. *"Go clean that up,"* she'd said, like she'd spilled tea.

I've never not *liked hurting people.* He pressed his face into his hands. *Did that plaything – did* Vera *– take that from me, too?* He forced down a sob. Dread boiled in his stomach. *Who am I if I can't hurt someone? What if I can't hurt people anymore?*

If he reached for the feeling, he could feel it in him, deep down, past the fear and the guilt and the horror of his father's death. He could feel that warm blanket of pleasure that waited to envelop him every time he took the knife to someone. Every time he made someone *suffer*. But it seemed shielded from him. It seemed taken.

His mother opened the door from the hallway and slid slowly into the room. She approached him with hesitant steps, her face pinched with worry. She stopped in front of him and ran her fingers gently through his hair.

"Oh, sweetheart," she murmured. "You'll feel like yourself again in no time."

He nodded miserably, leaning slightly into the touch. She smiled.

"I was right, she said smugly. "They *are* headed north." She sat on the couch next to him.

"Who?"

She raised an eyebrow. "You know who. Isaac and Vera and the rest." She sniffed delicately. "They're in some dirty little hovel a few hours north of here on the old turnpike at 52. Some... *safehouse."* Her lip curled. "I'm surprised it's taken them this long to get there."

His eyebrows drifted together. "How do you know that?"

She smiled and shook her head. "I should have known better than to tell you when you were medicated." Her hand went to his hair again and stroked gently through. His eyes slid closed for a moment. *I couldn't hurt someone. Why is she still being gentle?*

"There have been a lot of rumors of cities outside of our control, up north." She rolled her eyes. "We can't be everywhere. Who would want to live in such a miserable part of the country, anyway? It *snows* there." She sighed. "It's a big territory and I didn't particularly feel like scouring the entire damned north for them. Our people in Beringer were able to get a tracker placed on their car. Instead of just taking them, the Wilsons and the Torrs wanted to track them to whatever backwater they end up in, wherever they think is safe, and make sure it no longer is." Her mouth twisted into a sneer. "Send a message to everyone that would try to hurt us that doing so is incredibly unwise." She squeezed his hand. "But we've got time. Time to get you feeling back to normal again."

"I'm sorry, I just..." His face fell a little. "I... don't... I don't want this anymore. I don't think I... *can.*" A faint thrill of fear moved through him.

"Then what," she said evenly, "Exactly, do you plan to do once I've brought those wretched little shits home?"

He couldn't look at her. His eyes slid closed. "Please," he whispered. "Please, don't bring them here. I don't care anymore. I don't *care* about them. I never want to see them again. Please... if they're headed north, maybe we should just let them. There's no way they'd ever come near us again."

"No." He opened his eyes at the sound of her voice, sharp and steely. "I'm going to find them, and you're going to help me."

He raised his eyes slowly to his mother, hoping to find annoyance, or concern, or anything other than the coldness he found. "What?"

"The tracker is just insurance." She pursed her lips. "I want them to come to *me*." Her nostrils flared as she drew in a slow inhale. "I want them to think they've won. I want them to think they have the chance to end this forever and then rip it away from them."

His eyebrows pulled together. "…what could you possibly offer them that would make them think that?"

Her eyes softened for a moment and her hand went up to gently stroke his cheek. "You, honey."

His eyes went wide. *"What?"*

"They'd never get close to you, sweetheart," she soothed. "It would just *look* like they were going to, and then… we'd take them."

"You'd use me as… as *bait?*" His stomach dropped.

"Only to coax them in." Her eyes shone.

"How could you protect me? You don't know what they're *like*."

"Don't worry about that, sweetheart. Just know that in the end, we'd have them." Her face twisted. "We'd have them all. Especially…" Her lips pulled back over her teeth. *"Vera."* She spat the name like a curse.

Gavin leaned away from her. "How could you put me at risk like that? I'm safe now. How could you just… *dangle* me out there?"

She gently took his hand. "This is a chance to make the plaything that killed your father *suffer,* honey."

He pulled his hands away from her. "Dad's d-dead, mom," he whispered. "But I'm not. Why would you risk me to catch them… when I don't even *want* them anymore?"

She let her hands fall to her sides. "This isn't about what you *want,* Gavin. It's about what's *right.*"

"Is it worth it to you to risk me to do what's *right?*"

Her eyes narrowed and she tilted her head. "Yes. But it wouldn't be a risk. You'd be safe."

"I won't do it." He lifted his chin. "I don't want to." He shuddered as her eyes iced over again.

"I don't care what you *want,* sweetheart," she hissed. "Perhaps you don't care that your father is dead, but I do. I'm offering you the opportunity to crush the people who killed him."

"I won't do it."

"You don't have a choice."

He stared at her, his mouth hanging slightly open. He turned to go. "I'm leaving. I'm staying with Mark for a while."

"You will do this," she said softly, "Or you will find no door open for you. Don't turn your back on your family, Gavin."

He spun to face her. "It feels like *you're* the one turning your back on *me,* mom."

She stared him down. "We don't have a chance of bringing them to us unless I use you. You *will* do this."

A chill raced down his spine. He swallowed hard against the lump that rose in his throat. "No. I won't." He reached for his coat.

"Where do you think you're going?"

"I don't know," he threw over his shoulder, his eyes streaming with angry tears. "I'll figure it out."

"I'll freeze all your credit cards. Contact all our friends. I'll make sure not a single family door opens for you. Not until you come to your senses and help me with this." Gavin's hand froze on the door handle. "They killed my husband. Nothing will stop me from bringing them to justice." Gavin glanced back at his mother, at the rage that twisted her features. "Not even *you,*" she hissed.

"I'm still alive, mom," Gavin said, his voice breaking. "Call me when you've got your priorities straight."

"If you walk out that door, you will not be welcome here again."

His heart broke at the malice in her voice. "I won't be your bait," he said miserably. "Dad would have understood."

"Gavin." He flinched as her voice shot across the room. She stood. "Why do you think he let Vera get close to you?"

He turned to face her, paling. *"...what?"*

Her eyes narrowed at him. "He let Vera come to you because he knew she wouldn't be able to resist the opportunity to take your life." Her lip curled into a sneer, hostility coiling tightly in her eyes. "Because you couldn't leave well enough alone. You *had* to seek them out. You killed their friend. You kidnapped that bitch's little paramour. As soon as he saw Vera's picture he knew she'd come straight to you. So he let her come. He let her walk right into his trap." She jabbed a finger in his direction. "A trap *you* laid."

He threw his hands into the air. "So you see how dangerous this idiotic plan of yours is!"

"You underestimated her. You told him Vera would be yours as soon as she saw him. That she was weak. That she was *broken.* Your father is dead because you laid a *poor* trap," she spat. "Your father is dead because of *you.*"

His eyes blurred with tears. A sob moved through his throat. "Goodbye, mom," he rasped. He slammed the door behind him and pulled on his jacket as he made his way to the garage.

He walked straight to the fastest car. He opened the door and popped open the visor. The keys fell onto the seat. He climbed into the car, furiously wiping his eyes against his sleeve. A half-formed plan swirled in his mind. It wouldn't be any more dangerous than his mother's plan to dangle him out for Vera.

His chest burned with bitterness. *They were both willing to string me up to catch Vera.* He put the key in the ignition and started the car. The seat rumbled under him. He did some quick mental math. *If mom's right, I'll reach the house in a little less than four hours.* He revved the engine. *Maybe three.* He pulled out of the garage and onto the street. He hit 60 before he reached the end of the block.

Chapter 8

Vera held her hand out to Tori. "Come here," Vera murmured with a smile.

Tori took Vera's hand and sat down on the bed next to her, the foot of space between them yawning open. The crumbling, abandoned safehouse had four bedrooms, and this was the first time they'd been alone together since... Tori shuddered. The memory still felt like an open wound.

Vera's mouth turned down at the corners. "Come on, babe," she whispered. "I want..." Her fingers twisted through Tori's and she tried to pull her closer.

Tori pulled back a little. "Vera..." She chewed her lip. "I'm just..."

Vera stopped and leaned back, her face growing serious. "I'm sorry. Do you not—"

"It's okay." Tori's face twisted with concern. "I'm just worried about, about you. It's only been... what... a week and a half since...?" The unspoken words hung in the air between them. *Since you saw your captor again. Since he tortured you. Since you tore his throat open and watched him die like a slaughtered animal.*

Vera shrugged her shoulders up around her ears. "I'm fine," she murmured. She stopped when Tori quirked up an eyebrow. "I mean I'm not... *fine*... but I'm okay. And..." She ran her fingers along Tori's arm. "I miss you."

Tori moved closer, her hand moving along Vera's arm to wrap gently around her wrist. "I miss you too. I'm just... I know sometimes this sort of thing can... bring things up again. Pull things to the surface. Worse than before. I've seen it. I don't want you to..."

Vera took Tori's face gently in her hands. "If that happens, I'll tell you, okay?"

Tori pressed her lips together. She ached for Vera, too. She ached to feel Vera's hands, her mouth, her body, pressing and sucking and sweating and crying out... She shook herself. *It doesn't matter what I want if it hurts her.* She swallowed hard. "Okay. But we stop if something happens."

"Of course," Vera mumbled as she pulled Tori's mouth against hers.

They fell into bed together, Tori pressed against the length of Vera's body. She whimpered at the taste of Vera's mouth, the *familiar-safe-wild-sexy* smell all around her. Vera reached up and gripped the headboard. Tori whined softly as Vera moved her lips to her ear, down her neck, and she couldn't help the awakening feeling between her legs. She knelt between Vera's knees. Vera's legs immediately opened to her. Tori pressed her hips forward. Tori's hand made a fist in Vera's hair and she grazed her teeth over Vera's bottom lip.

"I want this," Vera whispered.

"I want you," Tori whispered back.

Vera moaned softly against Tori's lips. Her eyes fluttered closed and she opened her mouth to Tori's tongue, legs opening wider, falling back against the bed to either side. Tori shivered and rolled her hips against Vera's.

Tori's hand moved down Vera's chest to her waist and she gripped her there, pulling her closer against her. Vera whimpered softly.

"I want this."

"I want you too, babe." Tori trembled at the rush of blood between her legs, at her own wetness. *God, you're so beautiful. Please take me, please, please, god I need you. God, I want you.*

"I want this."

Tori froze and pushed herself away from Vera. Her stomach dropped at the sight of Vera's eyes half-open, glazed over, lips trembling.

Tori scrambled off of her and all the way to the other end of the bed. Vera lay on her back, her arms still above her head, chest moving with her gasping breaths.

"Vera?" Tori's voice shook. "Vera, where are you right now?"

Vera's lips trembled and she locked her jaw closed. A tear ran slowly down her face into her hair.

Tori bit down on her tongue, her stomach lurching. "Vera... y-you can speak."

"T-thank you, sir." Vera's eyes fluttered closed and two more tears coursed down her face.

"Vera, where are you right now?"

Vera's forehead wrinkled with confusion. "I... um..." She licked her lips.

"It's okay. You're in the safehouse. We're headed north, remember?"

"N-north...?"

"Yeah. We're going away from the syndicates. Do you remember all that?"

"Um..." Vera's whimpered, cringing in on herself. She kept her arms locked above her head on the bed.

"Vera, you can put your hands down. You don't have to... do that." Tori wrapped her arms around herself, biting down on her lip, trying to hold back her tears.

Vera brought her arms to her sides, her legs still splayed.

"Vera, would you be... more... *comfortable...* if you could curl up under the blanket? Are you cold?"

"Cold...?" Vera nodded.

"Okay." Tori moved closer to her, careful not to touch her. "Vera, sit up, and..." She looked around, shuddering as Vera immediately obeyed the command. "Sit against the headboard, okay? We'll get the blanket on you." Vera scooted back and sat rigid against the backboard, her knees coming up to her chest. She wrapped her arms around her legs and shivered. Tori pulled the hospital blanket they'd brought off of the bed and tucked it around Vera. She moved back and sat at the foot of the bed. "Better?"

Vera nodded slowly. "Thank you."

"Vera, can you tell me where you are? What you're seeing right now?" *I knew seeing him would do this. I knew it, and I still did this with her.*

"I..." Vera's voice broke. "I see... um... *him...* and I..." She swallowed hard, her eyes unfocused.

"Okay. You're safe, Vera. You're not with him. Okay? You're here with me, in this room. Can you feel the blanket around you?" Vera mindlessly grasped at the blanket, staring blankly at the opposite wall. She nodded mechanically. Tori forced down her tears. "Can you breathe with me? Can you do that?"

"Yes." Vera's voice was low and robotic.

"Ok. Breathe in…" Vera obeyed. "Hold. Good. Breathe out. Feel the breaths, okay? Feel them coming in and out. Breathe in… hold… breathe out." Vera trembled as she did it, tears spilling down her cheeks. "In… hold… out."

Vera gasped and went rigid, her eyes wide and staring off into space. Her breath huffed out of her and her mouth fell open in a silent scream.

Tori's hands jerked towards Vera. She caught herself, pulling back. "V-Vera? What happened?"

Vera's voice was strained into a ragged whisper. "There's…" She swallowed and shook her head.

"It's okay. What's wrong? What is it?"

Vera's eyes darted back and forth, uncomprehending and vacant. Her breaths came so fast and out of control that she rocked against the headboard.

Tori's hands shook as she dug her fingers into the sheets, rooting herself to the spot. She ached to pull Vera into her arms, smooth her hair, whisper in her ear that everything was alright. She trembled with tension and the tears started down her cheeks again. "Vera, please…" Her throat closed in a sob. She hardened her voice. "Tell me what's wrong," Tori ordered, hating herself.

Vera blinked and shook herself. "Yes sir. I… see…" Her tongue moved along her lower lip as she mindlessly tasted her tears. "There's… someone…" Her voice dropped to a whisper. Tori had to lean forward to hear her. *"There's someone else here with me."*

Tori leaned back. "I know. I'm here with you. There's no one else in this room, okay? You're stuck in that place again, but you're here. With me. No one else."

Vera shook her head. *"No,* I mean—" She flinched back and ducked her head. "I'm sorry. I mean…" Her eyes were fixed on the opposite wall. "There's… someone… *else."*

Tori shivered. "You mean there was… someone else… hurting you? When you were there with him?"

Vera's mouth gaped open as her eyebrows pulled together. "No… yes… I think…"

Did she know? Why didn't she tell me before? "Can you see this person now?"

"I can't... remember..." Vera's hands moved up to rub against her upper arms. "I... *feel*... them." Her mouth fell open. *"Him."*

Tori's eyes fell closed and sent tears cascading down her cheeks. "Was he... part of a syndicate?"

Vera shook her head desperately. "I can't remember, I *can't* remember, I'm sorry I'm sorry I'm sorry I'm sorry I'm sorry..." Her hands went up above her head and she cringed into herself. *"I'msorry I'msorry I'msorry I'msorry I'msorry..."*

"It's okay, Vera," Tori whispered. "You don't have to be sorry. You didn't do anything wrong." Vera sobbed incoherently, crumpling against the headboard, curling up on her side. "Vera, can you remember anything else about him? What he did? Did he hurt you?"

Vera's sobs grew louder. "I can't remember I can't remember I can't remember I can't remember I can't remember I'm not *allowed!*" The last word was a scream.

Tori jumped up, her stomach lurching with dread. She pressed her hands against her mouth and tried to force down the growing, suffocating terror that rose in her. "Vera," she hissed, voice tight with sobs, "Stay *here*. I'll be right back but stay *here*." She waited to see Vera nod before she turned and ran from the room.

She nearly collided with Gray just outside the door. Their eyes were wide. "What happened?" they gasped. "I heard her scream..."

Tori did her best to calm her voice, but she could do nothing to stop the tears. "Gray, it's bad, she..."

Gray brushed gently past her and into the room. Tori followed behind, shaking, a hand pressed to her mouth. Gray stopped as they saw Vera curled up at the head of the bed, heaving with sobs.

"We were just kissing," Tori whimpered. "We shouldn't have done it. I should have known it was too soon. I shouldn't have done it, I *know* that..."

Gray's hand went to her shoulder. "It's okay," they said gently. "It's not your fault."

"I tried to say we shouldn't, but she said she was okay. I'm sorry, I should have *known*..."

"Tori…" She quieted. "Stop. This is part of her recovery, okay? And… and yours. You can't blame yourself for this." Their thumbs wiped the tears away from her cheeks. "Let me help Vera and then we can talk about this, okay?"

"What happened?" came Isaac's voice from behind her. Tori turned as the others all appeared in the doorway.

She scrubbed her face on her sleeve. "Um… Vera… um…"

"How about everybody waits in the living room?" Gray held a hand out towards the others. "Let's not overwhelm her. She's going to be okay. She just needs a minute." They turned to Tori. "Do you want to go wait outside? Talk with the others?"

Tori hesitated, then shook her head. "No. Please. Can I be with her? Please?"

Gray turned back to Vera. "I'm not going to tell you you can't, Tori. Just wanted to know if you wanted to talk to someone while I help Vera."

"I'll be okay," she whispered. "I want to make sure she's okay." She turned to the door and watched the others slowly back away and into the hall.

"Vera," Gray murmured gently. "Vera, it's Gray. You can speak. What's going on?"

"I'm sorry," Vera whispered from where she was curled under the blanket. "I'm sorry."

"It's okay." They sat next to her on the bed. "Do you know where you are right now?"

"I don't *know!*" Vera cried, then huddled against the headboard. "*No, no, no, no, no I'm sorry… I'll be good, I'll be quiet… please…*"

"You're not in trouble, Vera." Tori stood and wrung her hands at the foot of the bed as Gray spoke. "Can you tell me why you're upset?"

"I'm not supposed to remember," she whispered. "I was bad. I wasn't supposed to remember."

"You weren't bad, and you won't be punished." Vera flinched at the word. Gray pressed on. "You won't be punished, alright? I'm telling you it's okay to remember. You're good, Vera. It's okay to remember whatever you want."

She whimpered softly. "I don't… *want*… to remember."

"What don't you want to remember?"

Vera mewled and curled up tighter into herself. Gray glanced at Tori, a silent question in their look.

"She remembered someone else," Tori mumbled. "She said she could remember another man. Another man in… *there*… with her."

Gray's face twisted. "Another man hurting her?"

"I don't know." Tori shook her head as her voice disappeared. "I don't *know*."

Gray turned back to Vera. "Vera, can you… what can you remember about him?"

She pressed her face into the mattress. "I… I can't… I remember… I can *feel* him."

"Did he hurt you too?"

"No… yes… I can't…"

Gray pursed their lips, thinking. "Was he a *bad* man?"

Vera answered immediately. "No."

"Was… was the other one a bad man?"

She whimpered. "I… *I'm* being bad. He made me good. He made me…"

"Shh," Gray murmured. "You're not being bad, Vera. You're being good. You're always good, no matter what you do."

"Bad…" she whispered. "Bad girl. Don't remember him. Don't remember. He was nothing. He was bad. Forget him, forget him, he never existed. There is no getting out. You imagined him, Vera, bad girl bad girl bad girl bad girl bad girl…"

"I can't," Tori sobbed, and ran from the room.

∴

Gray watched her go, concern pinching their features, and turned their attention back to Vera.

She was still whispering to herself. "Bad girl. Bad girl. Now I have to make you good. Now I have to make you better. I have to make you good, bad girl bad girl bad girl bad girl."

"Vera, *stop*," Gray ordered. Vera immediately fell silent. Gray bit their tongue and swallowed bitter shame. "Vera, I need you to come back to me now. Okay? Just like we've done before. I need you to leave that place you're in and come back to where you are now, with me. Take a deep breath, okay?" She obeyed. "Good. And out."

She blew out a shaking breath and immediately gasped in an inhale. "I'm sorry, please don't, I'm sorry, I won't remember I promise please no no *no…*"

"Breathe in, Vera," Gray said, a little sharp. Vera's mouth snapped shut and she dragged in a breath through her stuffy nose. "Out." She let the air back out. Gray paused for the briefest moment, seeing if she would start begging again. Vera trembled silently against the bed. Gray let out their own tiny sigh of relief. "In." She dragged in a breath and coughed on her tears. She gagged. "You're alright, Vera. Out." She slowly exhaled. Gray twisted their hands together. "In." They both took a slow breath in. "Good. Out." They pursed their lips and blew the air out slowly. Her shaking eased a little. "In." They could hear her ragged breath as it moved in. "Out." They exhaled together.

Over and over Gray breathed with Vera, in and out, in and out, slower and slower until she was no longer curled tightly into a ball but slumped in a pile next to the headboard.

Gray watched Vera's slow, trembling breaths. "Vera?"

She shuddered. "Yes."

"Are you back with me again?"

Her voice twisted into a sob. "Yes."

"Can you see me? Do you still see that other place?"

She lifted her head weakly. "No. I just see you." Her head dropped back down to the mattress.

"Okay. Can you tell me what just happened? If you think it'll put you back in that place then we don't have to talk about it."

Vera pushed herself upright and leaned back against the headboard. She shuddered and pulled the hospital blanket closer around her. "I…" She shook her head, squeezing her eyes shut and pressing her hands against her face. "I don't… know." Her hands fell and she looked up at Gray. "Why can't I remember?"

40

"Can I tell you what you were saying, while you were…there? Would that help?"

Her lips trembled. "…yes."

"You were saying there was another man in that place with you. Not a bad man. Does… that help you remember more?"

She shook her head, pressing her hands to her temples. "No. It's like… I reach for that space but there's nothing there. Or like there's…" She squeezed her eyes shut. "…a wall."

"What do you remember?"

"I can't…" She let her head rest back against the wall. "It's like… I can feel him. I remember… I remember feeling hands. And… if I don't try to think about it, if I just kinda… rest on it… I can remember… a smell… maybe? Like… sweat and… deodorant. He didn't smell like… the other one."

"Can you remember why he was there? What he did?"

Her mouth opened, shut, opened again. "I… no…"

"Did he hurt you?"

"I…" She shook herself. "I remember… pain… but not…" She bit down on her lip. "Not like… when I try to picture him, I don't get the… *sense*… of… pain. Well, maybe I do, but not… fear. No, that's not right…" She groaned in frustration. "He feels… safe?"

Gray spoke their next words very, very carefully. "Vera… Are you absolutely sure this person existed? And wasn't… um…"

Vera's eyes snapped to theirs. "Imagined?"

Their throat worked as they swallowed, doing their best to keep their voice even. "Um. Yes."

Her eyes fell closed again. "…yes. I can't picture him, picture his face, but I… I *know*. I remember how his hands felt. I remember… I can't hear his voice but I can get, like… the *feel* of it…" She tore her hands through her hair in frustration. "Why can't I fucking *remember*? Why is this just coming up *now*?"

"Hey, it's okay." Gray pitched their voice lower, soothing. "If this is something you buried, it might be coming to the surface because of seeing him again. He might have dug up all kinds of things."

"But I *killed* him," she murmured. "Why isn't he just… gone?"

"You know as well as I do, better maybe, that that's not how that works."

Her face fell. "I know. I just don't... understand..." Her brow furrowed.

"Don't push yourself," Gray said gently. "If this is a memory that's buried, or repressed or something, it might not come out all at once. But I'm sure it'll come." They pressed their lips into a hard line. "Don't try to force it."

"Fine." Vera wiped her face on her sleeve. "I'll just let that shit show up when I'm in bed with Tori." Her lips twisted bitterly. "Excellent." She pinched the bridge of her nose. "Where is she?"

"She had to leave," Gray said. "She couldn't... she didn't want to see you like that."

Vera ran her fingers through her hair and made a fist, pulling hard against the strands. "Why am I so fucked up?" she whispered.

"You're not fucked up," Gray said softly. Vera threw a dubious glance at them. Gray held her gaze. "You're traumatized. You're not fucked up, alright?"

She closed her eyes and clenched her jaw. "I want to talk to Tori. Make sure she's okay."

"I had everybody wait in the living room. Wanted to give you some privacy." Gray pushed themself off the bed, gasping a little.

Vera's cheeks flushed. "Of course they all know." Her head dipped. "Thank you, Gray. I appreciate it."

"Of course." They looked her up and down as she disentangled herself from the hospital blanket and stood.

She walked to their side and carefully folded into their arms. "Thank you."

Chapter 9

Isaac paced around the small living room at the back of the safehouse, his hand rubbing absentmindedly at the back of his neck. *Vera's in that place again. Seeing him put her there. If I had just—*

He was pulled back by Sam's hand on his arm, reaching out as he passed the couch. Their eyes were wide with concern, glassy and red-rimmed. He smiled tightly as he caught their hand and squeezed it.

"You okay?" they whispered.

"Yeah." Isaac shrugged. "Just worried about her." He looked over at Tori, weeping quietly on the couch next to Sam, her arms wrapped tightly around her legs. Sam had their free arm around her shoulders.

Isaac ran a tense hand through his hair and turned to the door. "I need some air."

Sam got halfway off the couch, their hand still reaching back, resting on Tori's shoulder. "I could come with you…"

"No," Isaac murmured, holding a hand back at them. He forced a smile, trying to disperse the tension in his face. "It's okay. I'll be back in just a minute. I just need a second alone."

"Okay." Sam fell back to the couch, their face a mask of worry. Their arm went right back around Tori's shoulders.

Isaac's hands shook. He clenched them into fists as he left the room. He moved in a daze down the hall to the front of the house. *We're all so fucked up. We're all so broken. How am I supposed to protect them? How can I help them when the damage has already been done?* He blew out a slow breath as his hand settled on the handle to the front door. *How do I keep them safe now?*

He pulled the door open and froze. His body locked in disbelieving panic. His breath felt punched from his chest.

There, standing on the front porch with his fist raised to knock on the door, was Gavin Stormbeck.

Isaac couldn't move. The ghosts of pain rose up and overtook him; the pain of broken bones and broken skin and the knife and the whip and Gavin's fists all swelled up inside him and nearly brought him to his knees.

Gavin grinned.

Something in Isaac's mind snapped. He lunged at Gavin, dragging him inside by his shirt and pinning him to the wall. He snarled wordlessly in Gavin's face.

Gavin grunted as his back met the wall. "Jesus, Isaac, at least buy me dinner firs—"

Isaac slapped his hand over Gavin's mouth as he yanked him away from the wall. He pushed the door closed with his foot and wrapped his arm around Gavin's neck. Isaac dragged him towards the downstairs door. He hauled Gavin down the stairs, his hand muffling Gavin's sounds of protest.

Gavin pulled against Isaac's grip, his feet kicking uselessly against the floor as Isaac flipped on the light, his other hand still locked around Gavin's mouth. As they reached the bottom stair Isaac let go and kicked Gavin to the floor. He fell hard onto his hands and knees.

Gavin cried out softly and groaned, pushing himself painfully upright. He wrapped one arm around his chest. Sweat beaded on his forehead. He looked up at Isaac, his breaths coming heavily, a sardonic smile shot through with pain on his face. "Well that's no way to treat—"

Isaac threw himself on top of Gavin and straddled his hips, pinning him to the floor. Isaac clapped his hand over Gavin's mouth again. *"Shut up,"* Isaac growled. "Just *shut up.*" Gavin's eyes flashed with dark amusement. Isaac's free hand went to Gavin's neck. It was as if he was watching his body do it, watching the hand wrap around Gavin's throat and press down all on its own. In a small corner of his mind, a voice screamed, *JUST KILL HIM! JUST KILL HIM AND END IT FOR GOOD! STOP FUCKING AROUND AND JUST KILL HIM!* Dark, bitter rage coursed through him. *No. I want to make him suffer first.* His lips pulled back in a snarl.

"I made a mistake," Isaac growled, his face inches away from Gavin's. "And so did Vera. We didn't kill you when we should have." His hand pressed harder against Gavin's throat and, for the first time, a flicker of real fear passed through Gavin's eyes. "I won't make that mistake again."

Gavin kicked weakly against the ground, pulling against Isaac's hands, gasping in breaths through Isaac's hand.

"Don't like being held down like this, do you?" Isaac's voice was venomous with rage. "When you had me, I *let* you do those things. I *begged* you to do those things because I had to protect Sam. But now…" He jerked Gavin's face to the side. "I'm stronger than you, Gavin. I was stronger then, too. How do you like being hurt by someone who has the upper hand?"

Gavin writhed under Isaac's grip, muffled screams rising and dying in his throat. Isaac's hand left Gavin's neck and went to search Gavin's pockets. His hand closed around a knife. A smile twisted his face as he flicked it open. Gavin's eyes went wide and he sobbed under Isaac's hand, tears running down his face. He yanked at Isaac's arm, trying to tear Isaac's hand away from his mouth. It sounded like he was begging. Something dark and terrible and good rushed through Isaac's veins.

"Do you want me to cut you open?" Isaac hissed, leaning over Gavin and pressing the knife under his chin. "You would *deserve* it after what you did to me… and Sam… and Tori… after what you did to *Vera*." Isaac's jaw clenched around her name. "You deserve for me to end your shitty little life in this *fucking basement*."

Gavin wailed under Isaac's hand, frozen with fear at the knife at his throat. He shook his head against Isaac's grip.

"This is how it felt," Isaac growled. *"This* is how it felt to be held down, hurt, almost killed by someone who had no fucking mercy at all." His blood thundered in his ears. His body burned with it. "You're not the first person I've killed, but you *will* be the only person I enjoy killing." Isaac pressed the knife harder against Gavin's throat. Gavin writhed against Isaac's hands, and Isaac's hand muffled his scream.

"Isaac!"

Isaac paused, his hands still itching to spill Gavin's blood. A shudder broke through him as he looked up to see Sam, clinging to the railing at the bottom of the stairs like they would fall apart without it, eyes wide and fixed on Gavin. The rest of the team filed in behind them, each staring at Isaac in shock. Vera's face was swollen and red. She stared at Gavin with blank horror. Edrissa stood frozen at the top of the stairs, her eyes darting around the room.

Gavin's eyes flicked between Isaac and the rest, desperate. He was white as a sheet and he trembled as Isaac pulled the knife back away from his throat.

Gray's voice shook as they spoke. "Isaac... what...?"

Isaac's throat tightened around a sob. "He was on the porch when I left to get some air. He tried to... I couldn't let him talk..." Tears stung Isaac's eyes. "I didn't want him to hurt any of you..." He slumped off of Gavin, the knife held loosely in his hand.

Gavin moaned with relief as Isaac released him. He painfully pushed himself upright, and his hand went up to rub his throat. "Jesus fucking Christ, Isaac," he muttered.

"Shut up!" Isaac roared, again turning his fury on Gavin. Gavin quailed back as Isaac rose up on his knees, leaning over him. *"Shut up!* You don't get to speak!" Isaac's voice trembled with tears. "You don't get to fucking *speak*. You don't get to hurt us like that anymore." His breath caught in his chest and his hands shook. "You don't get to hurt us anymore." Isaac crumpled into sobs.

Gray hurried past the others down the stairs, one hand pressed to their own wound. They placed a hand on Isaac's back. They took the knife from his hands and tucked it into their pocket, away from Gavin's reach.

Gavin stared at Gray in disbelief, his eyes darting over their chest, fixing on where he'd shot them. "You... you're not..."

Gray ignored him. "Vera," they said gently, their voice betraying only a hint of tension, "Get something to tie him up with. Everyone else get upstairs and start packing. If he's here there has to be someone else right behind."

No one moved for a moment. They all stood staring at Gavin. He trembled under their gazes.

"I'm here to help," Gavin whispered.

Isaac's hand lashed out and struck Gavin across the face. Gavin fell onto his side with a startled cry. "I said *shut up!*" Isaac screamed.

"There's no one else coming," Gavin panted, his lip oozing blood into the filthy, ancient carpet.

"SHUT UP!" Isaac lurched forward and his hand clamped over Gavin's mouth again.

"Isaac…" Gray's hand landed firmly on Isaac's shoulder. "We need to hear this."

"No," sobbed Isaac. "I don't want to hear another word. I don't want to hear his *lies*."

Vera approached Gray and laid a shaking hand on their arm. Gray turned towards the rest of the team, still standing motionless on the steps. "Everyone get upstairs! Now!"

"If he's telling the truth and there's no one else coming we need to know why," Finn mumbled. They were ghostly pale.

Gavin cringed away from the team as they all gathered at the bottom of the stairs. He whimpered against Isaac's hand.

"Then at least get something to tie him up with," Gray huffed.

"I'll go." Tori's voice shook. She all but ran up the stairs.

"Isaac…" Gray nodded at Gavin. "He needs to tell us why he's here."

"He's just going to lie," Isaac sobbed. "That's what he does… he just *lies*…" Gray looked at Isaac, their gaze gentle. Isaac whimpered. His hands fell away from Gavin's face and he slumped back on his knees. He wiped Gavin's blood on his pants.

Gray stepped in, putting a hand on Isaac's shoulder again and pinning Gavin with their gaze. "We're going to leave very soon, and when we go, we're taking you with us. Tell us what you know," they said quietly. "If you try lying to us, we will ask you a different way."

Isaac gasped softly and turned his gaze up to Gray. He'd never seen them look so dangerous, so completely full of disgust and hate, violence simmering below the surface. He'd never seen them look so *terrifying*.

Tori appeared over his shoulder and passed a length of rope into his hands. "It's a-all I could find in the car," she stuttered, and skittered back away from Gavin like he was going to lunge at her any second.

Isaac's hands shook as he uncoiled the rope. He seethed and gritted his teeth. "If you move, if you give me any reason to kill you, I *will*."

Gavin swallowed. "I'm here to help," he whispered. "I swear to god. I won't move."

Isaac's legs barely held him as he got to his feet and slipped behind Gavin, giving him a wide berth. "Put your hands on your head and get on your knees," Isaac muttered.

Gavin's hands trembled as he laced his fingers behind his head, clumsily maneuvering his legs beneath him until he was kneeling. Isaac slowly approached him, his stomach roiling. "Now put your hands behind your back."

Gavin grudgingly did. "I feel like this is maybe a *little* bit of an overreaction…"

Isaac's hand darted out and twisted in Gavin's hair, yanking Gavin's head back until he had to look up at him. "You're lucky you're still *breathing,*" Isaac growled. He shoved Gavin's head away and knelt, tying the rope tightly around Gavin's wrists. He reached for Gavin's ankles.

"Oh, come on, you're gonna hog-tie me? Really?"

"It's far from the worst way to be tied up," Vera hissed. She shook with tension, her hands locked tightly into fists as she stared Gavin down. He shrunk under her gaze and looked down at the floor.

Isaac walked stiffly around to stand in front of Gavin again, nearly paralyzed with fear and rage and hate. He pressed his lips together to stop them from trembling. Gavin raised his eyes slowly to Isaac's face.

"You have five seconds to answer each question," Isaac ground out through his teeth. "After five seconds I'm going to start hurting you. I'm going to do every *fucking* thing you did to me. Do you understand?" Gavin nodded jerkily. "*Good.* How did you find us?"

Gavin almost tripped over himself to get the words out. "T-tracker on your car!"

Isaac blanched. His ears buzzed. The others all gasped. *"What?"*

"Our p-people in Beringer put a tracker on your car."

Isaac's hands shook. "Then why aren't they here now? Why haven't they taken us?"

"We wanted to track you to the northern outpost." The words rushed from Gavin's lips.

"What?" Tori's mouth hung open in horror.

Gavin stared at Tori, almost apologetically. "They… um…" His eyes flicked to Isaac and he swallowed. "They wanted to know where people are going when they head north. And some of us… wanted to… destroy it. Make it so you couldn't be safe. My m-mom had, um, different plans."

"What plans?" Isaac breathed

"Um…" Gavin wet his lips. "My… mother… wants revenge…" He raised his eyes to Vera. "…on *you.*"

Vera's lips pulled back over her teeth. "Then she can come and *fucking get me.*"

Gavin shuddered. "She wanted you to come to *her,*" he said, looking at the ground. "By offering… um… me."

Isaac's lip curled. "You're lying." He took a heavy step towards Gavin.

Gavin jerked against the rope, nearly falling as he flinched away. *"No! I swear to god I'm not. I swear."* Gavin's breath quickened. "That's why I left. Because… she said… she was going to offer me as bait. And because…" His face darkened and tears shone in his eyes again. "My father already did."

"Your *father* answered your call so he could torture me again," Vera snarled. Her eyes were wild with dark rage.

"I know," Gavin whimpered, cringing back towards the floor. "But he… he knew he could bring you in… if you had the chance to kill me. So, he… he let you come. He didn't bring backup because he thought it was a perfect trap. And he… *I…* misjudged." The last words were almost a whisper. "And he… died… because he let me dangle out there like bait. He died because of *me.*" Gavin squeezed his eyes shut and tears ran down his cheeks.

"Oh, no," Vera said smoothly, the edge to her voice now rounded by cold, simmering rage. "Your father didn't die because of you. He died because of *me.*"

Gavin glanced up at her and wilted under her gaze. Isaac glanced at Vera. Her eyes were dark and wild, her lips pulled back over her teeth, her muscles pulled tight as piano wires under her skin. She looked prepared to tear Gavin apart the same way she did to his father.

Gavin cursed and curled in on himself, the rope pulling tight against his wrists.

"Then why would you come to us?" Isaac demanded, turning back to Gavin. "If you knew we'd come to kill you if you were offered, why come to us at all?"

"Because I..." Gavin swallowed. "Because my mother has... *plans*... for you... once she takes you. If she takes you. And I... can't..."

"What, she'll do something so bad even *you* won't partake?" Isaac's voice dripped with contempt.

"You don't understand," Gavin whispered.

"No!" Isaac roared, and everyone jumped. *"I don't!"* His body moved mechanically forward. He watched as his hand closed around Gavin's throat. "I don't understand... how you could... *hate* someone so much you'd hurt them the way you hurt me." Isaac could feel Gray's hand on his shoulder, gently pulling him away. He threw them off and knocked Gavin onto his side. His gut clenched at the twisted cry that punched out of Gavin's throat. Isaac aimed a vicious kick at his stomach. Gavin let out a ragged scream. "I don't *understand...*" Isaac fell to his knees and threw a blind punch. His eyes swam with tears. "I don't *understand* how you could enjoy *breaking* someone so much." He felt hands on him, pulling him back. He threw them off. "I don't understand how you could hurt me and hurt me and *hurt me* even as I begged you not to. I don't understand how you could *like* the sound of my begging... how you would *laugh* as you hurt me." Another punch to Gavin's ribs. Isaac felt hands dragging him back and he slumped back with them, sobbing.

Gavin convulsed with agony. Sweat shone on his skin. "I... I never *hated* you," he gasped. His lower lip trembled. "I'm *sorry.*"

Isaac's eyes snapped to Gavin's. "You're *sorry?*" Gavin's mouth snapped shut. Isaac jumped to his feet and lunged at him. He pulled his fist back, ready to break Gavin's face open again, ready to stain his knuckles with Gavin's blood again.

Someone stepped between them.

Sam.

Isaac stopped dead in his tracks, his fist still pulled back and hovering in the air. He met Sam's eyes, gutted by the look of fear and pain he found there. His fist fell to his side, loosened. He glanced at the look of terror plastered on Gavin's face. He brought his gaze back to Sam.

Sam stared at Isaac, a desperate plea in their eyes. "Please," Sam whispered. "Please don't do this."

Chapter 10

Isaac's mouth hung open. Sam reached out and rested their hands on Isaac's shoulders, pushing him gently back.

"Please don't do this," they repeated.

Isaac blinked in disbelief. "How can you... *defend* him... after what he did to you...?" His vision blurred with furious tears.

"I'm not defending him," they whispered. "I'm defending *you*."

He shook his head slowly. "I... don't..."

"I don't care if he deserves it or not." Sam's voice gained in strength. "I don't care if he deserves to be tortured. Maybe he does. I don't care. But don't..." They bit their lip, staring beseechingly up at Isaac. "Don't be the one to do it. Don't be like *him*."

"Sam..."

"Please." Tears welled in their eyes. *"Please.* I know you're not like him."

The fight rushed out of Isaac and he slumped to his knees. Sam fell beside him, wrapping their arms tightly around him. They buried their face in his neck.

"Please," they whispered. *"Please.* You can't be like him."

"I liked it," Isaac sobbed.

"You stopped." They squeezed him tighter. "I love you."

"I love you too."

After a long moment, Sam wiped their face on their sleeve and drew in a slow, deep breath. They stood and turned to face Gavin. He had scrambled up on his knees again, staring at Isaac in terror. Sam stopped in front of him. He couldn't seem to look at them, his eyes fixed on their shirt. Their hand went out and touched his chin, guiding his face up until he was forced to look at them. Their lips trembled and it took them a moment to speak.

"I am not your victim anymore."

They let his face drop and took a faltering step back. Isaac caught them as they dissolved into sobs, great heaving gasps that seized in their chest one right after the other. They threw their arms around him and muffled their cries against his shirt. He guided them away from Gavin to stand behind the others.

∴

"Tell us about this tracker," Gray said smoothly.

Gavin tore his eyes from Isaac and Sam in the corner to look up at Gray, the seething hatred in their eyes making him shudder. Pain tore raggedly through his chest and he struggled to take in a breath. "Um…"

"Now." They took a small step forward.

"No, no, no, *wait!* Okay, okay, Jesus…" Gavin swallowed hard. "We apparently have, like, spies or something in Beringer that found your car while you were… um…" His eyes flicked over Gray's chest. He bit his lip. "Um…" His voice grew quiet. "…recovering." Gray raised an eyebrow at him. "And… um… a few families decided that it would be better to track you north and round up the whole… uh… *operation*." His voice was heavy with implication.

"And that's how you knew where to find us."

"Um. Yeah." He stared at the floor. His knees were starting to ache, but it was nothing compared to the hole in his chest. He pushed down the pain. His shirt was damp with sweat.

"And tell me, once again, why you're here?" Gray's voice dripped with contempt.

Gavin trembled. "Um…" He shrunk lower against the ground. "Could I… maybe… get out of this?"

"No," everyone replied in unison.

Gavin's head drooped. "Okay. I… um…" Tears swam in his eyes and he squeezed them shut. "My mom… wanted to do her own thing. She wanted you all to come to her, so her plan was to… use me as bait."

"And you had a problem with this… why?"

"Because… you'd probably fucking *kill me?*"

Gray snorted. "And you thought somehow that *seeking us out* would be a better alternative? Alone? Without backup?"

52

"Well, yeah, I…" Gavin's eyes flicked up to Gray's face. "If I could… *explain* myself first…"

Gray waved their hand as if presenting the opportunity on a silver platter. "Well. Now's the time."

"Um…" Gavin looked shyly up at Vera. "When you… um… killed—"

"When I slaughtered your father like the animal that he is?" Her nostrils flared.

Gavin winced. "Um… when you killed him… and shot me…" The pain in his chest flared. He dragged in a breath. "It… messed me up. Like… *really* messed me up. The smell of blood now, it… and the feeling I used to get… from…" He shivered and looked down.

"Speak, Gavin." Gray's voice was thin with impatience.

"Sorry, I…" Gavin shuddered. "I can't… I can't… hurt people. Anymore."

A bitter laugh echoed through the basement as Isaac took a step forward. "That's fucking great. Fucking spectacular. You've been torturing and killing people your whole goddamn life. You nearly killed Sam, you *shot* Gray and nearly killed them too, you tortured Tori, you broke Finn's hands, you fucked with Ellis's head…" Isaac's voice rose to a shout. "You brought back the man who tortured Vera for *months*…" Gray stepped in front of Isaac. He pushed past them. "You *broke me*…" He shoved down a sob. Gray reached out and grabbed his arm, a deep look of concern on their face. He shook them off. "And now, out of *fucking nowhere* you decide that's not your thing anymore?" He grabbed the front of Gavin's shirt and jerked him upright. Gavin cried out in terror. "Just like that, you're… fucking *cured?*" Gray grunted in pain as they pushed Isaac back. Isaac dropped Gavin roughly to the ground. As he collapsed to his knees, Gavin screamed with the agony that exploded through his wound. Isaac stood behind Gray, chest heaving, his eyes fixed on Gavin with withering hatred.

Gavin's lips trembled. Tears sprung to his eyes. "I never…" His voice wavered. "I never *broke you.*"

Isaac shoved past Gray and threw himself at Gavin, bowling him over onto the ancient carpet. *"Yes, you DID!"* he roared. He grabbed Gavin roughly and shoved him onto his back. Gavin cried out. His wrists jerked against the ropes. "*You broke me!* You beat me and cut me open and made me beg. You made me think I was going to die alone!" Sobs broke up Isaac's words. "You took S-Sam away from us. You made me hurt for, for *months* after we got away…"

"Isaac, no!" Sam watched in horror. Vera stepped closer to Sam and they latched onto her in an instant. "Please…"

Vera bit her lip as she looked down at Sam, and let go. She crossed the room. She and Gray dragged Isaac off of Gavin. Gray cried out and clutched at their wound. They stepped away, gasping.

"I still have nightmares *every night* because of you. I *hurt Sam* because of one of my nightmares." Isaac lurched forward, trying to break Vera's grip on him. His face contorted with rage, tears streaming down his face. "I still hurt, and I still scream at night, and I still feel *broken* because you… you just wanted to *hurt me!*"

"I'm sorry," Gavin whispered.

"*I DON'T WANT TO HEAR YOU'RE SORRY!*" Isaac bellowed. "I don't want to hear you're sorry. I don't want to *hear it!*"

"What do you want me to say?" Gavin cried from where he was slumped on the floor.

Isaac fought Vera's hold on him, his eyes fixed on Gavin. "I want you to…" Isaac sobbed brokenly. "I want you to…" He collapsed to the floor. Sam darted to his side and threw their arms around him. He wailed into their shoulder, arms locking around their waist like they were an anchor in a storm. Sam's tears fell into his hair as they pressed their lips against his forehead. He trembled in their arms.

Gavin watched them with wide eyes. "I'm sorry," he whispered again, almost too faintly to hear.

"How could you expect me to forgive you?" Isaac whimpered, his face still buried in Sam's shoulder. "How could you come here and think we wouldn't kill you?"

Gavin shuddered. "You… you're going to kill me?"

"Yes," Isaac sobbed.

"No," Gray said firmly.

Isaac quailed. "You can't fix this," he whispered. "I don't care if you came to help. You can't ever fix this." He squeezed his eyes shut. "You tortured me for days. You tortured all of us... because it was *fun*." He spat out the word. "You can't fix *me*."

"I... I *did* come to help," Gavin whispered.

"What, you all of the sudden decide you're on our side now?" Isaac snapped bitterly.

"My parents fucking betrayed me!" Gavin cried, strangled with pain and terror. He bit his lip against the tears that started again. He looked warily around the room as everyone's gaze fixed on him. He swallowed hard and kept going. "My dad strung me out as *bait* to get..." He could barely look at Vera. "...to get *you*." He whimpered. "He was willing to risk my life to bring you back. And my mom... my mom *blames* me for that." He pressed the side of his face against the filthy carpet. "Maybe that's why she was willing to risk me to catch you. Maybe... if I died, then at least she wouldn't have to... have to *look* at me every day and think I killed my dad." He wept openly now. "And she fucking cut me off because I couldn't... I couldn't torture someone. She gave me someone to play with and I couldn't *do it*. She cut me off because I didn't want to see you again."

"You what?" Gray stared at Gavin with distrust.

"I... I didn't want to do it. She said she'd use me as bait so she could catch you all and so... so I could torture you all again. And I didn't want to."

"And just like that we're supposed to believe you?" Vera snapped. "We just have to take your word on it that you couldn't torture some poor idiot and now we're all good?"

"You don't get it," Gavin whimpered against the floor.

"No," she seethed. "I don't get it. I've never felt sad because I couldn't torture people anymore. You're right."

"It scares me now," Gavin whispered. "When I think about it, about cutting someone, about making them hurt..." He shuddered. "It just makes me feel scared. It makes me think of... of..." He closed his eyes and swallowed a sob.

"Makes you think of me ripping out your father's throat?"

"Yes." The word was barely a breath.

"Good." Gavin's eyes flew open and focused on her as she took another step towards him. "I want you to remember that forever. I want you to remember that *that* is what happens to people who fuck with me. Who fuck with *us*." She threw a glance over her shoulder at the rest of the team. "And I want you to remember that *that* is what's going to happen to you if you betray us." She took another step forward until she stood over him, hands clenched, trembling. She crouched in front of him and he flinched back, bleating in terror. Her hands shot out and fisted in his shirt. She dragged him up toward her until their noses were almost touching. "Do you understand, bitch boy? Do you understand what's going to happen to you if you ever even *think* about hurting me or my family again?"

Gavin nodded vigorously. "Yes," he gasped. "I swear to god. I swear I will never, never even think about it again. Please..." His voice broke as tears rose in his eyes again. "Please..."

She dropped him unceremoniously to the floor. He grunted as pain shot through his chest again.

"Good," Vera snarled. She stood and looked to the others. "I'd say it's time to move."

Finn and Ellis both heaved out a breath, clutching each other like they would both keel over if they let go. "Yeah," Finn breathed. "Let's move."

"You're taking me with you...?" Gavin looked frantically between them all. "I'm not... I'm not gonna fucking last out there."

"Oh, perfect." Isaac pinched the bridge of his nose between his fingers. "Now he wants our *protection*." His lip curled in a sneer.

"Please," Gavin begged. He pulled against the rope around his wrists. *"Please."*

Gray turned and fixed Gavin with a withering glare. "You're coming with us, alright," they said, their voice low and dangerous. "You're going to tell us all the tricks, all the checkpoints we don't know about. You're going to tell us all the places with your spies. You're going to tell us *everything* we need to know to reach the north safely."

"I don't really know that much about our oper—" Gavin cut himself off in a startled yelp as Gray took a furious step towards him. "No, no, no, wait, wait! I really don't know! I swear! I'm not really in charge of much. You..."

His voice grew petulant. "You fucking *blew up* everything I was in charge of. I haven't exactly had time to build up operations again."

"You figured your first priority after I wrecked your face was to go after us again?" Isaac snarled.

"Not… not all of you." Gavin shrunk away from him on the carpet. "Just… just you. And V-Vera."

"How'd that work out for you?" Vera snapped.

"Um…" Gavin looked away, his cheeks flushing. He pulled at the rope again, pain shooting through his chest as he did.

They all stepped away from Gavin. Finn and Ellis crept forward until they were in the circle, too. Edrissa remained frozen at the top of the steps, staring at Gavin in terror.

"What, are we just gonna…" Finn ducked their head. "…take him with us?"

"Yeah," Ellis snarled. "We're gonna take this fucking *nightmare factory* with us north? What if he's hurt people up there? What if they think we're with the syndicates when we get there?"

"I don't think we'll have to worry about that," Tori mumbled. "I know a few people up there that will be able to vouch for me."

"They won't vouch for *him*." Gray shot a glance at Gavin. He flinched away.

"So they don't have to." Vera's voice was venomous. "I'm sure they wouldn't mind getting their hands on a syndicate son up there."

"What?" Gavin squeaked.

Isaac threw a hateful glance his way. "Shut up."

"But, but you can't just…" Gavin writhed against the ropes, gasping in panic. "You can't just… *give* me to them…"

"Why not? Is that less than you deserve?" Isaac snapped.

"No," Gavin breathed. "Please, please don't…" Helpless tears started down his cheeks.

"Shh. Let the grownups talk." Gray turned away from Gavin. "Either way, you think we'll be safe if we bring him?"

"Yeah." Tori shook, clinging to Vera's side. "We'll be okay." Vera wrapped her arm protectively around Tori's shoulder and squeezed her tight. Tori winced, and Vera loosened her hold with a worried look.

"What about the tracker?" Ellis's eyes shifted between everyone in the circle.

"We'll find it and take it off," Vera said.

Ellis shot a nervous glance at Vera. "What if there is more than one? What if we miss one?"

"Hey, bitch boy," Vera threw over her shoulder. "Did you hear any *details* about this tracker?"

"No," he whimpered. "I didn't hear anything. Just that one existed."

"Okay." Vera pressed her lips together. "We'll just do a thorough sweep." She met Ellis's stare. "We'll be okay. Trackers with that kind of range aren't exactly tiny."

"Then what?" Sam latched onto Isaac, their hands clenched around his shirt.

"Then... we figure out how to kill mommy dearest," Vera growled.

"No," Gavin whimpered. "You can't, please... she's all... she's all I have left."

"What happened to *Mark?*" Ellis spat the name out with contempt. "You two seemed *so* close when we last saw him."

"He's not... *close* family..."

"And yet you took all six of us as revenge for 'taking your family away'," Ellis threw back at him.

"I was just..." The words died in Gavin's throat.

"Oh, do tell. *Please* tell us what you were 'just' doing," Ellis snarled.

"I was... just..." His voice dropped to a whisper. "...being dramatic."

"Now *that's* the understatement of the fucking century." Vera clenched her jaw in disgust.

"Enough," Gray said gently. "Do we all agree, then? We take him north, figure out our next step from there?"

Isaac quivered against Sam. "I wasn't aware this would come to a vote."

Gray fixed their gaze on him. "Of course. If we're going to take this risk, both to our safety and to our... mental health..." They swallowed. "...then yes, it should come to a vote."

"I say we take him," Vera said, "And let him suffer the consequences once we get north."

Gavin shivered.

"I say we leave him here," Ellis said bitterly. "Let him figure out how to survive. Trust fund jackass..."

"We should take him," Finn mumbled. "He might be able to give us information we need."

Gray turned to Isaac and Sam, held tight in each other's arms. "What do you think?"

Sam huddled closer against Isaac. "We should take him," they said softly. "He could help us."

Gray looked to Isaac. "Isaac?"

Isaac's jaw flexed, his eyes staring straight ahead at nothing. "I don't want him anywhere near me," he whispered.

Gray inhaled slowly and winced. "I think we should take him. He could prove useful. And I don't want him free to... get into trouble." Their face darkened. "As long as we know where he is, he can't surprise us." They put a gentle hand on Tori's shoulder. "Your vote counts, too. You're part of the family."

Tori squeezed Vera's hand. "Um..." Tori's hand drifted to her own neck, to the bruises there. "I... I can't."

"You can't have him around?"

"I can't *decide*," she whimpered.

Gray's expression softened. "Why not?"

"I don't want him near me." Her voice rose in a nervous whine. "I don't want him..." She squeezed her eyes shut and buried her face in Vera's neck. Vera stroked her hair gently, her gaze locked on Gavin. "But I think it's for the good of the... of the family. Of the resistance. To get him north."

"You wouldn't have to be around him," Vera murmured. "We'd keep him away from you." Tori nodded, tears wetting Vera's shirt.

Gray exhaled slowly. They looked up at Edrissa, still perched on the top of the stairs like she was about to run. Their brow furrowed. "What do you think, Edrissa? You're with us now, you should get a vote."

She shrunk back behind the railing, her hands clutching the bars. "We can't let him go," she whispered.

Gray paused. "Why not?"

"He's... he's seen me." Her hand went to wrap tightly around her forearm. "Please. He can't go back. He can't tell them..." Her lips trembled. She shrank back, a hand drifting up to protect her head as she crumpled into herself.

Gray made their way up the stairs and slowly approached her. She watched them with terrified eyes. "I think I understand," they soothed. "You don't have to say anything else. It's alright." She nodded jerkily, tears almost spilling over.

Gray turned back to the group, their gaze moving over each of them in turn. "It sounds like we have our verdict," they said softly.

"No," Isaac growled. He took a step towards Gray, Sam still hanging on his arm. "I... I *can't.*" His voice broke.

"We'll keep him away from you," Gray murmured. They walked slowly down the stairs and stood in front of Isaac. Their hands went to his shoulders. "You won't have to—"

"It's my job to protect *you,*" Isaac seethed, eyes brimming with tears. "It's... it's *my job.*" He swiped his hand over his eyes. "And I can't... protect you..." His chest heaved, his breaths coming faster. "...with *him* around. I can't..." He stumbled and Gray caught him. They winced and grunted with the impact. "I can't keep you safe when my mind is... is *broken...* because I keep seeing *him.*" He pointed an accusing finger in Gavin's direction. Gavin shivered where he knelt on the ground.

Gray's eyebrows pulled together, and they squeezed Isaac's shoulders. "We'll all take care of each other," they said softly. "I think it's for the best that we keep him close, keep an eye on him. Maybe use his knowledge. He won't have to be around you. And he won't... he won't *hurt* you again."

Isaac erupted into sobs and leaned against Gray, pressing his face into his hands. "I *can't,*" he wailed. "I *can't.*"

Gray ran their hands up and down Isaac's arms, over the sleeves that Gavin knew concealed rows of now-healed burns. His stomach churned.

"Yes, you can," Gray urged. "You can do this. You're strong, Isaac. You've done harder things than this. And I…" Gray bit their lip. "I hate to ask more of you, after everything you've done. After everything you've *given*. But please…" They pulled him to their chest, hiding a wince. "Please be strong for us one more time."

Isaac whimpered as Sam's arms went around him, too. "I'm sorry," Sam whispered against his shoulder. "Isaac…"

Isaac convulsed in a weak sob, raising his face to look at Gray. He looked so tired. So *resigned*. Isaac pulled his shirt up and wiped his face.

"Okay," Isaac said, gritting his teeth. "Fine. We take him with us."

"You won't have to be around him." Gray squeezed his shoulder.

"I won't have to be around him," Isaac repeated, as if reassuring himself. He blew out a slow breath from between his lips.

Gray's gaze lingered on him for another moment before they stood and walked to where Gavin still knelt, trembling. They towered over him. "Sounds like we've made a plan."

Gavin relaxed, his face pulling into a look of tentative hope. "Does that mean I get out of this?" He moved his arms against the rope.

"No." Gavin's face fell. "You stay tied up, and you're going in the trunk."

Chapter 11

Isaac clenched his jaw until his teeth ached as they sped along the dirt road walled in on either side with trees. The ground and branches glittered with frost under the moonlight. Finn, Ellis, Tori, and Vera sped along behind them in the other car, the headlights glowing in the darkness. Sam, Gray, and Edrissa sat quietly in their seats. Sam was up front again, pressed against Isaac's side for warmth. Gray stared out the window, their eyes far away. Edrissa huddled against the door, legs pulled into her chest, arms wrapped tightly around herself. She was trembling.

Gavin was in the trunk.

"Please," Tori had begged. *"I don't want him in our car, please..."*

"You sure, babe? You sure you don't want him close by so I can fucking gut him *if he gives us any trouble?"* Gavin had trembled on the floor as Vera bared her teeth at him in a vicious grin.

"N-no," Tori had stuttered, grabbing Vera's hand. *"Please..."* Her eyes filled with frantic tears. *"Babe, please... no..."*

Vera had turned to her, face twisting in concern. *"I'm sorry, I didn't mean..."* She'd looked at Isaac. *"Is it okay if he rides with you?"*

Isaac's lip had curled in contempt. *"As long as he stays out of my sight, I don't care."*

"He'll be in the trunk," Gray had repeated. They'd turned a disdainful look on Gavin. *"Don't worry."*

Finn and Vera had carried Gavin to the trunk and tossed him in. Before they'd closed the lid on him, Vera had shoved a gag between his teeth and tied it around his head for good measure.

Isaac put an arm around Sam and squeezed. Their head drifted up and they looked around. Their gaze landed on Isaac and their lips pulled into a clumsy smile. Their head fell against his shoulder and they leaned into his side.

They watched me beat Gavin. Isaac bit his lip. *They watched me turn into a monster right in front of them and they still love me.* He swallowed hard against the guilt that tightened in his throat. *Would they love me no matter what? They've seen me weak, so weak. They've seen me fail them, and beg for them, and nearly die when they needed me alive.*

Isaac's eyes filled with tears, blurring the road. He shuddered against the sinking feeling in his stomach that had been growing in him ever since Sam had found him in the basement of the safehouse, holding Gavin's own knife to his throat, relishing the hot, bitter joy that coursed through his body at the sight of Gavin's pain. At the power it gave him. The control. *Would they love me if they knew how much I liked it? If they knew how much like Gavin I was in that moment?* A tear coursed down Isaac's cheek. *Have I been like Gavin all along?*

Isaac lifted his chin, trying to keep more tears from falling. *Maybe Sam just doesn't know better. Maybe I've fooled them. They're so young, how could I expect them to know? Just because I saved them, once, and far too late to have actually kept them safe...*

He shoved down the sluggish drag of something far darker than regret, something that clung to his insides like tar, coating him, poisoning him from the inside out: the faint, bitter twist of resentment, the seething mass inside him that he couldn't stand to touch, that he couldn't bear to *think* about when it crept into his mind. His scars burned as if the wounds were fresh as shame pulsed in his mind in time to his thoughts: *If I hadn't gone... If I hadn't gone... If I hadn't gone...*

He flinched as a memory invaded his mind: Sam, trembling, beaten, half-dead, holding a gun in their shaking hand, pointing it right at Isaac's chest. Sam, delirious with pain, holding the gun to their own head when they couldn't kill Isaac, not even to save themself from the pain Gavin made them believe was coming. Sam, shaking with sobs, curling in on themself during nightmare after nightmare. *I'm not good to be around them.*

"Isaac?"

Isaac's hand slipped on the wheel and he jerked the car into the oncoming lane. He gasped, grabbed the wheel, and steadied the car, his hands shaking. He glanced at Sam. Their eyes wide in the dark as they looked up at him with concern written all over their face. They placed their hand on his shoulder. "Are you alright?"

He couldn't see the road. There was Sam, kneeling in front of him with their hands cuffed behind them, sobbing. Gavin's voice, so close he could have been standing next to him. *"I'm not going to hurt them, Isaac. Don't worry. I'm not."* That smile, that fucking *smile* Gavin always had as he tortured Isaac. *"You are."*

"Isaac!"

He gasped, hands numb as he let the car roll to a stop by the side of the road.

"It's okay, Isaac. It's okay. You can... you can do it. I can take it."

"No," Isaac sobbed. He fumbled the car into park and threw himself against the door, hands scrabbling for the handle.

"Isaac, it's okay... what's wrong?" He felt Sam's hands on his shoulder, heard their voice strained with tears. The door suddenly opened against his weight and he stumbled out, his legs almost collapsing under him. He staggered to the shoulder of the road and fell to his knees.

"Isaac, no! Please, Isaac, hurt me, please, Isaac please!"

He shook his head. *"Hear that? Sam wants you to hurt them. Do it, Isaac. Give them what they want."*

"I won't do it!" he screamed, his throat raw. His hands twisted in his own hair and he pulled.

A gun to the back of Sam's head, a bullet in the chamber. Sam, the closest thing he'd ever had to a sibling, on their knees in front of him, helpless, as Gavin grinned down at them both.

"Hurt Sam, or I kill them."

He was lost. He was fractured. Were there hands on him? He didn't know for sure. He felt the echoes of his pain rising in his body, flaring to life again. The pain in his back, shredded by the whip. The pain in his arms, seared by the heated flat of the knife. The pain in his chest, cut by Gavin's blade. His throat ached against his screams like it was being crushed. And, *god,* how every breath, every movement hurt from Gavin's beatings.

Sam, *his* Sam. The person who trusted him most in the world. *"Hurt Sam, or I kill them."*

It should have been me. It should have been me, my life. My life sacrificed so Sam could live. My life sacrificed so Sam would never have known

64

the monster I am. My life ended so Sam would never have found out that I'm just like Gavin.

"No..." He sank to the ground, his forehead pressed into the freezing dirt as he sobbed brokenly into his hands.

"I won't do it! Fucking kill me, Gavin, I won't do it!"

But I would beat Gavin nearly to death.

I would hold his own knife to his throat just to watch the fear in his eyes.

I should have died so Sam would be free, would be safe. So Sam wouldn't have to love me even as I became just like Gavin.

Maybe I always was.

"Please, please come, please make him stop this..." Pinned on his belly, Gavin dripping rubbing alcohol onto the lash marks on his back. *They watched me break and beg. What must that have done to them?*

"No... Gavin, don't... don't hurt them, please..."

"I'm not going to hurt them, Isaac. Don't worry. I'm not. You are."

"No. No. I won't. I... I can't."

A gun to his forehead. "Pretty sure you can."

"No."

"It's okay, Isaac. It's okay. You can... you can do it. I can take it."

"I... I won't..." Leaning harder against the barrel pressed to his forehead

"Then you die. Pretty simple."

"Then I die."

"Isaac, no! Please, Isaac, hurt me, please, Isaac please!*"*

"Hear that? Sam wants you to hurt them. Do it, Isaac. Give them what they want."

"I won't do it! Fucking kill me, Gavin, I won't do it!"

The gun pulling away from his head. "That wouldn't be any fun." Then, the thing that broke him. The thing that would kill him: the gun held to Sam's head. "Hurt Sam, or I kill them."

Sam's cry of terror. Their desperate sob as Gavin yanked them back against the gun.

"Sam..."

"It's okay, Isaac. Please..."

The burn of rope around his wrists. "Sam... I can't..."

"You really want them to die, then? You really want that to happen?"

A pull, harder, against the rope.

"You have five seconds to agree to do this, or you'll be cleaning Sam's brains off the floor. I have all six of you now. I won't cry over one dead Sammy." Sam, crying out as Gavin jerked them back again, staring down at them as they cried.

"No..." The tear of Isaac's skin as he pulled against the rope.

"Five..."

"No..."

"Four..."

"Please no!"

"Three..."

"No, no, no, please..."

"Two..."

"Sam!"

"One..."

"NO!" Isaac screamed into the dark, thrashing against the hands on him. He collapsed onto his side, sobbing until his chest hurt.

"What happened?!"

"I don't know!"

"Is he hurt?"

"I think he's... um..."

Hurt Sam, or I kill them. "No, no, no... Sam..." Isaac shuddered against the ground.

"Did he say anything?"

"He... he said..." A whimper. "'I won't do it.'"

"What does that mean?"

"I... I think..." A hand in his hair, moving gently through. Shaking. "He said that when... um... Gavin told him to hurt me. Or he'd kill him." A choked sob. "Then he threatened to kill *me*."

"And you think he's... maybe... seeing that again?"

"I think so."

"Why is this happening?"

"It's got to be *him*. Seeing him again."

"Sam *please!*"

"I'm right here, Isaac. I'm right here."

"No… you can't…" His chest ached. "Please…"

"I'm not going anywhere."

"But I… how can you…?" *How can you love me? How can you feel safe around me, after what you've seen me do?* "Please, go…"

"Go? Isaac, I'm not going anywhere." He felt hands on him, pulling him up. He fell against them. "Come on. Let me…"

"What are we going to do? We need to help him…"

"We can camp here tonight. We can push the cars off the road. We can conceal them in the trees just fine."

"And what about… *him?*"

"We'll keep him nearby. Still restrained. At this point I don't think he'd try to run."

"You believe all that bullshit?"

"Honestly, yes."

"Sam." I have to tell them, have to protect them. "Sam, please… you can't…"

"What is he saying?"

"I don't know… Isaac, you're alright! I'm safe. We're both safe. Because of you."

"I'm not…" *I'm not good. Not like you. I can't be your brother anymore.* "I'm just like him…"

"No." He felt hands tightening on his shoulders. "Don't do that. I don't know what's going on in your head, but you can't say that."

"Sam, can you help him while we move these cars? We really shouldn't stay on the road."

"Of course. Vera, can you—"

"Absolutely."

He felt hands on him, guiding him up. He limply let himself be moved. His legs quivered under him as he felt someone come up under his arm, supporting him. He felt someone else on his other side. Smaller.

Hurt Sam, or I kill them.

He sobbed. "No..."

"Come on, Isaac. Move your feet. There you go."

He could see two things at once, flickering in and out in front of his eyes. One moment, Sam was on their knees in that white room, Gavin's gun pressed against their head. Then, he was being guided off the road into the woods, the moon filtering through the trees. Vera on his left. Sam on his right.

His lips trembled. "Sam," he whimpered. *Sam, I have to protect Sam. From Gavin. From the syndicates. From myself.*

They looked up at him, the darkness obscuring their face. "What is it, Isaac?"

"I'm just like him," he sobbed. Sam opened their mouth to protest but he pressed on. "I liked it. I liked beating him... threatening him... It felt good, to hold his knife... to make him scared..."

"You're not like him." Sam's voice was firm.

"But I liked it," Isaac whined softly.

They both eased him to the ground, behind the line of trees that flanked the road. Vera bent over him, taking his shoulders in her hands as she looked down at him. The moon was just bright enough to show the worry in her face. "Isaac..."

"I'm like him," he whispered, sinking forward as his eyes slid shut.

"Stop," Vera snapped, putting a hand on his chin and jerking his face up. "Cut that shit out, Isaac, *right now.*" He opened his eyes. "I killed Joseph Stormbeck by tearing out his throat in front of his son. And I..." She faltered, her eyelids fluttering against sudden tears. "I *liked it.* You can bet your ass I fucking *liked it.*" Her hands shook. "No one is blaming you, Isaac. No one but you. Where is this coming from?" Her voice sank.

"I..."

Vera lurched forward. "*Joseph* Stormbeck. I..." She swallowed. "I remembered."

Sam looked from Isaac to her, tears rolling down their cheeks. "Vera?"

"I'm not allowed to remember," she whispered. "But I... I did. Joseph. His name was Joseph." She laughed, a broken, twisted sound. She leaned forward and pulled Isaac into her arms. He melted into her embrace. "Hey."

She pulled back and pushed Isaac's head up away from her shoulder so she could look him in the eye. She searched his face with her gaze. "You haven't forgiven yourself for any of it, have you?"

He crumpled against her again. "No," he whimpered. "I can't."

"Oh, Isaac." She wrapped her arms around him. Sam wrapped their arms around them both. Vera pressed a kiss against his forehead. "You've got a long way to go, my friend."

Chapter 12

Isaac's eyes flicked up to look at Gavin every few seconds, checking the restraints, again and again in the light of the fire. Gavin's wrists and ankles were zip tied, a rope passing through the space between his wrists in front of him and around his chest, tying him against a tree. His look of dejection made him look more petulant than menacing. It seemed to amuse Vera to no end.

"What's the matter, bitch boy?" she snickered. "You uncomfortable?"

"For your *fucking* information, yes," he snapped, the corners of his mouth turning down in a pout. He shivered just outside the warmth of the fire.

"My heart breaks for you. Truly. It does." Vera chuckled and turned back to her can of soup, warmed in the coals of the fire. Tori huddled closer against her side and munched on the bit of jerky she held tight in her hand. Vera dug her spoon into the can and fished around for chunks of meat among the vegetables. She scooped up a bite and offered it to Tori. Tori took it gratefully and nuzzled into Vera's shoulder.

Isaac sat opposite Gavin, eyes fixed intently on him. Isaac hadn't been able to take his eyes off him since Ellis tied him to the tree, staring him down as they did it. *"Honestly, I hope you try to escape,"* they'd hissed at him. *"Give us a reason to fuck you up."* Gavin had glared up at them but held still as they tied him up.

Sam bumped Isaac's shoulder with theirs, pulling him out of his reverie. "Hey," they whispered. "Are you okay?"

"Yeah." Isaac's jaw tightened. "I'm fine."

"We'll reach the north." Isaac felt Sam's gaze on his face. "We'll reach the north and then... We'll be okay. We'll have time to rest before we try to fight again. You can... you can get better."

"I'm *fine*," Isaac grumbled. He looked up to see Sam's eyebrow cocked at him in an expression of dubious amusement. "I mean..."

Sam shook their head. "Why can't you just—"

Isaac bristled. "Get over it?"

"—forgive yourself," Sam finished.

Isaac's shoulders slumped. "Sam, I—"

They put their own can of soup down. "I didn't mean get over it. I didn't say that. I would never say that." They leaned against Isaac. "Those things you said. About liking hurting him." They both threw a glance at Gavin, who stared back with an unreadable expression. "I think… I think it's okay to like it. He hurt you, Isaac. Really…" They closed their eyes for a moment, steadying their voice. "…really badly. And he can't fix that. But I think it's okay to…" They bit their lip. "…to enjoy hurting someone who hurt you, at least a little bit."

Isaac looked at them, tears welling in his eyes. "Would you like it?"

Sam chewed their lip. "I… I don't know."

Isaac waved a hand in Gavin's direction. "Go try it," he said bitterly. "Go hurt him and tell me it feels good. That you like it." He pressed his hand against his mouth. "Tell me you're just like me. Just like *him*."

Sam looked back to Isaac. They put a hand on his shoulder. "Isaac…"

He shrugged them off and stood. Without a word he turned and stalked off into the forest.

∴

Sam jumped up and followed him, half-running to catch up to him. Their breath fogged in the cold air as they left the warmth of the fire. "Isaac," they hissed. He didn't stop. "Isaac, *wait*…" They lunged forward and grabbed his arm, yanking him around to face them. Furious tears ran down Isaac's face.

"How can you not see this?" Isaac snapped at them, his eyes blazing with bitter rage. "How can you not see that I… Sam, you're so goddamned naïve sometimes, you can't even *see* that I…" His hands went up to his hair and pulled. "…you shouldn't be anywhere *near me*."

Sam stopped dead. Their mouth dropped open. "…what?"

Isaac paced in front of them, his voice tight with tears. "You're so trusting. You're so *good,* you can't even see what's right in front of your face." He sobbed. "How can you not see that I'm… I'm just like him? He hurt you, Sam. He tortured you for… for *sixty-three fucking hours,* and I thought I could

71

protect you. I thought I could be good enough to be your brother but this *whole time* I was... a monster just like him..."

"Isaac, *stop—*"

"I can pretend to be better, but fact is when I had him pinned, when I..." Isaac shuddered. "When I had his knife to his throat, I... I *felt* it. I knew exactly what it was, and I *liked* it. I *liked* his pain. There's no difference between... between what I am, and what he is." He squeezed his eyes shut. "And after everything you've been through, how could I... how could I *subject you* to... to *me?*" He whimpered and pressed his fists against his eyes. "I want to protect you, *god* I want to protect you, but I can't protect you from me! How can you want to be around me? How can you even... *look* at me right now?" He fell to his knees and sobbed.

Tears rolled down Sam's cheeks. "Isaac, please..."

"I don't care what Gray says about, about Gavin being around bringing all this up. I don't care what they say about it. It's been six months and I... I should be over this. I should be better. I shouldn't want to, want to *hurt* him so much... but it's all I want. I want to just... destroy him. I want to grind him out of existence so he can never hurt me again. So he can never hurt *you* again. But wanting that doesn't make me good. Ever since he showed up I just feel so... so..." His voice cracked. *"...weak."*

Sam's hands tightened into fists as they stared down at Isaac, their chest heaving with sobs, their breath fogging in the cold. "I get it," they whispered, their voice seething with quiet fury. Isaac's head snapped up to meet their eyes. They trembled with the effort of keeping their voice even. "I get it. I can be weak, but you can't because... what? I'm already weak? Because I'm somehow less capable of being strong like... like *you?*" Isaac's eyes went wide at the tightly packed rage in Sam's voice. Tears streamed down their face. "I can break, I can betray you, betray *myself,* but that's fine, no problem, because I'm already broken?"

Isaac reached out his hands to them. "Sam, no... I..."

"Shut up, Isaac," they hissed, shaking. "Just shut up and listen to me, for *once.*" They sniffled. "You're so committed to hating yourself, so committed to *punishing* yourself for breaking, you'll ignore everything we say, everything we tell you. You *know* seeing Gavin again brought this all up. You

know it's making you scared, and you're taking it out on *me*." They gasped, trying to catch their breath. "Of *course* you like hurting him, Isaac. He tortured me. He tortured you. He nearly *killed* you, nearly killed Gray. He hurt every single person you care about. You think I don't like the idea of him getting justice for what he's done? You think I haven't thought about revenge, even a little bit?" Isaac's eyes grew wider. "Of *course* I have. I'm not naïve. I know you want to hurt him. I'd be confused if you *didn't*. But it's just… one more thing, isn't it? One more excuse to hate yourself. And you'd… you'd push me away, just to punish yourself for it. You already have." They swallowed hard and their voice dropped to a whisper. "Is that why you love me? So you can… you can hold me up as this… *angel,* this perfect person, and hate yourself for being… *unworthy?*" A sob rocked their chest. *"Is that all I am to you?"*

Isaac stared up at them from where he knelt in the dirt, the knees of his pants already darkening with the melting frost. His throat worked as he held down his sobs. "Sam," he whispered. "No. That's not… I swear to god, it's not… please…"

"Then tell me what it is!" they wailed.

Isaac collapsed.

Sam stood rigid in front of him, tears coursing down their face as they watched Isaac weep into the cold ground. He bent forward at the waist until he was prostrate in front of them and heaved with sobs, pressing his face into his hands. Sam kept their hands squeezed into fists as they fought the urge to go to him, wrap him up in their arms, hug him. *I won't touch him. I won't touch him if that's all he sees about me.*

"I'm so sorry," Isaac sobbed into the dirt. "I'm so sorry, Sam."

Their voice wavered. "Sorry for *what?*"

He shook his head. "I don't… I don't love you so I can hate myself," he whimpered. "I love you because you're good, and I'm happy when I'm around you. You're my… my *sibling,* Sam. I don't want you to go. Please…" He pushed himself back upright on his knees, his eyes wide with desperation. "Please don't go, Sam, I'm sorry, I don't…" He pressed his shaking hands to his face. "I don't know what's… what's *wrong* with me." He shuddered against the ground.

"I just feel so scared," he whispered. "All the time. Scared that you... you'll leave me, that you'll figure out I'm just darkness on the inside and run..." He looked back in the direction of the camp. "That you all will. That one day you'll all figure out that I'm weak, that I'm nothing, that you'd be better off without me." He cringed away from Sam's gaze. "I don't know why, I don't know where it comes from, but it's just... *in me* all the time, and when I see him, when I remember all the things he did to me, all the things you watched him do..." He whimpered. "It just gets so much worse. And I don't feel... safe. I just feel like that moment is so much closer. That moment when you all walk away."

∴

Sam watched him for a long time. Long enough that Isaac started to shiver in the cold. But he didn't dare move, didn't dare get up from where he knelt in front of Sam. *I can't lose them. I can't fucking lose them.*

When Sam spoke again, their voice was heavy with sadness. "I... I'm not going to walk away."

Isaac crumpled again. He pressed his hand against his mouth and tried to quiet his sobs.

Sam knelt in front of him and ducked into his line of sight. "Isaac...?"

He drew in a shaking breath. "Yeah...?"

Sam chewed their lip. "Don't ever, ever do that again. Don't ever say you don't want me to be in your life unless you really mean it."

Isaac slumped forward. "I'm sorry," he whispered. "I'm sorry. I didn't... I didn't want you to go. I just felt..."

"I know." Sam scrubbed the tears from their face. "But it hurt."

"I'm sorry." Isaac met Sam's eyes. "Can I do anything to make it better?" Isaac trembled, his stomach roiling, his chest aching with the need to *do*. To *earn*. To *deserve*.

Sam leaned back, tears still moving slowly down their face. "Just... give me some space, okay? Just for a little while."

"Okay." Isaac nodded, his heart cracking in his chest. "I promise. I will. Tell me when you're, um... ready to talk to me again."

"I will." Sam tilted their head. "What can I do to make you believe I won't leave you?"

Isaac bit his lip, a fresh cascade of tears rolling down his cheeks. "Um… just… don't leave, I guess."

Sam's eyes bored into him. "…has someone left you before?"

Isaac's breath came punching out of him in a strangled moan. "Ah. Um…" *Gavin knows all this. Maybe Sam should, too.* "Um. My uh… my d-dad. And mom, kinda. And… my… the family I had bef-fore you…" His lips trembled.

Sam finally pulled him into their embrace. "Oh," they whispered. They squeezed him tightly.

"Uh…" A bitter, twisted laugh left his throat. "Yeah."

Sam's hand squeezed the back of his neck. "I'm sorry."

He sniffled. "Yeah. Me too."

"…I still need a little time."

Isaac pulled away and wiped his face. "Of course. Yeah. Take all the time you need." They stayed there together in the dark for a moment.

"Isaac! Sam!"

Isaac's head snapped up. "That's Gray." He staggered to his feet and pulled Sam up beside him. "Shit…" They jogged back to the camp.

Gray met them at the edge of the circle of light thrown by the campfire. They looked weary. Intense.

"Gray?" Isaac's voice approached the edge of panic. "What's going on?" His eyes moved past them to Vera, huddled by the fire. She was on her knees, her hands folded in her lap, her head bowed. "No…"

Gray nodded. "It's Vera. She's there again. Gavin—"

Isaac started towards her. "Gavin *what?*" he snarled.

"I don't think he even meant to." Gray's voice was pitched low. "He was giving Vera attitude and… called her *sweetheart.*"

Isaac turned and descended on Gavin.

"No!" Gavin squeaked, twisting as far away from Isaac as he could. "No no no no no fuck *please* I didn't mean to!"

Isaac grabbed the front of Gavin's shirt and pulled his fist back. "The *fuck* you mean you didn't mean to?" he growled.

"No, no, no, Je-Jesus *Christ*," Gavin babbled. "I didn't know that was a thing. I swear to god I didn't. I didn't know that would do that to her I *swear...*"

Isaac shoved Gavin back against the tree with both hands locked in his shirt. Gavin let out a strangled cry. "You thought you'd just call her what your piece of shit *rapist* father called her when he—"

Gavin dragged in a ragged gasp. "He didn't... *rape*..." Gavin's eyes were wide as Isaac slammed him harder against the tree.

"Yes, he *fucking did!*" Isaac roared, drowning out the sound of Gavin's scream. "He did, and he called it *making her good!*" Gavin cried out as Isaac slammed him back again. "What the *fuck* did you think he was going to have you do to her once he had her and Tori? You thought he'd stop then?"

"I didn't... *no*..." Gavin looked like he was about to throw up.

"You thought that wouldn't be part of it? Are you that *fucking stupid?*"

"No!" Gavin cried desperately. "I'm... I'm not a sexual sadist!"

Isaac's mouth fell open. "...are you fucking kidding? You think that matters to me? You think—"

"I didn't mean it, I swear," Gavin sobbed. "Please... I'm sorry..." He tried to look around Isaac at Vera. "Tell her I'm sorry, I didn't mean to..."

Isaac threw Gavin back against the tree. Gavin sobbed brokenly. His skin was pale and shone with sweat.

"If you *ever* call her that again, I'm going to *kill you,*" Isaac snarled.

He turned and approached Vera slowly. Everyone else watched him with wide eyes as Vera huddled silently beside the fire.

"Isaac..." Gray murmured disapprovingly.

"Yeah, I know." He waved his hand dismissively at Gray. He looked at Tori. "Has she said anything?"

"Of course not," Tori whispered. She stared at Vera with tears in her eyes.

"Oh." Isaac knelt beside Vera. She stared into the fire with a blank expression on her face. Isaac looked at Gray.

Gray licked their lips. "Vera, you can speak."

"Thank you, sir," she breathed.

Isaac squeezed his eyes shut. "We need to get her out of it," he murmured to Gray. He turned to look up at them. "It's not safe for her to be like this out here."

"I know." They looked at her with concern written across their face. "Vera, I need you to breathe with me."

Vera turned to look at Gray, her eyes staring sightlessly through them, at something only she could see. "Not allowed," she whispered.

"You are, Vera. You're allowed to breathe with me. Come on. Breathe in—"

She jerked her head from side to side, a muscle standing out in her jaw. Her lips trembled. "Not allowed to remember Ryan."

Chapter 13

Gray froze. "Vera... Who is Ryan? Is he the one you remembered before?"

She nodded slowly. "Ryan..." She bit her lip. "Ryan..."

Gray pressed their lips into a hard line. They drew in a slow breath, pain catching in their chest like a physical blow. "Okay. What do you remember about Ryan?"

Isaac balked. "Gray—"

"It's important for her to remember this. If it's buried, it will only hurt her."

"But—"

"Isaac..." Gray fixed him with a look. "Trust me. She needs to be able to remember this."

After a moment, Isaac sat back. "Fine."

Gray turned back to Vera. "Vera, what do you remember about Ryan?"

Her mouth fell open slowly. "I..." Her face screwed up in helpless concentration. "I..."

Gray glanced at Tori. She leaned back, away from Vera, her eyes squeezed shut and tears pouring down her face. "Did he work for...?"

"J—" She choked on the sound. She shook her head. "Not allowed to remember."

"We don't have to talk about him. Let's talk about Ryan. You're allowed to remember Ryan."

"Not allowed."

"Vera..." Gray bit their lip. "I say you are. Your memories are yours. They're all allowed. You won't be punished."

She flinched and groaned softly. "Ryan..."

"You said he was a good man. Did he help you?"

"Yes." Her mouth twisted. "He protected me."

"He protected you from... the other one?"

Her forehead wrinkled. "…he tried."

"Did he help you escape?"

Her jaw worked for a moment. "There is no escape. Ryan never existed."

"But—"

"You imagined him. Bad girl. Bad girl. Don't remember Ryan. You imagined him."

"Vera, you have to trust me. You're being good. He was real. Did he help you escape?"

Her lips trembled. "…he… he *tried*…"

"What happened to him?"

Tears rolled down her cheeks. "I don't *know!*" she wailed. "I don't *know,* I'm sorry, I'm sorry I'm sorry I'm sorry…" She pitched forward on her knees. Toward the fire.

"NO!" Isaac yanked her back, away from the flames, and sent her sprawling onto her back.

She shuddered and closed her eyes, reaching her hands up above her head on the ground and letting her legs fall out to either side. "I can be good," she whispered. "I'm not supposed to remember Ryan. I'm sorry. I can be good."

Isaac's hand closed around the collar of Vera's shirt and pulled her upright until she was sitting up. Without hesitating she pushed herself onto her knees again and bowed her head. He snatched his hand back from her like she'd burned him.

"I'm sorry," she murmured. "I won't remember Ryan. I can be good."

Gray crouched at her side. "Vera… You're being good. I promise, you're being good. I need to help you remember him or I need to pull you out. Can you do that?"

She cringed forward. "I can… I can be good. I can try to remember."

Gray hung their head and squeezed their eyes shut against their tears. "Okay. What can you tell me about him? Can you remember what he looked like?"

Her eyes closed as she concentrated. "…tall… taller than me. He was… stronger… could hold me down…"

Gray's head snapped back up as their eyes flew open. "What? Did he... did he hurt you?"

"I..." She bit down hard on her lip. "Yes... but... I understand..."

"What do you mean? Did the other one make him do it?"

She nodded emphatically. "Yes. Yes. He didn't want to. Wanted to help. Wanted to set me free. Save me."

"Did he do it?"

She folded forward and began to shake. "I'm sorry I'm sorry I'm sorry I know there's no escape. There's no way out. I imagined him. Bad girl."

"Okay." Gray looked up to where the trees ended and the stars began. "Okay. I'm pulling you out. Breathe in with me, Vera, and come back. Come back to our camp. Look around at the trees. And the fire. Breathe out."

Her eyes were dead as she breathed mechanically in and out. Her gaze remained far away.

"Good. Again. Breathe in, breathe out." She obeyed. "Good. In, out."

Tori knelt beside Vera, not touching her, but close enough that Vera leaned unconsciously into her warmth. "Good, Vera," Tori whispered. "Keep breathing with us. I love you."

They pulled breath into their lungs together with Gray around the fire, all of them. Finn, Ellis, Tori, Isaac, Sam. Even Edrissa. She sat at the edge of the fire as far as she could get from the others, and as far away from Gavin as possible.

As Vera came back to her body, her breaths came heavier, tears ran from her eyes, and her muscles coiled in pain. She shuddered and opened her eyes. She looked around at her family.

Her mouth fell open. "He raped me," she whispered.

She collapsed into sobs. Tori caught her as she slumped to the ground and pulled her into her arms. Vera wailed in anguish and threw her arms around Tori's neck. Vera buried her face into Tori's shoulder as she heaved forward, tongue clumsy. "I... don't..." she gasped. "I... don't... understand. I don't know why..." She shoved her face against Tori's shoulder to muffle her cries. "I know he didn't want to, I *know* it, but I can't remember what happened..." She choked on her tears. "Joseph must have, have made him. But I can't remember if he's the one who freed me." She ground her face into Tori's shirt. "Ryan… my friend…" Her voice trailed into a whine. "…*raped me*…"

Gray knelt beside her. "Can I touch you?" they murmured. Vera nodded and they wrapped their arms around her and Tori. "I'm so sorry," they whispered. "I'm so sorry. We'll keep looking. I'll try to help you remember."

"I don't want to remember," Vera sobbed. "I don't want to remember that. I remember Joseph… That was bad enough. I don't want to think of *him*. Ryan was my *friend*, I know that. I don't want to think of him doing that." She pressed a hand to her mouth. "I remember what it did to him. I remember how he… *hated* himself…" She whimpered. "But I can't even remember what he looked like. I remember how he smelled, I remember how his hands felt, I remember how it felt when he…" Tori stroked her fingers through Vera's hair as she sobbed. "But I can't even remember who he was. I just have fragments… of his voice, of him… holding me…" She shook her head. "But I can't remember anything else. How could I have forgotten that? How could I forget a whole *person?* My friend?" She pressed her face into her hands and wept.

Gray moved their hand over Vera's back in soothing circles. "The other one was Joseph Stormbeck, you said?" She nodded bitterly. "He forced you to forget, Vera. It sounds like he tortured you until you… couldn't think of him without pain. It's possible you completely buried the memories to keep yourself safe. Of course he wouldn't want you to think escape was possible. If he wanted you to be… compliant." Vera flinched at the word.

"I just…" Vera sniffled. "If he was the one good thing I had when I was down in that cell, I want… I want to remember him. Not what he did to me, but what… who he was. Who he was to *me*. I want to remember *that*."

"You can't force it," Gray murmured. "It'll come. But only if you let it."

"I don't want it to come up if I have to go there every time," she whimpered miserably.

"I don't think you have to. And we'll make sure no one uses that word again."

Vera stiffened. Slowly, she turned to face Gavin. He stared at her with terror in his eyes, and something like remorse. He swallowed hard.

"I'm sorry," Gavin whispered. "I'm so sorry, I didn't know... I didn't realize..." His eyes went wide as Vera carefully got to her feet, wobbling a little before she caught her balance. "I didn't know. I won't do it again. I'm sorry I used that word..." His voice rose to a terrified whine as she approached him. "I'm sorry! I'm so sorry!"

Vera bent down and slapped Gavin smartly across the face. He gasped and stared up at her. She leaned over him. He pressed himself back against the tree as she brought her face close to his until their noses almost touched. Gray rocked forward, ready to stop her if she moved to kill him. Isaac's body tensed, and Gray was certain he was ready to kill Gavin if Vera needed a hand.

Vera's voice was low and deadly as she pierced Gavin with her gaze. "If you – *ever* – say that word again, in my hearing or out of it, I will cut your heart out of your chest with your own knife and I will *eat it* in front of you. Do you understand?"

Gavin nodded frantically, his teeth clacking together. "Yes. I understand. I understand. Please don't kill me. I'm so... I'm so *sorry*." He trembled under her gaze, his eyes filling with tears of abject terror. "I didn't mean to. I'm so sorry. And I... I *swear*... I will never, ever do it again." He pressed his quivering lips together. "I'm sorry."

Without another word Vera stood and returned to her spot by the fire. She folded into Tori's arms again and wrapped her arm around Tori's waist. Finn and Ellis stared at Vera for a long moment, admiration and pride glowing in their eyes. Isaac kept his eyes fixed on Gavin as he took a seat across the fire from him. Sam sat several paces away. Gavin's gaze moved over all of them, and Gray kept a close eye on Gavin. Edrissa looked over at Vera with shining eyes. A smile tugged at the corners of her mouth.

Chapter 14

Isaac stirred. The ground was cold and uncomfortable under his bedroll, but it felt more normal than sleeping in a bed at this point. I've been on the run now for as long as I was at home with my parents. *The thought occurred to him through a thick fog of confusion.*

From the bite in the air, he figured the fire had died down. Weird. I wonder why Finn didn't keep it going. *They'd all gone to bed, leaving Finn to keep watch for the first four hours. Finn was supposed to keep the fire going, keep an eye on Gavin, and watch for anyone approaching the camp. Vera had tied a gag roughly around Gavin's head and triple checked the knots and zip ties around his wrists and ankles before she'd turned in for the night.*

Isaac painfully pushed himself to his hands and knees. I'll see what's going on. No need to wake the others.

The moon just barely filtered through the trees enough to illuminate the ground around him. He rubbed his eyes and looked around blearily for Finn. Where are they?

The coals where the fire had been glowed faintly in a deep, sputtering red. The hair on the back of his neck stood up and he forced himself to push out a slow breath. It fogged from his mouth as he turned in a circle, his eyes moving over the shadows between the trees.

His heart stopped as he saw Gavin was no longer tied to the tree.

He lurched forward, his hands feeling along the ground for the others. His fingers landed on an empty bedroll. Then another. Then another. His breaths came faster and faster as he checked each one. They were all empty. Every single one.

"Hey, Isaac."

He spun around, squinting into the dark at the vague shadow in front of him. His heart hammered in his chest. No. No no no no. This can't be happening again.

The fire sputtered to life behind Isaac. His stomach sank as the light flickered across Gavin, standing at the edge of the campfire's light. Gavin stood over Sam with a knife in his hand, already dripping red to the hilt. Sam, Sam was lying on their side at Gavin's feet, bound, gagged, bleeding heavily into the dirt below. Their eyes fluttered as they drifted towards unconsciousness.

Isaac roared and lunged towards Gavin. Gavin dropped to his knees beside Sam and held the knife to their throat. Isaac lurched to a stop. His eyes were wide and riveted on Sam.

I should have killed him. I should have killed him in that fucking basement. I should have ended his life. Sam... Sam, no...

Isaac fought down a sob as it clawed up his throat. "Gavin... let them go... please..."

Gavin grinned at him. "Or what?" *His hand tangled in Sam's hair and pulled their head up so Isaac could see their face. Their skin was pale and slick with sweat, agony dulling their eyes. The knife pressed harder into their throat.*

"What do you want?" *The words hurt as they made their way out.* "I'll do anything. Just... let them go. Please. Let me help them and let them go."

"Anything I want, huh?" *Isaac's stomach twisted at the darkness that coiled in Gavin's eyes.* "You'll give me yourself?"

"Yes," *Isaac breathed.* "You know I will. You know I'll do anything."

"You'd do it all again for them? You won't get away this time, Isaac. This time I'll have you until you're dead, and that's a promise." *Sam mewled weakly as Gavin wrenched their head to the side.*

"Sam," *Isaac whispered.* "Sam, it's gonna be okay. Sam, just... hang on..."

Gavin tsked. "Oh, I wouldn't be too sure about that." *He dragged Sam onto their back. Isaac gasped at the stain of red that soaked half the shirt they were wearing.* "I think I got their liver. Really not looking good for them."

Isaac barely felt the tears that streamed down his cheeks. "Please," *he whimpered.* "Let me help them. Let me get them to a hospital, please, and I'll go with you. I'll do anything. Please."

"I don't think they'll survive this one, hun."

"Then why—" *Isaac's voice broke.* "Why give me a choice? Why would you... do this? We spared you. I didn't kill you..."

Gavin laughed. "You are so slow sometimes, Isaac." He shrugged. "I did this because it's fun. It's in my blood." He pressed the handle of his knife into the wound. A twisted scream tore out of Sam. Their eyes squeezed shut against the pain before they slumped to the ground and their eyes rolled back.

"No!" Isaac screamed. "Gavin, no... please... Do anything to me, please, just... don't hurt them."

"God, I missed this." Gavin laughed. "Sam bleeding, you doing stupid self-sacrificing shit... I really do have your number, Isaac. You do stupid things for the people you love. And look where that's gotten you."

Isaac's knees buckled and he fell to the ground. "No," he sobbed, crawling towards Sam's limp form. "Sam... wake up, Sam, please..."

"They're not long for this world, Isaac," Gavin sneered. "You stab enough people, you learn where the important things are. And look at all that blood. They don't have an awful lot left."

Isaac was still several feet away from Gavin and Sam, but his hands were already wet with blood. It spilled out over the ground as Sam grew paler and paler. Isaac watched as they convulsed one more time against the wound in their side. They shuddered and lay still, their eyes staring blankly up at Isaac. Empty. Dead.

"NO!" Isaac screamed. He stumbled forward on his hands and knees and pulled Sam into his arms. Their blood soaked into his clothes. He cradled Sam against his chest, sobbing so hard he could barely draw breath. They seemed so much smaller. Lighter. Their eyes clouded over, the warm brown dulling to an empty darkness. Their curls fell over their face, leaving trails of blood on their skin. Isaac smoothed their hair back and pressed a kiss against their forehead. "No," he whimpered. "No, no... no... Sam..." He crushed them against his chest, rocking them. They hung limp in his arms. "I'm sorry. I'm so sorry."

"Say your goodbyes fast, Isaac. I want to get you back home. I miss having you under my knife."

"No," Isaac sobbed. He pressed his forehead against Sam's. His tears rolled down his face and onto theirs. He could feel the blood cooling on Sam's skin already. "No..."

Isaac felt a hand in his hair and Gavin yanked his head back. He stared up past Gavin at the stars above, tears blurring his vision.

"You should have known not to trust me," Gavin hissed. "This one's on you."

Isaac's eyes flew open. He was shaking.

He rolled to his side and tried to bring his hands to his face. His heart caught in his throat. His hands were tied behind his back. He pushed himself up onto his knees, his eyes blurry with sleep and tears. It took him a moment to comprehend what he was seeing.

Isaac's stomach dropped and he cried out as he saw Sam. They were pinned on their belly with their hands tied behind their back. A man knelt over them with one hand in Sam's hair, forcing their face into the dirt. His other hand – Isaac's stomach heaved – held a gun to the back of Sam's head.

Isaac's gaze snapped to the tree where they'd left Gavin. He was still there, his wrists and ankles still zip tied, the gag still in his mouth. He looked absolutely terrified. Isaac's chest began to heave in panicked gasps as he looked back at the others.

His family was lined up in the light cast from the still-burning fire, on their knees, gagged, their hands tied behind their backs. They stared at Isaac. Edrissa was on her knees beside them. She was sobbing, bent forward at the waist as tears streamed down her face. Another man stood behind the line of Isaac's family with his arms crossed in front of his chest. Isaac could see the shadow of a baton held loosely in the man's hand.

Isaac's mind went blank. He launched himself at the man pinning Sam to the ground. Rage and fear burned through his blood, razing everything else to the ground. He skidded to a halt as the man yanked Sam's head up off the ground and forced the gun harder to the side of their head. Sam's eyes were blank with panic as they stared up at Isaac.

The man with the baton rushed toward him. Isaac threw an elbow at the man's stomach. A growl ripped from between his teeth. The man's hand shot out with the baton. Isaac braced himself for the blow.

Agony ripped through him and he collapsed to the ground, his skin prickling with electricity. He moaned and rolled to his knees. His legs shook under him. The man struck him again, this time holding it there. A scream tore from Isaac's throat as his body convulsed around the pain. Suddenly he was on Gavin's table again as Gavin electrocuted him, his laugh loud in Isaac's ears. Then, abruptly as it started, it ended. Isaac lay on the ground, gasping. The man hauled him upright and half-dragged him to the line with the others. He was forced to his knees beside Vera. She was trembling, but Isaac could see a cold rage in her eyes that made his mouth go dry. *There are only two of them. As soon as Sam is clear…*

"I told you this was a good investment," the man with the baton mumbled as he turned to his partner.

"Not worth trading your fucking gun for, you idiot," the other one snapped. His hand tightened in Sam's hair and they whimpered. He shook his head and looked up at Isaac. "That's the last one awake then." He drew himself to his feet and dragged Sam upright by their hair. They cried out, shivering in terror.

Isaac lurched forward. He flinched as the man pressed the gun hard to the side of Sam's head again. A grin spread across the man's face. "Yeah, I figured you'd care about this one, too. Everyone else was *damned* concerned." He jerked Sam's head back and forced them to look at Isaac. Isaac thought he would be sick as he saw the desperate terror in their eyes.

"So," drawled the man with the gun to Sam's head. "I'm pretty damned sure I know who you are. I'm gonna say…" He flicked the gun at Isaac. "You're Isaac?" He waved the gun vaguely at the others. "And… let me see if I remember off the top of my head… Gray, Vera, Ellis, Finn… Sam?" His hand wrapped around Sam's chin and he pulled their face up towards him. "I'm assuming that's you." He glanced at Tori and Edrissa, and Gavin where he was still bound to the tree. "Can't really account for the three extras but they're probably wanted too, I reckon." He shrugged.

Isaac's lip curled. *Bounty hunters.* He swallowed as he wondered what they would say if they knew they had the person who could pay their bounties right here with them.

The man's gaze settled on Isaac. "I'm not in the mood to fuck around. I've been on the road for days, and I've barely slept with how *that* one—" He gestured at the man behind Isaac with his chin. "—snores like a motherfucker.

So, I'm gonna give you five seconds to tell me exactly who you are." He glanced down at Sam. "Or I start into this one."

Chapter 15

Sam's eyes went wide with horror as they met Isaac's gaze.

"No," he growled as he lunged forward. The man yanked him back and struck him with the baton again. A guttural scream ripped from Isaac's throat as he writhed on the ground. The shock ended and he slumped into the dirt. Sweat beaded on his face and prickled under his clothes. The man hauled him back up to his knees and held him still with a hand locked in his hair. Isaac's chest heaved as he looked at Sam, trembling in the man's hands. *Just the same. Just the same, but Gavin's not holding the gun.*

The man jerked Sam up onto their knees. "Five," he drawled.

"No," Isaac groaned.

"Four."

Isaac wrenched his wrists against the restraints. *Feels like a zip tie. Way too tight, even if I dislocated my thumb again.* "Please…"

"Three."

"No."

"Two."

"No no no *don't!*"

"One."

"Please!"

The man shrugged. "Fine." He threw Sam down onto their belly and kept his gun trained on their back. Sam grunted as they hit the ground. The man wound up and kicked them viciously in the side. Sam's scream was nearly drowned out by Isaac's own.

"NO! Fuck you, I don't… I don't know what you're *talking about!"*

Another kick to Sam's back. Sam's cry was a knife in Isaac's heart. "Really? Because y'all match the descriptions of six people the syndicates want *real* bad."

Tears streamed down Isaac's face. "Stop…" He swallowed the tearing feeling in his throat. "I don't…"

The man wrenched Sam's head to the side and pressed the gun against their cheek. They sobbed brokenly as their face was pushed into the dirt.

If I say who we are, we're all dead, including Sam. Isaac stared down at Sam, his mind going blank.

"Tell me who y'all are, and this can stop. We either go our separate ways, no hard feelings, or I pack you up nice and comfy and take you where you need to be. Nobody else has to get hurt." He jerked Sam's face up towards Isaac and dragged the gag out of their mouth. "Tell him to play nice with me."

Sam pressed their lips together and sobbed through clenched teeth. Isaac's jaw locked so hard his head began to throb.

The man sighed. "I can do this all day, you know?" He punched Sam in the back. They jerked and wailed into the ground.

"No," Sam sobbed. They screamed as the man kicked them hard in the leg.

"Ooh. That'll bruise."

"You *piece of shit,* you *leave them alone!*" Isaac roared.

The man laughed. "Or what? This is really easy. You tell me who you are and this stops either way." Another kick, this time to Sam's gut. They convulsed forward with a scream.

Isaac ground his teeth together as he looked up at the man with hatred that burned through his blood. He cried out with Sam as the man kicked them hard in the hip, sending them sprawling onto their stomach again.

"I don't know what you want me to say," Isaac forced out from between his teeth as tears streamed down his face. "Whoever you think we are…" He swallowed a whimper as his eyes flicked down to Sam again. "…I don't know who you're talking about."

The man stared at Isaac for a moment. He abandoned Sam on the ground and walked to stand in front of him. His partner pulled Isaac's head back as the man with the gun knelt in front of him. He surveyed Isaac carefully.

"I reckon," he murmured, "That if you *are* the crew the syndicates are looking for, you know the bounty is only good if I bring you in alive."

Isaac's jaw clenched tighter. He knew it. They all did.

The man's gaze moved over Isaac's face. "So you figure I won't kill this one." He motioned to Sam where they moved weakly against the ground with his chin. He blew out a slow breath. "And you'd be right. Six million is better than five million."

Isaac's eyes went wide. He hadn't known the bounties were *that* high.

"Here's the thing, though," the man continued. "I need to know exactly what I'm bringing in. Y'all might just be..." He chuckled. "...the unluckiest motherfuckers alive, matching the descriptions of wanted people. Hell, you might even be hunters yourselves, given how we found that one." He jerked his chin at Gavin. Gavin cringed back. "But I don't think that's the case. So, last chance, tell me who you are before I move on to something else."

What else would they do to Sam? Isaac looked past the man at Sam, who lay crumpled on the ground. They weren't looking to Isaac, anymore. Their eyes were closed, and their face was pressed into the dirt as they sobbed brokenly. *What more can I watch them do to Sam?* His eyes flicked along the line of his family. They were all looking at him with naked desperation. *They all depend on me. If I say anything, they all die. I watch Sam be tortured by the syndicates. I watch Sam die.* His eyes slid closed, sending a fresh stream of tears cascading down his cheeks. *I'm so sorry, Sam. I'm so, so sorry.* Isaac met the man's eyes.

"Fuck you," he growled.

The man straightened and sighed as he pulled a hand through his hair. He motioned at Isaac. "Jim, gag this one and we move on."

Isaac opened his mouth to scream and a gag was shoved between his teeth. He thrashed as it was tied tightly behind his head. He looked to Sam again. Their eyes were open slightly now. They moaned against the dirt. *No. No. What are they going to do to Sam?*

As the men moved away, Isaac watched Sam's chest heave. He watched the sticks and dirt and mud shift under their body. He watched as they shivered in the freezing air. He didn't notice the men until they spoke again.

"How about you, darlin'?"

His head snapped to the side as he saw them surrounding Vera. The man with the gun stood in front, and the man with the shock baton stood behind her. His lips trembled around the gag.

Vera stared up at the man with a curdled hatred in her eyes that made Isaac's blood run cold. The man laughed and whistled low. "Damn, darlin'. The way you're looking at me looks like you either want to kill me or fuck me, I can't tell which." He chuckled.

Isaac's stomach roiled. *No. No. I can't let them do that to her. Please... I'll tell them and we'll figure it out later...*

Vera growled low in her throat. Isaac shuddered. He knew without a doubt he was going to watch these men die if they gave Vera an inch. Tori whimpered. The man with the gun glanced at her, and turned his attention back to Vera.

The man pulled the gag gently from her mouth and knelt in front of her. "What'll it be, darlin'?" he asked gently. "You wanna tell me who y'all are?"

Vera lunged at him, her mouth open wide. The man jumped back with a hand to his face just as the shock baton connected between Vera's shoulder blades. She slammed onto the ground on her stomach. She convulsed with a scream. The man pulled the baton away, and Vera slumped to the ground with a weak moan. Tori sobbed as she stared helplessly at Vera.

The man staggered to his feet and pulled his hand away from his face. There was a distinct crescent ring of bloody toothmarks on his left cheek. Blood was smeared across the skin and over his hand. A trickle of blood ran from the deepest cut and he cursed.

"Son of a *bitch!*" He kicked Vera in the shoulder. She jerked, already trying to scramble to her feet. The man's boot landed squarely on her back and pressed her back down onto the ground. "Jim! Were you *planning* on holding her like we talked about? Like you held this one?" He jerked his chin at Isaac.

"Sorry, Lester. I didn't think she would..."

"Give me more of your fucking zip ties. We're hog-tying this one."

Tori screamed through her gag. Lester turned and looked at Tori, his mouth sliding into a grin as he looked back at Vera. "Hm," he grunted. "Seems this one's with that one. Good to know." He leaned more weight on Vera's back and smiled when Tori sobbed raggedly.

Vera writhed under Lester's boot as Jim pinned her legs down and bound her ankles together. They forced her legs to bend up until they could zip tie her wrists to her ankles.

"No!" Vera shrieked. "No no no no no *fuck!*" She sobbed and gasped for air as they dragged her back in line with the others and forced her onto her

belly. "Please no!" She dissolved into broken whimpers as they tied the gag around her head again. She whined into the gag as they walked away from her and moved down the line. Tori whimpered, her eyes fixed on Vera.

Isaac trembled as he watched Vera slip away. He watched her whimpers cease, watched the shuddering sobs that wracked her body quiet. Her cheek rested on the frozen ground and her gaze seemed miles away. She was perfectly still.

"How about you?"

Isaac looked up and saw the men standing around Gray. Gray trembled, their breaths seeming to come harder than they had before. Sweat shone on their forehead in the light of the fire. *I wonder if they made their wound worse.*

"I…" Each word that came seemed to cost them. "I don't have anything to say. We aren't who you think we are."

"Hm."

Their scream rent the air as the shock baton pressed against their side. They collapsed to the ground, shuddering and spasming after the baton had been lifted. Their mouth hung open in agony.

"Nothing?" The two men dragged Gray upright by their arms. They cried out, tears pouring down their face.

"What's this?" The man with the gun, Lester, prodded at Gray's chest. A dark stain spread slowly over their shirt. Finn lurched forward with a cry. "Looks like you…" He pulled Gray's shirt up over their chest and revealed the patch of gauze covering their wound. It was red and leaking blood.

The man laughed. "Huh. Yeah, that checks out. The one matching *your* description…" He let Gray's shirt fall. "…was seriously injured. Wanna make this easy and tell me who you are? We could get you to medical attention." He grinned.

Gray looked faint. "We're… not…" They squeezed their eyes shut against the pain and swayed on their knees.

"Hey, alright. We might come back to you." The man took another step to stand in front of Finn. "How about you? You ready to tell me something I can use?"

Finn glared up at the man. They quivered with rage. Lester laughed. "Okay. Got a fierce one here." Finn whimpered even as they bared their teeth at him. Lester pulled the gag from their mouth. "You wanna tell me what I need to know?"

"You're wasting your time, you son of a—" They convulsed as the baton struck them in the back. Ellis lurched forward with a muffled scream.

The man looked over at Ellis, staring at Finn with tears in their eyes as they quivered on the ground. "Ooh! Got another couple. You think maybe if I..." He kicked Finn in the shoulder.

Ellis jerked forward, a ragged scream tearing from their throat. The man laughed. "Jim, see if that worked."

Jim pulled the gag out of Ellis's mouth. Ellis screamed the words, tightly packed with hatred. *"Fuck you, FUCK YOU, you son of a bitch, touch them again and I'll fucking KILL YOU—"*

"Aw. Touch them? Like that?" Lester kicked Finn again.

"NO! Fuck you, I will KILL YOU—"

Finn lay whimpering on the ground as Lester stood in front of Ellis. "You wanna use that mouth to tell me who y'all are? Or are you just gonna keep screaming profanity at my sensitive ears?"

"FUCK YOU! You pathetic piece of shit son of a BITCH I'll tear you to pieces, I'll fucking—" They whined in protest as the gag was forced back between their teeth.

The man motioned to Finn. "Get them up, too." Ellis's eyes were wide and streaming with tears as they looked Finn over, mumbling wordless apologies into the gag as Finn sobbed. Jim stuffed the gag into Finn's mouth again and tied it behind their head.

Tori cowered, silent and shivering as the men stopped at her. Her face was wet with tears as Lester looked down at her. "And you? You don't match the descriptions of anyone the syndicates are after. What are you doing out here, honey? You with her?" He gestured to Vera with his gun. "If you're not a part of this, you have nothing to fear, right?" He pulled the gag from her mouth.

"I..." she whimpered.

The man ducked a little closer. "What was that, honey? I didn't hear you."

"I..." She swallowed. "I don't know what you're talking about." She trembled and squeezed her eyes shut as she said it. "Please—"

She screamed as the baton touched her arm. She fell to the forest floor, convulsing until the shock ended and she lay still. Vera didn't move at the sound of her screams. Didn't blink.

"I don't know anything," Tori whimpered. "Please…"

"Get her up," Lester sighed. She was roughly dragged up and forced to her knees. She wept quietly.

The man finally stopped in front of Edrissa. She was still sobbing, trembling. Her eyes were wide with terror. Lester knelt down in front of her.

"What about you, sweetheart? You seem like you'd be willing to tell me a few things."

Gavin's eyes went wide. His gaze snapped to Vera as the word *sweetheart* left the man's lips. Gavin's breath stopped for a moment and realization crossed his face as he saw, for the first time, that Vera was deep, deep under. He whimpered and looked back to the men standing around Edrissa.

Lester eased the gag from between Edrissa's lips. "Come on, sweetheart. You don't look like you're part of this. *God* you're so young. Tell me, honey. Can you tell me?"

"Yes," Edrissa gasped. "Please, please… I'll tell you. I'll tell you everything."

Chapter 16

Isaac rocked forward. *"No!"* he screamed. The word was caught and muffled by the gag. Burning tears of frustration spilled over his cheeks. *After all this, after everything, she's going to be the one to get us killed. I should have killed her before we even left Beringer. I should have kept my family safe.*

The bounty hunter looked over at Isaac with a grin. "Uh-oh, someone doesn't want you to spill the beans." He turned back to Edrissa and drew her hair back from her face. "Go ahead, sweetheart. Tell me who they are. I think I know, but I want to hear it from you."

Edrissa whimpered and glanced over at Gavin. He stared at her in terror, his mouth working against the gag. "Um…" She sniffled. She motioned to Gavin with her chin. "This is Gavin Stormbeck. He's the one who'd pay the bounties." Gavin withered. The bounty hunters both gasped and fell back a step.

Edrissa set her jaw and met the bounty hunter's eyes for the first time. "My name is Edrissa Worthington. I'm Gavin's p-plaything." Her lip trembled as she said it and tears shone in her eyes. She looked along the line of the others. "I don't… I don't know who these people are. They haven't told me their names, anything. They kidnapped me and G-Gavin and I… I don't know why." She shivered and tears spilled down her cheeks. "Please, I don't know if they're who you're looking for but… please… don't let them take me. I want to go with you." She whimpered softly.

The bounty hunters' eyes went wide. They both turned and stared at Gavin as he trembled against the tree. Lester crossed to Gavin and gently pulled the gag from his mouth. "Is this true? You're Gavin Stormbeck?"

Gavin took a long look at Edrissa. She met his gaze and held it.

Gavin took a shuddering breath and turned to the bounty hunters. "That's true. I have my ID in my wallet if you don't believe me. And as for *them*…" His lip curled as he glanced at the others. "I have no idea who they are. I don't know if they planned to ransom me, or what. But I'd *appreciate* it," he said through gritted teeth, "If you'd help me leave their... *custody*." He smiled. "I'm sure I could find a way to compensate you."

Isaac couldn't breathe. He couldn't move, couldn't *think*. He couldn't comprehend what had just come out of Gavin's mouth.

"Uh... yeah." Lester shook himself. He tucked the gun into the back of his waistband. "Sorry. Jim, uh..." He held his hand out. "You have those wire cutters? Get him out of those restraints. And..." He pointed at Edrissa. "...and her, too." His hand went up to rub the back of his neck. "Sorry about that. If I'd known who you were I think it, um... I think it speaks for itself that I wouldn't have... um..." He cast his eyes down guiltily.

"It's fine," Gavin grumbled. "I wouldn't exactly expect to find me in such an... *undignified* position, either."

Jim cut the zip ties around Gavin's wrists and ankles, and moved on to Edrissa. Gavin wormed his way out of the rope around his chest and staggered to his feet. He walked to Lester's side.

"So, Lester— It's Lester, right?" Gavin held out his hand. Lester shook it warily. He relaxed a little when an easy smile settled on Gavin's face. "No harm, no foul. I know you've got a job to do and it sounds like you're damned good at it."

Lester looked at his shoes. "Appreciate that, sir."

Gavin turned to face the others. Isaac looked up at him with a mix of fear and confusion burning in his chest – and not a small bit of hope. He felt dizzy. *Could he really be...?*

Isaac's gaze was drawn back to Vera. She lay silent and still on her stomach, eyes unfocused and far away.

"As for them. I'm sorry, but I think they just might be the unluckiest idiots ever. I've only been with them for a few hours, but they don't seem to be the ones I put out the bounty for." Gavin pursed his lips. "I think you might just have to keep looking." He rolled his eyes. "Although I fucking wish they were. I've got *plans* for whenever someone finally brings them in."

Disappointment hung on Lester's face. "Yes, sir. Well... would you like me to put them down for you? I mean... they kidnapped you, that's got to be punishable by *something*, right?" He turned his gaze up to Gavin, hopeful.

Gavin has more pull than I gave him credit for.

Gavin placed a hand on Lester's shoulder. "That might be warranted, yes. But... let me do it." Gavin turned to look at Isaac and the others, contempt twisting his features. "They haven't exactly been kind to me. I'd like to repay their treatment in Stormbeck fashion."

"Sure, of course, sir," Lester stuttered. He pulled the gun from his waistband and handed it carefully to Gavin.

Gavin took the gun, calmly surveying the others. His hands shook.

Oh, no. He's actually going to do it.

Isaac looked down at Sam. They lay sobbing on the ground, their forehead pressed into the damp earth, the frost melted by their breath. *"Sam,"* Isaac cried. A sound vaguely resembling their name made it through. They lifted their head, eyes raw from crying. They stared at each other for a moment, and Isaac knew they were both thinking the same thing.

I love you.

BANG.

Isaac jerked. His eyes flew up to Gavin. The bounty hunter toppled to the ground.

Gavin fired two more rounds into Lester's chest where he lay. Gavin was pale as he snapped the gun up to aim at the other bounty hunter. Jim turned to run.

"Stop," Gavin said forcefully. "Think about it. You don't have a gun and I *will* shoot your sorry ass if you try to run. Put the baton on the ground."

Isaac dove forward, throwing himself out of range and covering Sam's body with his own. He looked up. Tori scrambled away from Gavin and Jim. Gray weakly shuffled to the side on their knees. Finn was already on their back, working their bound hands to the front. Isaac flinched as Sam cried out weakly, trembling under him. His gaze snapped back to Gavin.

The bounty hunter shook as he followed Gavin's orders. He placed the baton on the ground and slowly straightened, his throat working in terror as he stared down the barrel of the gun.

"Come here, get out from behind them. Come here." Gavin jutted his chin at the ground behind him, away from the group. Jim wobbled on clumsy legs as he made his way there. "Get on your knees." The man all but collapsed to the ground. For the first time, his eyes fell on the body of his dead partner. A choked sob made its way up the man's throat. "Now—"

His voice was drowned out by Isaac's roar. Still bound and gagged, Isaac leapt up and descended on the bounty hunter. The man screamed as Isaac kicked him onto his back.

"No!" the man shrieked. "No, please! I'm sorry, I didn't—" Isaac's boot smashed into his face, silencing him. Isaac raised his foot and brought it down against the man's head, over and over again until he saw something clear leaking from the man's ears and nose, mingling with the blood.

"Isaac, stop!" Gavin shouted, tucking the gun into his waistband and throwing himself between Isaac and the body. Isaac blindly lunged forward. His eyes blazed with rage. Gavin shoved him back. "Fucking *stop!* He's dead, he's..." Gavin fell to his knees and shuddered. He squeezed his eyes shut. He lurched forward and retched into the grass.

Isaac stood still, transfixed by Gavin as he unraveled at his feet. Gavin dissolved into messy tears, burying his face in his hands and sobbing. "He's dead," he whispered. "I can't... no, no, no, *no*..." He crumpled in on himself.

Isaac felt hands on his wrists and jumped. Finn appeared at his shoulder with the wire cutters. Isaac let them cut the zip tie around his wrists and reached up to pull the gag from his mouth. He mindlessly wiped his boot on a fallen branch of pine needles.

"Isaac..." He spun around at the sound of his name, at the sound of the terrified voice that said it. Sam stumbled towards him, their face wet with tears. They tripped into him and he squeezed them tight, wrapping his arms around their waist and lifting them a few inches off the ground. They held each other and cried.

"Vera..." Tori whimpered. The spell was broken. Isaac set Sam down on the ground and turned to see Tori kneeling at Vera's side. Tori wept as she pulled the hair back from Vera's face. Isaac's hands shook at the blank look in Vera's eyes.

Gavin still has the gun.

His stomach dropped. He whirled to find Gavin on all fours, still heaving. Isaac stepped forward and snatched the gun from Gavin's waistband.

Isaac leveled it at him, and his eyes blurred with tears. His gaze snapped to Edrissa, standing frozen beside Gavin.

"What the hell was that?" Isaac bellowed at her. She flinched and cringed away like the gun was pointed at her. "What..." Isaac licked his lips. "What *was that?* Did you... did you *mean* for that to happen? And how did they...?" His eyes landed on Finn and they quailed under his gaze.

"I'm sorry," Finn whimpered. "I'm so sorry. They snuck up on me when I was getting firewood and gagged me first. They woke us up one by one and tied us up and gagged us. I'm so sorry..." Their voice wobbled on the edge of tears. "I wasn't asleep, they just... I swear... I just didn't see them!" They sobbed raggedly.

Ellis put their arms protectively around Finn and glared at Isaac. "It's true," they snapped. "*That* one—" They thrust their chin at the man Gavin had shot. "—held a gun on Sam as the other one woke everyone up one by one. Threatened to kill Sam if anyone made noise. It wasn't Finn's fault." Their hands went to cradle the back of Finn's head as Finn wept into their shoulder.

Isaac's head snapped back to Edrissa. His heart beat in his chest so hard it ached. *I thought I was going to watch Sam die. I thought I failed all of them.* He ground his teeth together. "Did you know...?" His eyes flicked between her and Gavin. "You better explain yourself *right fucking now.*"

Edrissa had her hands over her mouth, her throat working around sobs. "I'm sorry," she whispered. "I thought..." She looked down at Gavin, kneeling on the ground, finally finished retching. Gavin had his hands over his head as he stared at the gun. She looked from Gavin to Isaac, and back to Gavin. "I... thought..."

"*What* did you think?" Isaac screamed at her. His shirt was damp with sweat, and he shivered in the freezing air. Edrissa fell to her knees with a keening wail.

"Isaac..." He felt a hand on his arm, pulling the gun down slightly. He brought wide eyes to Sam. Their face was streaked with mud and tears, and they bit their lip like they were barely holding in a sob. "Isaac, please... can't you see you're scaring her?"

He looked at Edrissa. She was inconsolable, cowering on the ground away from Isaac. He clenched his jaw shut.

Sam went to her side, limping on the leg that had been kicked. She flinched when they touched her. "I'm sorry!" she wailed. "I'm sorry, I'll be good, please don't..."

"It's okay," Sam said softly, pain adding an edge to their voice. "No one's going to hurt you. We just want to know what you were thinking. Do you understand why it scared us?"

"I wasn't betraying you," she sobbed. "I couldn't. You've been good to me. Protected me."

"Can you tell me what you were thinking when you said those things?"

Edrissa pulled her face away from her hands and looked again at Isaac and Gavin. Gavin breathed hard, his hands still in the air, eyes still fixed on the gun in Isaac's hand. He looked like he was about to topple over. "I just... thought..." She pressed her lips together and shook her head.

"Edrissa, please. Help us understand. We need to know we can trust you." Sam's voice was soft, patient.

"I thought... they didn't think I was with you, and I thought if I could get out... and get... *him* out..." She looked at Gavin. "...I thought he would... I hoped he would understand, and... do something. He's *syndicate,*" she hissed. "I thought maybe he could..." She coughed on her tears. "I didn't have a plan. I just wanted someone to be untied so *someone* could do something." She looked to Isaac and dissolved into tears again.

Isaac's hands ached around the gun. His body buzzed with rage and adrenaline, his instincts telling him to kill Gavin right here and kill Edrissa immediately after. He felt ghosts of pain moving through him, tearing him open where he stood. He staggered and fell to one knee.

Gavin watched him with wide, horrified eyes. Isaac struggled to keep the gun pointed at him, tried to force himself to focus, to be okay. *I have to be okay.* His mind was on fire. *I have to be okay I HAVE TO BE OKAY I HAVE TO BE OKAY!* He whimpered and his hands shook around the gun. Tears blurred his eyes.

He felt a gentle hand on his wrist again and he looked up to see Finn, eyes wide, gently pulling the gun from his grasp. He collapsed to the ground in a heap.

He felt arms around him as he shook apart. Somewhere, in a faraway corner of his mind, he thought he could smell Sam as the arms tightened around him. It took him a moment to realize someone was sobbing.

"—thought I was going to watch you die," he whimpered brokenly. "I thought they were going to send us back and torture us again, and I ca—" He choked on his tears. "I *can't* watch that happen to you again, Sam, no... please..." His fingers dug into their back as he clutched at them. He registered a hiss of pain. He released Sam and curled in on himself. "I, I th-thought..." He sobbed. "He was going to kill you. I thought he was... *no*..."

"Isaac, it's okay, it's okay! I'm safe. He's not going to hurt us." Sam sounded frightened.

He could barely hear them. He was breaking open, he was going to *die,* he was being hurt and hurt and *hurt* by the man who was huddled in the dirt next to him. He couldn't see the woods. He couldn't see the bodies of the men he and Gavin had just killed. He could only see the inside of a dark room with chains hanging from the ceiling. He could only smell the blood Gavin drew from him. He could only hear Sam as they cried, *begged* Isaac not to hurt them. He wasn't safe. He would *never* be safe. There would always be people who wanted to hurt him and the people he loved. There would always be people who wanted to hurt *Sam.*

Sam's voice faded back in, on the edge of panic. "...please, Isaac, *stop.* You're okay. You're safe. You're never going back there. We're safe, Isaac. The hunters, they're... they're dead, Isaac, *please*..."

"Isaac, you're alright," came Gray's strained voice. "But we have to move. Someone might have heard the... the gunshots."

He barely felt the hands pulling him upright and guiding him to the car. When he blinked past the tears he could vaguely see Vera by the light of the fire, her face empty, being helped by Tori and Gray. Gray's warm black skin looked pale.

He could barely feel Ellis on one side, Sam on the other, supporting him between them as they walked. When he turned to look back, he saw Finn herding Gavin into the other car, the one that Vera and he weren't being helped into. He saw Edrissa behind them. Then he felt the car seat under him. He felt Ellis leave his side and jog to the other car to climb in with Finn. He watched

Gray stumble into the other car, too, clutching their chest. He could barely feel his body as Tori climbed into the driver's seat of their car, throwing a worried glance at Vera, who sat motionless in the passenger seat. He felt Sam press against his side.

Someone was still sobbing.

Chapter 17

It was light before they stopped again.

"Anyone need a break?" Tori said quietly. Her hands were tight on the wheel.

"Yeah," Isaac mumbled.

"Yes please," Sam said.

She guided the car off the road and Ellis followed suit behind them. Isaac leaned against the door even after the car had come to a stop.

Sam put a hand on his shoulder. "…Isaac?" Their voice was almost a whisper. "Are you okay? We're stopped."

He trembled and blinked slowly. "Yeah."

Sam bit their lip. "Do you want to get out?"

After a moment Isaac fumbled along the door handle. The door opened and he nearly toppled into the dirt by the side of the road.

Sam was at his side in seconds. Isaac put out a hand and held them at arm's length as he stood. "I'm okay," he whispered. "I need to be okay." His breath fogged and he shivered against the freezing cold.

"It's okay if you're not." Sam's forehead furrowed with worry. "Isaac…"

"I'm sorry," he whimpered. "I know you said you needed space. You don't need to be taking care of me…"

"I…" Sam took a step back. "I do still need space. But… Isaac, with the hunters… I know it scared you."

"I can't stop feeling scared." Isaac fought back tears. "I'm so scared, and sometimes it's just… it's too much, and I…" He glanced at Edrissa where she stood beside the other car. She watched him warily. He put his face in his hands. "What's wrong with me?"

"You, um…" Sam glanced at Tori. She stood protectively between Vera and everyone else. Vera still looked dazed. "Tori says you have PTSD." They tentatively reached out with one hand. The gently touched Isaac's arm.

"And you... you haven't forgiven yourself. I thought you were getting better, those months with Tori, but I don't think you ever let yourself... rest." Sam took a step closer and placed their hands gently on Isaac's arms. "I don't think you ever trusted us enough to really let yourself heal."

Isaac looked at Sam. Their eyes swam with tears. His jaw clenched tightly. "Sam, it's... not because—"

"I know. But you carry so much, Isaac. So much more than just..." They threw a glance over their shoulder at Gavin. He was standing a little away from the others. Unbound. Sam shivered in their jacket, the only thing they'd been able to take from the hospital.

"I almost killed him, Sam. And Edrissa," Isaac whispered.

"No, you didn't," Sam said gently. "You wouldn't have done it."

Isaac fell silent. *They don't know. They don't know how close I came to pulling the trigger on both of them.*

Sam's hand wrapped gently around Isaac's. "You need to let yourself heal if you want to be able to help more people." Then they dropped their voice so Isaac could barely hear them. *"You're not like him."*

Isaac shuddered against the rush of guilt and grief that rose up at those words. He shook his head. *Maybe grief is the first step.*

Sam squeezed Isaac's hand. Isaac rested his free hand on Sam's and squeezed back. His eyes went wide when they flinched. He gently took their hands and turned them. There were raw spots on their wrists where they had struggled against the zip ties. Isaac's hands started to shake. His eyes moved over Sam, really seeing them for the first time since he'd killed the bounty hunter. Their jaw was clenched in pain. They winced every time they took a breath. They were hunched over as if it hurt to straighten up all the way.

"Oh, shit. Sam..."

"I'm okay," they said, slightly breathless.

Finn appeared at their side. They kept their eyes down as they moved their hands quickly over Sam's injuries. "I'm sorry I didn't get the chance to check you before we—"

"It's okay." Sam winced as Finn pulled their shirt up. Isaac's jaw clenched at the bruises that stretched across their torso, angry and purple. Finn's hands checked the bruises quickly and firmly. They pointedly looked away from Isaac.

"Finn." Isaac bit his lip.

Their hands moved down Sam's left leg, then the right. "Yeah?"

"Finn, I'm..." His jaw worked against the words that pushed against his lips. *I'm sorry I lost control. I'm sorry I'm so damned volatile. I'm sorry I blamed you. I'm sorry I'm broken. I'm sorry I'm sorry I'm sorry I'm sorry...* He cleared his throat. "I'm sorry."

Finn froze where they knelt in front of Sam. Isaac saw the glimmer of a tear on their cheek before they swiped it away and stood. "'s fine." They turned to head back to the other car.

"No, it's not." Isaac followed them and they stopped short. "Look, I..." His throat worked. "I lost control. I'm sorry. I know it's not your fault what... what happened. I wasn't trying to blame you, I was just... scared. I needed to know how it happened, but I didn't have to ask like... like *that.*"

Finn stared at the ground beside Isaac. "Um. Yeah."

Isaac opened his hands. Relaxed his shoulders. Took a breath. "I know it wasn't your fault. I'm sorry for yelling, and for... um... what I said. I know that something's, um." He cleared his throat again. "Something's wrong. I know. And I... I'm going to get better." Finn looked up at him for the first time. "I'm sorry for taking it out on you. It was wrong, it was my fault, and I am going to do my best to never do it again."

Finn's eyes shone with tears. "Do you think, maybe..." they ventured, "You could... trust us? Depend on us?" They chewed their lip. "We're here for you, Isaac. Just like you are for us." They stepped forward and pulled Isaac into a hug. He wound his arms around them and shivered. "I hope you know that."

"I..." Isaac's throat worked. "I'm learning that."

"Okay," Finn mumbled against his shoulder. "Well, I say this as your medic and your friend, and I say it with love... Will you *please* stop being such a dumbass?"

Isaac chuckled wetly against Finn's hair. "Um. Yeah. Let me work on that."

"I love you, Isaac. We all do. Every single one of us."

"I know." Tears pricked Isaac's eyes. He blinked them away.

106

"Well, we should…" Finn cleared their throat and stepped back, wiping their face.

"Yeah." Isaac swiped his hand at the tears on his face, too. "Thanks, Finn."

Finn glanced over Isaac's shoulder. "Well, except for Gavin, maybe. I don't think he loves you much. But fuck 'im."

Another laugh, this one easier. "Yeah. Fuck 'im." He glanced back at his car. Sam, Tori, and Vera had already gotten back in. "How bad is Sam hurt?"

"Well, you saw." Finn's jaw worked as they looked at Sam through the rear windshield. "The bruising is pretty bad. I don't think they broke anything, miraculously. Maybe cracked a few ribs. But…" They rubbed the back of their neck. "I hate to say it quite like this, but if there was life-threatening internal damage, they'd be fucking dying right now. And they aren't. So, I think we're in the clear."

Isaac glanced at the other car. "How about Gray?"

Finn shook their head slightly. "They popped their stitches and were bleeding a bit, but I got that stopped. Same situation with them. If there was internal bleeding there would be signs. And I'm not seeing any."

"That's… that's good."

Finn moved their hand through their hair and, for a moment, they looked so much older than twenty-seven. *They've been through so much. They deserve to rest. They feel responsible for others, probably just as much as I do.* Their eyes went wide for just a moment when Isaac put a hand on their shoulder. "Once we get north, we'll all have time to rest for a while."

"Yeah," Finn snorted. "That's what we thought with Tori's place."

Isaac bit his lip. "We should probably get moving. We've still got a long way to go."

"Yeah." Finn turned and headed for the other car. Isaac walked a little unsteadily to his car. Tori stared at him as he closed the door.

"Everything okay?" Her eyebrows pulled together.

Isaac nodded. "Yup. Just wanted to check with them. Sounds like Gray is—"

"I checked with them. Yeah. Sounds like they're okay, too."

Isaac's mind still felt fuzzy. He hadn't felt right since they'd all been jumped in the woods. He couldn't quite think fast enough to keep track of everyone. "Right." He turned his eyes to Vera now, sitting still and dazed in the front seat. "You, um." His eyebrows pulled together. "You alright?"

The car started moving. Vera looked back at him, her face haggard with pain. "Um."

Isaac drew his hand through his hair. "Uh. Stupid question. I'm sorry, I'm not—"

"I remembered more."

Isaac froze. He looked over at Tori. "Oh."

"I remember what he looks like now. Ryan. I remember him. Um. Hurting me. But I…" Tears brimmed in Vera's eyes. She didn't seem to notice. "I remember him holding me. I remember he, um…" She swallowed hard. "After a party one time. He… he cleaned me up. Bandaged my wounds. He um, gave me water and… and held me. He gave me a blanket. Just held me."

Isaac's blood ran cold. "A… a *party?*"

Vera's eyes were still unfocused. "When Joseph would invite his friends over to rape me." She said it so robotically it made Isaac's stomach heave. Tori gasped out a silent sob. "But I remember him. Ryan."

"Do you remember what happened to him?" Isaac's voice was shaking.

"Um." Her face screwed up in a look of tortured concentration. "I… I… *can't…* It's like it's still behind a wall. I remember a plan. A plan to get me out. But I… can't… He was working with some people to get me out but I just… can't…" She whimpered.

Isaac's hand shot out towards her before he stopped himself. His hand squeezed into a fist and he sat back against the seat. His hand fell into his lap.

"Vera, um…" Sam said in a tentative voice. "It's okay…"

"I just… can't… *remember,*" she whispered. "I don't know if the people who pulled me out were there because of Ryan. I don't remember seeing him with them, but… maybe he was…" She pressed her hands against her forehead. "Augh…"

"It's okay, babe," Tori murmured, and stretched a hand out to rest on Vera's shoulder.

"Do you think it was…" Isaac's lips twisted. "…being… um… tied up like that? Or when the bounty hunter said… um…"

"It was being tied up like that," Vera whispered. "For one of the parties that's exactly how I was tied up. The first one."

Isaac shuddered. "There was more than *one?*"

Vera met his gaze with haunted eyes. "I remember at least three."

Sam whimpered beside Isaac and he ached to reach for them. *They said they need space. They'll come to me for comfort when they're ready.*

"I'm so sorry, Vera," he whispered. "God, I'm… I'm so sorry…"

"It's okay," she mumbled. Isaac's head snapped up to look at her, expecting to see a look of submission and fear. Instead he saw blazing eyes and bared teeth. "It's okay. Because no matter what I remember, no matter what… I killed him. I slaughtered him. Ripped him open. I tasted his fucking *blood.*" Her lips pulled back in a grin.

An image flashed across Isaac's mind, of her standing in the waiting room stained with that monster's blood, quivering with fear and relief and exhaustion. Of her folding into his arms after she'd torn Joseph Stormbeck open with her teeth.

"Yeah," he whispered. "You did."

"No matter what." Vera's hand rested on Tori's thigh, her eyes still a little unfocused. "I did that."

Chapter 18

It felt like hours since Isaac had seen something that wasn't endless hills stretching out into the distance. There was snow on the ground up here, several inches that made everything look so peaceful. Ice decorated the trees. The sun shone through the clouds as they moved through the sky, shimmering on the snow and making it light up so bright it was blinding.

Far ahead, a dark shape stood near the side of the road. Isaac squinted and leaned forward in the seat, staring at it.

"Tori?" he said softly. "What is that?"

"Um…" Tori leaned forward, too. "I think it's…"

"A horse," Vera said softly. Isaac looked over at her, at the broad smile on her face. "I think that's a horse."

"A *horse?*" Sam pushed past Isaac to stare out the windshield. "That's a… a horse?"

As the family approached, Isaac realized it wasn't one horse, but two, standing side by side next to the road. They were each wearing some sort of blanket that made them look like they were wearing a coat against the cold. Sam pressed their face against the window as they passed.

"A *horse,*" Sam breathed.

"Have you ever seen one before?" Isaac asked with a chuckle.

Sam didn't turn back around, but rolled down the window to poke their head out and watch as the horses fell behind. Once the horses shrank to a tiny dot behind them, Sam pulled their head back inside and stared at Isaac with a huge grin, cheeks pink from the cold.

"No," Sam said. "At least I don't think so? Maybe I… a long time ago." They smiled wider. "But never that *close!*"

"It's been a long time for me," Isaac said softly. "I haven't seen one of those since I was a kid. They…" He chuckled. "They look funnier than I remember."

"That means we're just passing into Crayton," Tori said with a small sigh of relief. Isaac fell silent.

They drove through more pastures, most of them empty. Then, houses. Spaced out at first, then closer together, a suburb instead of farmland. As the family passed through neighborhoods, quiet and serene, a car started to follow their little caravan. Another one pulled up alongside them as soon as the road widened into two lanes. By the time they reached the town center, another one had joined, just behind the first.

"What are they doing?" Sam swallowed hard as they looked out the window at the cars. Their windows were tinted, darkened nearly to black.

Tori's hands tightened on the wheel. "They're escorting us," she said tersely.

"E-escorting us?" Sam's eyes widened.

"These people essentially hold the line for the north, if the syndicates were to ever decide they wanted control up here, too," Vera murmured, staring straight ahead. "They're making sure we're not a threat."

Isaac ran his tongue over his lips. "It's alright, Sam." Sam turned to him. "They're not going to hurt us. They have no reason to."

"Their reason to is riding in the car behind us," Vera growled. She kept her gaze forward.

Isaac fell back into the seat. *They're right. If Gavin decides to act like a dumbass, which is highly likely, we might be shot right alongside him.* His jaw clenched.

"We've gone over this," Tori said as she blew out a slow breath. "They do this with everyone. They'll stop us in the main square and take us to their town hall for... well, not *processing* but, you know, to see what our intentions up here are and to take down our information. Find out where we're headed. And since they know me, know *of* me, anyway, the process should go pretty quickly."

"As long as Gavin doesn't act like an idiot," Vera grumbled.

"As long as Gavin doesn't act like an idiot," Tori conceded.

"I'd feel better if he was in the damned trunk still," Isaac ground out through his teeth. He shot a glance at the car behind them and could just make out Gavin's silhouette through the windshield.

"Bringing someone into the southern checkpoint tied up and in the trunk isn't exactly *subtle*," Vera grumbled. "If the point is to not be killed…"

"Yeah, I know," Isaac said, darkness clouding his face. "It just makes me fucking jumpy."

They pulled through the last intersection and cleared the buildings along the square, ringed by trees and light poles. Tori pulled over and slowed to a stop, Finn right behind her.

The cars following them followed suit. Two people climbed out of each of the three escort cars. They were all warmly dressed against the cold, and all had guns on their hips.

"As if it's not obvious," Tori said calmly over her shoulder, "Leave your guns in the car."

"Yeah." Isaac nodded. "I figured."

They all slowly opened the doors and stepped out of the car. Snow crunched under their feet. Isaac kept his hands out and open, showing he meant no harm. His breath fogged in the chilly air and he shivered under his jacket. He looked over at the others. They all looked as nervous as he felt. Except Gavin. Gavin looked *terrified*.

Fuck, I hope he doesn't get us killed.

One of the people in the escort cars immediately relaxed when she saw Tori. She turned to the others, and to the small crowd of people that had gathered around the cars already. "This is Tori Nasser," she said over her shoulder. "This is them." Everyone relaxed a little.

Tori hesitated for a moment. Her brow furrowed. "…Stephanie?"

The young woman smiled. Half of her mouth didn't pull quite as high as the other. Isaac noticed a scar running from her throat, below her ear, to just shy of the corner of her mouth. "Yeah. It's me. I made it north. Brian, too. He's around. The kids are in school right now."

Tori's mouth fell open in a delighted smile. "You have a *school* here? That's incredible. Stephanie, I am… I'm *so* relieved you made it. I know the Fosters were hot on your trail for a while."

"They lost the trail when we stayed with you." Stephanie stepped forward and pulled Tori into a hug.

Tori wrapped her arms tight around her and laughed. She pulled away and put a hand on her shoulder. "Guys, this is Stephanie. She and her husband stayed with me a few years back." Tori laced her fingers under her chin and her eyes shone with tears. "I can't believe…"

"Who else did you bring?" a taller man said. He still seemed a little twitchy. Isaac watched him, noticing how his hand stayed close to his gun.

Tori sniffed. "Oh. Sorry. Um. This is… Isaac Moore…"

Isaac's cheeks flushed at the quiet gasps that rose from a few people. He stared at the ground. Tori's hand rested on his shoulder and squeezed. She looked around at the others again. "Sam Vasterling. Finn Dunham, our medic. Ellis Price. Gray Uriah. Vera Novak. My. Um." Her cheeks flushed bright red and she proudly took Vera's hand. "My girlfriend." She looked to Edrissa. "This is Edrissa… Worthington?" Tori frowned. Isaac looked over at Edrissa. She was frozen, her eyes wide and fixed on the crowd of people gathered around.

Tori's eyes turned at last to Gavin. "And this is—" She stuttered. "This is Joshua." Isaac swallowed hard. *I hope to Christ it works.*

The people who'd gathered moved through the group, nervously shaking hands. Isaac felt himself quiver and shrink into himself at the light press of bodies. *No one here is hurting me,* he forced himself to think. *No one here is going to torture me.*

He turned to look at Sam. An older woman with graying hair pulled them into a hug and squeezed them tight, then did the same with Finn, then Ellis. They all accepted the comfort, dazed.

His stomach sank as he saw the nervous-looking man from before staring at Gavin with murder in his eyes. "You've got a Stormbeck in your crew," the man spat through clenched teeth.

Fuck.

Isaac found himself falling back a step. Standing between the man and Gavin. Reaching for his gun. It was tucked away safely beneath his seat in the car.

The mood of the crowd froze. Where there were friendly smiles before, there was now only fear and distrust. Anger twisted a few faces in the crowd.

Fuck. We're dead.

113

The man strode forward a few steps towards Gavin and again, Isaac found himself putting himself between them.

The man drew his gun. "I don't give a *fuck* who you are, *Isaac Moore.* You've got a Stormbeck with you that's reason enough to kill you right fucking here."

"Stand down, Lucius," another man from the armed guard said gently. He walked behind Lucius and stepped to his side, looking evenly at Isaac. His temples were silvered and he had calm, piercing blue eyes that passed over Isaac once. Surveying him. Lingering on the folds of his jacket, at the ankles of his pants. Isaac jolted with a realization: *he's looking for weapons.* Then the man stepped around Isaac towards Gavin.

Isaac moved towards Gavin again, and Lucius's hand twitched on his gun. Isaac froze. He turned slowly and watched as the other man approached Gavin. He spoke calmly. Perfectly in control, and clearly in charge.

"What's your name?" The man's blue eyes moved over Gavin's face, over the scars. Over the fresh bruises Isaac made days ago.

Gavin's lips trembled as he answered. "Um. J-Joshua, sir." Scared as he was, Isaac had to suppress an eye-roll. *Oh,* now *you start treating people with respect.*

The man tilted his head. "Hm." He looked at Gavin closer, at his eyes, at his jaw. The man's eyes moved over Gavin's hands, his build. Looking, clearly, for someone else in how Gavin stood. He took a step closer. Isaac's stomach clenched. "So you're *not* related to the late Joseph Stormbeck?"

Gavin's lips tightened, his eyes going a little wide and then a little narrow. Tears shone in them for a moment before he could blink them away.

The man's gaze hardened. He turned back to the others. "I agree, Lucius. This is more than just a *very* unfortunate, random resemblance." He nodded at his entourage. "Take him."

"No." No one could have been more surprised than Isaac as the word left his lips. Before he could move, Lucius had his gun halfway up to Isaac's chest.

"If you're harboring a Stormbeck, if you brought him *here,*" Lucius snarled, "You should die right alongside him."

The other people descended on Gavin. They dragged him away from the cars and further into the square. He writhed against their grip and screamed in terror. His feet skidded on the icy cobblestones. "*NO!* No, please... no... oh god..."

"*No!*" Isaac shouted. "He's with us now! He changed sides! He's not syndicate anymore."

"If his name's Stormbeck, he'll *always* be syndicate," a woman hissed at him.

Two men dragged Gavin to a light pole and threw him back against it. Gavin fell to his knees, gasping. They jerked him to his feet again.

Someone produced a short length of cord from a pocket. The men pulled Gavin's arms back behind the pole and wound the cord around his wrists. He sagged as they stepped away. Someone broke rank from the crowd and slapped him across the face. Another darted forward to spit on him. Someone else stepped forward and drilled a punch into his abdomen. Gavin gasped and fell to his knees again. His cheeks were red against the ghostly white of his face.

"*Hang him!*" someone screamed.

"*No!*" Gray tried to shout over the crowd. "We brought him north under our protection! He's working with us!" They pressed a hand to their chest and coughed. Finn was at their side in an instant and tried to pull them away from the fray. Edrissa trembled on the edge of the crowd, her eyes wide, frozen in place.

"Please!" Sam begged. "Please! We're telling the truth. He's good now. He's... he's trying."

Someone shoved Sam back and they nearly fell. Rage curdled in Isaac's stomach and he stepped forward, between Sam and the person who pushed them. The person paled and fell a step back when they saw the dark, seething violence barely contained in Isaac's quivering frame.

"*NO!*" Gavin shrieked. Isaac spun to look at him. His stomach dropped.

Someone had found a length of rope. He watched as a man tossed one end up and over the light post. Gavin flinched as the end hit him in the face as it came down. The man pulled the end down and tied a noose into the end.

Isaac lurched forward. *"No,"* he growled. "He's with *us*. He's *our* spy. You can't kill our fucking *spy*."

That made the man in charge pause and turn. "Your... *spy?*"

Isaac gritted his teeth. "That's right."

The man snorted. "You can't possibly ask me to believe that this boy, whom I strongly suspect is Gavin Stormbeck, has been torturing, mutilating, and killing people for years and it's all because he's been a *spy* for you?"

Isaac swallowed, but didn't back down. "He's the reason we made it here. He warned us about the spies in Beringer. He told us about syndicate checkpoints on the way up. He..." His voice faltered. "He helped us escape some bounty hunters on the way here. He *killed* one for us."

The man's lip curled. "That means nothing. All that could mean is that he's trying to gain your trust and you *gave it to him.*"

"Look at him!" Isaac screamed. "He's broken. One of mine *broke him.* And he's under our protection now." He threw a glance back at Gavin. The noose was around his neck. *"NO!"*

Isaac lunged forward and threw himself against the rope. It nearly lifted the man on the other end off the ground. He fumbled at Gavin's neck as he tried to loosen the knot. Hands closed on him and dragged him away from Gavin. The rope pulled tight around Gavin's neck. Gavin tried to cry out, but the rope tightened around his throat. Tears streamed from his eyes and his mouth gaped open, desperate for air. Isaac was forced to his knees. His hands were pulled behind his back.

"Please," Isaac begged. "He's our best hope of winning now. You're killing your best asset."

The rope tightened further. Gavin jerked in panic.

BANG.

A few people screamed. Everyone froze and turned towards the sound of the gunshot behind them.

Tori stood in front of the crowd, Isaac's gun held in the air tight in her shaking hand. The man's entourage all drew their weapons and raised them halfheartedly at Tori.

She was trembling and pale. "Oh, *go ahead,*" she snapped. "You're gonna kill me? Go ahead."

"No," Vera hissed. Isaac glanced at her and saw that she was also on her knees in the snow, a few feet to his left. Edrissa whimpered and stumbled a step towards Tori.

Tori gritted her teeth. *"I'm* the reason there's an organized system to get refugees north. *I'm* the one who sends your families to you. Go ahead and shoot." Sweat shimmered on her skin. She looked like she was on the verge of falling over.

She pointed at Gavin. He quivered against the pole, gasping around the rope. *"He* got us here. Yeah, he's a murderer and a bastard and a sadist but *we* broke him." Her eyes flicked to Vera. *"We* made him understand what it was to be hurt. To be afraid. Vera killed Joseph Stormbeck in front of him. Vera *shot* him. And he can't be the way he was anymore."

The man in charge stepped forward, tension trembling beneath his calm. "What do you mean, he *can't?"*

"He can't stand the smell of blood. Can't stand to even think about hurting people. His family cut him off, kicked him out. He works with *us* now." Tori's voice sounded a little stronger.

The man paused, calculating. He turned back to Gavin. "Let me see." He snapped at the men holding Isaac. "Get him up."

Isaac immediately realized what they were going to do. He let them do it. *If they see, we might get out of this alive.*

"Gordon, let go of that rope. For Christ's sake." The rope loosened around Gavin's neck. He dragged in a broken gasp.

The men holding Isaac dragged him to his feet. They pulled his right arm in front of him and yanked his sleeve up. One drew a knife from his pocket. Isaac's stomach clenched and he jerked back at the sight of the blade.

Gavin's not holding it. I'm not going to be tortured. They just need blood. He forced himself to blow out a slow breath.

"No, no, no," Gavin whimpered. "No, please, I'll—"

"Quiet."

Gavin didn't stop. "You don't have to do that, please, don't—"

The man slapped Gavin across the face. "I said *quiet."* Gavin sagged, sobbing. Red bruises encircled his neck.

The man pressed the blade to Isaac's arm and cut. Isaac gasped in a breath and bit his lip. His vision swam for a moment. *I have to do this, or they'll never believe us. They're going to kill us all.* The pain made him feel dizzy, slippery, like he was going to slide right out of his body. Blood ran freely from his arm and began to drip from his hand.

The men forced Isaac forward and shoved his arm into Gavin's face. Gavin cried out and turned away. A hand grabbed his hair and forced his head towards the blood. He held his breath. Tears rolled down his cheeks.

The man chuckled. "If you insist on holding your breath, we will just wait until you pass out and do this again. Another cut. Another time."

Gavin whimpered. He squeezed his eyes shut and breathed.

Gavin's eyes went wide, and he went rigid against the pole. His breathing sped up, catching in his chest, moving the wound there. He heaved forward and sobbed.

"P-ple-ease," he whimpered. "N-no..." He hiccoughed and gagged. The others jumped back, dragging Isaac with them.

Gavin fell to his knees and retched into the trampled snow. He bawled like a child. "I'm so-orry," he slurred. "Pl-please..."

The man watched Gavin with raw fascination. Isaac's eyes snapped between him and Gavin. Blood dripped from his fingers into the snow.

"Interesting."

"That's what I told you," Tori said at Isaac's shoulder. It brought him back a little. He shook himself. "We broke him, and he's with us now."

"What, like a..." One of the men's faces twisted. "...like a *pet?*"

The look of loathing that crossed Tori's face made the man wither. Isaac's lips pulled back over his teeth. "Say that word again," he growled. The man took a step back.

The man in charge turned to Isaac. "Very well. I'm convinced." A weak cry of protest rose up, but died just as quickly when he raised his hand. "As long as you're here, though, he will *not* have free rein of the town. You will keep him in your custody. If your custody does not satisfy me, I will make other arrangements."

"What the hell do you think we've been doing on the way up here?" Isaac snarled.

The man turned and leveled his gaze at Isaac. "He was completely unrestrained when you arrived, like he was one of you. *Don't* try to pretend that wasn't to avoid suspicion."

Isaac returned the man's gaze and clenched his jaw shut.

The man turned to Gavin. Gavin still knelt on the ground, his hands bound behind the pole, trembling and sweating. He had completely unraveled. The man grasped his hair and pulled his head up. "Look at me, syndicate boy." Gavin raised his glazed eyes to him. "If you betray us, lead any of your family to us, in any way jeopardize a single life during your time in my territory..." The man crouched and brought his face close to Gavin's. "...I will break you in ways even your twisted mind can't imagine. Do I make myself *perfectly* clear?"

Gavin nodded vigorously against the man's grip. "Yes. Yes, I understand. I swear to god I... I won't..."

"Swear to whomever you wish," the man said, his voice dropping lower. His gaze moved over Gavin's face. Then he stood and sighed. "Tori Nasser and her group are welcome here. They are taking responsibility for this one." He gestured to Gavin. "No one is to harm them or obstruct their movement when they choose to leave." He turned in a circle and stopped finally in front of Tori. "And if you are wrong, if he has somehow deceived you and I, I will hold you—" His eyes narrowed. "—and your family *personally* responsible. And you will break right alongside him."

Vera struggled on the ground, still held by the guards. She bared her teeth at him at the threat.

Tori lifted her chin and met his eyes. She looked like her old self again. Strong. Centered. "We risked worse than you to get here," she murmured. "And he's with us."

The man stared her down. Tilted his head. Stepped away. Smiled. He motioned to the men still holding Isaac and pinning Vera on her knees, and they were released. Isaac looked around and saw Finn and Ellis had been held, too. Sam clung tightly to Gray. Gray's head was bent, their breathing labored. Edrissa went to Tori's side and hovered at her elbow, careful not to touch Tori. She wrapped her arms around herself.

"My name is Daniel Schiester," the man said with a smile. "Welcome to Crayton."

Chapter 19

"Daniel!" came a woman's voice, harried and strained. Isaac looked around and saw a woman pushing through the small crowd towards them. "Daniel." She reached them and crossed her arms over her chest. Her gaze was hard. "You're going to just... let them go?"

Daniel tilted his head. "Yes, Mable. I'm going to just let them go."

"But *this one*—" She flung her hand in Gavin's direction. He was still on his knees, shivering and sobbing. "—*this one* has done... *terrible* things. You've heard the stories..."

"I have." Daniel nodded. "But they've broken him. Look at him." Daniel glanced down at where Gavin quivered in the icy mud. "He could do so much good for us now."

The woman's eyes filled with tears. "You know what he does," she whispered. "You know he... he tortures people, *kills* them, Daniel..." She turned to Gavin with fury. "How many *playthings* have you had, Stormbeck *shit?*"

Gavin sniffled and shuddered, the noose still hanging loosely around his neck. He didn't look up at the woman. "Twenty—" His voice broke. He swallowed. "Twenty-three." He turned his head up to Isaac and met his eyes a moment. He looked back down. Looked *ashamed*. "Twenty-four, including him."

Isaac's cheeks burned as everyone's gaze seemed to snap to him. He absentmindedly pressed his hand over the cut on his arm. His skin was slick with blood and sweat.

Daniel stared at Isaac with a new light in his eyes. "You... he tortured *you?*"

Isaac felt the shadow of the knife, the ghost of the whip. He shuffled his feet. He said nothing.

Daniel tilted his head. "So the rumors are true."

Isaac swallowed. "What rumors?"

"That you were held. Tortured. That you escaped Stormbeck captivity. I knew you're the one who marked up his face like that, but…" Daniel smiled and dipped his head a little. "…you did that from *within his captivity?*" His mouth pulled into a wider grin. "You're the first person I've ever heard to survive Gavin Stormbeck."

Isaac's eyes flicked to Sam, still clinging to Gray. "I'm *not* the only one."

Daniel turned to look for Vera. "And *you* killed Joseph Stormbeck? *You* shot this one?" He motioned to Gavin.

Vera took a step forward. "Yes," she growled.

Daniel grinned wide now. "Interesting." He flicked a hand at Gavin. "Cut him loose. He's with them."

"No," Mable whimpered, tears straining her voice. "Daniel, you have to… you have to do… *something…*"

The man rocked back on his heels and bit his lip. He looked at the ground for a moment, then up at Gray. They still gasped softly for breath. "You're the leader of your group?"

Gray nodded weakly. "Yes," they breathed.

"I do think it appropriate that this one be punished for his crimes, at the very least."

"No," Gavin moaned from where he knelt on the ground. "Please…"

"Quiet," Daniel spat. His eyes stayed fixed on Gray. "I do not feel content with sending you all along without seeing *some* kind of justice dispensed."

Isaac's body flared with pain again. He felt the knife, the whip, the burns. He felt the deep ache in his thumb where he had torn the skin open, and in his shoulder that had been dislocated as he escaped. He saw Sam, tottering on that chair. Sam, aiming a gun at his heart because Gavin had convinced them that Isaac was there to hurt them. He saw the blankness in Vera's eyes after Gavin claimed her— Isaac remembered that now. Gavin *claimed* her. *"You belong to me now. I claim you."* A dark curl of rage twisted his gut. *There is no justice for that.*

Gray sagged a little. Finn appeared at their elbow again. Their eyes widened with worry and their hands jerked slightly towards them.

122

"You want me to dispense justice to him?" Gray asked, sardonic.

Daniel's lips twisted. "He can never be fully brought to justice if you insist on keeping him alive. But yes. I do want *some* kind of justice, though it will be meager compared to the damage he's done."

Gray set their jaw. Isaac saw a small bloom of red on their shirt. His stomach lurched. *I hope they have what Finn needs up here to fix them up.* He watched Daniel's eyes flick to the spot, too.

"Alright. I can do it. Meager justice. Thirty lashes."

"Fifty," Daniel said evenly. He snapped at one of his entourage. "Get them a cane." They jogged off immediately.

"No," sobbed Gavin. "No, please…"

Daniel stepped around the puddle of Gavin's vomit and dragged Gavin halfway off his knees by his hair. "Do you believe you deserve less, Gavin Stormbeck? For ending twenty-three lives for your own pleasure? For torturing him?" He pointed at Isaac.

Isaac stepped forward with bitter rage still curdling in his stomach. "You don't speak for me," he growled at Daniel.

Daniel released Gavin's hair, his eyes fixed on Isaac in bemusement. He licked his lips and tilted his head. "My apologies." He threw a glance around at the crowd and gestured to no one in particular. "Get him up. Tie his hands in front of him, facing me."

Two people moved forward and yanked Gavin roughly to his feet. He sobbed piteously. "Please," he begged as they pulled the noose off his neck. "Please don't do this. I'm sorry… I'm sorry…"

Daniel snorted. "He's *sorry,*" he muttered. Someone returned with the cane and put it in Gray's hand. Their fingers curled around it as they looked down its length.

The northerners cut the cord tying Gavin's wrists behind the pole and wrestled him around to face it. They roughly stripped off his jacket. They pulled his arms around the pole and tied his wrists together again.

"Please don't do this!" Gavin sobbed, his voice rising in panic. "No, no, no… *no…*"

Daniel turned to Gray. "Fifty lashes." He gestured at Gray's chest. "Are you in a condition to administer them? I could have one of my people—"

"No," Gray said, a little breathlessly. "He's with us. I'm going to do it." They stepped away from Daniel and behind Gavin.

Everyone in the crowd could see Gavin's face. It was streaked with tears, and pale, except for the bruises Isaac had left there. He begged wordlessly now, twisting his wrists against the cord, cringing into the pole and away from Gray behind him. Isaac felt twin emotions rising in him as he stared at Gavin.

He felt a cruel rush of satisfaction. *He tortured me for pleasure for five days. He tortured Sam for information for three. He hurt every single person I love. He shot Gray. He brought his father in so they could own and hurt Vera together. He tortured Tori just for being our friend. He hurt Finn and taunted Ellis about their family. He killed* twenty-three people *before he ever got his hands on Sam.* His heart pounded in his chest and he felt the warmth pooling in his gut as he stared at Gavin's terror.

He felt a painful flood of empathy. He knew exactly how it felt to be bound, hurt, about to be tortured. He knew exactly how it felt to be told how and for how long he was going to suffer. He knew the terror that preceded agony. He knew the humiliation that came from having your power stripped away.

Rancor spiked in him again. *Maybe we should make Gavin count the lashes for us. It's only fair.* The cut on his arm burned as he squeezed his hand tighter over it.

Behind Gavin, Gray's eyes squeezed shut as their hand tightened around the cane. They took in a deep breath and winced. They opened their eyes. They drew their arm back and brought the cane down on Gavin's back.

Gavin jerked and cried out. To his credit, he stayed on his feet. Isaac threw a glance at Vera and saw her standing stock still, her hands bunched into fists by her sides. Isaac moved to stand next to her.

"You okay?" he said quietly.

She jumped slightly but nodded. "Yup."

His gaze moved over her face. "You don't have to—"

"I do." Her eyes swam with tears. "I do." Tori appeared at her other side and wrapped her arm around Vera's waist. Isaac turned back to Gavin.

Gray struck Gavin again. Gavin screamed. Tears poured down his face.

Again. A wail drew out, long and tortured, from his mouth.

124

Again. After his cry died on his lips, his mouth stayed pulled open in a silent scream.

Again. Gavin jerked forward, clutching the pole like a lifeline.

Again and again, Gray beat him. Brought the cane back and down again and again on Gavin's back. Gavin fell to his knees, sobbing and shaking. Isaac bit his lip. Gray gasped with each swing of their arm, one hand pressed to their chest. Sweat shimmered on their skin.

Finn looked at Gray almost desperately, wringing their hands, flinching with every blow as they watched Gray's face screw up in pain in time with Gavin's. *I can't let this happen. I can't let Gray hurt themself for Gavin.*

Isaac wiped his hands on his pants and stepped forward. A thin trickle of blood moved down Isaac's wrist still. Gray froze with their hand suspended in the air, the cane shaking in their grip. Isaac moved to Gray's side. "How many is that?" he asked Gray under his breath.

"Eighteen," Gray panted. Their face was pale and drawn with pain. Gavin looked behind him, an expression of painful hope on his face. He sagged as he saw Isaac reaching for the cane. Gavin pressed his forehead against the pole.

"Let me finish," Isaac murmured.

Gray shook their head, keeping their eyes fixed on Gavin. "No, Isaac. This is my responsibility. I don't want you to—"

"Gray," Isaac said softly. "You're hurt. Let me."

Gray paused for a moment and looked at Isaac. They searched his face for a moment, perhaps looking for fury. Rage. Bitterness. Looking, perhaps, for evidence that Isaac would use the opportunity to kill Gavin. Isaac met Gray's gaze steadily.

Gray sagged and passed the cane to Isaac. "Don't kill him," they said breathlessly. They stumbled back a step.

Finn darted forward and caught Gray as they staggered. "We're going," Finn hissed. "I need to see to you." Gray nodded and let themself be led away. Edrissa followed just behind, trembling violently, throwing glances at the crowd over her shoulder as she went. One man's eyes followed her to the cars, his brow furrowed.

Gavin was weeping now, shaking his head helplessly where he knelt. The snow beneath him was turning to freezing mud. "I'm sorry, Isaac," he sobbed. "I'm sorry, I'm sorry... I don't want to die..."

"You're not going to die from this," Isaac said through clenched teeth. *How many times did he beat Tori? How many times did his father beat Vera?*

"No, no, no, *no, no, no*..." Gavin quaked in the mud, sweat darkening his shirt. Steam rose from his skin. Blood stained his shirt in lines across his back. Isaac's stomach burned. He tightened his grip around the cane, slippery with the blood still on his hands. He raised his hand to strike Gavin. He froze when he saw Sam walk towards him, their eyes fixed on him.

"Sam," he said weakly. "What—"

"How many more does he have to go?" Sam asked softly once they reached Isaac's side.

"Thirty-two." Isaac's forehead creased with confusion.

Sam nodded once. They stepped to Gavin's left and knelt down in the slushy mud with him. They put their hand gently on Gavin's arm. He flinched when they touched him and sobbed harder when he met their eyes. Sam looked at Isaac and nodded again.

"Sam," he said and licked his lips. "Move. I can't—"

"You won't hit me," they said confidently. "It's alright. I'll stay out of the way."

"Sam—"

"It's alright, Isaac," they murmured. "I trust you. Do it."

Isaac adjusted his grip on the cane, grimacing at how the blood stuck to his skin as it dried. He bit the inside of his cheek. He looked at Gavin, then looked at Sam. He raised his arm and struck.

Gavin screamed, sagging against the pole. "Please," he begged. "Please, no, no, no, no..."

"You only have thirty-one more to go," Sam said softly. "It's alright."

Isaac's heart dropped in his chest. Tears pricked at his eyes as Sam glanced up at him with their wide brown eyes. Despite everything they'd suffered, they were still sweet and *good. This is why I went to Gavin in their place. This is why I would die for them, right here, if someone asked it.* He swallowed the lump in his throat. He raised his hand and brought the cane down on Gavin.

Gavin shuddered under the blow. "Thirty," Sam said quietly. "Thirty, Gavin. You can do it."

Another. Gavin writhed against the cord tying his wrists. Sam touched his shoulder. "Twenty-nine." They pulled their hand away. Isaac brought his hand up.

Again. Sam talked to Gavin through his screams. "Twenty-eight, Gavin. You're alright."

"No, no, no, no..." He whimpered. "Please..."

Again. "No!" Gavin shrieked. "Sam, please," he moaned. "Sam... please..."

Sam's eyes shone with tears. "Twenty-seven."

Again. Gavin wept in ugly, wracking sobs. "No, no, no..." He pressed his shoulder against the pole.

"Twenty-six," Sam said softly. "Remember, you've done this to other people. You did this to Tori." Their voice carried no anger. No judgement.

Again. Gavin jerked hard against the pole, making a dull thud. "I know," he whined. "I know I did. I'm sorry."

"Twenty-five." Sam's hand rested gently on Gavin's forearm. "You're halfway done."

Again. Isaac's hand tingled from the blows. Tears burned in his eyes. "Twenty-four," came Sam's soft voice.

Again. More marks soaked through Gavin's shirt, crossing over his back. Isaac's skin ached from the memory of the whip. His shirt clung to his damp skin under his jacket. Over and over, Gavin had beat him. Whipped him. *He deserves so much worse than this.*

"Twenty-three," Sam said gently. Gavin turned his head to look at them. His gaze bored into theirs like they were the only thing keeping him alive, keeping him sane. He whimpered.

Again. "Twenty-two." Isaac watched Sam, watched their softness, their gentleness. *He broke us both, and yet Sam is showing him mercy. Sam is forgiving. Sam is good.*

Again. "Twenty-one." The world tunneled away. The only thing that was real was the cane in Isaac's hand, the man kneeling on the ground taking the blows, and Sam kneeling beside him, guiding Gavin through the pain. Isaac could barely hear them over Gavin's screams, but Sam was his lifeline, too, as he drew Gavin's blood. His own blood fell from his arm with every swing, the cut bleeding freely again, dripping red and steaming into the snow.

Again. "Twenty, Gavin. Only twenty left. You're going to survive this."

Again. Isaac didn't try to stop the flood of tears. *Even though Gavin made them suffer, made them betray us, made them beg me to hurt them just to save my life... they're kneeling in the mud right alongside him. Helping him.*

"Nineteen." Sam's hand still rested gently on Gavin's forearm. Their hand and the pole were the only things holding him up now. Flakes of snow fell gently from the sky, melting on Isaac's skin.

Again. "Eighteen." Gavin's cries were being torn from his chest. Still, he kept his eyes fixed on Sam.

Again. "Seventeen. Just breathe. I know it hurts."

Again. *They know exactly how much this hurts.* "Sixteen. It's alright, Gavin."

Again. Gavin's sobs shook his chest.

"Fifteen. Breathe, Gavin. Breathe in." More stripes of blood crossed Gavin's shirt. Isaac didn't want to know what the skin looked like underneath.

Again. "Fourteen. There you go. You can do this." Gavin slumped against the pole, staring at Sam. Isaac's hand ached. He gritted his teeth against the familiar pain.

Again. "Thirteen." *After this, he won't want to help us anymore. We're ruining our only chance to make him useful. I am ruining it.*

Again. "Twelve." Sam's hand went to Gavin's and squeezed. Gavin squeezed back weakly.

Again. "Eleven." Gavin's screams barely sounded human anymore. Something shifted inside of Isaac.

Again. "Ten. Last ten, Gavin. You're almost finished." Gavin nodded weakly, his cry fading to a whimper.

Again. "Nine. Keep breathing, Gavin. You're almost there." Gavin sagged down, not even holding on to the pole anymore. Isaac swallowed.

Again. "Eight." Gavin's scream was softer, as if his body had made it without his mind giving the order.

Again. "Seven." Gavin's head fell forward. Sam looked up at Isaac, their eyebrows pulled together. *He's going to faint.*

Again. "Six. You're alright, Gavin. Stay awake." Gavin's head moved weakly from side to side.

Again. "Five." Gavin didn't scream. A low moan slipped from his mouth.

Again. "Four." His body jerked, and he slid a little farther down the pole until he was bent in half at the waist.

Again. "Th-three." Sam's eyes widened as they looked up at Isaac. He set his jaw and raised his hand.

Again. "Two. Gavin?" Sam lifted his head in their hands. It bobbled weakly on his neck. Isaac swallowed hard and lifted the cane.

Again. "Gavin? Last one. Gavin? Are you awake?"

Isaac brought the cane down on Gavin's back with a *crack*. Gavin jerked mindlessly against the pole. Isaac stood behind him, shaking, the cane still held tight in his bloody fist. His breath came harder, fogging in the cold, and he felt a sob building in his throat.

"Gavin." Sam shook Gavin's shoulder. "Gavin? Wake up."

The cane fell from Isaac's hand with a dull *thud* into the snow. His legs shook and it felt like there was a band constricting in his chest. Gavin's shirt was a mess of red stripes now, and Isaac could see some marks where the blood had started to run. The world tunneled back out and he could hear the noises of the crowd around him, the snickers, a few people clapping. He could hear Gavin's labored gasps as he slowly stirred against the pole, whimpering. He could feel the sting in his hand from how hard he struck Gavin. He very nearly fell to his knees.

Why do I feel so fucking guilty?

He lurched forward and fumbled at the cord around Gavin's wrists. Gavin was limp against the pole, his face dripping sweat and tears. His mouth hung open and his lips trembled. His eyes were halfway shut and glazed over.

129

Shit. He'll never help us after this. He's going to fucking betray us, because I did this to him. Isaac swallowed hard. *These people would never have let us go if I hadn't.*

As the cord came away from Gavin's wrists he slumped to the side. Isaac caught him just before he hit the ground. Gavin's wrists were rubbed raw and bleeding, the skin torn open in some places from how hard he had struggled.

Isaac felt someone at his side and he glanced up to see Ellis. Where he had expected to see satisfaction on their face he saw revulsion and horror. *They watched me do this to him.*

Vera appeared at his other side. "Let's get him somewhere away from all these people," she said under her breath. "Let's get out of here."

"Do we have anywhere else to go?" he hissed. "No one is going to let us stay anywhere near them."

"I have a house set up for us already," Tori said behind him. "It's near the other side of town. Out of the way. Stephanie gave me the key." She dangled it out in front of her. She stared at Gavin as she said it. She was pale and shaking.

"Gray, Finn, and Edrissa are already in the car," Vera said softly. "Finn's fixing Gray up. They tore their stitches again. I swear, if they don't take it easy Finn is going to kill them."

"Help me get him up." Isaac looped his arms under Gavin's armpits and around his chest. Gavin cried out as Isaac pressed against the split flesh of his back. Isaac winced in sympathy.

Vera stepped forward to take Gavin's legs. They stood and began to carry him to the car.

As they passed through the crowd, a few people threw taunts at Gavin. "Syndicate filth." "Serves the fucker right." "He's lucky we didn't tear him apart." Someone spat at Gavin as they walked past. Isaac kept his eyes fixed on the car and kept walking.

Tori pulled the door open. Isaac eased Gavin against the back seat and let him slump to the side. Isaac closed the door, cutting off the sound of Gavin's whimper. He turned and saw Daniel standing just a few feet away. Daniel's lips quirked into a smile.

130

"I must admit, watching justice dispensed on Gavin Stormbeck felt better than I anticipated. Now, as long as you stay here, you will not be bothered by my people. I expect you to keep him under your guard until you leave."

"I know," Isaac snapped. He could feel Gavin's blood soaking through his shirt. He pushed down his fury. "Thank you. For your hospitality. We won't cause any problems for you."

The man smiled wider. "I trust you won't." He turned back to the crowd and waved them away.

Isaac trembled as he made his way to the driver's seat. Sam climbed into the passenger seat, and Vera and Tori made their way to the back. Vera pushed Gavin upright and propped him against the window. Isaac didn't even wait to see if Ellis got into their car before he pulled away from the square. His right hand lay in his lap, still stained with blood, as he drove with his left. He made it a few blocks before he realized he didn't know where he was going.

"Tori, where—"

"You're going the right direction. I'll tell you when to turn." Tori's voice sounded thin and frightened.

He nodded, his left hand tight on the steering wheel. "Well," he said softly. "At least we're all still alive." He threw a glance in the rearview mirror. Gavin's eyes were open. He was crying.

Chapter 20

The car slipped slightly on the road as Tori made her way back to the ranch house. She was alone in the car, and alone with her thoughts.

She was torn between crushing sadness and a vague, faraway dread she did her best to force down. *I don't know for sure yet.* She shook her head to clear it as she turned onto the long driveway.

The snow was thicker here than it had been coming from the town hall, not worn down by the traffic of cars. She fishtailed and her hands locked on the wheel. *I've never driven in snow this deep before. If this is what we need to expect all winter...* It felt silly, to be preoccupied with something so mundane.

She couldn't help but breathe a sigh of relief as she pulled up to the house and put the car in park. She turned it off and walked to the front door, steeling herself.

Tori's hand closed around the doorknob on the front door and she paused for a moment. *Once I open this door, I can't undo what happens. I can't unknow what I learn. And I can't take back what I say.* She squeezed her eyes shut and pushed it open. Snow melted in her hair as she stepped into the warmth of the house.

Gray lay on the couch. Finn hovered beside them, wringing their hands and checking Gray's wound every few seconds. Gray gently pushed Finn away and sat up, wincing. Tori's eyes flicked to Sam and Isaac in the kitchen. They both turned when they heard her walk in.

She licked her lips. "Where's Edrissa?"

A flicker of fear passed over Isaac's face. His hand went to his bandaged arm. "In her room. Why?"

Tori set her jaw. "I need to talk to her."

The temperature in the room seemed to drop.

Isaac carefully made his way out of the kitchen to stand in front of Tori. He pitched his voice low. "What is it? Is she...?" His throat worked. "Is she...?"

Tori's eyes narrowed. "She's not syndicate," she said quietly. "No. She's not a spy or anything. I just…" She bit her lip and looked around at the others. All eyes were on her. "I went to talk to Daniel Schiester. To smooth things over and give him our information." Her jaw jutted forward. "Turns out he's the mayor here. Seems to enjoy quite a bit of control." She pushed down a flare of frustration. "Anyway, I got us registered with their town hall and um… someone recognized Edrissa in the square. He didn't say anything while we were all there, but he found me and asked me about her. I just… have some questions. I need to talk to her."

"Do you mind doing it in here, where we can hear?" Isaac's voice was tense.

Tori shook her head. "Not at all. I'll get her."

She made her way down the hall, past room after room. As she ran her hand along the wall, she felt the scuffmarks and dings under her fingers. She looked down at the worn gray carpet below her, and at the scribbles of crayons on the wallpaper like a mural. Tori smiled.

Her face fell as she reached Edrissa's door. Her heart clenched. She raised her hand and knocked.

She heard rustling and soft footsteps behind the door. The lock turned and the door opened. Edrissa looked out warily.

"Hey, Edrissa," Tori said gently. "I want to talk to you about something. Can you come out to the living room?"

Edrissa went pale and cringed behind the door. Her eyes flicked past Tori once, twice, probably calculating how far she could make it before someone caught her and held her down to hurt her. Tori put her hands up and stepped away.

"Hey. You're not in trouble. I just need to talk to you, okay? You're not in trouble. We're not…" The words died on her lips. "We're not going to hurt you."

Edrissa swallowed loudly and wrapped her arms around herself. Tori turned and walked to the living room. Edrissa followed behind, her head bowed like she was walking to her execution.

Everyone turned when they heard Tori walk back in. She went to an empty couch and sat, placing her hand on the cushion next to her. Edrissa's gaze moved warily over everyone as she sat down, huddled on the edge of the couch, as far away from everyone as possible.

Tori looked around at the others and cleared her throat. She took a deep breath and looked squarely at Edrissa. "Edrissa, you told the bounty hunters your name was Edrissa Worthington."

Edrissa's eyes went wide and she shot up on the couch, bracing as if to run. Isaac flinched and his hand went to his waistband. To his gun. It was still tucked under the seat in the car outside. Edrissa's eyes fixed on Isaac and she quailed. She sank miserably back to the cushions.

"Hey, sweetie, I told you you're not in trouble," Tori said soothingly. "Okay? We just want to know. Worthington isn't actually your name, is it?"

Edrissa's eyes filled with tears. She trembled as she pulled her arms tighter around herself, eyes darting to each person in the room in turn. Her breathing was fast and shallow. "Um…"

"It's alright," Tori murmured, her voice low and steady. "We aren't going to hurt you. We just need to know."

Edrissa's breath caught in a sob. Her eyes finally rested on Isaac, wary and suspicious. "No," she whispered.

Tori held her face and voice perfectly neutral, the way she'd done with her family when they'd all arrived on her doorstep months ago. "Okay. What's your real name? Can you tell us?"

Edrissa stared at Isaac. "I…" She shook her head. "I don't have that name anymore." Her voice shifted into a robotic murmur that was so *familiar*. Tori heard that tone in Vera's voice when she was under. "I'm… I'm Edrissa, that's all. I'm nameless. I don't have a family. No one's coming for me. I'm a plaything. I'm… I'm *nothing*…"

Tori couldn't conceal the tremor in her voice. "Oh." Her hands twisted around each other. "No, Edrissa. You'll never be that again. You're here with us, now. Free. You don't belong to us. What was the name you had before?" Her gaze flicked to Isaac and she stared at him, silently urging him to back down. He shrank back. He let his hands fall at his sides, open and empty. He looked at the floor.

"Please…" Edrissa whimpered. "Please, I don't want to get in trouble." She was crying now, openly, with tears rolling down her cheeks and into her lap.

Tori pushed down the urge to go to her and pull her into an embrace. She blinked back her own tears and tried again. "Edrissa… I might have news about your brother."

Edrissa's eyebrows shot up and her mouth fell open. Her arms unwound from her chest and she leaned forward, gripping the cushions. "Micah?" she breathed.

Tori's heart sank. She folded her hands on her lap. "Edrissa, I need to know your last name."

"Clark," Edrissa said, nearly tripping over the word. "My name is Edrissa Clark. Is Micah alive? Did he, did he make it? Is he alive?"

Tori looked at the ceiling, trying to keep the tears brimming in her eyes from falling. "Edrissa… um…" She pushed a slow breath between her lips. "Micah was killed."

There was a moment of crushing silence.

Edrissa collapsed. She shattered, and there was nothing holding her up now. She dissolved into sobs, pressing her hands against her mouth, bending forward until her forehead nearly pressed against the cushions.

"No," she moaned, and her voice broke. "No… Micah… *no*…" She dragged in a shuddering gasp and wailed, a terrible keening sound that tore at Tori's heart.

Tori pressed a hand to her lips and tried to force her tears down. "I'm so sorry, sweetie," she whispered. She cleared her throat. "I'm so sorry. Someone in the crowd thought you looked familiar—"

"Micah—"

"—and he knew your brother several years ago—"

"—no—"

"—when he saw you he thought he knew who you were—"

"—please—"

"—but he wasn't sure—"

Edrissa's breaths were coming too fast, panicked. Her eyes were wide, and she braced herself on the couch, gasping for air. Tori went to Edrissa's side and pulled her close.

Edrissa's wails dug claws of grief into Tori's heart. She slumped in Tori's arms, weeping, and curled her fingers into Tori's shirt.

"…he asked me if your name was Clark when I was at the town hall." Tori raised her voice over Edrissa's cries and pressed her lips into her hair. "He knew a Micah Clark who looked like you, and I thought I remembered Gray telling me your brother's name…" She glanced at Gray and they nodded. Tears shone in their eyes, too.

"Micah…"

"He said your brother was shot, and, um, succumbed to his wounds," Tori said miserably. "I'm so sorry, honey. I wish—" *I wish what? I wish your brother was alive? I wish you hadn't been taken? I wish you hadn't been used and tortured as a plaything for two years?* Tori pressed her cheek against the top of Edrissa's head. Tori's tears fell into her hair. "I wish I could change it," Tori whispered.

Edrissa struggled and pulled herself out of Tori's grasp. She dashed for her room, her hand pressed over her mouth, still sobbing her brother's name.

Tori's head hung low as tears ran down her nose. "Fuck," she whispered. "That poor girl… she had nothing but the… but the *hope* that her brother was still alive, and now she—" Tori cut herself off at the sound of a strangled sob. Her head snapped up. Vera stood in the doorway of the living room, her hand thrust out against a wall. Her other hand was pressed against her chest. Her eyes were faraway. Tears streamed down her face.

Tori was up in an instant. "Babe. What's wrong?" She crossed to Vera, but stopped several feet away from her, hands outstretched, helpless. "Vera? Are you there again? What is it? You can speak." Tori nearly babbled with panic.

"I…" Vera convulsed forward as another sob wracked her body. She slid down onto her knees and screamed. "I remember. I remember what he did. I remember what happened to Ryan." She slumped onto her side and pulled her knees to her chest.

Tori rushed to Vera's side. Vera cowered on the floor away from Tori. *"No!"* Vera screamed, curling tighter into herself. "No, no, no, *no*..."

Tori fell to her knees beside Vera. "Vera, what happened? What did you remember?" Her hands shook violently as she reached out to Vera, pulled back, reached out again. *What happened that hurt her this much?*

Isaac knelt beside Tori and without a word Tori folded into his arms. *I know he's here for her. He needs to be here for her. But...*

Tori had watched Vera suffer for months at her safehouse, unraveling the pain she'd buried, finding new limits to what Vera had thought she had endured. Tori had fallen apart right alongside her in the two weeks since she'd killed Joseph Stormbeck, had watched her fall into memory after memory that left her shaking and hollow inside. Had heard Vera say things that Tori wished she could burn out of her mind with bleach. *I can be good. I'm sorry. I didn't mean to scream. Bad girl. If you don't punish me, I can't be good. It hurts. It hurts where he fucks me. Do you want me on my back? Parties where Joseph invited his friends over to rape me. I remember at least three. I'm sorry I'm so fucked up. I'm sorry I'm so broken. Should I put the, the collar on? Bad girl. I can be good. I'm sorry, I know there's no escape. There's no way out. I imagined him. Bad girl. I'm sorry I'm sorry I'm sorry. He raped me. My friend raped me. I'm sorry. I can be good. Yes, sir. I'm sorry. I can be good. Should I get on my knees? Bad girl. I can be good for you. Please don't hurt me. I can be good.*

What could be worse than all of that?

Vera howled and pressed her hand against her mouth as she huddled on the floor.

"Vera," Tori whimpered, "Are you there in your mind? You can s-speak, babe, I... you can... you can speak..." She collapsed forward, out of Isaac's arms. He reached down and placed a shaking hand on Vera's shoulder.

"Ryan," Vera wailed. "Ryan, *no*..."

Tears blinded Tori as she lurched forward, sobbing. "Vera, babe... *please*..." She felt gentle hands on her shoulder, guiding her to her feet.

She stumbled back and bumped against Gray's chest. They grunted softly and eased her back, away from where Vera lay curled up on the floor. Isaac crouched beside Vera.

"You don't have to put yourself through this, Tori," Gray said softly.

"No," Tori gasped. "She's… she's *hurting,* Gray, let me—"

"You're hurting, too," Gray murmured. "This is hurting you, too. Let Isaac help her. You don't have to be strong for her every moment." Tori pressed her hands over her mouth and let Gray hold her.

Chapter 21

Years ago

As soon as she heard Joseph's footsteps approaching the door, Vera's heart went into overdrive. All night, every time she thought about morning coming and Joseph returning to hurt her again, her blood flooded with icy, paralyzing terror. *No matter what, after this morning I'll be out or I'll be dead. This will be over.*

She pushed herself up onto her knees, almost without thinking. *This is how he likes me.* Her mind shuddered around the thought as soon as it had formed.

She shot a glance at Ryan, standing to the side. His face was pale but set. The muscles in his jaw flexed as he clenched his teeth together. Her eyes flicked to the gun, concealed at his waistband, and back to the door.

"No matter what," he murmured under his breath. She closed her eyes and a shiver moved through her. Her fingers were white from how hard she was squeezing them together.

She held her breath as the door swung open and Joseph walked in.

"Good morning sweetheart," he purred. "You're looking rested. Excellent. I wanted you to be in good shape for tonight." She opened her eyes and a whimper made its way through her throat. He chuckled. "Pearson, you told her about the party tonight?"

She glanced at Ryan. *I can't speak. But he can.*

Ryan quivered with tension and avoided her gaze. "Yes sir," Ryan said with a shaky grin. "I'm sorry if you wanted to be the one to tell her, but it just kinda... slipped out."

Joseph watched Ryan, his piercing gaze looking Ryan up and down. From his face, his trembling hands, to his feet, positioned in a defensive stance. Joseph's eyes narrowed for a moment and Vera's heart stuttered in her chest. Joseph's gaze moved back to her. Her heart started again. Joseph shrugged.

"It wasn't a secret, Pearson," Joseph said, speaking a little more softly than before. The chill in his voice made Vera shiver – it was so much colder than the chill in the room. He took another step towards her and fumbled for the keys in his pocket. "Perhaps you'd like to help me bathe her this time. I've found the noises she makes when forced to feel pleasure are almost as good as the ones that come from her agony." He knelt in front of her and reached for her collar.

He has the keys. That's the signal.

Ryan's hand went back for his gun. He brought it up and aimed it at Joseph, his eyes blazing with furious intensity.

Joseph's hand shot into his pocket and he pulled out his knife. He dove behind Vera, shoving her in front of him by a hand on her collar. He crouched behind her and brought the knife to Vera's throat. Ryan's hands jerked. He froze as the blade pressed against her throat.

"God *dammit,*" Joseph hissed. *"Damien!"*

The door to the cell banged open and another man rushed through, his own gun held tight in his hands. His eyes went immediately to Ryan. He aimed his gun at Ryan's heart.

"No," Vera sobbed. She reached back, feeling for some kind of grip on Joseph's shirt. If she could just give Ryan a clear shot—

Joseph jerked her head back and dug the blade into her skin. Her body locked in icy panic.

"God *dammit,*" Joseph snarled. "God *dammit,* Pearson, I *knew* you were going to try something stupid like this. *Fuck!*"

Ryan's eyes were wide and streaming with tears as his gaze flicked between Vera and Damien. "V-Vera…"

"Drop your *fucking* weapon, Pearson," Joseph spat. "Drop it, or I cut her throat right now."

"You won't fucking do it," Ryan forced out between clenched teeth. "Fuck you. You won't do it. Let her fucking *go.*"

The knife pressed harder into her throat and she felt a hot line of blood move down her neck. She gasped.

"I will, Pearson. If you think I won't, you're more of an *idiot* than I thought. I have no qualms about killing her, and even fewer about killing *you*. Put down your weapon before I have Damien make this decision for you."

Ryan met Vera's gaze.

Vera nodded. *Shoot Damien. Do it. Take the shot. Let him kill me. At least one of us will get out alive.* Her lips trembled. Even now, even here with a gun pointed at Ryan's heart, she couldn't speak. *He hasn't let me yet. He'll hurt me worse if I do.* She whimpered and the knife bobbed with the motion of her throat.

The gun trembled in Ryan's hands. Tears fell from his face onto the floor. "Don't kill her," he whispered.

"Then put your *fucking gun* on the ground and step away," Joseph barked.

Ryan's hands dipped lower.

"Ryan, *no!*" Vera screamed. Joseph jerked the collar back. She gagged.

Ryan pressed his lips together. "If I put this down, don't fucking kill her. This was me. Not her."

Vera whined as the knife pressed harder against her throat, sending another stream of blood down her neck. *If he goes much deeper, he's going to kill me. Then Ryan won't have anything stopping him.* She reached up and wrapped her hand around Joseph's wrist, pressing the knife in harder. *I'm dead anyway.*

Joseph's hand jerked away from her neck. "*Bad girl,* Vera," he said in her ear. "*I'm* the one who kills you, nobody else. Not you. You belong to *me.*" She whimpered.

"Take the fucking knife away from her throat." Ryan's skin beaded sweat. He winced as some ran into his eyes. "I'm not dropping my gun until you do."

Joseph chuckled. "Alright. Damien, drop him if he doesn't put his gun down." Joseph pulled the knife away from Vera's neck. She rocked forward on her knees and sobbed with relief and despair.

Ryan raised his hands, his right hand still clutching the gun. He leaned forward and slowly lowered the weapon to the ground. He stepped back and his hands went back up above his head.

"Cuff him, Damien." Vera trembled in Joseph's grasp as his breath warmed the back of her neck. Damien stepped forward and yanked Ryan's hands behind his back. He pulled out a pair of handcuffs and clicked them onto Ryan's wrists. Ryan stared at her, tears rolling down his cheeks.

"Ryan, *no,*" Vera sobbed. "No, no, no... Ryan..." Joseph shifted behind her and stood. The hand on her collar moved up her neck to tangle in her hair. He snapped her head back, looking down at her as he forced her to look up at him.

"You were being so good," Joseph whispered, betrayal thick in his voice. "You were being so fucking good for me, Vera." He glanced at Ryan. "I thought he might be planning something monumentally stupid, but not..." He clicked his tongue. "...not *you. Bad girl, Vera.*" She shuddered under the weight of his words. He turned to look at Ryan, tilting his head as he considered him. "Get him on his knees."

"No," Vera gasped.

Ryan's eyes flicked to hers. Damien kicked the back of one knee and Ryan dropped to the floor.

Joseph released Vera's hair, and she collapsed to her hands and knees, staring desperately at Ryan. Joseph slowly crossed the cell to him, watching him closely the entire time. He paused in front of Ryan and twirled the knife idly in his hand. He looked up and nodded once at the guard. "Thank you, Damien," he said calmly. The man grunted and took a step back.

Joseph looked down at Ryan, tilting his head this way and that. Ryan glared up at him with vicious fury. Joseph reached out with one hand and slowly grasped Ryan's hair. Ryan went still at the touch and his lips pulled back over his teeth in a snarl.

Joseph pulled his hand back and slapped Ryan across the face. Vera cried out as Ryan gasped and nearly fell. Joseph's hand went back to Ryan's hair and jerked his head up again.

"You thought you could take my *fucking plaything from me?*" Joseph hissed. "After all I let you do to her, you thought you could claim her for yourself? You *stupid* fucking boy." Joseph's hand pulled Ryan's head back farther and exposed his neck. "You stupid, *ungrateful* boy. I gave you a job, I let you *fuck my plaything,* and you still thought you could take her from me?"

142

All the air rushed out of Vera's lungs. Every moment she'd spent with Ryan, every touch, every time his hands had moved over her, helping her, cleaning the evidence of Joseph's torture away from her skin, every time he'd held her as she cried, all loomed over her at once. Every time he'd *fucked* her. *Was he really enjoying it, this whole time? Was he lying to* me, *too?* She felt something crack inside her, something that threatened to shatter her completely. *This whole time, was he just using his power over me? Was he hoping to claim me for himself, once we were free? Was he going to put me right back into another collar, one that* he *chose for me?* Her skin crawled as every memory of his hands on her came rushing through her mind all at once.

She met Ryan's eyes, and the look she found there put her back together again. Her heart plummeted to the floor. *No. He really cared about me. The whole time.*

"I didn't want to fucking *claim her,* you fucking *rapist,*" Ryan snarled at Joseph. "I didn't want her like that. I *never did.* You…" More tears welled in his eyes and rolled down his cheeks. "You *made me do that.*"

Joseph laughed once. "As if you could resist," he said, drawing Ryan's head back farther. "As if you could look at her and not want her, after I've made her so good."

"I NEVER WANTED TO HURT HER!" Ryan roared.

Joseph leaned back. His hand relaxed in Ryan's hair. He glanced back at Vera, and down at Ryan again. His face broke into a grin.

"Oh my… *god,*" Joseph said softly. He bent closer over Ryan, his neck arched back by Joseph's hand. "Did you… develop… *feelings…* for my plaything, Pearson?"

Vera's mouth fell open with a cry. The breath was knocked from her lungs.

Ryan looked up at Joseph, and the loathing in his eyes could have withered Joseph where he stood. "I never wanted to hurt her," Ryan growled through his teeth.

"How sweet," Joseph mocked. He jerked Ryan's head to the side, so he had to look at Vera again. "I hope she was worth your life."

"Joseph, *no!*" Vera gasped, and threw herself forward.

Joseph's head snapped towards her and his eyes narrowed with rage. *"Joseph?"*

"Please, no!" Vera begged. "Please no, he... he's good, he didn't... do anything *wrong*..." Tears burned in her eyes.

"He tried to take you from me," Joseph said, his voice going low and dangerous.

She looked only at Ryan now. The desperate terror in his face and the unwavering determination in his eyes threatened to tear Vera apart. "I'm sorry," she whispered.

"You've proven you can't be trusted when you're not chained down," Joseph said softly to her, contempt twisting his features. "Glad I made the decision to chain you when I did." He stepped behind Ryan and jerked his head back again with a hand in his hair. Joseph held the knife to Ryan's throat.

"No!" Vera shrieked. She shot forward and gagged when the collar jerked her to a stop.

Ryan flinched and tried to stand. Joseph pressed the knife harder against his throat. The skin opened immediately, and Ryan froze, a gasp of pain seizing his chest.

Joseph fixed his eyes on Vera. Venomous satisfaction pulled the corners of his mouth up into a deadly grin. "Your real punishment will come tonight at the party, Vera," he hissed. "Until then, take this as punishment. His death is on you."

The knife cut deep into Ryan's throat.

"NO!" Vera screamed. She threw herself forward against the chain. A choked sob tore from her own throat as Ryan slumped to the floor, blood pouring from the gaping slash in his neck. "No, no, no... *Ryan!*" She reached for him, tried to pull him away from Joseph. Tried to staunch the bleeding. *Something. "No,"* she sobbed. "No, Ryan... I'm so sorry... *please*..." The collar closed around her throat, seeming to drag her back away from Ryan's body. Ryan shuddered and choked on the floor, blood gurgling in his throat. She strained against the collar, eyes streaming, trying to touch him, reach him. Her hands left smears in his blood.

Chapter 22

"Vera," Isaac urged, his voice tight with worry. "Please, tell me what's going on. What did you see?"

Vera wailed wordlessly on the floor, cowering away from Isaac, her hands flung up over her head. She had her eyes squeezed shut as she shuddered, sweat dampening her skin.

Isaac heard a gasp and he glanced up, further down the hall. Ellis stood in the doorway of the room they shared with Finn. They lurched forward and hurried to Vera's side.

"What happened?" Ellis said, tears wobbling their voice. "What *happened?*"

"I don't know," Isaac said, lowering his voice. "She remembered something. We're trying to figure out what."

"Ryan, *Ryan,* I'm so sorry, *no,*" Vera heaved out. *"NO!"*

Isaac found himself leaning over Vera, shielding her from everything and everyone else while she fell apart. "Let's just back up a little bit. Give her some space." He didn't move from her side, but the others moved back hesitantly.

"No," Vera sobbed into the carpet.

"Vera," he murmured, sitting by her side. "Please tell me what happened?"

"He's... he's *dead!*" she screamed, her voice muffled by her hand over her own mouth.

Isaac's eyes slid shut over the sudden burn of tears. He sagged back against the wall, pressing a hand to his face and keeping a hand on her. Steadying her. Grounding her. *"No,"* he whispered.

"He, he was going to get me out, he *promised,* he was going to get me *out!*" Vera wailed. "He hired people to get me out. He was going to get me *out,* we were going to run and... he was going to save me, he *protected me* from Joseph, he did those things to me so..." She cut herself off with a whine.

145

Isaac's hand shook as he gently squeezed her shoulder. He bit his lip, half expecting her to pull away, but she pushed into his touch.

"He did those things so Joseph would..." She choked on her tears. "So he would... let Ryan get *close* to me. He h-had to earn Joseph's trust, so he could help me..." She shuddered and pressed herself into the floor. "And he... he died... for *me*..."

"Vera, can I get you up off the floor?" Isaac murmured as he moved his thumb over her shoulder.

It was like she didn't even hear him. "Joseph was... was going to have another *party*." The word came out as a tortured wail. "Ryan said he'd get me out, no matter what. He'd get me out, or we... we would die, but that was alright... I would die with my friend." Vera reached out and grabbed Isaac's wrist. Isaac went still for a moment, certain that she was going to shove his hand away. She dragged herself upright towards him and clutched at him, wrapping her arms around his waist.

She took a shuddering gasp. "And Joseph found out. Somehow, he found out, and... as Ryan was going to shoot him... Joseph pushed me in front of him and..." She cringed into herself. Isaac wrapped his arms around her. "Ryan... put down his gun... for *me*." She moaned softly. "He died for *me*," she whispered.

Isaac glanced up and saw Gavin standing in the hallway. Even in the dim light, Isaac could see Gavin was pale. Sweat shone on his face and a dark bruise encircled his neck. He leaned against the wall, still weak from the beating. Gavin's gaze fixed on Vera where she was slumped against Isaac. Isaac's lips pulled back over his teeth in a silent snarl.

Gavin froze, wincing, and held his hands out to his sides in supplication. Isaac felt his heart speed up, could feel the fear spreading through his brain like poison. *I'll never be safe he's going to hurt me going to hurt US I need to stop him I need to put him in the fucking ground.* Isaac trembled as his muscles coiled to spring, his hands curled into fists, and his chest burned with the need to kill. To *protect*.

Vera whimpered beside him, and his heart dropped. He shuddered and glanced down at her as she clutched his arm, her face raw and wet with tears. He trembled as the fear ran bright and hot through his mind, almost forcing him

146

to stand, to stride over to where Gavin leaned on the wall, to beat him to death with his bare hands *the way I should have done from the start. Should have killed him. Should have kept them safe.* He squeezed his eyes shut and felt Vera against his side, warm, shaking, afraid. He opened his eyes.

"Finn, help me get her up," he murmured over his shoulder. Finn jumped forward, hands extended. They knelt on either side of Vera and lifted her under her arms. She wailed as they pulled her up and moved towards the couch. Her feet dragged behind her and she staggered between them, tears pouring down her face.

They eased her down onto the couch. Isaac sat beside her and she latched onto him, sobbing.

"My friend," she wept. "Joseph cut his throat just because he *helped me,* just because he wanted to save me." She coughed hard and buried her face in Isaac's chest. "He died for *my mistake.* He died because I wasn't strong enough. He died because I *begged him* to get me out before... before Joseph had his friends rape me again..."

Isaac heard a sniff from the other couch and glanced over. Tori sobbed quietly into Gray's shirt. Gray looked haunted as they watched Vera, tears rolling down their cheeks.

"If I hadn't... *begged*... if I had just held on... if I had just waited, if I'd waited for the plan... he might... still be..." She convulsed forward in a scream. Isaac's arms wrapped around her and pressed her to his chest.

He heard the shadow of two voices: his and Sam's.

"I— If I had d-died if... i-if I'd ma— made him ki-ill me... he would n— never... you... never..."

"I went to Gavin to keep them safe and they still ended up getting hurt. Because of me. Because I... couldn't..."

We all carry the same scars.

"No," he murmured. He pulled Vera closer and pressed a kiss to the top of her head. "*No,* Vera. This wasn't your fault. Do you hear me? None of it. You didn't kill him. *Joseph did.* This *wasn't your fucking fault.*" His voice slid into a whisper as tears tightened in his throat.

"No," she moaned. "Ryan... *no...* He did, he did everything... e-everything he could to keep m-me safe. He... *blamed himself...* for torturing me. It w-wasn't his, his *fault...*"

"And it wasn't yours, either, Vera. He died and that doesn't mean anything about you. It just means something about..." Isaac swallowed. "...about Joseph."

"He *loved me,*" Vera whimpered. "I... I don't know if... if it was... like *that...* but... he died because he cared about *me.*" She wailed miserably.

Isaac shivered. *Is this what it's like, to die for them? Is this what you leave behind?* He shoved the thought away and laid his cheek on the top of her head.

Isaac's eyes drifted up again to Gavin. He stood in the doorway of the living room, still leaning against the wall. Acid churned in Isaac's stomach. *If he's here because he's* getting off *on her pain...*

Gavin's face was pulled into an expression of horror. His arms were wrapped around his middle and Isaac could see him trembling from across the room. *That could be from this, or it could be from the beating.* Isaac watched him for another moment, calculating. That same feeling that shifted in his mind as he'd beat Gavin wobbled and moved again. He looked away, turning his attention to Vera. She sagged against him. Her fingers locked into his shirt.

"I'm so sorry," he whispered to her. She whined softly. "I'm so sorry."

"Ryan," she whimpered. *"No..."*

Isaac tightened his arms around her. She sobbed against his chest, murmuring Ryan's name over and over.

"Ryan," she whispered. *"Ryan.* I'm so sorry. I'm *so fucking sorry."*

Chapter 23

Vera's convulsing sobs slowly quieted to whimpers. Isaac held her close, pressing his cheek against the top of her head, rocking her gently as she trembled. His eyes slid closed and he breathed slowly, silently encouraging her to breathe with him. After a while, her breathing started to match his. In, and their lungs expanded together. Out, and their bodies relaxed a little more. In and out. In and out.

Tears had long since soaked through Isaac's shirt. He didn't mind. He held her gently, smoothing her hair away from her face, slowly rubbing circles over her back. Her fingers loosened from the fists she'd made in his shirt. Her head fell onto his shoulder as she wept softly.

Vera hadn't let him touch her this much since... Well, since seeing Joseph. They'd always been open with each other – gentle hands on shoulders, hugs, huddling together for warmth while they were on the run. It had been... difficult for her, after Gavin claimed her. She'd been jumpy, flinching or going still at his touch in a way she never had before. She had slowly recovered, over the almost six months they spent at Tori's house. She'd slowly started to let him touch her again. Slowly regained that silent part of their friendship that had always been there.

After Joseph...

After Joseph, Vera hardly let anyone touch her at all. Isaac understood.

Vera sank into Isaac's embrace. It soothed his own fear, sharp as glass under his skin, as he looked over at Gavin, still leaned against the wall like nothing else was holding him up. Gavin's eyes were downcast, his face dark with something Isaac couldn't place.

Vera whimpered softly and pressed her cheek against Isaac's chest. *I wonder if I remind her of Ryan sometimes?* he thought. Isaac was gripped with horror. *What if I had to hurt her to save her? What if I had been in his position? What if I had to—* He ferociously broke off the thought. If he thought about it any longer, he would disintegrate in her arms. He couldn't do it. Not to her. Not with the history they had together.

Not even to save her life?

He shuddered and pulled his arms tighter around Vera. She shifted and looked up at him. Her eyes were red and swollen, her face slick with tears. There was a heaviness in her that dragged at Isaac's heart. Her eyes moved over him, and her eyebrows pulled together in concern.

No. I can't let her worry about me. Not now.

She wet her lips to speak. "Are you—"

"Do you need a tissue?" Isaac interrupted, his jaw clenching.

Finn practically leapt forward with a box of tissues. Vera looked at them and took one. Her eyes returned immediately to Isaac. "Are you—"

"I'm just... I'm sorry you're hurting," Isaac whispered, and pressed a kiss into her hair.

Vera bit her lip as he pulled away. Another tear coursed down her cheek. Her face twisted and she sobbed again. "Ryan..." She crumpled against his chest.

He held her again and she wound her arms around him.

Sam walked stiffly from where they'd been standing near the kitchen, their own face wet with tears. They sat down gently on the couch on Vera's other side. She stirred and looked at them.

"Can I..." Sam's voice faltered. "Can I, um, touch you?"

Vera nodded. Sam leaned gently against her and wrapped their arms around them both. Vera sniffled softly and rubbed Sam's arm.

"He sounds like he was a good man," Isaac murmured.

Vera sobbed. "He was."

"Would you...?" Isaac paused. Vera lifted her head. "Would you... maybe... want to have a funeral for him?"

Vera's face crumpled and she sobbed again. "Oh. Um..." She wiped her nose with the back of her hand. "I..."

"You don't have to," Isaac said quickly, biting his lip. "I'm sorry if I overstepped."

"No, no." Vera sniffed. "I mean... that would be... really nice."

"Okay. Maybe we could… have a…" Isaac's gaze moved to the hallway where Edrissa had disappeared. His eyes fell on Gavin again and stayed for a split second. He pushed down the wave of unease that moved through him. "We could have a funeral for Micah, too. Let Edrissa mourn him properly."

"And for your dad."

Gavin's words went through Isaac like a thunderclap. Isaac went rigid. His hands curled into fists and his jaw clenched shut. *"What?"*

Gavin's eyes went wide, and he went a shade paler. "I'm sorry," he mumbled. "I didn't mean…"

"Isaac…" Sam said quietly.

Isaac tore his eyes away from Gavin and fixed them on Sam. Their eyes were wide and filled with tears.

"I didn't know your dad *died…*"

Isaac swallowed hard. His throat felt too tight. He couldn't breathe. "I…"

"We should do that," Vera said softly, wiping her face on her shirt.

"But…" Isaac's eyes went back to Gavin where he stood, looking ready to bolt. Isaac wondered how far he'd make it without falling. *He used my dad's death. He used the thing I told him. He used the thing he* took from me, *with a gun to my head.* He trembled as he held Gavin's gaze. Tears welled in Isaac's eyes and ran down his cheeks.

Gavin stared at the ground. "I'm sorry," he whispered. He turned and disappeared down the hall.

Gray looked between Isaac and the hallway. Their eyebrows pulled together. "What was that, Isaac?"

Isaac worked to hold down furious sobs. "I… he…" He swallowed and a whimper escaped his throat. "He knew… my dad d-died, because… while he was, was *torturing me…* he…" His eyes squeezed shut against the memory of being tied down to Gavin's table, a blindfold over his eyes and Gavin's gun pressed to his head. Vera squeezed his hand and he opened his eyes.

"He took that from you?" she whispered.

He whimpered. "He took *everything* from me." Something in Vera's eyes tightened as he said it. "Oh, fuck, Vera, no… I… I'm sorry…"

"It's okay."

"No, it's not. Gavin never… he… never…"

She shook her head and closed her eyes. "That's okay. There isn't a comparison, Isaac."

He bowed his head. "I don't want to feel this anymore."

Vera sobbed out a laugh. It twisted as it came out. "Fucking preach."

Isaac reached for a tissue. He blew his nose and settled back on the couch. He was shaking. He could feel Vera trembling, too.

"How the fuck do we move on from this?" he whispered, pressing a hand to his face. "With the guy who tortured all of us in the next fucking *room?*"

"Carefully," Gray said ruefully. "Although he didn't actually torture *me.*"

Isaac snorted. "No, he just shot you. No big deal."

Gray shrugged. "Technicalities." Their eyes turned to Vera. "I'm so sorry, Vera. I didn't… I didn't know things would… end… like this."

"They haven't ended," Vera said softly. "I still have no idea what made me forget him in the first place."

Gray's expression darkened. "I can guess."

She nodded, ducking her head. "I know. But I… want…" She drew in a breath and slowly pushed it out through her lips. "I want to remember him. Honor him. For what he did for me."

"Babe…" Tori murmured, still pressed against Gray's side. She had her eyes fixed on the floor. "If Ryan never got you out… how did you escape?"

Vera shrugged, her shoulders pulling painfully up around her ears. "It must have just been protesters, like I thought. I was thinking maybe he had something to do with it, but…" She shook her head. "Now I… I don't know." Isaac squeezed her hand. She squeezed back. "I remember him. I remember Ryan." More tears formed and rolled down her cheeks. "And I fucking killed the man who murdered him."

Chapter 24

Isaac shuffled his feet nervously in the snow. He was warm in his new coat, and in the warmth of the fire they'd built on some cleared ground. "I… I'm sorry. I've never done one of these before."

Tori's hand rested gently on his shoulder. "That's okay. Just… say whatever you'd like to say. If you want to talk about him, or… a good time you had together, or something you miss?"

He looked down at the small bouquet of flowers he held tight in his hands, crushing the stems until they drooped. He bought them in town from a greenhouse that kept flowers blooming all winter. "I, um…" He shrugged. "I don't think I even… remember that much about him at this point. I'm sorry." He shivered and fell a step back. "I should just—"

"Isaac…" He stopped at the sadness in Sam's voice. "Please don't go."

Isaac took a step further into the circle, closer to the fire. He raised his gaze to Sam, then to Vera. The dying light of the sunset lit their faces just as much as the fire they'd built. Vera's face was already glazed with tears and she stared at him with broken hurt in her eyes. He let his head fall forward. "Okay. I'm sorry. Um." He swallowed hard and took a deep breath. "So…" He looked at Tori as she squeezed his shoulder again. "My dad's name was Jonathan. Um. He died when I was, uh, twelve. Um. In a car crash." He couldn't help but glance at Gavin. Gavin stared into the flames, head bent, his eyes studiously away from Isaac. "He was, um…" Isaac shrugged. "He was a mechanic. He liked his um. Boat. Had a rowboat. And… he would take me out on the lake in it sometimes." He bowed his head, finished.

Tori looked at him, her hand never leaving his shoulder. "Is that all you want to say, Isaac?"

He felt the sting of tears forming in his eyes and jerked his head in a nod. "Yeah. I think so." He held out his hand and dropped the flowers into the fire.

He watched them burn. The petals fluttered and browned and burst into flame as the fire licked along the stems, curling them and turning them black. The light dusting of snowflakes falling from the sky melted several feet above the fire, the logs sizzling as each drop disappeared into the flames.

Something very old rose up in Isaac, climbing up through his lungs from his stomach, tightening his throat. Something he hadn't felt in a long time. Something that was wrapped up in blue uniforms and the smell of gin and the very faint feel of his father's rough hands gently tousling his hair. He panicked and tried to push it down. *Not in front of them. I haven't felt this in years. I can't, not in front of them...* He shuddered as Tori squeezed his hand. He squeezed back and closed his eyes tightly. *If I feel it, it'll level me.*

He felt her warmth as Tori took a step closer. *Maybe it's okay to be leveled with them.*

He opened his eyes and looked into the fire. The flowers were burned to ash. Two tears rolled down his cheeks. "Um..." He drew in a shaky breath. "Um. He'd take me out on the boat in the summer. We... we couldn't fish in the lake, but he would have me row. He said it would make me stronger. And sometimes he would row and I'd just, um." He shivered. "I'd lay in the bottom and stare at the sky and feel the cool on the bottom of the boat and we would just talk. And... he always cooked, not my mom. Except for steaks. She cooked the steaks. But... he cooked for us, all the time. And, um." Tears rolled freely down Isaac's cheeks. "He helped me work on my bike. And took us out for ice cream after it would hail." He sobbed out a laugh and shrugged. "I don't know why he did that. But he, he would look outside at the hail and say, 'It's an ice cream day!'" Isaac licked his lips.

"And when he, um." Something bitter rippled through his chest. "When he, um. Died. The, the cops, they..." He pushed down a sob. "They um. Came to the door. And t-told my, my mom he was..." Isaac shuddered and whimpered. "...he was... was *dead*." His arms wrapped around his stomach. "She um. She screamed and the... cops, um... told me and... they said they were, were *sorry*, that it was a car accident and someone ran a red light, and I just thought, there's no way, there's no way someone could run a red light and kill my dad, he was a *good driver*, and I didn't even know you *could* run a red light. I thought you *had* to stop." The words spilled out of him now. "And I, I

154

didn't understand, he was just here, he went out to buy some *milk,* and now he was *g-gone,* and he wasn't coming back, and he was *dead…*" He sobbed and trembled as Tori rubbed his arm. Sam pressed against his side and he immediately opened his arm for them. "And I didn't under, understand that… he wasn't gonna *be there* anymore." Sam buried their head against his chest. "And I… I lost my mom that day, too, because she… she never came back either. After that she was always drunk and never came back. She… she… she didn't hit me, or… but, but she, she said… terrible things, and… said it was my f-fault, and… I n-never, never had my mom again…"

Isaac gasped and looked down. "I'm sorry. I'm sorry. I don't know if she's dead, and this is… this is for…"

Tori's hand tightened on Isaac's arm. "You lost her, too. It's okay."

Isaac slid to his knees and pressed his face into his hands. Snow soaked into the knees of his pants. His chest shook with deep, wracking sobs that came from the core of him. Came from that place where he still wanted to feel his mom and dad's arms around him, their voices telling him they loved him. He had almost forgotten. He hadn't let himself feel it in over ten years.

He felt torn open all over again at the wash of memory of his second family, the ones who took him in and taught him to fight – and of the mission he'd been too cowardly to carry out. What should have been his *first* mission. The mission where only some of them came back.

He sank further into himself. Rancid, familiar guilt dragged at his insides. *Jordan. My fault.*

He felt the press of bodies around him. Hands on his shoulders, hands on his head. Whispers. "We love you Isaac." "Thank you for telling us." "I'm so sorry." Sam knelt beside him and pulled him into their arms. He turned and wrapped them in an embrace, burying his face in their hair. Hands at his shoulder pulled him up to standing and he reached out an arm for them, too. He pulled Vera close. She was trembling.

After a while, Isaac quieted. He pulled away from the tight embraces. He wiped his face with his hands and raised his eyes to the dusky sky. Snowflakes landed lightly on his face. "Um." He swallowed. "Thank you." He glanced over to see two figures standing uncomfortably still in the circle around the fire, away from the others— Gavin and Edrissa.

Everyone returned to their spots and Isaac bowed his head. He felt raw. Not torn apart, but like an infected wound had just been cleaned. He raised his gaze to Tori as she started to speak.

"I lost my mom to breast cancer when I was nine," she said softly, tears standing in her eyes. "We had a good memorial service for her, and I've had a long time to mourn her." She nodded. "But I miss her. I miss her so much. She had the most beautiful singing voice. And she loved flowers. Daffodils, especially." She glanced down at the flowers in her hand. "That's why I picked these." She smiled and two tears ran down her cheeks. "Yellow." She dropped them into the fire.

Vera squeezed Tori's hand. "Is that all you wanna say, babe?" she said softly. "You can... you can say more, if you want..."

Tori shook her head and rested it on Vera's shoulder. "No, it's... it's alright. It's been a long time." Tears ran into Vera's shirt. "And I'm okay."

Vera stared into the fire and clutched the flowers in her hand tightly. Tears welled in her eyes and ran over. "Okay. Um." Her throat worked as she swallowed a sob. "I. Um. Lost my sister. Asa. In the, in the fights." Her eyes slid shut, sending another cascade of tears down her cheeks. "She w-was killed... two years after I... escaped." Across the fire, Gavin's eyes closed. "I didn't find out un, until... years later." She opened her eyes and looked down the circle to Gray. "I heard it from one of your friends." Gray nodded. "In the militia we were helping in '24. She was... was shot... fighting the syndicates." Vera blew a breath out through trembling lips. "Doing what she thought was right. Trying to avenge me." She bit down on her lip and stifled a sob. "And I... regret... being too broken to go back home and, and see my family again."

She shuddered. A sob ripped from between her clenched teeth. Tori rubbed her back in gentle circles.

"And... and *Ryan*..." The word was a sob. "I... I didn't know that he was... was dead... this whole time..." She pressed a hand to her mouth. "He, um. He died. Trying to help me." Her face went horribly blank for a moment. "And Joseph fucked me in Ryan's blood."

Gavin flinched. Edrissa whimpered and squeezed her arms around herself.

Vera slammed her eyes shut. "Oh, fuck. I'm... I'm sorry. I didn't mean—"

"It's okay," Tori said softly.

"No, I... I don't wanna *talk* about that stuff. I wanna talk about Ryan. How good he was." Vera opened her eyes and laced her fingers through Tori's, squeezing hard. "He... he was my friend. He was a good man. He didn't hurt me because he wanted to. He tried... *so hard*... to get me out." She let the tears run freely down her face. "He found my handler, paid the guys to get me out. He was with me *every night* in that cell. I was never alone." She lifted her chin and drew in a deep breath. "I've been trying to... remember... everything about him. He had light blond hair and... really clear blue eyes. He... he was taller than me, I remember that. He... We didn't laugh very much, but he had a nice laugh. And he smelled like some cheap deodorant bodywash thing. I can't remember what it was called but..." She smiled. "I remember how it smelled." She let her eyes close. "He always wanted me to be warm. And he... he worried about me drinking enough water. He helped me remember who I was. Remember... there was a world outside the basement *Joseph* put me in. He would..." Her voice wobbled. "When it got really bad, he would clean me up after. And he never..." She bit down hard on her lip. "He *never* let me lose faith entirely. He always promised he would get me out. Right up until... until the moment he died, he was trying to get me out." Her eyes opened and focused on the fire. "He was a good man." She dropped the flowers into the fire. They sent up a puff of embers and ash.

Vera folded against Tori, whimpering softly. Tori smoothed her hand through Vera's hair.

Gray cleared their throat. "Um. I... I've lost a few f-friends. In the, in the skirmishes." They nodded, their mouth twisting. "Marci. Aaron. Todd. Candace. Adam. Rehka. Mike. The other Mike." They smiled ruefully. "Mike Gates and Mike Johnson." They pressed their lips together and took a steadying breath. "They were fighting for something they believed in. It doesn't bring them back. I miss them every day." Gray sniffed. "But I have to think that's how they would have wanted to give their lives. I have to believe that." Their hand opened and they dropped their flowers into the fire.

Everyone was silent for a moment, watching the flames. One by one, they all looked at Edrissa where she stood next to Ellis. She shivered in her coat, biting her lip and keeping her eyes down. The coat was a size too big, making her look even smaller than she was.

"Edrissa?" Tori said softly. "Is there anything you'd like to say? You can talk about anything you want."

Edrissa stared into the flames, tears rolling down her cheeks one by one. Finally, she raised her eyes and looked at Vera across the fire. Softly, she said, "I'm like you."

Vera went still against Tori's side. "Wh-what?"

Edrissa's eyes flicked back down to the fire. "I... They... they d-didn't torture me, a-as much as you. But they... *hurt* me and I... um..."

Vera stared at Edrissa in horror.

Tori's lips trembled. "But you're a... a *child*..." she whispered.

"Old enough to know how," Edrissa said flatly. She shuddered and focused again on Vera. "But I hoped my, my brother was alive for two years. I didn't know he was... was *dead*..." She convulsed forward, her arms going around her stomach again.

A silent look passed between Vera and Tori, and they both walked around the fire to stand at Edrissa's side.

"Can I touch you?" Vera whispered to Edrissa. She threw herself into Vera's arms, sobbing like her throat would tear open at any moment. Tears ran down Vera's cheeks as she slowly wound her arms around Edrissa.

"Can I touch you?" Tori said softly, on her other side. Edrissa nodded against Vera's chest and Tori wrapped herself gently around them both, holding Edrissa in her embrace. Edrissa sobbed long and hard as they held her together, as if everything she had been through was being torn out of her chest, flowing out with her tears. Vera and Tori held her and swayed with her gently, matching their breathing to each other, deep and slow, just loud enough for Isaac to hear across the fire. He found his own breath matching theirs. After a while, Edrissa's breathing slowed to tremulous, hitched sobs, then to soft whimpers. Eventually she was quiet, still wrapped in Tori and Vera's arms. She lifted a hand to wipe her nose. The flowers brushed her face, forgotten in her hand.

"Oh." She laughed, a little painfully, and tossed them into the fire. She turned back and wormed her way a little deeper into Vera's arms.

Ellis was already crying. They let the tears fall as Finn leaned in to press a kiss to their temple. When Ellis opened their mouth to speak, their voice was low and husky. "Um. I... miss... my children. Galen and Chloe. They would be fourteen and eleven now. Chris and I would have been, been married for fifteen years this year." They whimpered. "And there are some days when I feel like... I can't breathe without them here." Ellis laid their head on Finn's shoulder. "And I will... will *always* love them. And miss them. And I like to... imagine... they're all alive somewhere else. Living. Not being afraid." Finn lifted their head and smiled, tilting their head back and blinking against the tears that shone in their eyes. "*God,* I miss them," Ellis sobbed. They threw the flowers into the fire and turned against Finn's chest, sobbing. Finn ran their fingers through Ellis's hair and let them cry. Their own eyes shone with tears in the firelight.

Ellis's sobs eased and quieted. They stood in Finn's arms, weeping softly. Finn wet their lips. "Um... I don't even know who I lost. After the Junior Defense Corps base got destroyed I... I was too scared to... go back home, even. After a few years I went back home, but... I..." They looked up, blinking rapidly. "My parents weren't there anymore. I um..." They gulped. "I don't know if they're still alive. But my school..." Their face crumpled. "I don't know who escaped the death squads and who didn't. My medic education instructor, Instructor Grant..." They pursed their lips and blew out a slow breath. "He, um. Sacrificed him, himself. For us. So we could get away. I wa-watched him get shot." Ellis's arms tightened around their waist. Finn squeezed back. "I wish I knew who was still alive from my class. If any of them are—" Their mouth snapped shut and they heaved a shaking sob. They bowed their head and dropped their fistful of flowers into the fire.

Sam bit their lip and took a small step forward. "Um..." They looked around the fire. "I... I don't think I've really... *lost* someone. I... don't remember my parents, and I... I mean, I've had homes, and people who loved me, but I never really had a... a real *family* before you guys. I've known people who died, but... I was safe, for a really long time. I was... really lucky I guess." They looked down at the flowers in their hand. "But I... I do miss them. I miss

159

Corey. He was the one I was closest to in the group I was with when…" They swallowed. "When I had to run. So, I don't know if he…" They gasped softly. "Anyway. This is for him. And all the others I never knew what happened to." They dropped the flowers into the fire and watched them burn.

Everyone was silent for a moment. Isaac looked around the fire and saw everyone's eyes averted from Gavin. Gavin looked down into the flames, shining lines of tears on his cheeks. His flowers were crushed in his grip. His lips were pressed together like he was terrified of opening his mouth.

"Gavin?" Gray said softly. Isaac's head snapped to look at them. "If you have something to say, you can say it. This is for all of us, including you."

Gavin raised his gaze to Gray. "How can I—" Gavin's voice broke and he tried again, shaking his head. "How can I speak when… when the people I've lost… destroyed your lives?" He hung his head, staring down at the flowers in his hand.

Gray's voice was stiff. "You still have your grief. It's alright to have… complicated feelings about it."

Gavin shuddered and nearly pitched forward in a sob. "I…" He whispered. "I've lost… *everyone*." He tossed his flowers into the fire, sending up another shower of sparks. He pressed his hands to his face and sobbed.

Isaac stared at Gavin, open-mouthed. He'd seen Gavin lose control when Isaac beat him and when Isaac killed the bounty hunter, but it had never occurred to Isaac before that Gavin might… *feel* something besides pain or anger or just goddamn *delight* in hurting people. The world shifted a few degrees.

Gavin sank into a crouch, covering his head with his hands as he sobbed. Everyone around the fire stood still, stiff, uncomfortable. Gavin shuddered on the ground, cowering away from the eyes on him, pushing down his sobs until they came out in strangled whimpers.

Sam wiped their hands on their pants, staring down at Gavin. They bit their lip. They took a step closer and knelt down, gently resting a hand on his shoulder. Gavin jerked away from the touch, a low wail rising from his throat. Sam's hand squeezed into a fist. They took a deep breath and rested their hand on Gavin's arm, making slow circles. Gavin slowly raised his head from his hands. When he saw it was Sam kneeling beside him, he dissolved into sobs again and covered his face with one hand. With his other, he reached out and clasped Sam's.

"I'm sorry," he whispered. "I'm sorry, I'm so, I'm *so sorry,* Sam…" he moaned. "I didn't, I didn't know, I swear I didn't know what… what I *did,* I didn't know… I didn't fucking… I'm so goddamn stupid, I didn't fucking… *realize*… the… the *damage.* I didn't know what it meant when someone hurt, I didn't know what it *felt like,* I just knew it felt good and I… god fucking *dammit,* I'm so *stupid,* I should have fucking figured it out, and I'm so *sorry*…" He pitched forward onto all fours, his face getting close to the flames. He crawled backward and settled back on his heels. "I didn't know how it felt, I should've just known but I *didn't,* and I regret it, I'm so, I'm so *sorry, Sam!*"

Tears shimmered on Sam's face as they rubbed Gavin's arm. Isaac stared at them both, dumbfounded.

Gavin raised his gaze up to Vera. She stared at Gavin in disbelief. "I didn't know my dad was doing that to you. I'm a fucking idiot but I *swear* I didn't fucking know. I should have, I should…" Gavin shuddered and froze into a full-body tension. "If I had known, if I had, I could've helped, I could have, I could have… *done* something, and I didn't, and I… oh, *fuck*…"

Gavin convulsed forward with a wail and pressed himself against the ground. "Oh my, oh my *god,* I didn't…"

Vera's face was pinched and tense. Her arms tightened around Edrissa.

"And I… I wanted to hurt you, I *know* I did, I'm not saying I didn't want that, but… *fuck.* And how can I, how can I miss my dad, how can I miss him when he did that to you? I believe you; I know he did, I know it in my *fucking soul.* I know he hurt you like that, and how can I… how can I say I miss him, that it fucking kills me that he's dead, that I *watched him die,* when he… he strung me up as bait for you, after he…" He keened brokenly into the snow.

"Gavin…" Sam said softly.

"No, no, no, no, *no,*" Gavin sobbed. "I lost my entire, f-fucking family. I'm… I'm fucking dead to them. I can *never* go home. My mom, my fucking *mom* wants me dead because she, she fucking blames *me*…"

Sam's hand settled on Gavin's shoulder and squeezed.

"I can never go home. My family, my mom told them all to close their doors to me and I can't…" Gavin gasped. "I… I've lost… *everyone.*" He

161

collapsed into himself and sobbed. Sam moved their hand in circles on Gavin's shoulder again, silent. Snowflakes landed in their hair.

There was a flicker of moment in Isaac's periphery. He looked up to see Gray take a hesitant step around the fire towards Gavin. They stopped, their hands tightened into fists. They took a step. Paused again. Finally, they blew out a slow breath and made their way around the circle to Gavin. Gray knelt at Gavin's side, their hand hovering slightly over his head. They bit their lip. Their hand settled in Gavin's hair.

Gavin glanced up, his eyes widening when he saw Gray. He looked back down at the ground. His hand went up to wrap around Gray's wrist and squeeze, keeping their hand pressed gently in his hair.

Everyone else watched, silently, until the fire started to die down.

Chapter 25

Tori lifted the axe. Swung it. Cracked it down into the log teetering on the massive tree stump. The axe buried itself in the chunk of wood. Sweat chilled on Tori's skin in the cold, biting air. Tori twisted and shook the axe free, steadying the wood on the stump and raising the axe to swing again.

"Hey."

She jumped and nearly dropped the axe. She spun around to see Isaac slowly approaching her, hands up. She pressed a hand to her chest. "Fuck, Isaac. You scared me."

"I'm sorry." Concern darkened his features. "You, um…" His gaze moved over her face. "You okay?"

She put the axe down on the tree stump. "Yeah. I'm good. You just scared me."

"You scare a lot lately," Isaac said softly. He sat down on the frozen ground next to the stump.

Tori looked away.

"Hey." Her eyes flicked to Isaac. He held out his hand. "We don't have to talk if you don't want, although I really, really think you should. Let's sit for a minute. None of us have really gotten to just… sit."

She sighed and took his hand, letting him pull her gently to the ground beside him. She groaned softly as she sat. Sweat dampened the shirt she had on under her sweater. She shivered and met Isaac's gaze.

Isaac's eyes moved intently over her, lingering on her face as she tried to force down the grimace of pain, on her throat and how it moved with each breath. Her hands, how they shook. She swallowed. The motion still sent ghostly panic through her as her throat remembered the feel of the collar, even weeks later.

Isaac finally looked away, toward the house. He wet his lips. "You were there for us for months."

"Isaac…"

"Taking care of us. Keeping us safe. Listening to us while we cried. Holding us."

"Isaac, please…"

"And now, I think you're making a mistake."

She turned to look at him, her mouth falling slightly open. "…what?"

Isaac's gaze was warm as he looked at her without judgement. Without demand. He didn't need anything from her.

That terrified her.

She swallowed again, the movement feeling rough, like it always did now. "What do you mean?"

Isaac kept his gaze on her and reached for her hand. She let him take her hand in his. He squeezed gently. "I mean… you're keeping to yourself. Withdrawing. Trying to make it look like you're fine, when…" His gaze moved over her again. "…you're not."

Tears pricked at Tori's eyes. She pulled her hand out of Isaac's grasp. She squeezed her eyes closed for a moment, blowing out a slow breath. It fogged in the crisp air. "I… I'm… I'm fine."

Isaac chuckled. Her eyes flew open and fixed on him, her stomach boiling with sudden rage. "What?" she demanded.

Isaac's smile faded. "I'm sorry. You just… you sound just like me. Like I did seven months ago."

She sighed and let her head drop back, blowing the breath out slowly, watching it fog into the air, forcing herself to be calm. "But I really am fine."

Isaac took her hand again and squeezed harder. "I know you're not. And that's okay."

She bit her lip against the tears that threatened to spill over. "How can I…" She cleared her throat and tried again. "How can I… *complain*… about what I went through… when it was only for a few hours? How can I complain when… when…" She sniffed and pulled her hand away. "…when he did that…" She gestured at Isaac. "…to you?"

Isaac smiled gently. "The same way I can complain about what I went through, when Vera went through it, too, and so much worse… for months." He put a hand on her back. "There's no comparing it."

He rubbed her back, and she tensed. She tried to push it down, tried to ignore it like she always did. His hand pressed into the almost-healed skin that Gavin had split with the cane. The flesh had nearly knitted together again, although she always hurt, now, when the marks were touched. When she stretched her hands over her head. When she was on her back beneath Vera, just kissing, because Vera hadn't been able to have sex in weeks. It hurt. It always hurt.

She looked up at Isaac. The corners of his mouth were turned down. He pulled his hand away from her back. "Does that hurt?" he asked.

Again, a slow breath. In, and out. Just like she told Vera. In, and out. Everything was fine.

"Tori… are you still in pain?"

She looked up to the sky, praying the tears in her eyes wouldn't fall. "You went through so much worse, Isaac," she whispered. "And I… I want to take care of you. All of you. I don't want to be the one that's… that's…"

"A burden," he murmured.

"Yeah. Yeah, exactly. I don't want to be—" She glanced up and saw the look on his face. She blanched. "I didn't mean…"

"I know what you meant, Tori," he said gently. "But… did you think I was a burden when I couldn't even feed myself? When I lay in bed for days, just crying? Did you think I was a burden when you had to change my bandages, check my shoulder every day? Did you think I was a burden when I kept everyone up with my nightmares?"

"No, Isaac, I—"

"I've been the biggest burden on this team since Gavin tortured me," he pressed on. "I've needed the most help. The most medicine. I've woken everyone up with my nightmares for months. Only five days with Gavin, and I caused *months* of fallout for my family. And do you think…" He had to stop to steady his voice. "Do you think I'm a burden?"

"No," she whispered. "But it's… it's different. He only had me for a few *hours*…"

"And yet he marked you."

She shivered as the wounds on her back spiked with pain, on her arms, her legs, her chest. Gavin hadn't spared anything. She had scars, now, everywhere.

"Tori... you were the first person I told about Gavin's torture. They all know now, but... you were there for me. Please. Let me be there for you." She looked over at him. She trembled and bit her lip.

"Um..." *Where would I even fucking start?* "It... it hurts sometimes. A lot. The marks he made..." For a moment, her hands drifted to the hem of her sweater. She paused, shaking. *No one but Vera has seen these.* She took a deep breath and lifted the back of her shirt slightly, turning so her back was exposed to him. She knew it was streaked with still-fading bruises and new pink scars that stood out against the brown of her skin. She could feel Isaac's gaze on her back. She lowered her shirt and turned back to him.

She was afraid to raise her eyes to meet his, terrified of what she would find there. *He's been through so much worse.* She gritted her teeth and looked up at him.

Still, he wore that expression of softness, without judgment.

She released a breath.

"I don't know how to get better," she whispered.

Isaac smiled sadly. "Neither do I. If I did, I would be better by now." His mouth twisted.

"And having him... *here*..." She glanced at the house. "He... he fucked with my head, Isaac. He said things and I... I believed him."

"What did he say?" he asked gently.

Her vision blurred with tears. "He... said..." She gulped. "He said... Vera was only with me... because she needed to be *owned* again. And I was... *taking advantage*... of her. He said I... I *like them broken*." She shuddered. "He said I liked that Vera would be my plaything if I... if I wanted."

Isaac tensed. "You... you believed that?"

She sniffled. "Um. I... I did. He was... he was *hurting* me, and... I felt... *so fucking guilty* that she was coming for me. I thought Gray was *dead*. She *told* him Gray was dead. And I... I thought she was going to die for me, too. I wasn't thinking straight, Isaac, I... I wasn't..." She shuddered forward into a sob.

He wound an arm around her shoulders. "Hey. You're alright."

"No," she moaned. "You don't... I thought Gray was... was *dead.* I thought they were both dying for *me.* And I couldn't stop it. I felt so fucking *helpless* and I just kept praying I could be brave, like... like Vera."

Isaac squeezed her shoulder. "You know Vera gets scared, too, right?"

She laughed out a sob. "But it's *different!*"

He squeezed her tighter. "You're allowed to be scared, Tori. You're allowed to break."

She turned and wrapped her arms around his neck. "But with him with us—"

"I know. I'm, um. Struggling. With it, too."

"Do you think he would try to hurt us again?" she whispered. "Do you think he's going to...?"

Isaac was silent for a long moment. Finally, he murmured, "I don't know."

"He's done such fucked up things," she whimpered into his shoulder. "He's hurt *all* of us. He's a fucking *monster.*"

Isaac's jaw clenched. "I know. But... I think..." He blew out a breath. "I don't know what I think. He's... he's different now. I think he... I think he... maybe... understands?"

"How can he fucking understand? He's... he's..." Her hands tightened in his shirt and she whimpered. "He *hurt me,*" she whispered.

"I know," he said gently. "I know. But... we'll just have to keep an eye on him. He's... different. I don't know what it means."

"But what if he—"

"If he even tries to hurt any of us again..." He held her tight to his chest. "I'm going to kill him. I won't let him hurt us again. If he tries again, I'm going to kill him."

Chapter 26

Isaac listened contentedly to his family's low voices and soft laughter from the living room as he washed the dishes from dinner. Gray and Tori had done the shopping. Sam and Edrissa had been busy all morning shucking corn and drying out meat for later. Vera had chopped the vegetables. Even Gavin had worked on making bread. Finn and Ellis were off on their own, eating dinner in town – their first-ever proper date. Isaac had been content with doing the dishes after dinner if it meant having the afternoon off.

The night was calm. Everyone was seeming to adjust to their new, if temporary, lives up north after a week in the ranch house. It was as close to peaceful as Isaac had been since they started running missions again, months ago.

Someone bumped into his hip and he jumped slightly, knocked out of his thoughts. Sam smiled up at him with their brown eyes shining with something Isaac hadn't seen since the woods. He smiled and turned slightly back to the dish in his hand.

"Hey, Sam. What's up?"

"You've been getting better," they said softly.

Isaac's lips curved up, but he kept his eyes on the plate. "Yeah. I have."

"And I... I want to start talking to you again."

He stopped washing the plate, the brush still held tight in his hand. He blew out a shaky breath. "Yeah?"

"Yeah," they said. Isaac set down the plate and brush in the sink and turned to them. They smiled. "You've been... you've been different. I don't think..." For a moment a corner of their mouth turned down. "I don't... think..."

"...I'll explode at you like that again?" Guilt weighed heavy in Isaac's stomach.

Sam shifted their feet and leaned against the counter. "Yeah."

Isaac chewed the inside of his cheek. "Well, I… I won't. I never should have. I'm sorry."

"I know you are." Sam's hand was gentle as it rested on his arm.

The touch made him shiver. *I haven't really been touched by any of the team the way I used to. It's like they're all afraid to get close to me. It's like they all think I'll…* The thought brought tears to his eyes and he blinked, looking down.

Sam ducked into his field of vision. "Hey. Um. I know you're having a hard time."

"No hard time justifies what I did," Isaac rasped, still staring at the floor. "No matter how bad I feel, or how… how *lost* I feel, *nothing* justifies pushing you away like that."

Sam smiled, a hint of sadness in their eyes. "It's not the first time we've pushed each other away because of pain, Isaac. It probably won't be the last."

Isaac shifted his gaze away. "But you've never… you've never *hurt* me like that, Sam. You've never done anything like what I did."

"Isaac, I pointed a gun at you when you rescued me from Gavin the first time," Sam said with a chuckle.

"Oh." Isaac's hand went up to rub the back of his neck. "I guess you did. I kinda forgot about that."

"And if I had killed you?" Isaac looked back at Sam, tears shining in their eyes, too. Their arms wrapped around their chest. "We've both done… really stupid stuff to each other. I punched you in the face, too, remember?"

Isaac opened his mouth to protest. Sam's eyes narrowed and their mouth twisted, their lips still pulling up a little in the corners. Isaac closed his mouth again.

"I think you're healing," Sam said softly.

Isaac blew out a breath. "Yeah."

"And you're… you're trying."

Isaac laughed once, bitter. "Kinda pathetic that I have to be convinced to try to not hurt."

"It's how you've always lived, Isaac."

Tears welled in Isaac's eyes, too quickly for him to blink away. One coursed down his cheek, then the other. "I don't want to feel this way anymore," Isaac whispered.

"I know. And that's why I feel ready to talk to you again. Because... you're not holding onto that pain anymore, Isaac. You're not keeping it around to punish yourself with. And I'm not... I'm not afraid of you."

Isaac's heart clenched. He squeezed his eyes shut. "Have you been... afraid of me? Lately?"

"Um, yeah." Sam said with a deep breath. "A little. After the thing with the bounty hunters... and how you've reacted to Gavin a few times... I've been a little worried that you were..."

Isaac nodded, his eyes still closed. "Yeah."

"No, please let me say it."

Isaac opened his eyes, steeling himself for whatever was about to come out of Sam's mouth. *You're dangerous. You're a liability. You're weak. You scare me too much for me to want you around.* He nodded.

Sam bit their lip and searched Isaac's face with their gaze. "I was afraid I was... um... losing you."

Isaac wet his lips. "Yeah. I—"

"Please let me just... say all of it. Please." Sam's gaze moved over Isaac's face. He nodded again.

Sam took a deep breath and pushed it out slowly. "I've been... scared, because..." Sam looked away and their chin quivered. "I've always trusted you. From the very beginning. And you've always, always kept us safe. Kept *me* safe. But when Gavin showed up... I... you started to..." Sam gulped. "I started to wonder if, if pain was... all you could let yourself feel. Pain, or, or anger. At Gavin, at... at Edrissa... anyone who stood in the way of..." Sam's gaze returned to Isaac's face. "And... it *scared me,* Isaac. It scared me that you might be... losing yourself." They unfolded their arms and placed one palm on Isaac's chest, over his heart. "Your *goodness.* And when you..." Their hands fell to their sides and their eyes filled with tears. "When you said... when you said those things, in the woods, I thought— No. Sorry. I just... I thought you were... pushing me away. For good. Because maybe you went through..." They bit down on their lips. "Maybe you went through too much pain to want to be around me anymore."

"Oh," he said softly.

"And I… I haven't known how to… to *help* you, Isaac. I can't… I can't help if you… if you just… won't let me in. I didn't know you were hurting so much. I didn't even…" They pitched their voice lower, their words gentle. "I didn't even know your dad died, Isaac."

Isaac hung his head. "I know. I… I *know* that. I've just been so scared… that… that if you all knew what, what I felt sometimes… that I had… so many damned *weaknesses…*" He swallowed hard. "You would…"

Sam tilted their head. "Isaac, when have we ever left someone behind because we thought they were *weak?*"

Isaac's lips trembled. He curled his hand into a fist. "*You* haven't, but… you don't…" He shuddered and caught himself on the counter. "It feels like the hurt never ends," he whispered.

"Well… maybe if you let yourself just, just *hurt* sometimes, without getting… without pushing us away, maybe it would stop piling up?"

"How can I feel that much hurt?" he said, his eyes finding Sam's and holding them desperately. "How can I… *let* that happen? What if… what if I feel something, and I… I break, and I never come back, and I'm not… *useful…?*"

"You don't have to be useful to be worthy," Sam said quietly.

Isaac looked up, recognizing Tori's words. He smiled brokenly, his mouth twisting. "I prefer to be useful, though."

Sam huffed out a breath. "Don't we all?" They hesitantly reached out a hand towards Isaac. "I should have asked, before. Can I touch you?"

Isaac let out a breath. "You never have to ask, Sam. You *never* have to ask."

Sam held back for a moment, chewing their lip. "I… I do, Isaac. You've been… you jump when we touch you sometimes. You… flinch."

Isaac's eyes went wide. "*What?* I didn't… even… I didn't even *know.*"

"Seeing Gavin again messed you up, Isaac. You've been different."

"I know." He felt the pull towards guilt, towards pushing Sam away and telling them to leave him alone for their own good. *I'm dangerous to them.*

I'm a threat. A liability. What if Gavin makes me angry and I lash out, and hurt Sam? I could never forgive myself. He clenched his jaw shut and shook his head.

I will never let that happen.

He straightened slightly, only realizing now how the guilt and exhaustion had pulled his shoulders down, how his head bent against the dread. "Um. Yeah. You can touch me. Thank you."

Sam stepped forward and pulled Isaac into a hug. Isaac carefully wrapped his arms around them, more aware than ever of his strength, his height, how he could hurt them, *so* easily, if he ever lost control. *It's selfish of me to try and make them stay. They shouldn't be around me. I can't lose control, can't lose control...*

He shook his head as if to clear the thought. He rested his cheek on the top of Sam's head, holding them tight. Sam buried their face against his chest. *I won't lose control. Not anymore. Never with them.*

Isaac squeezed Sam tighter, a piece of himself falling back into place as they tightened their arms around him, too. He ran his fingers gently through their hair, his heart aching. *God, I missed them.*

He swayed slowly with them, holding them tight. After a long moment, he pulled away and stepped back. Sam wiped their face on their shirt.

"You haven't..." Isaac's voice faltered and he started again. "You haven't been... *affected*... by Gavin being here as much, I don't think."

Sam bit their lip, mulling over the question buried in Isaac's words. "Yeah... I don't know why. I mean, I still sort of... I still think about what he did, I think about it all the *time,* but... he's so different now, Isaac. He's not the same person."

"Yeah, Vera made sure of that," Isaac said under his breath.

"No, I mean..." Sam ran a hand through their curls. "He really is... *different,* Isaac. He doesn't want to hurt people, yeah, but... haven't you seen him? He... he *hurts*. It's like... now that he understands, now that he's... made the connection, he's sorry. And... he wants what we have."

Isaac took a full step back, shuddering, his mind rebelling at the thought. "What... *we...?*"

Sam shook their head. "No, not... not *you and I,* specifically, but... what we have as a family. He wants... I think he wants something that he... doesn't have to earn by hurting someone."

Isaac snorted. "He's never had to *earn* a thing in his life. He's never—"

"Isaac, you're not *listening.*" Isaac's mouth snapped shut. "You know his parents torture people, and... his mom *cut him off* for not wanting us captured and tortured. Do you think he had a choice as a kid, either?"

"We *always* have a choice," Isaac ground out. "*Always.* He tortured Vera when he was *ten years old.* How can you say he—"

"Does a kid have a choice between a parent's love, and anything else on the planet?" Sam's hands clenched into fists at their sides.

Isaac choked on the rage that swept up through his chest. "This wasn't about his parents' *love;* this was about how much he wanted to *hurt people.* It made him happy, to, to *hurt.* Nothing could have... have *changed* that..."

"What if he'd been raised by Gray?" Sam lifted their chin. "What if he'd been raised by someone like Tori? Do you think he would have turned out the same?"

Pain punched through Isaac's gut, as real as a bullet. Isaac fell back against the counter, paralyzed. The rage burning in his throat ran down his arms, made him ready to *fight,* fight Gavin, fight the pain, fight *Sam,* if they said one more *goddamned thing* defending Gavin...

At the same time, tears pricked his eyes. *If I was raised by someone other than my mom, if Rosa and Michael and the others hadn't left me, would I hurt the way I do? Would I feel so broken? Would I be so fucking* hollow *on the inside, if someone like Gray raised me? If I had someone to teach me I wouldn't be left if I wasn't good enough? If I had someone telling me they loved me, even if I was weak?*

He saw a brilliantly clear picture in his mind of himself, twelve years old, and *loved.* Held, when he missed his father. Protected, when the world started to hurt him. Soothed, when he was in pain. The way it should have been.

The damage was done. Could never be undone.

Sam's arms went around him and he was suddenly sitting on the floor, sobbing until it felt like his lungs would collapse. A throbbing ache, torn and inflamed, crushed his chest.

"—c-couldn't, I... I n-never, oh, oh *god*..."

"I'm so sorry." There were tears in Sam's voice.

"Wh-what if, what if I, oh *no,* I just... my mom, if my, my *mom*—"

A sniffle, beside him. "I wish... I wish you could have known, then, that you... you deserved so much better."

"...sh-she never, she, *never,* and... Rosa, Lexi, Michael, William... they all... they were *fine*... with leaving m-me... and J-Jordan was... was *gone*..."

"I'm so sorry," Sam whispered, wrapping their arms around him and cradling him as best they could.

"...what if, if I *had* Gray, what, what if, someone *loved me* the whole time, what if I didn't... *hurt* so much... *no,* Sam, I'm fucked up, I'm... I'm *broken,* I... I hurt *so fucking much,* how am I... how am I *ever* supposed to..."

"I don't know," Sam said softly. "But we'll help you. We'll help you get through this, Isaac. I promise... we are never going to leave you. We *love* you."

Isaac clutched at Sam. "I'm sorry, I'm so sorry, I ca-can't, I, can't, I..." He pressed his hand against his chest. His heart raced so fast it made him dizzy. He couldn't slow his breathing, no matter how hard he tried. Tears poured down his face and he rocked forward, clawing at his throat, sobbing so loudly it sounded more like a scream.

Then more hands were on him, cradling his face, pushing back his hair. And voices, and bodies around him, but he couldn't *see* what was going on, couldn't make sense of it. The world spun in a horrible kaleidoscope of color and jagged feeling that he couldn't get a grasp on. He panted and sobbed against the cabinets.

"Sam?"

"I don't know, he, we were talking about—"

"About... Gavin?"

"Well... I mean yeah, but... I think... he's... I think it's the abuse."

"…I'm sorry, I'm, I'm *sorry,* I, I'll do it, I'll *do* it, please d-don't leave I'm *sorry…*"

"Oh, god. Oh. Oh, no…"

"Oh, Jesus. I… shouldn't be here."

"You *think?*"

"Easy, Vera. Gavin, it might be best if you leave for a bit. Just until we find out what's going on in his head right now."

"*…I tried to be good…*"

"*Fuck.*"

"Vera, go. It's not the same thing. You're alright."

"No. I need to… um… I, I need to be here… for…"

"*…I'm sorry, I tried, I tried to be good…*"

"*No…* F-fuck, I…"

"Vera, go."

"It's okay, babe. Gray's got this."

"*…no no no no please don't leave, please, please don't go…*" Isaac's hands reached out blindly.

"She's not going anywhere, Isaac. Just into the next room. I'm staying right here with you. So is Sam."

"*…I'm sorry, I'm sorry I'm sorry I'm sorry I'm sorry I'm sorry…*"

"Isaac, I'm… I'm sorry, I can't… *listen…*"

"*…please…*" A whimper. "*…please…*"

"Vera's going to be just behind that wall. Here, give me your hand, Isaac. I've got you."

"*…n-no…*"

"Isaac… we're both right here. Oh, um. It's Sam. We're in the kitchen of the north house. You're, you're safe, Isaac."

"Isaac, breathe with me. Can you do that with me? Just breathe. In… come on, Isaac, try to slow your breathing down and take a deep breath in."

"*…I can't, I can't I can't I can't—*"

"You just did, Isaac. Do it again, deep breath, now hold… No, shh, just hold the breath for me. Good. Now out. Good, Isaac. In again."

"Just squeeze my hand if you need to. Oh, ow… Yeah, just a little looser… Thank you."

"Breathe in again, Isaac. Big deep breath. All the way down into your lungs. Hold it for just a moment. Now out. Good. Perfect."

In.

Hold.

Out.

In.

Hold.

Out.

In.

Hold.

Out.

"I'm sorry," Isaac whispered.

"Shh." Gray kissed his forehead. "Don't be sorry. I keep telling Vera this: it was hidden for a long time. It's alright if things come back out a little rough."

"I… I'm so sorry…" Isaac's voice wobbled. "I didn't… know that was…"

"Now you know," Gray said softly. They groaned as they lowered themself to sit on the floor beside him. They leaned up against the cabinets and let their head fall back. Sam squeezed Isaac tight from where they sat on his other side. "Now you know the pain is there. You don't have to push it down. You felt it, and it didn't kill you."

Isaac winced, curling forward around the pain in his chest. "Why does it… *hurt* so much?" His face was still wet with tears.

Gray laughed gently. "You pushed it down for years, Isaac. It's going to hurt when it comes back up." They squeezed Isaac's hand. "But you did it. And I'm proud of you."

Isaac let his eyes close, sending more tears coursing slowly down his face.

Chapter 27

Years ago

The fire was dying down. Isaac got to his feet to put on another log, and the world tilted. He staggered and put a hand to his head. "Whoa."

"You good?" Vera slurred from her seat by the fire. Her eyes followed him slowly.

"Uh. Yeah." He giggled. "That ssstuff Gray got is um." He giggled again, his chest feeling warm and fuzzy.

"I told you I know good whiskey," Gray said earnestly, sitting straight up and staring at Isaac as if they had just delivered the plan for world peace. "I *told* you. I *told* you I know good whiskey and it's *good.*" They held up the empty bottle.

"We also gained 4000 vertical feet today," Finn said, grinning, their eyes shining. "So the alll… cohol affects you more. The partial pressures of the oxyg—"

Ellis dragged them into a kiss, their movements clumsy. "You are so smart," Ellis murmured, their voice low and urgent. "You are so, so, so *smart* Finn Dunham. You are my sexy smart nerd medic." They pulled Finn into another, deeper kiss. Finn laughed and pulled Ellis close.

Isaac spun, suddenly remembering his mission. "Another log!" he exclaimed. He pointed at the stack of firewood. Now there was just one log left, and plenty of kindling. He gasped. "I have to find more logs. I'llll be right back. With more logs." He placed the remaining log as gently as he could in the fire. *This is what brain surgery must feel like. Place the log. In the fire. Carefully.*

He stood up and took a step to the side as the world spun around him again. He turned towards the woods and began walking.

Vera scrambled to her feet. "I'll come with you! I wanna come with you to get the looogs." She laughed, high and loose in a way Isaac had never heard before. Her cheeks were flushed, and her eyes sparkled.

He grinned. "Bros. On a mission. Get the logs." He struck off again in the direction of the trees, Vera close behind.

"Be carefully—" Gray cleared their throat. "Be careful of the woods!" They waved their hand around them in a circle as if demonstrating their point.

Vera grinned. "We will be ssooo careful of the woods."

Isaac stumbled over the underbrush, finding himself in the middle of bushes more often than he found himself on the path. His gaze bounced over the ground. *"Logs. Wood. Firewood,"* he mumbled under his breath. His eyes settled on a small fallen tree, its bark stripped away by animals, its wood bleached from the sun. "Wood!" He grabbed the tree and dragged it towards the camp.

"You found a whole tree?" Vera asked, perplexed. "We're going to burn a whole tree?"

"I will…" Isaac made a chopping motion with his hand. "Break it. And then we can use it."

Vera put her hands on her hips, swaying slightly. "I don' believe yyou. Show me."

Isaac shrugged. "Okay." He braced a branch of the tree under his foot and wrenched the end upwards. The branch came away from the rest of the tree with a satisfying *crack*.

Vera smiled. "Okeee. I was wrong. We'll break the tree." She stepped forward to tear another limb off.

"We should break the tree at the camp," Isaac insisted, his eyebrows pulled together in concern. "We need to carry the tree there, so we don't have to carry the wood instead."

Vera's eyebrows shot up. "Ohhh that makes sense." She bent down to grab another branch.

They dragged it through the underbrush together, laughing as they tripped over roots. The tree lurched to a stop. Vera turned slowly, squinting at the tree in the near-darkness. Isaac's gaze moved from her to the tree and back again. He blinked.

"Um."

Vera pointed at the tree, looking utterly perplexed. "…ssstopped."

Isaac scratched his head. "Uh-huh."

"Um…" Vera took a clumsy step to the side. "Why…"

In a flash of insight, Isaac found the problem: the tree was wedged against another tree.

"Vera!" he cried, pointing. "Look!" She stumbled to his side, looking intently in the direction he was pointing. "It's stuck!"

"Haaaaaa." Vera held up her hand for a high five. "Figured it out. Nice."

Isaac grinned and aimed a high-five at her hand. He missed.

Vera turned and grabbed a branch. "Come on, Isaac!" she said, her voice comically deep. "Let's dooo iiiit."

Isaac grabbed the tree and yanked. Vera dug her heels into the ground and leaned against the branch, straining to dislodge the tree. With a sudden jolt, it moved, and she toppled to the ground with a thud.

Isaac gasped and immediately bent down to pick her up. "Vera! Oh nooo…" he whined softly. "Are you alright?" He grabbed her arms and pulled her upright.

She wobbled, grinning. "Yep. I'm sso good. Just fell." Isaac's hands were still on her arms. She swallowed.

"Uh." Isaac looked down at his hands. "I'm sorry. I shouldn't… yeah." His hands fell to his sides.

Her gaze was fixed on his face. "Huh?"

"Uh. Well… sorry. I um. Well, you… you know?"

Her eyes flicked down to his lips. "Nope."

He bit his lip. "So, you're like… my friend? Best friend, maybe?" She nodded. He grinned. "So, I want to, you know. Be respectful. Cuzzz I'm kinda drunk. And you are also."

Vera's mouth fell open, wounded. "I am not! Watch watch watch." She scampered a few steps away from him to a clear patch of ground. "I'll walk the line. See? I'm wwalking." She staggered across the ground. "And… I can do roadside tests. I know *aalll* the roadside tests. I know the date it is…" Her forehead wrinkled. "It is March 20, 2027. And we're in the forest, and if I have a pen, I can…" She patted her pockets. "No pen. Oh well, but if I, I had it I could follow it with my eyes. And I can count backwards from forty-seven to thirty-nine. See? Forty-seven forty-six forty-five forty-four forty-three forty-two forty-one forty thirty-nine. See? I'mm not drunk. And I can say the alphabet backwards. See? Z, Y, X, W—"

Isaac cut her off with a hand over her mouth. "I believe you. You're not drunk."

"Okay." She smiled and pulled her face away from Isaac's hand. "Shhhouldn't drive, but… I'm not drunk. Okay? So we can."

Isaac blinked slowly. "We can… what?"

"Um." Vera took a step closer. "If you want to. We don't, um. Have to."

Isaac cast around in his mind for what in the world she could be talking about. "We don't have to… what?"

Vera stepped close enough that Isaac could feel her against his chest. "Fuck," she said, matter-of-factly.

Isaac's eyes went wide. "Oh."

"I mean it doessn't have to be weird," Vera slurred. "I mean, like we're friends, it doesn't have to be, you know." Her hands drifted to the hem of his shirt. "Do you want to?"

Isaac swallowed. "Do you?"

Vera blinked. "Umm. Yeah." She pulled Isaac close and pressed a kiss to his lips.

Isaac's mind went perfectly, blissfully blank.

Then his hands were on her, sliding around her waist, tangling in her hair to pull her head back. He deepened the kiss. She moaned.

"Not gonna be weird," Isaac said against her lips. "I just want—"

"Me, too," she sighed. "It'ss been a long time and I just wanna… see…" She pushed Isaac back against a tree.

"I wanna stay friends," he murmured as he kissed down her neck.

"Me, too. This won't change that. Fffucking promise me."

"I promise." He found her hand and wrapped his pinky finger around hers. "Won't change that. Best friends. I just… right now… I…" He groaned as she pressed her hips into his.

"You know I love you as my best friend," she whispered against his ear. He shivered.

"You, too. But I… I want you right now…"

180

Vera smiled and stumbled a step back. She eased Isaac to the ground, sitting him down. The ground was soft with pine needles. He leaned back against the tree, his eyes sparkling in the fading dusk as he looked up at her. She slid to her knees and straddled his hips.

His hands went to the hem of her shirt. He started to pull it up over her back. "Can I—"

She wrapped her hands around his wrists and stopped him with gentle pressure. "Uh-uh."

His hands left her shirt immediately and went to her face, cradling it as he pulled her in for another kiss. "Can I touch, um." He whimpered as she nibbled his lower lip. "Can I touch you over the shirt or—"

"Yeah," Vera murmured against his jaw. "I just wanna keep it on. Cuz I don't... um..." She sucked along his neck.

"Yup." Isaac's hands moved up her back, over her shirt, to cradle the back of her neck. She shrugged his hand off, grasping it and moving it to her waist. He pressed his lips to her throat and she gasped.

She rolled her hips against his. They both moaned at the friction, and she rolled them again, and again, getting into a rhythm. Their warmth seemed to hold the chill back as they panted against each other's skin. Isaac felt himself straining against his pants, and he whimpered.

"Do you have a condom?" Vera whispered against his neck.

He groaned. "Oh. No. I um. No."

"I have an IUD," she said as she trailed her lips up to his ear. "I keep it up, up to date. I know this, uh, this doctor who helps... you knooow, with people on the run and... and I... I mean, I haven't really slept with anyone... since..."

"Oh. Um." Isaac tried desperately to clear his head, but his mind swirled with the whiskey. "I mean I've... um... always used condoms, and—"

"I know I'm clean," Vera said as she pressed her lips to Isaac's cheek. "I got tested after... after last, last time."

"Okay. Are you, are you okay with...?"

"I trust you," she murmured as she nibbled his earlobe. "I trust you."

"O-okay," Isaac sighed, shivers moving down his body as she licked her way from his collarbone to his jaw.

"You want to?"

Isaac whimpered against her chest. "Please. But only if you want to."

She sighed against Isaac's neck. "Y-yeah," she whispered. "I... I want you." She stood and kicked off her boots. Then she unzipped her pants, and pulled them off her legs.

Isaac stared up at her with his mouth open, his eyes following her hands as she pulled her panties off, too, and threw them on top of the pile. His eyes caught on dark stripes across her thighs, and silvery lines on her hips. She knelt and straddled him again.

Her hands moved to his belt and she fumbled at the zipper. He *very* helpfully reached down to help her, desperate to feel her against him. His hands got in the way and his pants hung only halfway open. They laughed together.

Vera finished unzipping his pants and Isaac groaned as he was freed from the restriction. Isaac could smell the whiskey on her breath as Vera rose up over him, grasping his cock gently with one hand. He moaned as she positioned him against her and slid slowly down onto him.

She gasped out a shaky breath and her arms wrapped around his neck. He felt her trembling against him and wrapped his arms around her waist. Her breaths came fast and heavy against his hair as she clutched him. They sat still together for a moment.

"Will you just talk to me, please," she said in a small voice.

Isaac's tongue was clumsy in his mouth. It was so *much,* the feel of her body against his, the feel of being inside her, warm and soft and so fucking *close,* the sheen of sweat on her skin, how her chest moved with each breath... He blinked and tried to arrange his thoughts in any sort of order.

"Um," he tried. His mind went blank. "Oh. Uh. You, um, feel good."

Her arms loosened around his neck for a moment. "Can you tell me I'm, um... safe."

"Oh." His hands rubbed in circles on her back. "Oh. You're safe. I don't... I don't know what, um..."

"Please just... keep going. Or talk to me about... I don't know. I just want to hear your, um, voice. *Your* voice."

"Okay. Uh... You're safe. We're just... uh... just two best friends, in the woods, with our, um... naughty bits..."

182

They both burst out laughing. Isaac moaned at how it made Vera spasm around him.

"I just want to hear that you, um… want me to… um… feel good. And safe. Please?" There was a tremulous vulnerability to her voice that made Isaac suddenly want to punch whoever it was that hurt her. But he couldn't. Not when he was inside his friend. He could just be with his friend. That would be good.

"Okay. Well… I do. I want you to feel good and safe and… and happy. You are my beautiful friend and you are very scary and I love you. You could kick my ass if you wanted." It was so, so hard to concentrate.

"I want you to be safe, too," she murmured, her lips pressed into his hair. She took a deep breath. She began to move.

They both groaned as she moved against him, grinding her hips hard against his. Her hands never left him. They were in his hair, on his face, reaching back to brace herself against his leg. His hands moved to her hips and he pressed his fingers against her bare skin, easing her up, guiding her back down, his vision nearly going white. Her mouth was on his and she was tasting his lips and she was all around him. A sort of strangled whine escaped his throat as she ground herself down harder against his hips.

The more moans she drew from his lips, the more she sank down onto him, pressing him back against the tree, devouring him, drawing her lips and teeth down his neck. He let his head fall back, his mouth open to her, helpless. He could smell her hair and her sweat and the whiskey and it all melted together into warm curls of pleasure that moved through him, beginning where he was deep inside her, her hips pressed against his. His eyes rolled as she drew his head to the side and bit down gently on his neck.

"V-Vera," he murmured, his hands tangling in her shirt.

"Oh, god. Yeah?" She pushed him back against the tree and worked her hips harder into his.

"I am, um, thank you. This is, uhh, is good. Really good. I'm glad you're my, my friend."

She laughed gently, then shuddered and picked up the pace. "Isaac, *fuck*, I… oh god…"

He could feel Vera tightening around him. He twitched and jerked his hips upward, into hers, desperate to come, trying more desperately to hold off.

It would be cool if she would come. That would be good. She's my friend. That's what friends do.

"Can I… um… touch you, to help you… uh…"

"Yes."

He moved a clumsy hand across her thigh to the front of her pelvis, his fingers fumbling like they were twice their normal size. He found her clit and moved his thumb in a slow circle.

She convulsed around him with a whimper. "Oh Jesus *Christ,* please, faster…"

Panting against her open mouth, Isaac sped up the circles on her clit. The world spun dizzily around him, and he could barely tell which way was up. The only thing that kept him on the planet was the warmth of Vera's skin, the heat of her breath on his neck, the growing, unbearable waves of pleasure moving through him, rising as she rocked her hips against his again and again.

Her head fell back, and she moaned. "Oh, *fuck,* I didn't know I… could still… Isaac, *fuck…*"

"'m doin' my best," he mumbled, pressing his face against her chest. She wound a hand through his hair and tugged.

"Isaac, *yes,* Jesus fucking Christ, Isaac, *please…*"

He moaned wordlessly, his climax rising in him as she moved with him, clutching him against her. His hand was pressed between them both.

"Isaac, *fuck,* I…" Vera shuddered and came with a low cry.

The sound of her moans, the feel of her arms holding him tight, and the sight of her pleasure all brought him to the crest of his climax.

She stopped moving, taking deep, sighing breaths as she came down.

Isaac's climax eluded him. His mouth opened. He was beyond the edge of sanity. He couldn't form words. He whimpered.

"Hm?" Vera's voice was low and dark with pleasure.

Isaac's hands closed around her hips. "V-Vera, I, um," he panted. *"Please…"*

"Oh." She laughed, delighted. "I want to. I *want* to. Let me do this…" She rolled her hips again.

Isaac gasped. She quivered and whined against his neck. She moved against him, guiding his body up into pleasure again, before he tipped over the edge and completely came apart, pulling Vera's mouth against his as he moaned.

They slumped together against the tree, panting and shuddering. Isaac's arms wound around Vera and he held her gently to him. His hands moved slowly over her, pressing gently against her skin, running his fingers through her hair, kissing her chest through her shirt.

Their breathing slowed and the sweat started to dry on their skin. Vera still held Isaac tightly against her.

"Umm… Vera?" His voice was muffled in her shirt. "Are you… okay?"

"Yeah," she breathed. "Holy shhit. I didn't know… I could… still…" She sighed. "Thank you, Isaac. That was, um. That was really good."

He felt drops in his hair. Confused, he reached up and pulled her gently back. He couldn't quite tell in the darkness, but it looked like two tears rolled down her cheeks. His head swam. *Uh… She's crying from the sex?* Embarrassment swept through him. *I hope it was good…*

"That was fucking good," she sighed.

Isaac's mind went blank, blissfully forgetting the last thought that had crossed his mind. Without thinking, he pulled her in for a kiss, and she met his lips with an open mouth.

"If it never happens again, is that—"

"That'sss fine," he slurred. "The sex was, um, was good. But no. We're… um. Don't wanna make it weird. Never have to. Might get weird, or… I don't know." He wasn't sure what he was saying.

Vera smiled and pulled him close again. "Best friends?" she murmured against his hair.

"Best friends," he said back.

Chapter 28

Gavin was home again.

He knew it immediately. The walls, the pictures, the carpet, the light, the smell, it was all exactly how he remembered it. Years ago, or weeks ago? He wasn't sure. He just knew he was home again.

He wandered through the front door, dragging his fingers along the white wall, looking around.

When's the last time I was here? Years ago, or weeks ago?

He shrugged and kept moving.

He passed the grand staircase that disappeared into shadows upstairs. Where his bedroom was, and his parents' bedroom. And his playroom, now turned into a study for when he wanted to visit his parents in the summer and work from home, though he hadn't done that in years. He passed a coat closet to his left. A bathroom to his right. Passed a corner, into the living room. The kitchen, off to his right. The room at the end of the hallway, where he spent hours playing under his father's desk while he worked. Where he learned to be a syndicate son.

He could hear the echo of his father's voice. "Come here, Gavin. Look at this map. We'll learn the cities together. Soon it'll be yours."

It was exactly the same as he remembered it— Years ago, or weeks ago? What did it matter? It was perfect. He ran his hand along his father's desk, along the low set of drawers along the wall.

The hair on the back of Gavin's neck stood up. He heard breathing behind him, wet, ragged.

Icy terror poured down his spine as his hands clenched into fists.

"Gavin."

The sound of his father's shredded voice clutched Gavin's heart. A shudder rippled through him. He closed his eyes, praying that if he didn't look, it would go away. That he wouldn't have to see it. Tears rolled down his cheeks and he felt breath on the back of his neck.

186

He spun around in a panic, his hands flying out in front of his face to protect himself. Still several feet away, his father stood, looking at him.

His throat was completely torn away, gaping raggedly, blood bubbling in the deep tear that disappeared into his neck. His father's eyes were blank and clouded, like he was already gone.

Gavin pressed himself back against the drawers, his heart beating out of his chest. "D-dad…"

His father's voice gurgled out of him. "Hello, son."

"P-please, no, I don't… please…"

His father grinned. "Want to see me make her good again?"

Gavin's stomach dropped, and he gagged. "No. No, no, no, no, I don't want that, dad. No."

Gavin blinked.

There was someone else standing beside his father. She looked like Vera, felt like Vera. He knew she was Vera.

Her mouth gaped open with razor sharp teeth.

Gavin shivered. "No. No, no, fuck, Vera, I'm sorry, please no…"

His father's hand closed around Vera's hair and forced her to her knees.

"No, no, no, dad no…" Gavin staggered a step forward, his hand outstretched.

Vera lunged forward and snapped her teeth at Gavin's hand.

He screamed and fell back, bashing his head against the drawers behind him. His father barked out a wet, shrieking laugh. "I told you. She's feral." He jerked her back to her knees and stared down at her with a smile on his otherwise vacant face. "This is why I had to make her good."

"Dad, you…" Gavin got to his feet, forcing down the bile that clawed up his throat as he stared at his father. "You made her like this!"

His father chuckled and loosened his hold on Vera's hair. "You want me to let her go, then? You want me to let her get you?"

"N-no, please, just… Why did you…" Gavin choked down tears. "Why did you do this?"

"I told you, son," his father croaked. "I told you from the beginning. What you feel is right, no matter what. They exist to be our—"

"No!" Gavin shouted. "They don't! You... she wouldn't be this way if you didn't..." She lunged at Gavin. He gasped and fell back a step.

She fought against his father's hold, writhing against the hand in her hair, clawing her way towards Gavin. Her eyes bored into his, and blood dripped down her chin from her teeth. She snarled at him wordlessly.

"Please," he whispered to her. "I'm sorry. I didn't know."

Her lips pulled back over her teeth. She yanked out of his father's grasp and threw herself at Gavin, pushing him down and snapping at his throat.

"No!"

Gavin pushed at her frantically, sobbing. "No no no no *no please!*"

"Gavin."

He knew that voice.

"Gavin."

"No," he whimpered, flailing in the dark. The wound in his chest ached dully, more like an echo of the wound than real pain.

"Oh, for fuck's sake..." The weight disappeared, and Gavin slumped back to the bed, sobbing with relief. He clawed at the scar on his chest, almost healed after two months. The light snapped on. Gavin flinched back, covering his eyes. The sheets tightened around him and he thrashed, panicked.

"For *fuck's* sake, Gavin, calm the fuck down. It's me."

Gavin shuddered. "I-Isaac?"

"Yeah, dumbass." Gavin's eyes slowly focused. Isaac stood by the door, his arms folded over his chest.

Gavin trembled and pulled at the sheets. "I... Fuck, I'm sorry. I didn't mean to wake you."

Isaac gritted his teeth. "Well, you did. I'm going back to bed." He reached for the light switch.

Gavin's stomach lurched. "Isaac, *please.*" Isaac stopped. "Can you just... just wait?"

Isaac stared into the hallway. A muscle stood out in his jaw.

Tears burned in Gavin's eyes, and he looked down, mortified. "I... I'm sorry," he whispered. "I'm... just really fucking freaked out right now."

Isaac dragged his hand across his face. "You've got to be fucking kidding me," he mumbled, so quietly Gavin almost missed it. Then he turned and leaned up against the doorframe. "Okay. What do you want?"

I want to not be so goddamn scared all the time. "Please. I just…" Gavin's head fell forward into his hands. "I don't know. I'm sorry."

Isaac crossed his arms across his chest. His hands were squeezed into fists. He stared at Gavin with a look that could have been disgust, if there wasn't that flicker of fear behind it. Gavin's heart clenched with shame. *Yeah, no shit, dumbass. You fucking tortured him.*

Gavin picked at the bedspread. "I'm sorry it was, um, you." Gavin stole a glance at Isaac where he stood.

Isaac's eyes narrowed. "Sorry *what* was me?"

"I'm um, sorry you're the one I woke up. I guess I…" Gavin fell silent.

Isaac blew out a scornful breath. "It's not exactly like you have your pick here of people you haven't fucking *traumatized.*"

Gavin swallowed. "I… I know. I'm s—"

"Don't," Isaac growled. "Don't fucking say you're *sorry.*"

Gavin chewed his lip. "Then what the hell do you want me to *say?*"

Isaac ground his teeth together and for a moment, Gavin thought Isaac might beat him to death right here. *If I've gotta go out some way…*

Isaac slid down the wall to sit on the floor. He pressed his face into his hands. "Ugh." The sound came out muffled.

Gavin twisted the sheets between his hands, his heart still beating hard in his chest.

"I…" Isaac dropped his hands and stared at the ceiling. "I want you to say…" Isaac shook his head. "I don't know what the fuck I want you to say. The damage has been done."

Gavin's throat tightened. "I… I kn-know I, um, damaged you."

Isaac's eyes snapped to Gavin's. "Oh, *fuck you.*"

Gavin swallowed. Tears burned in his eyes. "I'm sorry."

Isaac smoothly got to his feet and took a step towards the bed. "You don't know fucking *damage.* You don't know a fucking *thing.*"

Gavin pressed himself back against the headboard. "I—"

"Shut up," Isaac snapped. "You don't know how it feels to watch your two best friends fucking *break* because of something some entitled, sadistic *asshole* decided to do because he wanted to have fun on his fucking *Saturday.* You don't know how it feels to watch every single person you love dragged into the middle of a room and tortured in the *worst possible way.* You don't know a fucking *thing.*" Isaac's hands curled into fists. "Do you *fucking understand?*"

A tear escaped to run down Gavin's cheek, and he nodded, cringing back. "Yes. I'm… I'm *sorry.*"

Isaac shuddered forward. "I don't understand why Gray won't let me fucking *kill you.*"

Gavin held a hand out in front of him, as if he could protect himself from Isaac. As if he could *try.* "P-please don't," he whispered.

Isaac squeezed his eyes shut, his chest heaving. *"Fuck,"* he whispered. He blew out a slow, forceful breath. *"Fuck."* He took a step back. Then another. He opened his eyes. His face was pulled into such a look of anguish that Gavin felt it with him like physical pain. Isaac fell back another step, against the doorframe, and slid to the floor again.

Gavin cast around for something to say. "Um…" He bit his lip. "I'm… I'm not a sadist anymore?"

Isaac looked at him, murderous.

Oh. I fucked up.

"Oh, fuck. I mean, um, I… I won't do it again. And… and I don't *want* to do it again. I just want—" He cut himself off as Isaac turned an alarming shade of red. Gavin's mouth snapped shut.

"What," Isaac snarled through his teeth, "Do you want? I'm *dying* to fucking know."

Gavin's vision blurred with tears. He bit down hard on his lip, trying to keep the tears from spilling. *If I tell him, he's going to kill me.*

He's never going to trust me until I do.

Gavin swallowed, pressing the sleeves of his shirt against his eyes. "Um. I…" He blew out a shaky breath, considering for a moment it might be his last. "I… just… want to feel like I have a family again."

Gavin held his breath. He waited for Isaac to launch himself across the room and bash his skull in. Gavin didn't move an inch.

He started to get dizzy from the lack of oxygen. He dragged in a gasp and dared to peek over his hands at Isaac's face.

Isaac had gone a ghostly white, looking at Gavin with something that surpassed horror. Gavin's heart sank in his chest.

"And you want... you want... *my family?*" Isaac rasped. His lips trembled.

"I don't want to... to *steal them,* or anything, I mean..." Gavin wrapped his arms tight around his chest. "I mean..." He shook his head. "I thought..." His voice wavered. He tried again. "I realized over the past couple months everything about my family was, um. Was a lie. I thought they loved me. I thought they, they gave a fuck about me. But I'm, um... I'm starting to realize... they only ever loved me when I was, um. Like *them.* They... they ignored me when I did anything else. When I, um. *Wanted.* Anything else. And I..." He gasped, holding his hand out to Isaac. "I'm not trying to say I had it worse. Okay? I'm not. I swear. But... I never knew there was, um, anything else. I should have fucking known, okay? But... it... um... h-hurting people was, was all I was ever good at. And I was *good at it.* I never had to do anything else. I never had to, um, learn to be anything else. And then... when I didn't want that anymore..." Gavin swallowed the burning in his throat and closed his eyes. "Um... as soon as I was, um, someone else, someone who was, um, broken, they... *she*... threw me out. But you..." Gavin shuddered, sure he was pushing too far, that he would say the wrong thing, that somehow he would ruin everything more than it was already ruined. "Everyone's, um, broken here. And you all..." He choked. He couldn't say it.

"We *what?*"

Gavin opened his eyes and looked at Isaac. Isaac had his hands at his sides, still curled into fists, his breaths moving fast through his chest. Gavin steadied his breath.

"Everyone's broken here. And you all still love each other."

Isaac leaned back against the doorframe, his eyes still fixed on Gavin. He crossed his arms in front of his chest again and breathed slowly.

Gavin swallowed hard. "And I want that, too."

Isaac opened his mouth to speak. Closed it. Opened it. Closed it again.

Gavin buried his face in his hands. *Fuck.*

"You wanted a family, so you went and found the family you tortured?" There was something in Isaac's voice Gavin couldn't place.

He didn't raise his head. "You're, um, good people. Good people are easy to hurt but, um, I don't want to, uh, hurt you."

"You almost took my family away from me," Isaac whispered. "Do you fucking remember that? Is that even real to you?"

Gavin lifted his head. The pain that dragged at Isaac's face made Gavin's throat feel tight.

"Do you fucking remember holding a gun to Sam's head and telling me you'd kill them if I didn't fucking *torture them?* My fucking *sibling?*"

Gavin clenched his teeth together. He nodded.

"Do you remember torturing my *best friend* with the man who raped her and tortured her for *months?*"

Gavin opened his mouth to speak.

"Don't fucking say you didn't know about the rape. I've already fucking heard it. If you didn't know, then you're an idiot."

"I *am* an idiot, Isaac," Gavin whispered. "That's what I've tried to fucking *tell you.*"

Isaac laughed once, bitterly, and rolled his eyes. "Are you even the same fucking *person?*"

Gavin swallowed. "Yeah. Just… minus everything that made me who I was, yeah."

Isaac snorted. "Then there wasn't much to you in the first place, was there?"

Gavin's mouth twisted. "Don't be an asshole, Isaac."

"God forbid there be two in the room," Isaac snapped.

Gavin laughed darkly. "See, this is why I—" *OH GOD DON'T FUCKING SAY THAT!*

"Why you *what?*" Isaac's eyes narrowed.

—why I loved torturing you. The rapport. Gavin shook his head. "Can I just say it was something really, really stupid that I don't wanna say and we call it good?"

192

Isaac stared at him for a moment, then let his head thump back against the doorframe. "Sure. Why the hell not."

Gavin breathed out a desperate sigh of relief. "Thank you," he wheezed.

Isaac tapped his fingers against his legs. "Dare I ask what your fucking nightmare was about?"

Gavin's eyes widened. "Um. No. Oh no, no, no." *He really* will *kill me. I can't tell him that.*

Isaac tilted his head. "No, I really wanna know. What scares Gavin fucking Stormbeck?" His tone was taunting, but he wasn't radiating the murderous rage he usually had around Gavin.

"Um..." Gavin closed his eyes. An image of Vera with teeth like an anglerfish flashed through his mind, and his eyes flew open again. "Ugh. Fuck. You have to, um, promise not to get mad."

Isaac's face darkened. "No, I fucking don't."

Gavin bit his lip. "Well, I... I can't fucking *help* what my subconscious thinks of, right?"

Isaac said nothing, just stared at Gavin with a snarl on his face.

Gavin's head fell back. "Fine." Just thinking of it made his stomach clench with a fresh wave of fear. "Um... I had a dream I was um, at my house, where Vera, um... where my, uh, dad was killed. And he was there, looking all bloody and fucking horrifying. And Vera was there, too, looking like... well, like a fucking nightmare, with sharp teeth and shit, like she always does..."

"Wait... 'like she always does'?" Isaac's eyes narrowed.

"I, um." Gavin looked down at the bedspread thinking, for not the first time tonight, that this was when Isaac would kill him. "I, um, ha-have nightmares about Vera, um, killing my dad. Every..." He drew in a deep breath and blew it out. "...every fucking night."

Isaac leaned back. "Oh. Holy shit." A smile quirked at his lips. "She'd be goddamned thrilled to know that."

"Yeah, I bet she fucking would," Gavin grumbled. He glanced up and saw Isaac's eyes fixed on him again. *Agh, fuck.* He shook his head and kept going. "So, she, um, was there, with my dad, and my d-dad said he would, um, let her..." Another slow breath. "Let her get me if I didn't want to..." Gavin's eyes flicked to Isaac's again. *Yup. He's gonna murder me for this.* "He said he would let her get me if I didn't, um, want to watch him…" He squeezed his eyes shut, terrified to look at Isaac. *"…make her good."*

Gavin flinched back at Isaac's soft intake of breath, his eyes still desperately squeezed shut. He braced himself, shivering against the headboard.

"And what the fuck did you say?" Isaac growled.

"I… I didn't want him to. I wanted him to stop." Gavin shuddered. "I just wanted him to fucking *stop.*"

For a moment there was nothing but the sound of their breathing.

Then there was a rustle of movement and Gavin's eyes flew open. Isaac pushed himself away from the doorframe and stood.

"I…" Isaac said softly. He wet his lips and tried again. "I don't know how I can ever *trust you.*"

Let me earn it.

Can I earn it?

I want to earn it.

"I… I know." Gavin's voice creaked out of him.

"No. Do you understand what you've done to me and my family?"

Gavin was silent.

Isaac shook his head. "I don't know how I can trust you," he said again, quieter. He turned to leave, his hand reaching for the light switch.

"No, *please,*" Gavin breathed.

Isaac paused in the doorway.

Gavin swallowed. "L-leave the, um, the light on. Please."

Isaac dropped his hand and left.

Chapter 29

When Gavin woke in the morning, he had the oddest feeling that someone had just been there in the room with him. He looked around the room blearily, his skin feeling too-tight and warm, like someone had just touched him. Like he could still feel their hand on his skin.

He rolled to his side, groaning as the motion stretched the mostly-healed hole in his chest and the scars on his back, and swung his legs off the side of the bed. He scrubbed his eyes with his fists. He felt heavy and slow and exhausted, unsettled by the nightmare and by Isaac's presence after it even more so.

He didn't know what to feel about Isaac. What was there to feel about someone so good, someone so strong and honest, someone shot through with anguish, who kicked a man to death right in front of Gavin's eyes, after Isaac held Gavin's own knife to his throat and *relished* his terror? What was there to feel about someone Gavin had hurt so deeply?

Gavin was sure that he'd never broken Isaac. How could he not be, when he'd seen over and over how strong Isaac still was? How devoted he was to his family, to keeping them safe? *Broken* would have meant Isaac betraying them. *Broken* would have meant Isaac caring more about keeping himself safe than about his loyalty to them.

Broken couldn't mean anything else.

But that wasn't all that Isaac was. He was more than his devotion to his family. So much more than that.

No, Isaac was an entire lifetime of being hurt by the people who should have kept him safe. Isaac was death, and abuse, and pain. Isaac was being trained to be a weapon by the first people to care about him after his dad died, and even if Isaac couldn't see that, Gavin could. Isaac was desperation. Isaac was protection. Isaac was survival. Isaac was darkness, and rage, and fear.

Under all that, Isaac was *kind*.

After everything I've done to him, after everything I've done to his family, he still sat with me last night. He still came to me when I woke him up with my screaming, and he stayed.

I've been a fucking monster to him, and he still at least acted like he cared.

Gavin rolled his neck, blowing out a slow breath. Isaac could have been faking it. Could have been pretending, putting up with Gavin until he thought he could leave without Gavin waking him up again. He could have been coddling Gavin because he thought Gavin needed that now.

Maybe he thought Gavin was broken now, too. Maybe he thought Gavin was weak.

I mean, shit, maybe I am.

Despite everything he'd been fucking *handed* in his life, he couldn't do what Isaac could do. He couldn't prioritize other people. He couldn't push through crazy amounts of pain. He couldn't single-handedly protect an entire family of people and ask nothing in return. He couldn't sacrifice himself the way Isaac had. He couldn't even sacrifice himself for his own *mother.* Not even to make her happy. Not even after he killed his own dad, or at least was responsible enough for it that it didn't matter if he ripped his throat out himself or not.

He couldn't even stop hurting people, even after seeing they were truly fucking good. He couldn't stop hurting people just because he wanted mommy and daddy to love him.

No. It was more than that. He couldn't stop hurting people because he fucking *liked* it, and needed his brain scrambled just to make him *stop.*

After everything Isaac had been through, he never became a sadist. After losing both his parents, after being abused by his mother, he still prioritized other people. *My parents never abused me. They didn't exactly love me, but they never abused me.*

After being handed everything for his entire fucking life, after only giving up torturing people once the pleasure it gave him had been ripped out of his head with Vera's teeth, Gavin still couldn't be as good as Isaac. Sometimes he hated himself so much it made his bones ache. Sometimes – like now, his hands pressed to his face, his skin aching in all the places he had hurt and battered and *broken* Isaac – he felt like nothing.

But Isaac?

Isaac was *everything*.

He shook his head to clear that thought.

Isaac isn't everything. He's just one of the first people who's ever stood up to my bullshit before.

Gavin pushed himself out of bed and stood, swaying for a moment as his head went fuzzy. *Ugh. That nightmare fucked me up worse than I thought.*

As he crossed to the chest of drawers, he passed in front of the mirror. He kept his eyes down like he always seemed to these days. The scars on his face didn't *bother* him, he told himself, over and over and *over* since Isaac put him in the hospital. Why would they bother him? They made him look sexy. Dangerous. *Right?*

He ran his hand over his face, his fingers lingering on the slight indentation of a scar across his cheekbone. Across the bridge of his nose. Stretching from the corner of his eye out to his temple. They were so much better than they had been months ago, before the purely cosmetic surgeries had smoothed them out, rearranged his face a little, so it was closer to how it had been before Isaac had fractured Gavin's skull.

He lifted his chin and forced himself to look into the mirror. He forced his eyes to move over the lines on his face, the slightest way his left eye pulled a tiny bit higher than the right at the corner, the scar there puckering his skin. He forced himself to look carefully at the damage Isaac had done. At the damage he'd been *forced* to do.

He pulled his shirt off and turned away from the mirror, averting his eyes from his body. He couldn't force himself to look at the pink scar just below his collarbone. He angled himself so he couldn't see the marks from the cane. *God dammit. God fucking* dammit. *Why am I so stuck on this this morning?*

He pulled a drawer open and reached for the first thing he saw. He pulled the shirt on over his head, then quickly changed his underwear, and his pants. He turned and put his hand on the doorknob.

He took a deep breath. He always needed to steel himself before seeing the others. Whether it was Ellis's glares or Vera's snarl or Isaac's fucking *fear,* he always hated how they reacted to him. He wondered, briefly, how long it would take for them to stop seeing the sadist in him, the torturer. How long it would take for them to start seeing the broken fucking idiot he was. He wondered if they ever would. He stood at the door, wearing the clothes the others had bartered for from the people who lived in this little town in exchange for odd jobs. Even after everything, they were still clothing him, feeding him, and, for the most part, including him. He squeezed his eyes shut. He took another deep breath and pulled the door open.

The smell of frying bacon and eggs wafted over him. His stomach growled and he licked his lips, his head turning in the direction of the kitchen. He closed his door and padded out into the hall.

He nearly collided with Edrissa as he walked into the kitchen. She squeaked and leaped away from him, all but hiding behind Vera. Vera smirked a little, and her lips pursed like she was pushing down a smile.

The whole family was either packed into the kitchen or seated at the barstools that lined the counter looking in, talking and laughing. Isaac and Sam were busy at the stove, cooking breakfast together like a well-oiled machine. Tori was toasting an entire loaf of bread in their small toaster two slices at a time, adding the slices to a plate that was already stacked high. Finn and Ellis were squeezing oranges – *real* oranges, *for Christ's sake, where are they getting oranges up here where it snows?* – into a massive pitcher on the counter, a slice in each of their mouths, their lips pulled back over them in giant orange grins. Their faces fell for a moment when Gavin walked in.

He ducked his head. "Um. Good... good morning."

There was a moment of excruciating silence, the only sound coming from the sizzling food on the stove. The toaster popped up, making all of them jump.

"Morning, Gavin," Gray said gently from their barstool, and sipped a cup of coffee.

Gavin glanced at them, meeting their gaze for a moment. He looked back at the floor. Every time he looked at them, *every fucking time,* he felt a sharp lance of guilt, worse almost than when he looked at anyone else. He shot Gray. With his own hand. With his own gun. And Gray had been the first one to pull Isaac off of him when Isaac nearly killed him at the safehouse on the turnpike. Gray had been the one to let him mourn his father at the funeral. Gray had been the one to comfort him as he grieved for everything he'd lost.

He swallowed hard. "Um. Good morning."

Sam looked over from where they stood at the counter, stirring a pan of scrambled eggs. "Do you, um, want some breakfast?" they said.

Gavin's face flushed with a mix of shame and gratitude. "Um. Yeah. Thank you. Um…" He lifted his gaze to look around the kitchen. "I could have, um. I'm sorry. I would have, uh, helped, with breakfast, I just didn't…"

"It's okay," Isaac said. "We wanted to let you sleep. You had a rough night."

Gavin's face blushed a furious red. He stared down at the floor, his eyes watering. "Oh." He glanced up in time to catch a look between Isaac and Vera. "Um. Thank you."

"Now that you're here, though, lazy-ass, you can set the table." Vera passed Gavin a stack of plates and silverware.

Gavin's fingers fumbled and he nearly dropped the stack. *Isaac told them all about my nightmare. He told them I have nightmares about Vera. He told them I'm so fucking weak that I asked him to stay, I asked him to stay, why the* fuck *did I do that?*

He swallowed, looking up at Vera with leftover terror in his eyes. "Okay." He walked into the dining room and set the plates in front of each chair. His skin prickled with humiliation as he tried desperately not to imagine everyone's eyes on his back, all of them smirking about his nightmare and his fear. He straightened the knives and forks until they were perfectly spaced around the plates, dreading when he would have to face them all around the table, their eyes averted from him, their voices hushed.

A moment later, Ellis walked by him carrying the pitcher of juice in one hand and some cups in the other. Finn followed right behind with more cups. Gray came after them, carrying only their own cup. They'd been careful not to strain themself since they arrived north. *I remember where I shot them. Their wound was worse than mine.*

He walked past the steady stream of the whole family as they filed into the dining room, carrying huge plates of eggs and bacon and toast, laughing, making plans for the day. It's Sunday, Gavin remembered. That's why they were eating breakfast together like this. They'd done it that way last Sunday, too, and the Sunday before that, every Sunday since they'd arrived north.

He walked back into the kitchen to get his own cup of coffee. *I should just grab my plate and eat in here. They don't want to see me. They won't want me around. Jesus Christ, I wouldn't want me around.*

He was alone in the kitchen with Isaac. He froze.

Gavin's throat grew tight with panic and shame as he made his way to the coffee maker. He considered turning around and going to his room with just his coffee and only coming out when they'd left. He hoped there would be leftovers.

"What?" Isaac said. Gavin turned and saw Isaac staring right at him.

Fuck.

Isaac cocked his head, a strange look on his face. "What?" he repeated.

What if I just jumped out the window? I wouldn't have to talk to him then.

"Um…" Gavin's voice shook. The window was sounding like a better and better idea. "Uh…"

"I didn't tell them," Isaac said gently.

The empty mug in Gavin's hand clattered to the counter.

Isaac's eyes flicked to Gavin's hand and back up to his face.

"Um…" Gavin's voice broke. He swallowed the lump in his throat. "W-why not?"

Isaac leaned back against the counter, his eyebrows pulling together. "Why would I?"

"Uh…" The window was *right there.* "Because… um…"

"I told Vera. But only because I thought it would make her feel better around you."

Gavin's face fell into his hands. "Oh, fuck. Oh, no."

A soft laugh. "She's not mad."

"She doesn't have to be *mad,* now that she knows, she… she…" Gavin heaved a deep breath. "Oh, fuck." His head snapped up, a sudden question burning on his tongue. "Did you tell them you… um…"

"…stayed?" Isaac's gaze remained steady on Gavin's face.

Gavin dropped his head forward. "Yeah."

Isaac was quiet for so long Gavin thought maybe he hadn't heard him. He looked up and Isaac was looking at the floor, biting his lip. After another moment, he shook his head. "No."

"Oh." Vague relief washed through Gavin's limbs.

Isaac looked up at him again. He wet his lips. "You know we aren't all... waiting for a reason to kick you out, right? Or... or kill you, or something?"

Gavin let out a hysterical peal of laughter. "What?"

Isaac rubbed the back of his neck. "I mean... if you betray us, yeah, we'll kill you, but..." He waved his hand in the general direction of the dining room. "We aren't... I mean..." He sighed. "We aren't all... *out to get you*, Gavin. We're not..."

...like me. The unspoken end of the sentence hung in the air.

"Ellis hates me," Gavin whispered. "And Vera. And Edrissa. And I understand—"

"Vera doesn't hate you," Isaac said.

Gavin scoffed. "Yeah she—"

"She's my best friend," Isaac said, his gaze back on Gavin's face. "I know her better than you do. She doesn't hate you. She's wary of you, she's definitely first in line to kill you if you betray us, but she doesn't *hate* you."

"But I—"

"Gavin..." Isaac pinched the bridge of his nose. "Will you stop being a dumbass for all of two fucking seconds and stop trying to convince me we should all want you dead? We have plenty of reason to, okay? We don't need you to convince us."

Gavin's mouth snapped shut.

Isaac drew in a deep breath. "Look. This is a weird fucking situation, okay? I get it. Probably weirder for us than it is for you."

I doubt that.

"But after what you said last night..." Gavin's face flushed red again. Isaac leaned back against the counter. "I didn't..." Isaac shook his head. "I didn't know all that. About your parents. About the nightmares. I didn't realize you, um..." Isaac fell silent. "Anyway. It just... gave me a lot to think about."

"So... what did you tell them?" Gavin's voice shook.

Isaac shrugged. "I told them you had a rough night, we talked a little, and I don't think you're gonna hurt us."

Gavin's eyes went wide. "You told them we *talked?*"

Isaac's eyes narrowed. "Why wouldn't you want them to know that?"

Because if they know we talked they'll think I'm lying to you. That I've tricked you somehow.

Or maybe they'll think other things. Gavin wasn't sure exactly *what* he was scared of them thinking, but his gut burned faintly with dread.

"I just..." Gavin licked his lips. "I'm just... worried... they won't trust me."

"Fuck, Gavin, *I* don't think I trust you. But... I do a little more, now. I guess."

Gavin's face fell into his hands. "Oh. Fuck, I... Fuck. I don't know what to think. I'm sorry. I shouldn't have... I'm sorry. I didn't want to wake you up."

Isaac was quiet for a moment. "This... whatever *this* is..." Gavin's head snapped up and he saw Isaac gesturing between himself, Gavin, and the dining room. Gavin's heart stuttered. "...will be a lot easier if I can trust you, Gavin. I don't know if I can. Or if I... if I *should.* But I'm glad we talked last night. I'm glad I know all that about your parents." A grin flashed across his face. "I'm glad I know you're scared of Vera."

"Who fucking wouldn't be?" Gavin muttered under his breath. He sagged back against the counter.

Isaac chuckled. "Hell, I'm scared of her." He shrugged. "We should get to the table. They won't wait for us and I want there to be food left." He pushed himself away from the counter and left the kitchen.

Gavin groaned and pressed his face into his hands, bracing his elbows up against the counter.

Isaac wants to trust me.

Gavin's chest ached. He wanted Isaac to trust him, more than he wanted anything else.

Chapter 30

"Um. Is anyone gonna eat the last piece of bacon?" Gavin's gaze flicked around the table, barely resting on each person before he stared back at the table and up again. Gray smiled at him. Sam shook their head. Vera crunched her own piece of bacon.

Ellis wouldn't look at him at all.

"Um."

Gavin flinched slightly as Finn spoke up from the other end of the table.

"I'll um. Split it with you." Finn looked down at the lone piece of bacon on the plate, twisted and just a little burnt. They looked up at Gavin. A tight, uncomfortable smile pulled at their lips.

Gavin heaved a deep breath. "Yeah. Yes please." He reached for the bacon and broke it in half with his fork. He grabbed the smaller half and pushed the plate towards Finn.

Finn took the piece and ate it in one bite. They crunched it and threw a grin at Ellis. Ellis wouldn't look at Finn, either. Gavin looked down and stared at the table.

Gray cleared their throat and stood. "Thank you for breakfast," they said with a smile. "I'm going to go for a walk, see if I can get my heart rate up a bit. Anyone who wants to can join me." As if dismissed by Gray's words, everyone else stood, grabbing their plates, talking about what they were going to do for the rest of the day.

"I wanted to go into town and see if there are any new arrivals," Tori said softly, bumping Vera's arm. "Do you want to come with me?"

Vera wrapped her free arm around Tori's shoulders, resting lightly to avoid the marks from the cane that Gavin left. Gavin noticed that Tori still flinched when they were touched, even though they were long since healed. Gavin winced at the memory of breaking Tori's skin open.

"Yeah, babe," Vera said, pressing a kiss into Tori's hair. "Sounds good."

"Can I come?" Edrissa whispered at Vera's elbow.

Tori and Vera smiled at each other. "Yeah," Vera said, grinning. "We can all go."

Gavin shuffled uncomfortably as he walked to the kitchen with his plate and put it in the sink. He wouldn't be going anywhere. He knew that if he left the house, even for just a minute, he and everybody else in the house would pay for it with their lives.

But at the same time, staying in this big ranch house with the others had given him a sense of security he didn't think he'd ever felt before. He did miss the outside, though. He missed the ability to go wherever he wanted in his parents' territory, whenever he pleased. He missed the freedom.

He hated to admit it, but he missed being the heir to the fucking kingdom.

He shook his head and turned the tap on hot as the rest of them piled their plates and cups by the sink. Since he hadn't helped with breakfast, he'd be on dish duty. He didn't mind. Even being included in the chores made him feel safer. He was working with them. Trying to pull his own weight, even if it was doing something as mundane as washing dishes.

He had his back to the rest of the kitchen as he rinsed the first plate, trying not to listen as the others filed one by one out of the kitchen behind him. Off to their adventures. Off to the trips into town, the walks down the lane between the road and the ranch house, off to the snowball fights they had in the yard that Gavin watched from the windows. Off to their lives, where he couldn't follow.

I don't need to follow. I came here as a hostage to give them information about the syndicates. I'm lucky the family doesn't have me in chains right now.

He wasn't sure when he started referring to people like his own family as 'the syndicates.'

He wasn't sure when he started thinking of these people as his family.

He wasn't sure if they would ever feel the same way about him.

His shoulders relaxed as the kitchen went quiet. At least when he was alone, he didn't have to worry about scaring anyone or making anyone feel threatened or accidentally triggering someone into hurting him, or killing him.

If he was completely honest with himself, that's probably how he was going to die. Someone living in this house was going to kill him one day.

He couldn't bring himself to feel scared of that anymore. Every day he'd been here, someone had shown him in some small way that that possibility was fading. The sharp tone in Gray's voice had dropped away. Last week, Sam brought him chocolate from a trip into town. Today, Finn shared that piece of bacon with him.

Isaac stayed with him when he was scared last night.

Sure, Ellis hated him and Edrissa looked at him like she was waiting for him to launch himself across the room and start beating her at any moment. Sure, Isaac's hands still twitched to his waistband when Gavin moved too fast, even though Isaac never carried his gun on him in the house. Sure, every time he entered a room the conversation died down for a moment, and sometimes stopped altogether.

Despite all that, despite every moment of awkwardness and guilt and wondering if today was going to be the day someone's fear or rage would overcome them and they'd kill Gavin for everything he'd done to them... He felt safer here than he ever had before. The people here cared about each other. Would die for one another.

And Gavin couldn't quite convince himself that they were all faking the small kindnesses they showed him.

Gavin chewed his lip, realizing that he'd been scrubbing the same plate clean for the past several minutes. He put the plate on the dry towel next to the sink and reached for another.

"So, I hear you're scared of me."

Gavin let out a shriek and spun around, pressing himself back against the sink as he realized he was now alone in the kitchen with *Vera*.

Welp, I guess I'm dying today.

Vera laughed at his reaction, crossing her arms in front of her chest and looking him up and down. Gavin flushed, mortified. His hands shook with the realization that Vera had cornered him in the only room in the house with a linoleum floor. *Oh, shit. She's gonna bleed me out, just like she did to dad.*

Vera's gaze pierced through him and his mouth went dry. He swallowed, trying frantically to unstick his tongue from the roof of his mouth so he could beg. For what, he didn't know. Mercy, forgiveness, a fast fucking death, anything. His chest ached as his heart all but threw itself against his ribs. His blood pounded through his ears. Every instinct in him screamed at him to run, to hide, to get as far as fucking possible from the predator standing between him and the door. His hands clenched into fists, even as he knew he couldn't fight her.

His muscles locked against him and he froze.

The smile slid from Vera's face.

She raised her hands out to the side, empty and open, and took a step back. "Jesus Christ, Gavin. Breathe. You're good."

Gavin dragged in a ragged inhale and realized he'd been holding his breath. He slumped back against the counter, the rushing of the hot water in the sink making its way back into his ears.

"Jesus Christ," Vera breathed. "Isaac wasn't kidding."

"About what?" Gavin said thickly.

Vera's gaze moved over him, uncertainty passing over her face. "About you being scared of me. Like… Jesus. You'd think I'm the one who tried to kill you or something."

"You *did* try to kill me," Gavin mumbled through numb lips.

Vera huffed out a breath. "Fair enough. You had it coming, though."

"Yeah, I fucking know." Gavin's jaw clenched and he stared at the floor.

Seconds ticked by before Vera spoke again. "Do you… do you really have nightmares about me every night?" Her voice was low, gentle, uncertain.

His eyes blinked shut for a moment and he blew out a slow breath. "Yeah. Yeah, I fucking do. But I don't wanna talk about it, okay? I don't wanna talk about why. Because I know my dad was a terrible fucking person and I know he hurt you and I know I deserve every fucking nightmare because of what I did to you and Tori and what I was *going* to do to you…" His eyes burned with tears. "Okay? I fucking *know it*. So, can we just—"

"Whoa, whoa, whoa, Gavin, stop." He looked up at her. "Just… slow down. Okay?"

Gavin sniffed. "Okay." He reached behind him to turn off the water. He wouldn't meet Vera's eyes.

They stood together in silence for so long Gavin's legs began to fall asleep. Finally, he raised his gaze up to Vera. She chewed her lip, staring at the floor, her eyebrows pulled together. She opened her mouth to speak.

"I don't know if I can ever forgive you for torturing and collaring Tori."

Gavin wilted. "I know. I'm—"

Vera held up her hand. "Just… shut the fuck up, for a second? Please?"

Gavin flinched at the words but relaxed a little at her gentle tone. He nodded.

Vera looked down at the floor and crossed her arms over her chest again. "I don't know if I can ever forgive you for what you did to Tori. But I… I want you to stop beating yourself up for what you did as a kid. Okay? You've got so much other shit to atone for. At least let that thing go."

Gavin drooped, his eyes sliding closed.

"Look…" Vera paused. Gavin looked up at her as her face twisted. "I don't know what went fucky in your head to make you like hurting people. Okay? I don't. I don't really care, either. And I don't know what made you stop. I don't really care. But I know you couldn't help how you were raised. I don't know how they were to you. I don't really want to know. But I… I… I guess what I'm trying to say is…" She met Gavin's gaze and held it. "I know what it's like to turn into something twisted trying to be good for Joseph Stormbeck."

Vera bit her lip and stared at him for a moment. Then, she turned and left the kitchen. Gavin was alone.

Chapter 31

Vera closed the car door, slightly dazed. The inside of the car was already warm. It took her a moment to realize Tori was staring at her. "What?" Vera rasped.

"How'd it go?" Tori said, her eyebrows pulled together in concern. She reached out and squeezed Vera's hand.

"Um…" Vera licked her lips. "That boy's *real* fucked up."

"Hm." Tori regarded Vera carefully. "What does that mean?"

"I mean…" Vera threw a glance back at Edrissa, sitting in the back seat. She leaned forward, holding onto Vera's every word. "I mean… he's terrified of me. Like, *terrified*. Like, nightmares-about-me-every-night terrified. And… his parents really fucked him up. I mean… they… I don't mean his dad *made* him a sadist, but… he definitely made sure Gavin had no other choice. I um… hit on something with him, I think. I told him I understood trying to be good for Joseph Stormbeck. And he, um… ran to his room. He's sobbing in there right now."

"Gavin's a bad person," Edrissa whispered from the back seat. She wrapped her arms around her middle and squeezed. "He, um, he hurt you." She looked at Tori. "And you."

"I know he did," Tori said softly, her hand going to brush her neck. The bruises were long gone.

"Pain makes you do bad things," Vera whispered, her gaze far away. There was something there. Something swimming beneath the surface. Forms moving in the dark, a whip, a rope, a lie.

"Babe?" Tori squeezed Vera's hand. "Are you here?"

"I'm here," Vera mumbled. Every time she reached for the shadows in her mind they skittered away, pushed back by the light of her focus. "I'm just… trying to remember something."

"Okay." Tori's hand stayed in hers.

"Sorry. Um." Vera shook herself. "I shouldn't force it. I know that. We can go. If it comes, it comes."

"Okay." Tori pulled her hand back and put the car into gear.

The drive was quiet and long. The roads were still icy from the last snow, but the ice had finally started to melt with the warmth of the coming spring. The house was far on the outskirts of the town, but that was good. It gave them space to rest and recuperate before they headed south again.

It gave them space from the people who wanted Gavin dead.

The houses became closer together, the yards smaller, as they entered Crayton proper. Businesses. Shops. Restaurants. Things that seemed so foreign now, so out of place. Things Vera never thought she would see again. Things that only existed in syndicate-occupied territory, or here.

Tori pulled up to the town hall. Vera stared out the window, unaware that they had stopped until she felt a hand on her shoulder. She jumped.

"Sorry, babe," Tori mumbled, and pulled her hand back.

"No, no. I'm good. Sorry. It's just…" Vera shook her head. "There's something coming up. I'm not sure what. It's kinda big."

"We can go back if you need," Tori said. "We can come another day. It's okay."

"No." Vera reached over and took Tori's hand. "I want to get out. It gets claustrophobic in that house. And I don't want to be here on a weekday. I don't want to see that Daniel asshole."

A look of irritation crossed Tori's face. "Yeah. If we never see him again, that would be fine." They all got out of the car.

As they walked up to the front door, Edrissa drifted to Vera's side. Vera smiled, her lips curving up only slightly, hoping Edrissa wouldn't notice. Vera took Tori's hand as they climbed the steps and walked inside.

The hall was cool inside, and quiet. Their steps echoed through the atrium, going up three floors. Vera wasn't sure why a small town north of the syndicates needed such a large town hall, but she didn't really care. She knew where Tori was headed.

Tori walked slightly ahead of Vera and Edrissa, her shoulders tensing with excitement. It made Vera smile to see Tori so happy about new arrivals. Every one, a life saved. Every one, a life preserved. Once the team went south to fight Colleen, Tori would be helping people full time again. She'd run a safehouse out of the house the team was staying in now. She would help people heal, recover, before they were sent out to their permanent homes. Vera's heart swelled with pride.

She pushed down the sadness that swelled in her, too. Over the past few months, Vera had grown comfortable. She loved seeing Tori every day. She loved having Tori in her arms at night, every night, in their bed, even though she couldn't bring herself to have sex just yet. Soon she would be back on the road, only seeing Tori in the brief downtime between missions. She missed Tori already.

Tori guided them to the room where the records of the new arrivals were kept. She went straight to the ledger on the small table near the door, the record of every person who passed through Crayton on their way to the places beyond it. Tori turned the page back, her finger brushing over the nine names of the family, placed just two months ago. Vera looked over her shoulder as she browsed. There were only seventeen names on the list after theirs.

"Winter's a slow season," a voice said behind them.

The three of them jumped. Edrissa skittered behind Vera, peeking around her as Daniel Schiester, his majesty, royal motherfucker himself, stood in the doorway. Vera's lip curled. *He reminds me of Joseph.*

Tori had a hand pressed to her chest. "Jesus Christ. Scared us."

"I'm sorry. I should have announced myself sooner." Daniel smirked, his cold blue eyes moving over the three of them. "People who've been victims of the syndicates are often jumpy. I should have remembered you're affected too, even though you've got one as a pet now."

Vera's hand itched towards her hip, where her gun would have been if she was wearing her holster. "Say pet again," she said quietly.

Daniel finally took a step back, raising his hands. "Alright. That was in bad taste. I apologize." He gestured to the ledger. "You checking on new arrivals?"

"I wanted to know how often you get them," Tori said quietly. "Once I've got the safehouse up and running I'll—"

"That's right. You were planning on running a safehouse." Daniel smiled. "We should discuss that before you make any plans."

Vera glanced at Tori as her eyes narrowed. "Why?" Tori said, uneasy.

Daniel crossed his arms over his chest. "The presence of your... *guest*... complicates your intentions of running a safehouse. Once the rest of you move on, where does he go? Do you intend to send him further north? I expect that will bring a whole new realm of challenges you have not *begun* to face here."

Vera was painfully aware that Daniel still stood blocking the doorway. She was stepping forward before she'd realized what she was doing. "Speak like a fucking adult, Daniel, and stop trying to be so damned political. *What* challenges? Is that a threat? What should we expect further north?"

Daniel leveled a smile at her that made her skin crawl. "Very well. I'll speak like a fucking adult." He tipped his head towards the door. "Here, our people are used to a constant flow of strangers that may or may not do them harm. Our job is to weed out the threats from the refugees. And believe me, we get our fair share of threats. Your Stormbeck is not the first syndicate agent we've had come through here."

"He's not an *agent,* he—"

"But once you go further north, people are much less... understanding. They are *used* to their safety up there. They are used to not having to think too hard about the syndicates that keep my people up at night. So, if you try to take your boy further north..." Daniel shrugged. "I think you'll find more hostility and less willingness to listen."

Vera's hands curled into fists. "Right, like your willingness to listen when we first arrived?"

"Vera..." Tori put a steadying hand on her arm.

"Your boy is alive, isn't he?" Daniel said softly.

"No thanks to you," Vera snarled. "We're the ones that had to stop your fucking *mob*."

Daniel's eyes narrowed. "You show... an *astonishing* level of protectiveness towards him, considering your past."

Vera's throat worked as she swallowed. "What the fuck is that supposed to mean?"

Daniel tilted his head, fixing her with an icy stare. "Vera... why did you kill Joseph Stormbeck?"

Vera's heart froze in her chest. Her face hardened into a look of abject loathing. She smiled when Daniel took the slightest step back. "So that's what this is about."

"Daniel, back off," Tori snapped.

"No, it's okay," Vera said coldly, and shrugged off Tori's hand. "You think Joseph fucking Stormbeck fucked me up so much that I still belong to him in my mind. You think I want *Gavin* to own me now."

Daniel's eyes widened a fraction. He pressed his lips together, pitching his voice low. "No, I—"

"You think this whole fucking thing is just about me being fucked up."

Daniel's gaze moved slowly over Vera's face. Finally, he said, "I hope you can understand my confusion."

"Oh, I do," Vera seethed. *He's not Joseph. He's not Joseph. He's not Joseph.* "I understand. In your head, once someone is broken, they're broken. That's it. No fixing it. It's why you think I'm defending Gavin. It's why you refuse to believe he's changed."

"I told you that you were free to go once I saw that he'd changed," Daniel said, the first hint of irritation coming through.

"But not without threatening to torture us to death if we were wrong," Vera growled, taking another step forward.

"What would you do if it was you, Vera?" Daniel snapped. There was something about his tone that cut her straight to the bone, made something in her quail and shrink back. Rage boiled in her blood, filling her back up. "I have an *entire town* to worry about. What would you do for your family?"

"I think we're done here." Vera moved to push past Daniel. He stepped smoothly in front of her, blocking her. Vera's hand went to her hip again. She felt an icy stab of dread in her stomach.

"I didn't want to have this conversation with you like this," Daniel said gently, rounding out the sharp edges of his voice. "But I saw you all come in and I wanted to see where you stood. I think I have a good idea of it now."

"And what is that?" Vera snarled, unconsciously pushing Tori and Edrissa behind her. "Where *exactly* do you think we stand?"

Daniel's lips pulled into a shadow of a smirk. "I think it would be unwise for you and your family to bring Gavin Stormbeck farther north."

"We can't exactly send him home," Vera said, willing herself to be calm. "They'd kill him, and not before making him tell them about everything he's seen up here."

"You really think they'd kill their own?" Daniel cocked an eyebrow.

"You don't know the family like I do," Vera said softly. "Yeah, I fucking do think that. We've been watching him for the past few months. His parents were *monsters*. What, you thought he just woke up one day and decided torturing people was for him? They... they fucked him up. We're working to fix him."

"If you can't send him north, and you can't send him south, there is a solution that I would suggest. I could even offer my own services to get it done, if you find the job distasteful." Daniel shrugged.

Vera's lip curled. "You said he'd be safe here as long as he stayed with us."

"I did." Daniel nodded. "I did say that." He met Vera's eyes. "So, you'd better keep him with you, wouldn't you say?"

"What do you think we've been doing?" Tori said, stepping out from behind Vera. "We've got him going absolutely stir crazy in that house. We're doing everything we're supposed to. So, what the *fuck* is the point of this exercise, other than to piss us off?"

Daniel raised his hands. "It's my job to stay updated on what goes on in my town," he said. "Your *guest* poses quite the threat to me and my people. I won't apologize for continuing to ensure he is being properly handled."

"You could apologize for being a grade-A prick," Vera snapped, and pushed past him out of the room.

She didn't look back until they were out of the building and halfway to the car. Edrissa practically jogged to keep up with her on her short legs.

"What the *fuck* was that?" Vera snarled. "What the *fuck*. Why the *fuck* would he—"

"That went beyond protecting the safety of his people," Tori said fiercely. "What a piece of shit."

"Shouldn't we be careful of him?" Edrissa said softly, her voice shaking. "He's, um, in charge and—"

"Fuck him and his fucking power," Vera said darkly, and stopped short when she saw the look on Edrissa's face. "Hey, I'm… I'm sorry… I shouldn't have said it like that to you. I'm sorry."

Edrissa's eyes filled with tears. "You're planning on going south anyway," she whispered. "But if M-Mr.— What if D-Daniel says I can't stay?" She shivered. "I can't go south. I *can't*. Not with this." She pulled her left sleeve up, revealing the now-healed scar over her old brand on her forearm. "If you, um, make him so mad that he says we can't stay—"

Vera took Edrissa's shoulders between her hands. "Hey. No. We are *not* going to let him do that to you. If he says you can't stay, we'll just send you further north. We'll find a place for you."

"We won't let you be taken again, Edrissa," Tori said, smoothing Edrissa's hair back from her face. "No matter what, we will keep you safe."

"But you're, um…" Edrissa cringed forward, curling into herself. "I'm sorry. I'm sorry. I shouldn't…"

"Please," Vera said softly. "Please tell us. We're not going to hurt you for saying it. We aren't going to leave you." She ducked and met Edrissa's eyes. "Okay? Please tell us."

Edrissa's gaze flicked between Vera and Tori and she bit her lip. "Um…" She shivered and wrapped her arms around herself. "You are, um…" She took a step back. "You're prioritizing Gavin. He could get us all killed and you're… you're doing it for, um. For Gavin."

Vera opened her mouth, and closed it again, just as quickly. Tori took in a quick breath.

"I'm sorry," Edrissa whimpered. "I'm sorry, you've been, um, good to me," she whispered. "You've been, um, nice…"

"Edrissa," Vera said quietly. Edrissa immediately stopped talking. "You are our family now, too. Even after we leave and go south, you're our family. Gavin is…" Vera swallowed hard. "Gavin is with us, but he's syndicate. He hurt all of us. So if it comes down to it…" She took a step back. "If it comes down to it, you are our priority. If he poses a threat, he will be eliminated. Not you. Okay?"

"B-but you don't think he poses a threat right now." Edrissa's voice was weak.

Vera blew out a slow breath. "No. I don't," she said finally. "I think he could… I think he could be one of us some day, too." Vera shot a glance at Tori. Tori's lips trembled. "Babe? I'm sorry, was that… did I…?"

"No," Tori said softly. "I'm, um, scared of him. And I don't think that will ever go away. But watching him, knowing how scared he is of you, seeing how his… his guilt, and pain, and… and how he *regrets* it, I truly believe he does…" Tori shuddered, and Vera wrapped an arm around her shoulders. "I know what he's done. Believe me, I know. But… he's different. Truly different. And I want to believe he could be… good."

Edrissa whimpered. Tori and Vera both turned to look at her. "But you… you'll make sure he…?"

"Believe me," Vera said, a wry smile pulling at her mouth. "If he steps a toe out of line, he's got a long, long list of people who will kill him."

Chapter 32

Gavin slammed his door shut and crumpled to the floor, heaving with sobs. He pushed himself back and leaned against the door, pressing his hand to his mouth, shuddering and rocking forward as each sob broke over him.

"I know what it's like to turn into something twisted trying to be good for Joseph Stormbeck." Vera's words still rang in his ears.

He reached out in his mind for the memories of feeling good when he hurt someone. Cutting Sam. Drowning Isaac. Beating Tori. He remembered how it felt, the warm, wrenching glow in his chest that shimmered and moved through him as the sound of their screams rose. He remembered what it was like, even as a creeping nausea clutched his stomach. He remembered how it felt.

Tentatively, terrified, he reached out in his mind for a different feeling: the feeling he got when his father told him he was *good* when he was a kid. When his father ruffled his hair and smiled and pulled him into a hug and said, *"You're my good boy, Gavin."* He reached out for the feeling of his father's love, of his approval. He reached out and remembered how it felt to have his father's hand on his shoulder as he smiled at him. He reached out for the memory of his mother's soft hands on his face, beaming down at him in delight and approval. He remembered how it felt when she smiled at him and said, *"Gavin, sweetheart, you're so good."*

It was the same feeling.

He lurched forward with a horrified gasp.

But he wasn't trying to be *good,* was he? He wasn't trying to be *good* when he hurt those people. He wanted it. He *deserved* the family's ire, their judgment, their hatred, because he really did *want* to hurt people. No amount of justification, no amount of *lies* could ever take that fact away. He liked hurting people, and his father let him. That was that.

But...

What if Gray had raised me? What if they found out what I was, found out I was a monster, and helped me? What if they found out I liked hurting people and found a way to love me anyway, without making it worse? *Without making me feel like that was the only way to be?*

He slumped to his hands and knees and curled up on his side, his back pressed against the door. He covered his mouth to muffle his sobs. *I can't let anyone hear this. I can't let anyone hear me crying and think I'm trying to gain their compassion. I don't fucking deserve it.* He curled tighter into himself and buried his head in his arms.

My parents didn't have to let me do it. They didn't have to fucking encourage me. It was… it was my responsibility not to, but they… He shook his head. *It wasn't their fault, was it? It wasn't their fault I was like this. There was something wrong with me from the start, deep down, deeper than anyone else could go. I can't remember ever* not *being like this. I've always been this way. I've always been fucked up.*

I've always been broken.

It had never, never been a problem before. He was a syndicate son, and syndicate sons and daughters took playthings and pets. Syndicate sons and daughters played with people in their spare time, just like their parents. It was the way it was, and as far as Gavin knew, the way it always had been. He had never known it not to be true. He had never *not* been the master of everything he knew. He had never once had to consider that other people didn't deserve the torture he felt like dealing out. It was like his mother said: he was syndicate, and so everything in the world was at his feet and for his pleasure. It was the way of things. He had never had to – or wanted to – consider anything else.

But now, surrounded by these people who had spent their *lives* being tortured and used and brutalized and broken by the syndicates… surrounded by them, things were different.

When had he started to care about them? He couldn't remember a time or a moment where he'd decided it. He couldn't remember looking at any one of them and thinking, *I care about you now.* And yet, it had happened. Somehow, in the past two months, it had happened.

He sobbed harder. Now he was surrounded by these people, these decent, kind, *good* people, and he *cared* about them. He hadn't made the decision. He simply *cared*.

And they hated him. He certainly couldn't blame them. He couldn't tell them they were wrong, and that he had changed, and that they should get over it and love him now. He had hurt them as deeply as one person can hurt another, each and every one of them. Except for Edrissa, but she had been broken, too. Not by his family, he knew that, but by another family so much like his that it didn't matter. She hated him for his syndicate blood and his syndicate name. And she was right to.

It was easier before he realized how much he cared for them. It was easier, when he was just their prisoner. His days had been filled with a sort of dull, buzzing terror that they could kill him at any moment, and his nights were always shot through with nightmares. But it was *easier* knowing they meant little to him, and he meant less to them. It was simple. He was a traitor to his own family, to his own world, and he had nowhere else to go. He had information that could help them, so they were willing to keep him alive. That was it. That was all there was to it.

But he cared about them. And that changed *everything*.

Walking away from his mother was hard, but it was necessary. Walk away or die by the hands of the people he tortured. They may have made it hurt, or they may have done it quickly. Those were the only two possibilities if he stayed. They would not have listened to his pleas for mercy.

Once he left, more possibilities opened up: staying alive, escaping the torture that probably awaited him. He could have gone anywhere. He could have run and found some place, somewhere, far enough away that nobody knew his name.

He hadn't done it. He still didn't know why. He'd sought out the people his mother was going to sell him to. He'd submitted himself to their wills. He'd assumed his value as an informant would have been enough to keep him alive for a while. Gavin understood the politics of information. He understood the tightrope he was walking between telling them all what they needed to know, and keeping enough to himself to stay alive.

And he *was* still alive. They hadn't tortured him for information, or even really asked. They'd used his knowledge to navigate the syndicate checkpoints, and that was it. That was all. What was he still *doing* here if they weren't going to use him?

And yet somehow, he doubted they would kill him once he stopped being useful to them. He wasn't even useful *now*. They didn't *ask* him anything. Didn't *want* anything from him. So what was he still doing here? Why was he still alive? He knew they didn't care about him. They couldn't. They had no reason to.

He wasn't lying when he told Isaac that he wanted a family again. He didn't know if he'd ever been so honest in his life. And Isaac hadn't killed him for saying it.

But the idea that his father loved him when he hurt people, when he was a *monster* like him, and no other time? The thought alone threatened to destroy him.

He could rebuild himself with this new family, he thought. Maybe they would let him live, even after he outlived his usefulness. They weren't the kind to kill people once they'd been used up. They weren't like *him*.

He wasn't that way any longer, though. Was he?

There was no way he could ever prove that to them. He could never really prove he had changed. Vera broke him, yes. Vera had planted a terror in him that he couldn't push away, a terror wrapped up in torture and blood and pain that made it so he couldn't hurt people anymore. She had taken that away. But he couldn't prove his change beyond that.

He couldn't prove that he had kept growing. She had ripped out of his life the one thing he was good at, but something else had come in to fill that gap. He wasn't sure what it was. He still wasn't sure *who* he was if he wasn't a syndicate son, a sadist, the master of his world and everyone in it. He wasn't sure who he was without torturing people. But he *was* someone.

He could be someone else, here. These people would let him be something else. They would let him live, be who he was now. And they could accept that. He was sure of that, now. They weren't going to kill him, not unless he gave them reason to. Isaac had put himself in the way of a bullet for him. Isaac had let the northerners cut him and bleed him just to prove Gavin wasn't a threat. Gavin had watched Isaac's eyes fog over, had watched him leave his body for a moment as the knife drew his blood. Gavin had watched Isaac go back to his basement, under his knife, under his torture. He'd seen it, before the smell of blood had gripped him with panic.

But what now? They wouldn't kill him. But they wouldn't *care* for him, either. Ellis wanted him dead, he could see it every time they looked at him, or more accurately, refused to look at him. Edrissa was terrified of him. With the brand on her skin and the scar on her arm where her tracker had been, she was terrified of everything he represented. And Isaac...

For the hundredth time, for the thousandth time, for the millionth time, Gavin's thoughts turned to Isaac. He'd hurt Isaac worse than anybody else in the family. Isaac's body was permanently scarred because of him. Isaac's *mind* was scarred because of him. If Gavin hadn't seen the panic attacks for himself, he wouldn't have believed it. Over and over and over, he'd told himself he hadn't broken Isaac. He hadn't made him betray his family. He hadn't shattered him.

He couldn't live with himself if he ever believed he had.

Isaac was... good. Despite the darkness, despite the rage and the bodies that lay in Isaac's wake, despite the scars Isaac had left on Gavin's face and on his mind, despite very nearly dying by Isaac's hand... Isaac was everything that Gavin wanted. Isaac was loyal, and strong, and... he was *there*. After everything he'd survived, he was still alive. He was still *there* for his family. He hadn't abandoned them. He hadn't sold them out or betrayed them. He was *there*.

Gavin wanted Isaac to be there for him, too.

He didn't know what that meant. He didn't even know what he *felt,* not if he got down to it. He still felt for Isaac what he had from the start: he valued his strength, his courage, his absolute, unwavering dedication to being an idiot when it came to his family. He marveled at the lengths Isaac was willing to go for people who weren't even his own *blood*.

There was something else there, though, something new. Something about how when Isaac cried, Gavin was torn with guilt instead of pleasure. Something how he *ached* when he thought about Isaac coming to his room last night, drawn by the sound of him screaming, like Isaac *cared*.

He gasped against the stab of longing. He wanted Isaac to care, more than anything.

A fresh wave of tears poured down his face. He wanted them all to care, not just Isaac. He wanted Gray to… to be *proud* of him. He wanted Vera to like him, as fucking pathetic as that was. He wanted Tori to stop being so scared of him, and to understand that he would never hurt her, now. He wanted Finn and Ellis to just accept him. Finn had a little, this morning, when they shared that piece of bacon. But Ellis looked like they wished he would choke on it.

And Sam? Gavin shuddered as he thought about their hand in his during the caning, their hand on his shoulder while he sobbed about losing his father in front of the person his father raped and terrorized.

Gavin whimpered miserably and pressed himself down into the carpet, wishing the floor would open up to consume him, wishing he could disappear.

He'd escaped Vera's bullet and his mother's revenge. He'd escaped the life that would have trapped him in an endless cycle of blood and panic and torture. He'd escaped north, where he could be safe from his own people.

He'd escaped into the arms of a family that didn't want him. He'd escaped one family that lusted for his death and found another that felt nothing for him at all. He knew he was better off here. He knew he was safer.

He knew the loneliness would burn him alive.

Chapter 33

Finn made their way slowly through the woods, tilting their head up to enjoy the feeling of the sun dappling on their face. They breathed in deep the clean, cold air, sky and pine and melting snow. It was colder up north than they were used to. They shivered in their coat. The woods were more pine than oak and maple, unlike the forest around Tori's house.

Finn felt a pang of loss still when they thought about Tori's house. It was their home for almost four months before they'd started up running missions again, and it was their home base they returned to for the two months they'd been active after. It was the one place Finn had felt safe in years, at least. Maybe since they escaped the death squads that destroyed the Junior Defense Corps. But Tori's house was a place they would never see again, now that Gavin's people knew where it was. It was no longer safe. No longer home.

Anger moved sluggishly through Finn's gut. Anger at Gavin, at the system that had created him. Anger at Gavin's father, who guided him to torture Vera when he was ten. *Ten.* A *child.* At that age Gavin should have been playing with his friends, climbing trees, building forts and getting underfoot. He should have had a childhood. Instead, his father had taken him down into the basement Vera rarely talked about and taught him torture.

Joseph Stormbeck broke Gavin. Finn had no illusions about that.

Sometimes it snuck up on them, the bitter resentment at Gavin for what he had done. Finn's left hand still ached when a strong storm came through. Their brain had healed completely, but they still felt a terrible sense of dread that everything they were, every memory, every aspect of them could be erased in a moment with a well-placed blow to the head. Finn had been dizzy and foggy for weeks after Gavin gave them a concussion. They knew too well that the damage could have been much worse.

And yet, the deepest fury they held for Gavin was for what he did to *Ellis.* Finn had known going in that Ellis was hurt, wounded, torn apart by the loss of their family. Finn had been prepared to be with Ellis through it, to hold them when the loneliness crushed them. They hadn't been prepared for the damage Gavin had done.

Finn shook their head and pushed the thought away. This wasn't the place for pain, for ruminating on the past. This was the place they went with Ellis to be alone together, to remember their walks near Tori's house, the surreptitious love they made in the only place they had true privacy. On these walks they bundled up with scarves and warm winter boots, protected from the cold but feeling so alive with it, too. These were the walks where they came back with red cheeks and cold ears, ready to curl up on the couch together with something hot to drink. These walks were for them, and no one else. These walks weren't for thoughts about Gavin.

Finn glanced at Ellis. They didn't look nearly as happy to be out here as Finn was.

Finn stopped and took Ellis's hand, searching their face with their gaze. "Ellis?" Finn said softly, squeezing Ellis's fingers. "You okay?"

"I'm fine," Ellis grumbled. They pulled their hand out of Finn's grasp.

Finn ran their hand distractedly through their hair. "Okay... You seem mad."

Ellis crossed their arms and took a step back, away from Finn. "Well, I..." They blew out a slow breath through their nose. "I'm sorry. I'm not fine. I'm fucking pissed."

Finn swallowed. "Okay. About what?"

Ellis refused to meet Finn's gaze. "About... about *you*."

Finn's heart beat a little faster. "About, um, me?"

"Yeah." Ellis shook their head, still staring at a snow-covered bush to Finn's left. "You..." Ellis's jaw worked. "How can you... be so fucking... *nice*... to Gavin Stormbeck?"

Finn's eyebrows pulled together. "What? I'm not... *nice*... What?"

Ellis rolled their eyes. "At breakfast this morning? The bacon?"

Finn balked. "You think that was being...? Ellis, I don't..."

"You shared with him. You shared your fucking *food* with him. After everything... everything he's *done*..."

"Um, yeah, Ellis," Finn snapped, defensiveness creeping up their limbs, pulling their shoulders higher around their ears. "I shared my food with him. He's gonna be with us for, um, a long time. We have to share our shit with him."

"Well, you..." Ellis stared at the ground. "You didn't have to be so fucking *nice* about it."

Finn threw their hands in the air. "What about that was *nice?* He asked if anyone wanted the bacon, I did, we split it. What's the matter with that?"

Ellis ground their teeth. "I don't... I don't *know,* okay?"

"Babe..." Finn's voice dropped, grew softer. "I'm not... I'm not cozying up to him, okay? I'm not... forgetting what he's done. But he's different. And I think—"

"He's *different?*" Ellis shrieked. "Are you fucking *kidding?*"

Finn bit down hard on their retort.

"Are you..." Ellis tore their hands roughly through their hair. "Are you... has he fucking *brainwashed* you, or something? Are you out of your *mind?*"

"Stop yelling at me," Finn growled.

Ellis flushed, bright red spreading over the pale skin of their cheeks, creeping down their neck. Shame twisted their features, dampened their rage.

"I know he's fucked with us," Finn snapped. "I fucking remember, okay? I wore a brace on my hand for *months* because of what he did. I remember watching him torture Isaac. I remember Sam nearly dying. Okay? *I'm* the one who placed the chest tube in Gray. *I'm* the one who pulled Sam back from sepsis. *I'm* the one who cleans up what he did to *all of us.*" Finn's lips trembled and their hands shook. "*I'm* the one who put you all back together again."

Ellis pressed their lips together and stared at the ground, the flush burning a deeper red on their skin.

"So don't..." Finn's hands curled into fists at their sides. "Don't fucking say I'm *brainwashed.* Don't..." Their throat closed around a sob. They forced it down, ignored the way their eyes burned. "Don't say... don't say he *fucked with my head.* Okay? He... he *didn't.* I'm still... still *me.*" They swallowed the lump in their throat, cursing the tears that fell down their cheeks.

Ellis's head snapped up and they met Finn's gaze, regret and guilt heavy in their eyes. "Oh," Ellis breathed. "Finn, I didn't mean... I didn't mean that..."

"I know you're angry," Finn said, their voice tight. "I know you hate him. And I don't blame you. I don't. You can hate him forever. I don't care. But... I *fix people,* Ellis. I know when someone is broken. And Gavin is... is *broken.* You've seen him and if you deny it..." Finn shook their head.

"I..."

"You saw him with the bounty hunters. You saw how Gavin reacted to Isaac's blood, when the mob nearly hanged him. You've seen how he flinches around Vera. You've seen it, right?"

"Yeah," Ellis whispered, their voice thick with something Finn couldn't place.

"And you heard what Isaac said this morning, too, right?" Finn said, their voice still tight but not as loud. They breathed slowly, forced the tearing pressure in their chest down. "You heard him talking about how Gavin's not sleeping well. And you've heard him screaming at night, I *know* you have."

Ellis nodded slowly. "I know."

"I know he's done some terrible fucking shit, Ellis," Finn said heavily. "I'm aware. But... look at who his parents are. His father was willing to let him die so he could capture Vera again. His mother was hoping we'd kill him the first chance we got. He's been raised from birth to be exactly who he was and once he got his shit scrambled, he *left.*"

"That doesn't fucking excuse it," Ellis mumbled, their own eyes shining with tears.

"I didn't say it does," Finn said through their teeth. "All I'm saying is..." They pushed out a slow breath through their lips. There was a tightness in their chest that wouldn't be relieved. "All I'm saying is, he's changed. And I'm... I'm willing to give him a chance. Even if that chance is just sharing food with him."

"He doesn't get a chance with me," Ellis sneered.

"Well..." Finn gulped, trembling at the wave of terror and rage rising in themself. They took a step back from Ellis. "I..."

Ellis's eyes went wide. "*Finn*... Are you...?"

"He didn't fuck with my head," Finn whispered. "He... he *didn't.* I'm not... crazy, I'm not confused..."

Ellis held their hands out plaintively, biting their lip, taking a half-step in their direction. "I know, babe... I'm sorry..."

"He didn't... do you... seriously... think...?" Finn gasped, gulped at the air that seemed to have all rushed out of the forest at once. They stumbled back and tripped on a branch buried in the snow. Ellis lunged forward and caught them.

"I don't, babe," Ellis whimpered, tears rolling down their cheeks. "I'm so—"

"How could you... *say that...?*"

"I didn't mean it..."

"You *did*," Finn sobbed. "You think he's tricked me. You think I..." They slowly slid to their knees, pressing their face into their hands. Snow soaked through their pants. "I didn't know this was, still in my, head..."

"I swear to god, Finn, I didn't mean it," Ellis said as they pulled Finn into their arms. "I swear. I'm so... I'm so *sorry*. He just gets me so fucking *angry*..."

"I know." Finn shuddered and choked out a sob. "I know he does. He hurt you."

"That doesn't mean I get to hurt you," Ellis said against Finn's hair.

"Ever since... every time I... forget something, or get confused, or get dizzy, *anything,* I worry he did lasting damage, that he... he damaged me..."

"He didn't, babe," Ellis soothed. "You're the smartest person I know. You got a little concussion a few months ago and now you're fine. Everyone gets confused sometimes."

"But I..." Finn hiccoughed. "I understand why you hate him. He... he b-brought back... he... with the pictures of, of Chloe and Galen and Chris... and he tortured all of us... but I swear to god, Ellis, he's different now. He's changed." Finn swiped their hand at the tears running down their cheeks. "I see it more every day. He's not who he was. He can't be."

"I know," Ellis sniffled. They pressed their forehead to Finn's temple. "I think that's part of why I'm so... mad. He gets to do all that, be a fucking monster, and then he... he heals. He gets better. He gets *us*. And I..." They swallowed. "When I... um... went dark..." They pressed a kiss to Finn's

226

forehead. "There was no one there for me. I was alone. I had *nothing*. Now he gets… he gets *everything*."

"It's not everything for him," Finn said softly. "He lost his family, in a different way, and he's stuck with us. He probably walks around wondering when we're going to just waste him, every single day."

Ellis sat back, their eyebrows shooting up. "Why do you think that? Why would he think that of us?"

"Um…" Finn chewed their lip. "We've nearly killed him twice?"

Ellis scoffed. "I mean, yeah, technically, but it was fucking warranted and *self-defense* both times."

"And we've threatened to kill him more times than I can count since he came to us."

"Only if he betrayed us!" Ellis's mouth twisted. "I think that's kinda obvious!"

"Ellis…" Finn sighed. "It doesn't matter to him what we think. All that matters is he's watched us kill people who hurt us, and he's on that list."

Ellis's eyes narrowed. "How do you know so much about what goes on in his head?"

"Because I'm constantly trying to think of how to *fix it,*" Finn said, exasperated.

Ellis studied Finn's face. "Do you…?" Ellis began tentatively. They cleared their throat and tried again. "Do you think he can really change?"

Finn looked down at their hands twisted in their lap. Ellis reached out to lace their fingers through Finn's. "Um…" Finn bit their lip. "I th-think… he already has. I think if we just… give him a *chance*…"

"I don't trust him enough to give him a chance to hurt us," Ellis said quietly.

Finn squeezed their hand. "Maybe we won't have to."

"But he'll have to come south with us," Ellis said, their voice shaking. "He can't stay up here. He can't go further north. They'll kill him. He's got to stay under our protection, for…" They swallowed hard. "*Forever.* And there's no way Isaac would trust him enough to ever bring him on missions."

Finn laughed, and Ellis's shoulders relaxed an inch. "Oh, no. We'll definitely have to take him with us, but yeah, there's no way Gavin goes on missions. The day Isaac trusts Gavin is the day I'll know I really *have* gone insane."

Ellis smiled and held Finn tight. "I'm sorry," Ellis said quietly.

"Me too," Finn murmured, and pulled Ellis in for a deep kiss.

Chapter 34

Vera yawned as she crawled into bed with Tori, the room lit dimly by the lamp on her nightstand. Tori sat on top of the blanket, her eyes unfocused, not having spoken since they got back to their room. She chewed idly on a fingernail, not seeming to notice when Vera drew close.

"Tori?" Vera said softly. "You okay?"

"Uh, yeah," Tori murmured. She drew in a deep breath. "Yeah, babe. I'm good."

Vera tucked one of Tori's tight curls behind her ear. "Do you want to talk about anything?"

"I..." Tori huffed out a breath. "I've been... um... thinking about Gavin."

Vera leaned back slightly. They hadn't seen Gavin all day. He'd been in his room, sulking according to Ellis, and *processing* according to Gray. Something trembled at the corner of Vera's mind, something she'd pushed down, something she'd told herself was stupid. Something that was part of her stupid, fucked up conversation with Danny boy. Something that should never have come to mind in the first place, with all the things Gavin had done to her family.

Vera drew in a slow breath. "Okay. What about him?"

Tori brought her gaze to Vera. A chill moved through Vera's stomach at the guilt that she saw in Tori's eyes.

Tori opened her mouth but took a moment before she spoke. Finally, she whispered, "He's really changed...?"

Vera froze. Slowly, she reached over and took Tori's hand. "Um... is that a question, or a statement?"

Tori pressed her other hand to her face. "I don't know. Both. Neither. Um. I mean..." She swallowed and kept going. "I mean... if he had th-that... *reaction*... to what you said... about becoming bad for Joseph Stormbeck..."

"It was stupid. I was being fucking dramatic. I shouldn't have—"

229

"But what if that's true?" Tori whispered.

Vera sat back. Her gaze moved over the bedspread as she drew in a deep breath, let it out, and squeezed Tori's fingers.

"I…" Vera felt something between them, a tremulous idea that, once spoken, would harden into something that would remain in their minds like an insect in amber. If she spoke what she thought Tori was saying, and it was *true*…

Vera felt torn. She wanted to rip Gavin's throat out. She wanted to pin him down until she saw the fear in his eyes that Isaac had seen, and then tear him to pieces. She wanted to *crush* him out of existence for what he'd done to her, to her family, to *Tori*. Tori bore the scars of Gavin's torture still, scars that cut across her skin in lines of fire, that *still* hurt, all these months later. Tori woke from nightmares that left her gasping in a cold sweat, nightmares where Gavin tied her down and made her watch as he killed her family, one by one. Tori had come back to her nervous, quiet, frightened. Tori was still who she was before, but now she trembled under a shadow of fear and pain that shattered Vera's heart. And that was *Gavin's* fault. That was *Gavin's* doing.

And yet…

She remembered, as clearly as if it was happening now – she couldn't fall back in, she *couldn't* – the things she did to stay alive when being good was the only handhold she had as she dangled over the abyss. She *remembered* – it was in pieces, in flashes of memory that seared her mind like a brand, but she *remembered* – the stinging, acerbic despair of betraying herself. Of giving herself up, piece by piece, until there was nothing of her left. There was no reserve of strength she kept for herself. There was no scrap of her essence she preserved when she was down in that cell. By the time Joseph was done with her, she was a shell, ghost, something with skin and bones and scars but *nothing* that he had not carved from her pain. She was a body, and he was the mind that drove it.

There was no mercy in that man. What did he do to his own son?

Vera glanced up at Tori, and saw Tori staring at her with a desperate, pleading look.

Ah. It was *a question, then.*

Vera cleared her throat. "Um…" She shifted uncomfortably under Tori's gaze. "I…" She steadied herself, prepared herself for the denial, the anger, the fear. She gritted her teeth. "Y-yeah. I think he's really changed."

Tori let out a breath. Her other hand went absentmindedly to Vera's and Tori squeezed with both hands. "Yeah," she whispered. "I've been thinking that, too."

Shock shot faintly through Vera, like a lightning strike miles away. "You… think…?"

"I've seen it," Tori murmured. "I've seen that he… he holds back because he knows we're scared of him touching us. He's careful when he's around Sam. The way he is around Gray…" Tori's swallowed and shook her head, her eyes unfocused, her voice low. "…he… *admires* Gray. He asks what he can do to help. He learns from us. And… Vera, the… the way he looks at us… *all* of us…" Tori's brow furrowed. "…it's like… he's seeing something for the first time. He, he *carefully* watches how we all talk to each other. And touch each other. He looks at us, and… it's like he's seeing a *family* for the first time in his life. And… and how he looks at *Isaac*… It's like he sees Isaac for what he is, instead of just a plaything, and he… *regrets* it. He *regrets* hurting all of us."

Vera laughed gently. "'Sees Isaac for what he is'? What is Isaac, other than a dumbass?" Vera's lips quirked into a smile.

Tori grinned and pushed Vera's shoulder playfully. "I mean…" She grew serious again. "It's like… he looks at Isaac and realizes… if Isaac can heal from what Gavin did to him… maybe Gavin can heal from it, too."

Vera chewed her lip and settled back against the headboard. "Um… huh."

Tori's gaze snapped to Vera's. "Am I totally missing something? Do you think he—"

"No, you're right," Vera said softly. She shrugged. "I guess I just… didn't see it from that angle before."

Tori's mouth twisted, uncertainty trembling in the movement. "What did you see, then?"

"Um…" Vera shook herself at the ghost of a memory, Joseph's fingers trailing along her throat. "Uh…" She forced it down. "I've been thinking about it from… uh, his parents." The touch faded away.

"His parents?"

"Yeah. Um… I just…" Vera set her jaw. "What kind of parent… takes a *ten-year-old* to torture another human being? What parent… *encourages* their kid to hurt other people, and… I mean, for Christ's sake, you heard what Gavin said. His mom just… *gave* him someone to help with his 'recovery'. And what did she do when he couldn't? He didn't just refuse. He *physically couldn't*. And… she cut him off. She cut him off because he refused to, to *die* to make her feel better because Joey was dead." Vera blew a breath out through her lips. "If she was willing to do that… I mean, Jesus Christ, all the kid did was puke at the smell of blood and not want to die. What do you think she did to him…?" Vera's head fell into her hands. "Fuck. *Fuck.* I'm defending him. I'm *defending* the fucking sadist who hurt you, and, and hurt *me,* and was going to—"

"He was," Tori said gently, and guided Vera's head up until Vera looked at her. "He was going to do that. And… you know as well as I do that he was going to be killed the moment he refused to rape us. He would have been happy to do…" Tori shuddered. "…*everything* else, but that would have crossed a line for him and then…"

"…he would have died."

Tori pressed her lips into a hard line. "Yeah," she breathed out.

They both sat in silence for a long time. Vera stared at the wall, her mind churning with thoughts that burned as they passed through. *He is the things he did. He is a sadist. He is a torturer. He…*

He was a child, once. And he could have been different. Vera drew in a deep breath and held it. Her chest ached, but not from the breath frozen in her lungs.

Vera looked up to see Tori staring at her. "What?" Vera said softly.

"Is it…" Tori pulled her hands away and wrapped her arms around her chest. "Is it… *possible*… to, to see what he's done… and… and still…" Tori's voice dropped to a whisper. "…*forgive* him?"

Vera's breath rushed out of her. She felt dizzy.

"I… maybe," Vera said heavily.

232

Tori hugged herself harder. "Joseph is dead," she rasped. Vera nodded, the white-hot stab of vicious joy she always felt at the thought burning through her chest. "But... Colleen isn't." Tori's face was twisted, dark with bitterness, her jaw set in a sort of fury Vera had only started to see in the past few months. Vera swallowed hard.

"No," Vera said softly. "She's not. That's why she's our next target. Next threat, obviously, because she wants us dead... but she's also the last Stormbeck left. She's the only one controlling the region anymore. You've heard what Gray's been hearing in town. The east is falling apart. She's got the west and south handled, but when we kill her, there will be a power vacuum. The whole region will be destabilized. We could—"

"I want to help," Tori said, a sureness in her voice and in her face that made Vera go still.

Vera held her gaze. "Okay," she said softly. "And... what about the safehouse?"

Tori slumped back, looking down at the bedspread, her hands clasped firmly together in front of her. "Um... yeah. Th-that, um, had me thinking. The talk with Daniel, I mean. I..." Tori shrugged awkwardly. "I know a safehouse is important. I know it'll help. I *know* that. But..." Tori met Vera's eyes. "Colleen Stormbeck has caused so much suffering. So many of the people that pass through here are families of her victims. She kills hers, just like Gavin does— did. She runs the western sector. She crushes the dissenters. She keeps the cities running, yeah... but... *none* of those people are free. And..." Tori's voice dropped so low Vera could barely hear her. Vera leaned forward. "...she *hurt* Gavin. I know she did. No one... I have to believe no one turns out the way he did without being hurt. And if Gavin's with us now..."

Vera sharply drew in a breath. "So you... you want to come south with us... to help kill her?"

"Um... yeah," Tori murmured. "I do."

Vera's hands shook as she reached for Tori's again. Tori wasn't trained for the field. Tori couldn't carry a gun with the ease that Vera and Isaac did. She wasn't versed in syndicate tactics. She didn't know how to survive on the run, with nothing but what you had with you when you had to leave. Tori wasn't meant for danger. Tori was meant for safety, and warmth. As much as Vera wanted her near and felt the crushing press of longing when she wasn't there, she wanted Tori out of danger. She wanted Tori to stay north.

Vera reached out and cupped Tori's face. Her heart ached as Tori's dark brown eyes met hers, nearly black in the dim light of the room. Vera bit her lip and forced down the burn of tears.

How much of that is me trying to keep her safe? How much of that is me trying to take away her choice, because I want her out of danger? Because I want her away from the blood and death I've lived with for nearly fifteen years? This isn't my choice. It's hers.

"Tori…"

Tori's hand went up to wrap around Vera's wrist. Tori gently caressed the scars there, faded almost completely away after fifteen years, but there all the same. Tori kissed Vera's palm. "Y-yeah?"

"I…" Vera bit down on her lip until it hurt, trying to keep the words inside. *Please don't come with us. Please stay here, with Gray, with Edrissa. I'll come back to you, I promise, just please, please don't follow us into this. You could be hurt. You could be taken. You could be* killed. *Please, Tori, please…* "If that's what you want to do…"

"Yeah," Tori said with finality. "It's what I want to do."

Vera pulled Tori into her arms and pressed a kiss to her hair so Tori couldn't see the tears that pricked Vera's eyes, the terror that flashed across her face. Her hands trembled as she held Tori close. Tori held Vera just as tightly.

"When we come back," Tori said softly, "I'll start the safehouse. I'll start helping people that way again. Once Colleen is dead…"

"Will you stay with Gray? Run a safehouse with them?"

"Hell no," Tori said with a tight laugh. She pressed her face against Vera's shoulder, and Vera could feel tears soaking through her shirt. "Gray's been through enough. They deserve a nice, quiet retirement. But… maybe next-door neighbors? Maybe just down the road? We can't have it here in Crayton. Daniel—"

A sudden flood of sharp, piercing rage burst through Vera. "Don't let that asshole make you feel like you can't have it. Fuck him. You can—"

"I don't *want* it around him," Tori said. She pulled out of Vera's embrace and cuddled against her side. "He... there's something not good about him, Vera. I know you see it, too, but—"

"He's a piece of shit," Vera hissed. "He's an absolute motherfucker and the further you get away from him—"

"Vera," Tori said gently. She ran her fingers through Vera's hair and gently tilted her head down until Vera looked into Tori's eyes. "Come back to me."

Vera blinked. The fiery pit of rage in her cooled, fizzled. She drew in a deep breath and let it out. Then another. Her throat was tight as she swallowed the last of the poison that had suddenly bubbled up her throat and burned her tongue. "Yeah," she rasped. "Sorry."

"It's alright," Tori said, and pressed a kiss to Vera's lips. "It's alright. It's not your fault."

Vera drew in another breath, deeper. She blew it out slowly, the rotten bile that had overtaken her for a moment coming out with it. "Sorry," she said again. "I agree. Safehouse. Not in Crayton."

"Yeah," Tori said, cuddling closer to Vera. "We'll go south and kill Colleen. And when we get back, I'll have a safehouse, close to Gray, with maybe a little garden in back, and, and we could get a dog—"

"A German shepherd?" Vera said softly. A wave of longing washed over her, and tears came to her eyes.

"Yeah," Tori said, and Vera could hear the smile in her voice. "Yeah. A German shepherd. And... maybe chickens. We'll have a huge house and we'll help people and... and we'll be together."

"Yeah," Vera whispered. The image in her mind felt as sharp as any pain, a fierce joy that her body could barely hold. "Yeah. We'll have all those things."

"Promise," Tori sighed, and brushed her lips against Vera's cheek.

Chapter 35

Years ago

Gavin padded softly down the hallway, the bottoms of his pajama pants brushing against the wood floor. He wrapped his arms around himself and shivered. Where's mom and dad?

He made his way to their room, his stomach hurting. The air was cold on the back of his neck.

A floorboard creaked behind him. He gasped and spun to look, but there was no one there. His skin was freezing. He turned and began to walk faster.

He turned a corner, then another. He saw the door to his parents' room. He put a small hand on it and pushed it open.

There was no one there. Gavin's forehead wrinkled in confusion. Maybe they're downstairs playing with someone? *For a moment he felt a bitter wave of sadness.* They didn't invite me. *He didn't get to play with people yet. They said eight years old was too young. But they let him watch. His head drooped and tears sprang to his eyes.*

The door slammed behind him. He cried out and skittered away.

There, standing in front of the door with a bloody knife in his hands, was a man Gavin had seen before. The man had been in dad's basement two days ago, chained up and bleeding. Dad let Gavin watch as he stabbed the man in the heart, the first man Gavin had ever seen die.

The man's skin was pale grey, the same color it had been after all the blood had been drained from his body. A dark red stain spread across his shirt right where he'd been stabbed. His eyes were completely black, but Gavin knew the man was looking at him.

"Gavin Stormbeck," the man croaked. His voice was raw and broken, the way it had been at the end.

Gavin shook his head as he backed away. "No," he whimpered. "No, no, no..."

The man took a heavy step forward and raised the knife.

Gavin screamed and leapt onto his parents' empty bed, desperate to get away, to run, to hide. He felt fingers on the back of his neck. He leapt off the bed and dashed into the bathroom off his parents' room.

He felt heavy breaths on his skin. He screamed and twisted away, covering his eyes, hoping desperately that if he couldn't see the man, he wouldn't hurt him. A hand clamped down on his wrist and pulled his hand away from his face. The man's blank stare was inches from his. The man's eyes were still that empty black. They threatened to swallow Gavin whole.

Gavin shrieked and dashed past the man, back into his parents' bedroom, and then out the bedroom door. His heart pounded as he tore down the hall, running desperately to the basement. His mom and dad would be there, and they'd protect him.

He turned corner after corner, looking for the basement. The halls stretched on for miles, and no matter how much he ran, he didn't get any closer. He looked over his shoulder. The man ran after him, the knife held high, breathing hard but always just behind Gavin. Gavin willed his legs to move faster, willed the door to the basement to suddenly appear. Terror jangled in his mind as he tore through the hallways.

"MOM!" he screamed. "DAD! HELP! PLEASE!"

No one could hear him. He ran, and he ran, and the dead man chased right behind. The man aimed a vicious stab at Gavin's back.

Gavin lurched forward and dragged in a desperate gasp. He tangled in the sheets, damp with his sweat. His heart pounded so hard and so fast in his chest he could hear his pulse in his ears.

His gaze darted around the room, lit by his nightlight. A dead man was waiting in the shadows. He was waiting to catch Gavin. He was waiting to hurt him. To kill him.

"Mom!" he wailed. He dove under the blanket and pulled it up over his head, hoping that would hide him enough that the man wouldn't get him. *"Dad!"* He reached for his pillow and hugged it tight against his chest.

He's going to get me. He's going to get me. Gavin trembled and sobbed into the sheets, praying his father or his mother would walk through the bedroom door, not that man that his father had killed. It felt *so good* when it

237

happened. The man had only been in the basement for a few days. *"He's been plotting against our family,"* his dad had said. *"He's been moving guns that he was planning to use on us. He was going to hurt us, Gavin."* Gavin had shivered against his father's side. If there were people out there going to hurt him, he was glad this man was in his father's basement instead, where he couldn't even touch Gavin. Not with the ropes tied tightly around his wrists, his arms pulled so high over his head that his toes barely touched the floor.

His father let Gavin watch as he whipped the man, cut him, hit him with his fists until the man started crying, and then screaming, and then finally started telling his father things. All kinds of things. The names of the people he was working with, the types of guns he was moving, the cities they were in. The address of his home. The names of his children. Then, finally, when the man had already been begging for death for several hours, Gavin's father stabbed him in the chest with the knife that Gavin loved, pure black from hilt to blade. And the whole time the man suffered, the whole time he screamed and bled and begged, Gavin had felt *so good*. The sounds of his pain, the blood on his clothes, every moment of it made Gavin's chest flutter and his mouth water. His hands itched to hurt people. *"Not yet,"* his father said. *"Not yet."*

He's going to get me.

"MOM!" Gavin screamed, as loudly as he could. *"DAD!"* He wailed and curled tighter into a ball. Was the man in the closet? Under his bed? Waiting just outside his door?

Dad said it didn't even *matter* what the man said while he had been hurting him. He said it didn't even *matter*. *"Some of the information will be good,"* dad had said. *"Some of it won't. It doesn't matter, though. We'll follow all leads, pick up what we can. But, Gavin, do you understand why I did that, even though some of the things he said might not be true?"*

Gavin had stared up at his father with wide eyes, and slowly shook his head. *"Um...?"*

His father had knelt in front of Gavin and gently placed his hands on Gavin's shoulders. *"Really?"* he'd said softly. *"You can't think of a single reason why?"*

"Um..." Gavin had looked at his shoes. If he told his father his feelings, would he get in trouble? Maybe dad just had to do this for work. But... was it

okay to like it? Was he being bad? Being wrong? *"Um... did you... um... did you like it?"*

A smile had spread across his father's face, and the relief that coursed through Gavin made him dizzy. *I'm not being bad. I'm being* good.

The man is in the closet coming to get me.

"Yes, Gavin, I like it. Do you?"

The man is dead, and I really liked watching him die, and now he's going to stab me and it's going to hurt and I'm SCARED!

"Um... yeah. I... um... I, I liked it."

The man is going to get me.

"MOM! DAD! PLEASE!" Gavin cowered under the blanket. His door opened.

Gavin nearly threw up as a hand landed on his shoulder. He keened softly and squeezed his eyes shut. *Please please please be my mom or my dad and not—*

"Gavin, sweetie, what's wrong?"

Gavin's heart nearly burst with relief. *Mrs. Shaney.* Dad said she kept the house safe. Gavin threw back the blankets and leapt into her arms.

The hard vest she wore over her work shirt was rough on Gavin's cheek as he sobbed into her neck. Her hand moved through his hair and she rocked him stiffly.

"Gavin? What's wrong? Did you have a nightmare?"

"Y-*yes!*" Gavin sobbed. He clawed at Mrs. Shaney's vest as he tried to crawl into her lap. "I, he, the, the man who, who dad, I... Can I have my mom? Please? I... or my dad? Please, I want them, I want them, please, Mrs. Shaney, please please please please—"

"I can go get them, Gavin," Mrs. Shaney said tightly. "Or you can go to the basement. They've got someone to play with right now, and they're not close to being finished for the night."

"N-no, no, I..." Gavin couldn't leave his bed. The man was everywhere. He'd grab Gavin's ankle as soon as he dangled his foot off the bed. He'd snatch Gavin and drag him into the closet. He was hanging from the ceiling, and he'd drop onto Gavin and stab him when Gavin walked beneath him. The man was everywhere, and Gavin didn't feel good about his pain anymore.

Gavin whimpered. "Can you, can you go get them? Please? Please? I…" He couldn't stop his chest from heaving, pulling in breaths too quickly. He felt dizzy.

Mrs. Shaney nodded. "Sure, I can do that." She stood and walked to the door.

Gavin cried out softly. He didn't want her to leave. He didn't want her to leave him alone with the man that was lurking somewhere close, waiting for him to be alone. But he couldn't leave his bed. Under his blankets he might be safe. He might be alright. But out there…

If he didn't come with Mrs. Shaney, he'd be left alone.

Terror paralyzed him until she was already out of the room.

Gavin realized in a wave of despair that he desperately wanted the lights on. Fear froze his tongue as he tried to call after her, to beg her to come back and turn on the lights, to chase away the shadows that could be concealing the man. The man had a knife. He was going to find Gavin and get him. Gavin whimpered with unbearable panic.

His heartbeat and his trembling sobs were the only sounds he could hear. He didn't hear the ragged breathing of the man with the knife, didn't hear the rustle of clothes nearby giving away someone trying to stay concealed. He tried to force himself to not be scared. The man was dead. Gavin watched him die. The man couldn't get him now.

The sound of footsteps echoed from down the hall and got closer. Closer. Closer. Gavin shivered and pressed himself back against his headboard, holding his pillow in front of him like a shield. *Please be mom. Please be dad. Please be Mrs. Shaney.*

His mother pushed his door open, and Gavin sobbed in relief. She flipped on the light. Gavin gasped.

His mother's shirt and pants were streaked with blood.

Gavin's lips trembled. "M-mom, I—"

"What is it, Gavin?" his mother said, and her voice had a syrupy flatness that sent a chill through Gavin's insides.

Tears pricked his eyes. "I, I had a nightmare."

"Oh." His mother's eyebrows drew together and she sat down on his bed. "What about, sweetheart?"

"Um…" Gavin swallowed as he looked down at his mother's hands. They were stained with blood as well. "The, um, the man that d-dad, um, k-killed a few—"

"Ah, yes. Taylor, I believe. Yes, he proved to be staggeringly unhelpful."

"Um…" Gavin's hands twisted together in front of him. "I h-had a nightmare he, um, had a knife, and was going to…" He trailed off as his mother stared at him. "…um…" He pulled his knees in toward his chest. "I, um… m-mom, will you just, um, stay with me?"

His mother snorted. "I'm in the middle of playing with someone, Gavin."

"Oh." Something was crushing his chest. "Um… but… but he—"

"That insurgent is dead, Gavin," his mother said curtly. "He's never coming back. He's not going to hurt you. That's why your father killed him, so he can never hurt you or anyone in our family again."

Gavin's heart pounded painfully in his chest. He bit down hard on his lip and tried to hold back his tears, tried to be brave. "But… I…"

"Gavin…" His mother reached out to touch his hand, then paused as she noticed the blood on hers. She laughed easily as she pulled it back. "That man was a threat to you. A threat to this family. Aren't you glad he's dead?"

Gavin nodded vigorously. "Yes. Yes, I'm very glad he can't, um, h-hurt us."

"There's nothing wrong with what we do, sweetheart," his mother said softly. "We are Stormbecks. And he was a threat to our family line. Didn't you like it, when your father hurt him? Didn't you feel good?"

The warm, fluttery feeling he'd gotten in his chest as he watched the man scream and beg momentarily pushed away the aching chill. A smile pulled at Gavin's lips. "Yeah," he rasped. "That was, um, good."

"Good," his mother said, as if that settled it. She stood.

"Mom," Gavin whimpered. He was still scared, why was he so *scared?* "Can you still… um…?"

His mother rolled her eyes. "Gavin, I'm in the middle of something. Come join me if you wish, but I can't be away for this long."

The man was dead. He was dead, and Gavin liked watching him die, and that was good. And yet, his muscles locked against him when he tried to push himself off the bed and follow his mother into the basement. "I... I can't..."

His mother fixed him with a stare for another moment. Then she turned on her heel and headed for the door. "Come get me when you're finished being ridiculous, sweetheart," she said, warmth and coldness twisting in her voice until it was too confusing for Gavin to think about. She turned off the lights again and was down the hall before Gavin could unstick his tongue from the roof of his mouth. He sobbed in the darkness and pulled the blankets up over his head. He shivered, tears running from his eyes until he slumped back in bed, exhausted. His heart still pounded in his chest.

Chapter 36

Gavin made *sure* he was awake before the rest of the team. As he went to bed the night before, his eyes still a little raw from crying, he demanded of himself to wake up at the crack of dawn, before anyone else would reasonably be up. He kept the blinds open so the sun would light up the ice on the trees and stream into his window as it rose, and all night he had nightmares of a dark figure with razor sharp teeth and burning eyes standing at his window, looking in at him.

He shot upright in bed. For a moment he completely forgot where he was, casting his gaze around the dark room, his sleeping clothes slightly damp with sweat. *Am I at home?*

He rubbed the sleep out of his eyes and pushed himself out of bed. He let his gaze move once more around the room, more slowly, his eyes adjusting to the dim light of the coming sunrise. He looked out the window at the clouds just starting to turn pink in the east, at the deep indigo that stretched across the sky. He shook himself and changed into his clothes for the day. He shivered in the cold of his room, the chill that crept into the house at night.

He wasn't exactly sure *what* he intended to do with being up so early. He knew he would struggle with the task of making breakfast for the whole family. He'd never had to cook before he came here. He was learning, but it was a slow process. He'd helped make the mashed potatoes for dinner last night, and he hadn't even burnt anything. How you could burn mashed potatoes was a little beyond him, but he'd been surprised all the same.

He was getting better at it, though, at being part of the family. He was pulling his own weight. Earning his keep. A desperate thought flashed across his mind: *maybe if I can prove to them I'm useful, they won't kill me when they've extracted all the information they need.* He shook his head and squeezed his eyes shut, running a hand roughly over his face. *I need to stop thinking like that.*

Not that it wouldn't happen; Gavin had long since realized his death was an inevitability. He'd realized it as soon as Isaac held the knife to his throat. What he needed to stop doing was *ruminating* on it. The rest of the family had spent their lives with the understanding that they could be killed, or worse, at any moment. If Gavin kept thinking about it, all it would do was stress him out more. All he could do is look forward to the little things before they killed him.

He stumbled gracelessly into the kitchen and flipped on the light. He went to the counter and reached for the container of coffee. If he could do nothing else, he could make coffee. It was just a matter of following steps: take out the old filter, replace the filter, scoop in the coffee, put the thing back into the coffee maker, fill it up with water, hit the green button. It was simple and hard to screw up. *Perfect for me,* he thought bitterly.

But Gray told him earlier last week that they really liked his coffee. That somehow it tasted better than when anyone else made it. Gavin had no idea what that meant. As far as he was aware, coffee was coffee. They didn't have the good coffee he was used to, but he didn't mind. The idea that someone could somehow make coffee that was *better* than everyone else's, when they were using the cheap stuff and it was such a simple, step-by-step process, was weird to Gavin. But when Gray said it, Gavin latched onto the praise like his life depended on it.

Maybe it does.

Stop it.

He went through the motions of making the coffee, hoping today it would still be as good as Gray said it was. *If this is one thing I can do right, one thing I can do that makes them all happy...* He distractedly flipped on the coffee maker and took down a mug for himself. He leaned back on the counter and waited for it to brew.

A door in the hallway opened. Gavin froze. He couldn't run and hide; they'd would know someone had been here. The coffee pot was running, for Christ's sake. Although, wasn't there a setting where you could set up the pot the night before and it would turn on by itself in the morning? Gavin could *swear* he'd seen someone do that before. But had anyone actually set it up like that? No, of course not, the coffee pot had been empty. So, if he ran and hid, they'd get suspicious. They'd wonder why he was hiding. Maybe they'd think he was working against them, sending messages to his mother. Maybe they'd think he betrayed them. Maybe his life would end this morning.

Before Gavin could decide what to do, a small figure wandered out into the hall. Their curls stuck out sideways from their head and they yawned.

Gavin slumped back against the counter and breathed a sigh of relief. *Sam is probably the one that wants me dead the least.* He clenched his jaw and swallowed against the familiar wave of guilt that moved over him at the thought. *They're the kindest of all of them, the most forgiving, and I broke them first.*

Sam rubbed their fists into their eyes as they walked into the kitchen. "G'morning, Gavin," they mumbled.

"Um." Gavin stared at the floor. "Hi, Sam." *They've never been alone in a room with me before. How can they feel safe like this?*

"You making coffee?" Sam raised their eyes blearily to Gavin.

"Um." Gavin looked at the coffee maker, then to the mug still held tight in his hand, and then back at Sam. He had no idea what to say. "Um. Yeah."

"Cool." Sam yawned. "Can I have some?"

Gavin yawned, too. "Yeah, of course."

Sam smiled at him. "You make good coffee."

Gavin blushed and glanced at the floor. "What is everyone doing today?"

Sam shrugged. "I'm not sure. I think Vera and Tori are headed back into town again today. Sounds like their plans were cut a little short yesterday."

"Yeah, I heard that Daniel Shit-ster guy was an asshole to Vera."

Sam laughed. "Shit-ster. I like that." They shrugged. "Why anyone would be rude to Vera is beyond me. But she said he said some… um… really bad things to her."

"Oh." Gavin's mouth twisted. "Like what?"

"Um…" Sam blushed and looked down. "I probably shouldn't say. It's her thing to tell."

That bad, huh? "Okay."

Behind him, the coffee pot started to gurgle.

"Coffee's done," Gavin mumbled, and turned to the cabinet to pull down another mug for Sam. It occurred to him that Sam might have needed help getting the mug down themselves, they were so short. The thought that he could do something nice for Sam was like a bubble of warmth in his chest. He reached for the pot and started to pour. "How do you like your coffee?"

Sam laughed once. "Lots of room for cream, please."

"Lots of room, coming right up." Gavin smiled tightly, still facing away from Sam. He poured his own cup. He turned back with Sam's cup in his hand. "Here you go, Sammy."

Sam froze.

Oh, fuck.

"Come on, Sammy, let's try this one more time. What's Isaac's last name? Makes it so much easier to find him. Help me out."

"Hey, Sammy, let's go again. I wanna see if you can hold your breath for long enough this time."

"I have all six of you now. I won't cry over one dead Sammy."

"Sam, I… I'm so sorry…"

"No." Sam took a step back, their eyes wide and brimming with tears.

Gavin put the mugs back on the counter and took a step towards Sam, his hands held out to them. "Sam, I…"

Sam stumbled backwards, colliding hard with the wall and slumping down. They held their hands out in front of them, as if to protect themself from Gavin. Tears rolled down their cheeks. "P-please, no… no… please *don't,*" they whispered.

"Sam, Sam I'm *sorry,* I won't call you that again. I promise. I'm so sorry. I… I'm not gonna hurt you… I *swear…*"

"Please, n-no," Sam gasped. "Not again. Not now."

Gavin tore a hand through his hair. "No no no, no *fuck,* no…" He stood in the center of the kitchen, frozen, staring down at Sam as they cringed away from him against the wall. He knew what he had to do. He knew he'd probably die for this.

For a moment, he considered just leaving Sam there. Maybe going back to his room. Maybe Sam wouldn't remember. Maybe everyone would assume Sam had a flashback, and Gavin hadn't *really* been there.

Gavin's stomach roiled. *I can't do that to them.*

Gavin lowered his voice. "Sam, don't move, okay? Stay *here*. Do you hear me?"

Sam nodded where they sat crumpled against the wall. Their eyes were wide, fixed on Gavin. *I wonder if they think I'll hurt them if they move.*

He swallowed hard and walked out of the kitchen.

He made his way down the dark hall to another room. The closer he got, the more his hands shook. It felt different, walking to his death, instead of waiting for it to come to him. But he couldn't leave Sam like that.

He stopped in front of a closed door. He took a deep breath and knocked three times.

"Uugh." Something rustled behind the door.

Gavin shivered and knocked again.

"Muh. What."

Gavin's lips trembled. "Isaac, it's, um. It's Gavin."

A loud sigh from behind the door. "What d'you want?"

"It's, um." Gavin blew out a slow breath. "It's Sam."

Behind the door, Gavin could hear fast movement. A thump as Isaac got out of bed. Rapid footsteps to the door. Gavin pressed himself against the opposite wall as the door opened. Isaac's hair was messy, his clothes rumpled, his eyes angry.

"Oh, shit," Gavin whispered.

"What's wrong with Sam?" Isaac growled. He looked down the hall towards Sam's room. The door was open, the lights off.

Gavin glanced toward the kitchen. "Um, they... uh..."

Isaac brushed past Gavin and headed for the kitchen. "What happened?"

"I..." *Why is it every time I open my fucking mouth I'm terrified he'll murder me?* "I... accidentally called them... um..." *I need to tell him before we reach Sam.* "I called them Sammy. It was an accident, I swear to god, I didn't mean..."

Isaac stopped and glanced back at Gavin. "'Sammy'?"

Gavin looked down at the floor. "It's a name I called them when I... um..."

Darkness passed over Isaac's face. "When you tortured them."

247

Gavin's mouth went dry. "Um. Yeah."

Isaac turned on his heel and walked into the kitchen. Gavin followed right behind.

Sam cowered back against the wall, their face red and wet with tears. As Isaac approached them, they whimpered and covered their head with their arms. A miserable wail filled the kitchen.

"Hey, Sam," Isaac said quietly, soothingly. "Sam, it's Isaac."

"N-no," Sam sobbed.

"Sam…" Isaac crouched beside them, leaning against the wall. "Sam, you're safe. It's Isaac. You're in the kitchen in the north house. Can you look at me?"

Slowly, Sam raised their head and looked at Isaac. Gavin's chest ached with the trust he saw there. Sam looked at Isaac like he was the sun after a year of darkness. Their hands reached out unconsciously and grasped at Isaac's shirt.

"Can I touch you?" Isaac said softly. Sam nodded. Isaac sat against the wall beside them and pulled them into his arms.

"What happened?" snapped a voice behind him. Gavin's blood ran cold. Vera pushed past him into the kitchen. Tori was right behind.

Isaac looked up, a sort of casual sadness on his face. "It's okay. Sam just had a flashback. They're alright."

"What set it off?" Tori said, and she glanced at Gavin. In her eyes he saw something like a flicker of suspicion and shattered trust. It baffled him, and devastated him, all at once.

He swallowed hard. "I…"

"Shit," another voice said behind him. Gavin quailed back against the wall, as far from Sam and Isaac as he could get. Ellis wandered into the kitchen, too, the blanket from their bed wrapped tight around them. Finn pressed themself to their side, barely awake.

"Sam had a flashback," Isaac said. "They're alright."

"Why?" Ellis rasped.

"Um…" Gavin trembled. "I'm sorry. I didn't mean to."

"You didn't mean to *what?*" Ellis snarled. "What the *fuck did you do?*" They took a step towards Gavin, their teeth bared.

"I called them Sa—" His eyes snapped to Sam and he cut off the word. "I called them, um, something I called them when I was, um…"

Ellis stepped forward and got right in Gavin's face. "When you were torturing them, you piece of shit? How could you slip up like that? What the fuck is *wrong with you?*" Finn tried to pull them back and Ellis threw off Finn's hand. "I thought you were trying to be *different,* you fucking trust-fund *shit.*"

"I didn't mean to," Gavin whimpered. "I'm sorry. It just slipped out—"

"'Slipped out'?" Ellis growled. "That isn't just 'slipped out.'" They jabbed a finger toward Gavin's face. "That is fucking…" Their words ran out and they snarled wordlessly at him.

Rage and fear flooded through Gavin as Ellis backed him into the corner. For a single, horrifying moment, an urge punched through Gavin: to take the knife to Ellis, *punish* them, *hurt* them for making him scared. He whimpered and shoved down the urge, the fraction of a moment where he pictured them bleeding and screaming at his feet. *NO! I don't want that anymore. I don't want to* be *that any longer.*

He shuddered and flinched as Ellis pushed in closer. *They're not Vera. Ellis wouldn't kill me. Or maybe they would.* He threw a glance at Isaac, sitting on the floor with Sam, running gentle fingers through their hair and murmuring softly to them. *Maybe Isaac wouldn't kill me, but he might let Ellis do it.*

Gavin turned his gaze back to Ellis. They took a step back, glaring at him, before they turned and looked back at Sam. Their posture instantly relaxed.

"I'm sorry," Gavin whispered. "I tried to help them, I tried to, to calm them down…"

"I think you've done enough," Ellis snapped over their shoulder. "Why don't you just go back to your room, let Sam come down from the flashback they had of you *torturing them?*"

"Ellis, take it easy," Isaac said, holding a hand to them. "He didn't mean it. Let's just everyone… stay calm."

"I know he didn't fucking *mean* it," Ellis snapped. "I know he's *good* now, he's *perfectly fucking innocent.*" Ellis's eyes streamed tears. "I know he didn't *mean* to fucking traumatize all of us."

249

"Ellis," Isaac said calmly. "Now we're getting into your shit. You're not talking about Sam now. Let me just... help them, and then we can talk about your stuff, okay?"

"I can talk about it," Finn said, still a little sleepily. "Ellis, let's go talk." They took Ellis's hand and gently pulled them toward the hall.

"I'm okay," Sam said quietly. "I'm s-sorry. I'm doing okay now." Isaac squeezed them and pressed a kiss to their forehead.

"I'm sorry," Gavin whispered. "I want to, to help... what can I do?"

"Take a long walk off a short pier?" Ellis said bitterly. Finn pulled a little harder and guided them from the kitchen.

Gavin hung his head and turned, walking down the dark hallway to his room. He left his coffee in the kitchen, untouched.

Chapter 37

Gavin was alone in the house and alone with his thoughts.

He'd been alone more often than not the past few days. With spring fully upon them and everyone's injuries healed, he knew the family was planning on leaving the ranch house soon, and they needed to prepare. They went into town every day now to meet with people who had recent updates on the syndicate movements, to gather food and supplies, and to set up a home for Edrissa and Gray once they left. Gray would be retired and Edrissa would be safe, for perhaps the first time in her life.

Gavin assumed the rest of the team would head south when they were ready. He heard Tori talk about possibly starting a safehouse up here, but he doubted she would follow through. Not that he didn't think she could do it; he'd just assumed Tori would be going south with Vera. He saw how they were together. How they touched each other whenever they could. How they would position themselves protectively in front of the other when one of them suddenly couldn't breathe from panic. How they shared a bed. How sometimes at night Gavin could hear the noises they made in bed together.

It all made him burn with longing.

I'm never going to find anything like that, he thought to himself fiercely. *There's no one who could ever feel that way for me, not after what I've done.*

He tried to return his attention to the line he'd been reading for the past twenty minutes. It was a book Gray brought him, something about recovery from trauma. *The others need this more than I do. I haven't been traumatized. At least, not by anyone but Vera.* He sighed.

The front door opened. *That's weird. I didn't expect anyone back for hours.* "My room," he called.

He'd gotten into the habit of announcing where he was when someone walked in alone. He figured it made them feel safer, knowing where he was.

And it didn't hurt so much when they walked in knowing he was there, when they didn't jump and look at him like he was something under their shoe.

It was really only Ellis who did that anymore, and even then it wasn't as often.

Whoever had come in was quiet, unlike after most trips into town. *Are they doing that on purpose? Why would they be sneaking around? They know I know someone's home.* He looked up at the door, his head slightly tilted, listening intently. It sounded like at least two people were home, but they weren't talking to each other.

The hair on the back of Gavin's neck stood up.

"Guys?" he called, putting the book down on his bedspread. "Gray? Isaac, is that you?" He swung his legs over the side of the bed and slowly stood. Whoever it was, they were in the hall now. Coming towards his room. His heart felt like it was stuck in his throat. "Sam?" He walked slowly to the door.

He looked through the doorway and into the hall. His eyes went wide as he came face-to-face with a dark-clothed figure, tall, massive. Someone he didn't recognize. He fell a step back into his room.

Hands closed on his shirt, dragged him from his room, and slammed him against the opposite wall. Gavin cried out as his head cracked against it.

"No, no, no, no..." he pleaded. A heavy hand clamped over his mouth as the man dragged him into the living room. Gavin screamed as the man wrenched one arm behind his back. He looked around, terrified, to see another man dressed in black, just like the first. A gun was holstered at his hip. He looked down at Gavin with pure hatred in his eyes.

The man holding Gavin threw him to his knees and he hit the ground hard. He groaned and tried to scramble to his feet, his shoulder throbbing. *"No,"* he sobbed. "Please no, *no*..."

A slap rocked his head to the side and he fell to the floor, his head spinning. He tasted blood. His stomach lurched.

"Shut up, you syndicate *fucker*," the man snarled.

"No, no, no *please*, I didn't... no, *please*..." Gavin sobbed. He tried to crawl away from the men, tried to get to the couch, just to put something between him and them. A hand grasped his hair and yanked him backwards, back to his knees. He cried out and his hands came up to pull against the hand in his hair.

"Let's just fucking do it and get it over with," the other growled. "I'm tired of this piece of shit *breathing*."

"*No,*" the first said from above Gavin's head. "I *finally* fucking have the chance to get a little bit of justice for Tina. No fucking way I'm giving up on that."

"I…" Gavin gasped. "I never knew a Tina—"

"*Shut up!*" he roared. He yanked Gavin's head back viciously. Gavin was forced to look up at him. "Shut the *fuck up,* you syndicate *prick*, your fucking *father* slaughtered her for *fun.* And you used to do the *same fucking thing.* Sounds like Stormbeck senior is fucking worm food right now, but I don't mind you standing in for him, you little *bitch.*"

"Please," Gavin sobbed. "Please, no."

The man released his hair. "Put your hands behind your back, Stormbeck."

"*No.*" Gavin pitched forward on his hands and knees again, trying desperately to escape the two men. The second man aimed a kick at Gavin's stomach that pitched him onto his side. Gavin shuddered and wheezed.

The man who had found him yanked Gavin up to his knees and pulled one arm behind his back again, the man's other hand fisting in Gavin's hair to hold him in place. He forced Gavin's arm up higher, until his hand was nearly pressed against his opposite shoulder. Gavin screamed.

"Put your other hand behind your back or I break this one off," the man growled in his ear.

Gavin wailed as the man jerked his arm back harder. "Okay okay okay!" he yelled. "Please…" He put his other hand behind his back. He sobbed in relief as the man stopped wrenching his shoulder. He whimpered as the man held both his wrists in one hand and slid a zip tie over his hands. The man pulled it tight around Gavin's wrists and stood up again, walking around to Gavin's front. Gavin twisted his wrists against the restraint, his heart pumping despair through his body. *They're going to kill me. The family won't even know what happened.*

"I'm sorry," Gavin moaned. "I'm… I'm *sorry* my dad did that to Tina, I'm sorry I—" He gasped as his head snapped to the side with another blow. His ears rang.

"You don't get to say her name," the man snarled, suddenly kneeling in Gavin's face. "You don't get to *fucking say her name,* you syndicate *bitch.* You thought you could spend your whole life torturing people, hurting people, and it wouldn't come back on you? You thought you could *ruin lives* and it would never come back on you?"

Gavin sobbed, tears streaming down his face. "No," he whimpered. "I'm sorry, I'm *sorry…*"

The man stood and snorted at his partner. "He's *sorry,*" he said with a snarl.

His partner's lip curled. "The idea of playing with him for a bit is sounding better and better. Schiester said they wouldn't be back for hours."

"I fucking told you," he said, and drew his gun from its holster.

"No!" Gavin screamed, shaking his head, scrambling backwards on his knees. "No, *please!*"

"We should tie those feet, too," the second man mused. The taller man laughed and stepped back around Gavin.

Gavin lurched forward, trying desperately to get to his feet before they could restrain him even further. The first man's hand closed on Gavin's hair and pulled him back down hard onto his knees. He stepped on Gavin's calf and *leaned,* grinding Gavin's kneecap into the floor. Gavin froze and cried out in agony. The man made quick work of tightening a zip tie around Gavin's ankles.

The man got to his feet. Gavin knelt on the floor, shivering and sobbing. Tears dripped down his face and onto the floor. *They have hours to torture me before they get back. Before they kill me.*

"So," the taller man said, drawing his gun again, "How do you want to die, syndicate *bitch?*"

"P-please," Gavin whispered, his throat too constricted with fear to make a sound. "Please, no…"

The man held the gun to Gavin's forehead. Gavin cried out and pulled away from the gun. The man's hand shot out and grabbed his hair, dragging him forward until the gun was pressed against Gavin's head again. "You wanna die like this?"

"N-no," Gavin moaned. *They're going to have to clean my brains off the walls.* "No, don't... don't *do this...*"

The man laughed and tapped the gun against Gavin's forehead. "Hm." He moved the gun to press against Gavin's cheek. "How about this?"

Gavin trembled against the man's iron grip on his hair. "Please just... t-take me outside. *Please.* Don't make them see this, *please...* don't make them see this in their own home..." *The last thing they need to see is more death.* "Don't get my b-blood all over the..." Gavin rocked forward, gagging hard at the thought of his blood running in rivulets across the floor in the hallway, soaking into the carpet in the living room and the pad underneath, ruining it forever. Thinking of the family finding his body, cold, empty, the room so full of the stench of blood it would *never* come out.

The man grinned. "What do you wanna bet I can make this look like you did this to yourself? What do you wanna bet I can make this look like your suicide?"

Gavin met the man's gaze and yanked hard against the zip tie around his wrists. They might stage this like a suicide, maybe even put the gun in his limp hand after they killed him, but his family would see the red around his wrists and know. *They have to know I wouldn't kill myself.* He didn't know *why* that was so important, but they had to know. They had to know that he...

Tears pricked his eyes and he swallowed. They had to know he wouldn't *leave* them. That he wanted to be with them, as miserable as it was. *I love them. I love them all so fucking much. Why did it take me so fucking long to say it, I love them...*

Gavin yanked harder. He felt the skin of his wrists break open and bleed.

The man pulled the gun away from Gavin's cheek and smiled wickedly. "Open your mouth, syndicate *bitch.*"

Gavin sobbed and tried to twist away from the hand in his hair. The man only tightened his grip. He forced Gavin's head forward. "Open your mouth," the man growled at him. "Do it. *Now.* Or I blow your fucking head off right now."

Gavin clenched his jaw shut and pressed his lips together. He shook his head against the man's grip, tears streaming down his cheeks, his eyes fixed on the gun hovering inches away from his face.

The man snapped Gavin's head back and shoved the barrel of the gun against Gavin's forehead. "You really wanna die right this second? Let us play with you, you little *bitch*. Stormbeck *fucker*. The longer you let us play with you, the better chance they'll come and save you, right? Your stupid fucking *traitor* family. You want that, right? *Open your fucking mouth.*"

They're not going to save me. They're going to find my body and forget about me. Why would they risk themselves to save me? Even if they caught you, they'd just stand back and watch me die. He blinked tears out of his eyes and did his best to stare the man down.

The man ground the barrel of the gun into Gavin's head. Gavin winced. The man's finger was on the trigger. The safety was off. *"Open. Your. Fucking. Mouth."*

Gavin shuddered at the thought of the bullet in the chamber, the bullet that was inches from his face. All the man had to do was pull the trigger, and the bullet would tear through Gavin's skull at 2500 feet per second. It would obliterate his brain, tear up everything that had ever made Gavin *Gavin*. He wouldn't just be dead; he'd be *destroyed*. All in less than a second. He squeezed his eyes shut.

He whimpered and opened his mouth.

The gun pushed past his lips, pressing down over his tongue, shoving all the way to the back of his throat. Gavin's eyes flew open as he gagged.

"That's what I fucking thought, Stormbeck *bitch*," the man growled. "That's what I *fucking thought*. Fucking coward. Fucking piece of *shit*."

Gavin sobbed, the steel-oil-gunpowder taste laying heavily on his tongue and making him sick. The man grabbed the back of Gavin's head and forced the gun harder into his mouth. Gavin's eyes streamed as he gagged again, his spasming throat twisting a sob as it forced its way out. He couldn't beg with the gun in his mouth, couldn't plead. He could only cry and choke.

"I'm gonna fucking kill you like this," the man rasped in his ear. Gavin cried out and shied away. The man's grip tightened on his hair. "I'm gonna pull this trigger and kill you. How many people have you killed, little bitch? How many people have you killed? Now, I'm gonna bring that shit right to you. You're finally gonna know what it feels like to die."

I bet it hurts. He tried to form the word 'please' around the gun. He gagged again as his tongue pressed up against the barrel.

"Maybe I shouldn't kill you just yet though, yeah? What if I just fucking cut you apart, piece by piece? That way when your fucking family comes home, they have to go on a little Stormbeck treasure hunt. Maybe your hand between the couch cushions, your ear in the shower…" The man chuckled. "Your dick hanging on the front door." He snapped the gun up against Gavin's teeth. "Maybe I should put your head on a spike outside."

Gavin squeezed his eyes shut. *Please, please no. Please just kill me. I know I deserve it but please no…*

"Maybe I shouldn't kill you here at all," the man mused. Gavin forced his eyes open. The man's gaze moved over Gavin's face, over his eyes. "Maybe I should just drag you to the square and hang you, properly. Maybe we could do it slowly."

"Maybe we should just send him piece by piece to his darling mother," the other man sneered. "I'm stuck on the dismembering idea."

Gavin wailed around the gun in his mouth, tugging hard against the zip tie around his wrists, pulling against the hand fisted in his hair.

"Or maybe," the first man said softly, easing the gun a centimeter out of Gavin's mouth, "We just take you back to the town hall. Chain you up in the basement. Keep you there for a month or three. Your family would never fucking know where to find you. Maybe we should just keep you like the fucking *bitch* you are, see exactly how you like it."

Gavin shook his head slightly. The man forced his head back and pushed the gun all the way into his mouth.

"Naw," the man said, his finger tightening on the trigger. "I think I'm just gonna do this here."

Gavin closed his eyes.

The front door opened.

Gavin's eyes flew open. He groaned in despair as Isaac walked through the door.

Isaac's eyes went wide, and his hand jumped to his waistband, to the gun Gavin knew wasn't there, because Isaac never carried his gun inside the house. Isaac fell a step back, his eyes fixed on Gavin.

"Sam!" Isaac shouted over his shoulder. "Gun! Now!"

The second man snapped his own gun up to point squarely at Isaac's chest. "Back the fuck off," he grunted. "Back off right now. Turn around and go."

Gavin whined and pulled against the hand in his hair, trying to plead with Isaac to save him and hating himself for it.

Isaac slowly raised his hands to waist level, but no higher. He hadn't looked away from Gavin since he opened the door, but now he raised his gaze to the gun in the second man's hand, then to the man's face. "I want you to think about what you're about to do," he said gently. "If you kill me, you permanently damage the north. My family will never work with you again. They'll stop bringing your families to you. They'll stop bringing you refugees. They'll stop risking their lives to harbor your spies, move your equipment. You kill me, and you cripple your operations up here. You kill me, and you're fucked. Do you understand that?"

"But this *bitch*—" the man with the gun in Gavin's mouth started.

Ellis burst through the door behind Isaac. Gavin flinched as the door slammed against the wall. Ellis's jaw dropped, their gaze darting between Gavin, the man holding him with the gun in his mouth, and the man pointing the gun at Isaac's chest.

"What the... *fuck*..."

Isaac pushed Ellis behind him. "Ellis, get *back*," he said urgently. "Get *back*. Tell everyone to stay back."

Sam walked in just behind them, holding Isaac's gun out. "Isaac, what—" Their eyes went wide at the sight of the men. Their hand began to shake and they nearly dropped the gun. Isaac's hand shot out and snatched it away from Sam, then aimed at the man forcing the gun into Gavin's mouth.

"Sam, get *back*," Isaac said, his voice taking on a hint of desperation. "Please..."

"Isaac, what...? Gavin...?" Sam stood frozen in place.

Isaac pushed Sam behind him with one hand while the other kept the gun pointed squarely at the first man. "Ellis," he said calmly, just a hint of tremor to his voice, "Is the other car here yet?"

Ellis shot a glance out the front window. "They're just pulling up."

Isaac swallowed. "Go tell them to stay outside. Please. Go tell them—"

"What the *fuck* do you think you're doing?" Ellis snarled at the men, completely ignoring Isaac. Gavin looked up at them in shock. Ellis took a step towards the men. "What the *fuck?*"

"Stay back," the second one growled. "Stay back, or we blow his fucking head off."

"No, fuck you," Ellis snapped. "Fuck you *very much.*"

"Ellis," Isaac said through his teeth. "No. Tell the others—"

The door pushed open again, and the rest of the family appeared in the doorway. Vera jumped and dragged Tori away from the door, then dashed off. Gray pushed Edrissa behind them and guided her back to the car. Finn lunged forward, their hands reaching for Ellis.

"Answer my *fucking question,*" Ellis snarled, and Gavin shrank back. "What the... what the *fuck?*"

"What the fuck do you care what happens to this Stormbeck prick?" the man demanded.

The other man pushed the gun hard into Gavin's mouth. Gavin felt his upper lip catch between the gun and his teeth. He whimpered and tried to pull away, eyes streaming.

The second man's hands tightened around the gun pointed at Isaac. His hands were shaking. "What the fuck do you care about him? He's a..." His eyes filled with tears. "He's a *monster.*"

Ellis's eyes blazed with fury. "Yeah, mother*fucker,* but he's *our monster.*" They lunged forward and bowled the second man over. The gun went off as Ellis slammed the man's hand against the floor. The bullet buried itself in the wall. Sam leapt into the fray, landing squarely on the man's crotch with all their weight. The man groaned and doubled over.

Vera burst through the door, her gun held tightly in her hand. Her eyes went wide at the screaming, clawing fright that was Ellis, and Sam, wrestling the gun out of the man's grasp.

The man still holding Gavin looked between Isaac and Vera, his eyes darting quickly, his hand tightening in Gavin's hair. Gavin could feel him trembling. He waited for the gun to go off, to tear through his mouth, punch through his brainstem. Gavin whimpered.

"Think very carefully about what you decide to do next," Isaac said, raising his voice. "If you kill him, it's gonna take you a few seconds to bring your gun around to aim at us. I have a *very* fast reaction time. Kinda twitchy. Must be the trauma." His eyes flicked down at Gavin and for a moment, Gavin could swear Isaac *smiled.* He whimpered as the man pushed the gun down hard against his tongue.

"Hey," Isaac barked, and the man jumped. "If you're cool with dying over this, fine. Just know that if you shoot him, you're dying in this house today." Isaac raised his chin at the other man, now groaning and sobbing on the floor, holding his crotch as Ellis and Sam kicked him over and over. "We'll even let that one go, for good measure. Take the gun out of his mouth. Right now."

"No," the man growled. He yanked Gavin's head back. Tears ran from his eyes and into his hair. "This fucker destroyed *everything I love*—"

"Was it actually him, or someone else in the syndicates that this poor idiot is standing in for?" Isaac said calmly. "I've heard people talking in town about using him as a stand-in, don't for a *second* think I haven't. I understand if it was him. If it was, we can work something out. Some kind of justice." Gavin's eyes went wide, and he looked at Isaac, just as the man looked down at him. Isaac shook his head slightly. Gavin sobbed.

"Or," Isaac continued, "You kill the one useful syndicate member alive in this world just because you wanted to stick your gun in *something.* And then you leave this house in a body bag. Up to you."

The man stared down at Gavin, hatred twisting his face into something terrifying. His hand shook around the gun. He forced Gavin's head back further, until Gavin started to bend backwards. He whimpered and gagged against the gun.

"Come on, man," Isaac murmured, pitching his voice low. "Up to you. Put down the gun. Let him go."

The man trembled. Gavin was sure the man would kill him. He braced for the shot, tried to think of something good for his last moments. He shuddered and looked past the hand holding the gun in his mouth.

All Gavin could see was Isaac.

The man hunched his shoulders and bowed his head. He forced down a sob. *"Fine,"* he growled, and pulled the gun from Gavin's mouth.

Gavin pitched forward with a sob, his jaw aching. Isaac darted forward and twisted the gun out of the man's hand, bending his wrist until he was forced to kneel. Vera jumped in to roll the other man onto his stomach and lean on his back.

"You have something to restrain yourself with?" Isaac asked the man, his voice intense.

"What the fuck, you said—"

"I'm not gonna kill you, you *idiot,*" Isaac spat through his teeth. "I'm gonna *restrain* you and drive you back into town. Then I'm gonna have a long fucking conversation with your *mayor* about *exactly* what the word 'hospitality' means. Got it? *Do you have any extra restraints?*"

"Y-yeah," the man stuttered. "Zip ties, left pocket."

"Perfect." Isaac stuffed his hand in the man's pocket, still holding him at gunpoint with his other hand. "Hands behind your back. Now."

"But—"

"I will make this *very fucking simple* if you don't do what I *fucking say,*" Isaac hissed. "Hands. Behind. Your back. *Now.*"

Gavin swallowed hard as the man obeyed Isaac. Isaac tightened the zip tie around the man's wrists, his eyes fixed on Gavin. Moving over him. Checking for injuries. Gavin felt his skin burn under Isaac's gaze.

Isaac turned his gaze back to the man and dug his hand into his pocket again, pulling out another zip tie. "Here," he said, holding it out to Vera. Gavin looked up to see Finn still standing in the doorway, their mouth slightly open, a look of amazement on their face. They stared at Ellis where they now stood, towering over the shorter man on the floor. Vera tightened the zip tie around the man's wrists as he groaned.

261

"Finn," Isaac said, and snapped Finn out of their reverie. "Can you handle this one? Get him to the car?"

"You bet." Finn grinned, stepping forward to pat the man down before jerking him to his feet with a hand clamped down on the collar of his shirt. "You fucked with the wrong family, moron. Our people are fucking *nuts*." They smirked and shoved him through the front door. The second man came next, supported between Vera and Ellis, who were *not* being gentle. Sam panted on the floor, their skin flushed and shiny with sweat, a wide grin spread across their face.

Isaac quickly knelt beside Gavin and put a steadying hand on his shoulder. He grabbed the knife in his pocket and cut away the zip tie from Gavin's ankles. Isaac reached for Gavin's wrists. The zip tie snapped under the knife. He tucked the knife back into his pocket.

"Isaac," Gavin sobbed, and threw his arms around Isaac's neck.

Isaac froze. He took a breath. His arms wound around Gavin's waist.

"Isaac, *thank you*," Gavin gasped, his breaths coming too fast. "Isaac, they... he was... *fuck,* I'm so sorry..."

Isaac squeezed Gavin gently. "Why are *you* sorry? They..." Isaac pulled away, his gaze moving once again over Gavin's body. His gaze returned to Gavin's face, to the red mark that probably spread across his cheek. "They... they tortured you, right?"

"N-no," Gavin mumbled. "It was nothing. It wasn't a big deal. They only—"

"Gavin..." Isaac said gently. Gavin's heart lurched uncomfortably. "They *tortured you.* It's okay. You're allowed to say it."

Gavin let out a twisted sound halfway between a laugh and a sob. He pressed his hands to his face. "Why..." He shuddered, and his chest ached as he heaved a sob. "Why did you save me? He could've just... killed me, and it would've been over."

"I didn't want to get blood on the carpet," came Isaac's reply.

Gavin's head shot up and he met Isaac's gaze. Isaac smiled gently. "Kidding. Because... fuck, Gavin, it's fucking weird but you're with us now. No one fucks with you but us. No one murders you but us."

Gavin flinched.

Isaac's face fell. "Okay, that was maybe in bad taste." He stood and held a hand out to Gavin. Gavin took it and painfully got to his feet. His hand felt cold when Isaac let go. "I want you to stay here with Finn while we handle this mess." Isaac waved his hand in the general direction of the cars. "Maybe we'll leave Vera here, too. Just to be safe." He took a step towards the door. "Does that sound okay? Will you be okay until we all get back? Gray and Edrissa will be here, too."

"I-Isaac..." Gavin's tongue felt too big for his mouth. "Vera, um... she..." He wrapped his arms around his stomach and winced. "Could you... I mean, could you... please...?"

Isaac stared at Gavin. "Could I... what?"

"Um." Gavin swallowed. "Could you be the one to, um, stay?" His cheeks burned.

Isaac chewed his lip as he regarded Gavin. After a moment, he said, "Sure. I can stay. Just let me check with Vera and Gray and send in Finn, okay?" He touched Gavin's shoulder for a moment before he seemed to think better of it and pulled his hand away. "Will you be okay for just a second?"

"Yeah," Gavin breathed, swaying where he stood. "I'll be, I'll be fine." He watched as Isaac turned and jogged out the door.

Chapter 38

Gavin trembled where he sat on the couch, his hands shaking, his stomach still churning with dissipating waves of terror. He winced as Finn pushed against his abdomen. Isaac looked on, his gaze unfocused and far away. Gray and Edrissa had gone out on a walk to calm Edrissa down. The others were out taking the men back to town.

"Sorry," Finn mumbled. They adjusted their hands and pushed again. "Deep breath."

Gavin breathed in, doing his best to hold his face in a neutral expression. His stomach *hurt*. Under the pain, though, was a heavy, warm awareness that Gavin had barely been touched in a way that felt *good* since he left his home and his birthright. Almost everything since then had been pain and torture. Up to this point, almost no one had touched him without the intention to do him harm.

No one except Sam when Isaac had beaten Gavin. And Gray and Sam together, at the funeral.

And Isaac when he'd let Gavin hug him. Gavin's throat tightened at the thought.

Finn watched his face carefully as they pressed in. "That hurt?"

"Um." Gavin cleared his throat. "A little."

"Where exactly did he kick you?"

Gavin leaned back and placed his hand on the left side of his stomach. Finn pulled up Gavin's shirt.

"Hm. Not much bruising, that's good."

"Um." Gavin ducked his head. "It's fine."

Finn laughed softly. "There are only a *few* important things on that side. But if you're still okay in a few hours, you're probably in the clear." Finn held Gavin's wrists up to inspect the torn skin. "*This* I can do something about."

Finn pulled their bag closer. Isaac stood back with his arms crossed over his chest, watching Finn out of the corner of his eye. After a moment he dropped his arms and started pacing the living room.

"Isaac," Finn said gently as they pulled some ointment out of their bag, "Stop pacing."

"I'm not…" Isaac sighed. "Fine." He plopped down on the other end of the couch. "What's the verdict, doc?"

Finn smirked. "He *probably* doesn't have a busted pancreas, but that's really all I can tell with the tools I have. These—" They held up one of Gavin's wrists as they smeared the ointment on. "—will be fine."

"Good." Isaac pinched the bridge of his nose between his fingers. Gavin's heart skipped a beat.

"Wh-what does this mean?" Gavin said, his voice tight with pain as Finn gently wrapped Gavin's wrist with gauze. "What do we do now?"

Isaac sighed. "Well, we obviously can't leave you alone again. My bigger concern is that they *knew* we were all gone. They were watching the house."

Gavin swallowed hard. "They said they knew you wouldn't be back for hours. Why did you… um… come back?"

"I forgot the store we wanted to go to would be closed today, so we just decided to scrap the day and come back early. I'm fucking glad we did."

"Um. Me, me too." Gavin hissed as Finn slathered the ointment on his other wrist.

"Oh, hush," Finn said gently. "You're fine."

"Yeah, sorry," Gavin mumbled. Finn glanced up at him with a hint of a smile.

"This definitely means we have to move our timetable up," Isaac said, passing a hand over his face. "I thought we'd have more time to prepare, but the sooner we leave, the better for you." He met Gavin's eyes.

"Do you mean we… um… Am I coming with you?" A lump rose in Gavin's throat.

Isaac blew out a slow breath. "I'm not sure what other options we have. You can't stay here. They'd kill you within a day. And you can't go further north. I have a feeling your name would follow you there, too, no matter how hard you try to keep it a secret." Isaac rubbed the back of his neck and glanced at Gavin apologetically. "I can't ask you to run missions against your family. I don't know if I can... *trust* you to do that. I wouldn't trust me."

"You can trust me," Gavin murmured. "They're not my family anymore."

Isaac looked at Gavin steadily as Finn wrapped his other wrist. "You're still a Stormbeck, Gavin."

Gavin looked at the floor. "But I don't... don't *want* to be. Everything they— we— are is... is *bad*. I'm exactly who those men said I was." Gavin glanced up and caught Finn and Isaac sharing a look.

Isaac wet his lips. "Not... not anymore... right?"

Gavin shook his head. "I don't want to be. I don't want to be those things. I'm still a Stormbeck, but they're *not* my family."

Isaac narrowed his eyes. "Who is, then?" He looked at Gavin like he already knew the answer.

Gavin swallowed and awkwardly met Finn's gaze as they finished tying the bandage. Gavin licked his lips and opened his mouth to speak, then closed it again. "I..." he whimpered helplessly.

"Gavin..." Isaac's gentle tone belied the command.

"I didn't really know before they, um..." Gavin mumbled at the floor. "I didn't know. I mean, I *did,* but I didn't know how *much* I..." He shivered. "I don't have to be your family. But I want... um, was hoping... you... could be mine." His cheeks burned as he met Finn and Isaac's eyes in turn.

Finn's mouth fell open. "I..."

"It's okay," Gavin said quickly. "It's okay if you don't want me. I understand. I do. I've done... fucking awful things to all of you. But you, um, you gave me another chance. You l-let me live, you let me... be a part of you. You, um, saved me when they were going to hang me. And I kn-know it's been hard with me around, because I, um... I remind you of, of things... but you let me stay anyway. You, um, care. I... I thought I was going to die. He, um... he told me he was going to, um, kill me and make it look like a suicide. And I just... I thought..." Gavin's eyes filled with tears and he shoved his face into his hands, mortified. "I just thought, I wanted to tell you all that I..." He choked off the word and shut his mouth with a snap.

266

"Wanted to tell us what?" Finn said gently. They reached out to touch him, then pulled back.

"Um." Gavin shook his head. "It's not important. Thanks for cleaning me up, Finn. I, um, appreciate it." Gavin pushed himself up off the couch and turned to leave the room.

"Whatever it is, it's something so important you thought about it as you thought you were going to die," Isaac said to Gavin's back. "May as well share. I just had a gun pointed at me for *you*. I figure you're in too deep here to give a shit about being *embarrassed* now."

Gavin paused. He turned and looked back at Isaac, standing in the middle of the living room with his arms crossed, and Finn, looking after him with something like concern in their eyes. Gavin swallowed reflexively, his stomach churning with fear as his chest ached with the feeling he'd had before. He loved them all, even Ellis. Ellis launched themself at someone with a loaded gun for him. Sam risked being shot jumping into that fight, too. And Isaac was right; he could've caught a bullet in the chest, for *him.* Isaac could have died, for *him.*

Is there no one he wouldn't protect?

Gavin licked his lips. *I might not have the chance to tell them again if the people up here are willing to watch the house and send people to kill me.* His cheeks burned. *And I'm not afraid of Isaac killing me anymore.* "Um. I... I guess... I guess I just realized I, um, wanted you to be my family. And that I, um... l-love you all."

Isaac's eyes went wide as Finn's cheeks flushed bright red. "But..." Finn murmured. "I thought..."

"I'm sorry," Gavin whispered, and turned to go. "I'm s-sorry..."

"Wait," Isaac commanded.

Gavin froze.

"I..." Finn breathed. "You're d-different. I knew you were different. I knew you were getting better, but... you *love us?*"

"Don't tell Vera," Gavin said quickly, his voice shaking.

Isaac burst out laughing. Gavin jumped and grimaced at him. "What's so fucking funny?"

Isaac pressed his lips together, a smile on his face. "I'm sorry. That was rude. But you... you almost *died,* you almost got your fucking head blown off and you don't want me to tell Vera that you... you *love* us?"

"She'll kill me," Gavin whispered. "She'll, um, she'll kill me for saying that."

Isaac's lips quirked up. "Why do you think that?"

"Because she, um..." Gavin wrapped his arms around himself and winced. "She just will. I know she will. She'll k-kill me, she'll think I'm lying..."

"*Are* you lying?" Isaac asked, a strange edge to his voice.

"No!" Gavin took a step forward. "I swear to god, I'm not. I swear. When that man put the, um, gun..." Gavin shuddered. "I thought I was going to die. And I wanted you all to know that I, um, love you. And..." He turned his gaze to Isaac. "And..." *Your face was the last thing I wanted to see as he killed me.* "And I wanted to, um, see you all again."

"*Why?*" Finn breathed.

Gavin whimpered, humiliation and fear making him shiver. "B-because... you're *good.* You're all so *good.* And you, um, you love each other. No matter what. No matter how, um, *broken* you get. You love each other. And, um, fix each other. And I... I've never had that."

A look passed between Isaac and Finn, like a confirmation. Gavin pressed on.

"I, um, I watch you with each other. You're so kind and you... you don't *take* from each other. You *give.* You, um, protect." He flicked his gaze to Isaac. "And I, um..." Raw pain welled up in his chest. "And I... I've never had that before. I want to feel something *good.* I... I want love that doesn't *hurt.*"

He bit his lip as he looked back up to Finn and Isaac. His stomach dropped as, for a moment, an image flashed across his mind: Isaac, choking on the floor, bleeding, *dying,* because of Gavin. Isaac, gasping around a hole in his chest, drenched in his own blood. For Gavin. Isaac could have died today, because of Gavin.

Gavin drew in a shuddering gasp. He turned to leave and didn't look back.

Chapter 39

Gavin flew awake with a scream, throwing his hand out in front of him to protect himself. His heart hammered in his chest. There wasn't enough air in the room. He lurched forward, gasping, clutching his chest.

There was a monster in the dark with him. A monster with Vera's eyes and a thousand pointed teeth, that would feast on his flesh and blood until he was nothing but bones, that would tear his body open and bleed him out onto the floor.

There was a rustle, and Gavin gasped again.

"Who's that?" His eyes widened in the dark. "H-hello?"

"It's just me, Gavin," came the reply. It wasn't Vera's voice.

"Isaac?" Gavin breathed. He flinched back as the light flicked on.

Isaac stood in the doorway, his arms crossed over his chest. Gavin's mouth went dry. Isaac's hair was still mussed from sleep, his sleeping shirt stretched over his muscles like he was flexing on purpose. Gavin's gaze fell to the bedspread and he swallowed.

"Another nightmare?" Isaac sounded gruff, but… there was something under it that made Gavin's heart beat a little faster. Something gentle.

"Um." Gavin swallowed drily. "Yeah."

"Wanna talk about it?"

Gavin let his eyes flick up to look at Isaac. Isaac looked at him evenly, calmly, like he really would listen if Gavin told him.

"Um…" He swallowed. "N-no. Thank you."

"Okay." Isaac turned to go.

Gavin's heart squeezed painfully in his chest. "No." He threw his hand out towards Isaac. "Please. Please stay."

Isaac paused. He turned back and surveyed Gavin carefully. His gaze moved around the room and finally settled on the foot of Gavin's bed. "Mind if I sit?"

"Um..." Gavin's voice cracked like he was sixteen again. "Yeah. Yeah. That sounds good."

Isaac nodded and closed the door.

Gavin's eyes widened. Isaac slowly approached his bed and sat down on the end. There was a good four feet between them, but Gavin could swear he felt the heat coming off Isaac's skin, even from so far away. Gavin trembled.

Isaac laughed gently. "What?" His light brown eyes burned into Gavin's green.

Gavin gasped softly and looked down again. "Sorry. I. Um. Was just thinking."

"About what?" A small smile pulled at the corner of Isaac's mouth.
Fuck.

Gavin shook his head. "Don't, um, don't worry about it."

Gavin's gaze dropped to a scar on Isaac's forearm. It cut across his skin from the edge of his left wrist halfway to his elbow, in a straight, thick line. Gavin's eyes narrowed. He'd never noticed it before. "Um..." Isaac followed Gavin's gaze down to his arm. "That... that wasn't one of... of mine."

Isaac turned his forearm and looked at it. "Oh. No." The scars from Gavin's knife, rows and rows of burns down Isaac's arms, shimmered on the other side. "That was from the bullet."

Gavin looked up at Isaac. "The bullet?"

Isaac nodded. "Yeah. When you almost shot Sam. You ended up shooting me."

Gavin's eyes widened. "Oh. I... I had no idea that hit you."

Isaac nodded. "Yup." He held Gavin's gaze, a calculating look in his eyes. Finally, he wet his lips. "Wanna see?"

Gavin's felt like his skin would combust. "Um, what?"

Isaac grinned at him. "My scars. Wanna see?"

Gavin's heart couldn't have beaten faster. His mouth was bone dry. "Um. Yeah."

Isaac reached for the hem of his shirt and pulled it up over his head.

Gavin gasped and bit his lip, his eyes moving over the planes of Isaac's body. His strong arms, his taut chest, the way the hair below his navel disappeared into the waistband of his pants...

Gavin gasped again, and louder, at the sheer number *of scars that crossed Isaac's body. Long lines from Gavin's knife crisscrossed Isaac's chest and abdomen. Stripes of scars ran up and down his arms from the heated-up blade of Gavin's knife. A ragged line stretched across Isaac's right hand from the top of his wrist to the base of his thumb.*

Isaac turned to show Gavin his back. Gavin's chest ached at the whip scars that crossed Isaac's back, dozens of them. There had to be close to a hundred. Each one slightly raised, a silvery line where Gavin had split his skin. Each one, a reminder of Gavin's torture. Gavin wanted to... to kiss *each one. He swallowed hard and reached out, letting his fingertips trail over the scars on Isaac's back.*

Isaac shivered when Gavin touched him. For a moment Gavin wanted to pull his hand away, until Isaac took a deep breath in and relaxed his shoulders. Gavin pressed his fingers harder against Isaac's back.

Isaac turned back to face Gavin. Gavin pulled his hand back slightly when he saw something in Isaac's eyes that he couldn't place. Something that scared him. Something he wanted more of.

Isaac lunged forward and pinned Gavin to the headboard by his throat.

Gavin's hands went up to wrap around Isaac's wrist to pull his hand away, so he could breathe. *But didn't he deserve this? Hadn't he choked Isaac, over and over and over, when he had him in his basement? Hadn't he put him through indescribable pain, for his own* pleasure?

"You tortured me," Isaac rasped against Gavin's ear.

"I know," Gavin whimpered. Tears sprang to his eyes.

"You made me beg you to kill me. You hurt me. Made me hurt for months *after. You made me fail my* family. *You... you* broke *me, Gavin Stormbeck."*

"No," Gavin sobbed. "I never did. You know *I never did."*

"I begged for my family to come for me," Isaac whispered. Gavin shivered as Isaac's lips brushed his ear. "You drew that out of me."

"But you never betrayed them." A tear rolled down Gavin's cheek.

"How am I supposed to trust you?" Isaac whimpered. "How am I...?" He leaned forward against Gavin, pressing his body in close to his.

"You can kill me," Gavin whispered. *"I understand. You can do it. I...
I'm sorry."*

Isaac's *fingers tightened around Gavin's throat and he gagged.* This is
it. Isaac is going to kill me. I couldn't have asked for anything else. I fucking
deserve it.

*Isaac trembled and gasped against Gavin's shoulder, his fingers tight
around Gavin's throat. Gavin's hands were still wrapped around Isaac's wrist.*

"I..." Isaac whimpered. *"I don't want to kill you. I c-can't."*

"Why not?" Gavin croaked. *He didn't want Isaac to. But if that is what
would stop Isaac's pain, save him from it... Gavin would do anything.*

"B-because I..." Isaac's *fingers loosened around Gavin's throat, and
his hand slid down to rest against Gavin's chest.* "Because I..."

*Isaac raised pained eyes to Gavin's. Gavin thought his heart would
shatter with the depth of the agony he saw in Isaac, of the suffering that still
ravaged him, almost a year after Gavin tortured him.*

"If killing me is what will end your pain, Isaac," Gavin said softly,
"Then do it." He moved Isaac's hand around his throat again. *"Please."*

Isaac whimpered. "I can't. I... I can't."

Isaac leaned forward and pressed a firm kiss to Gavin's lips.

Gavin couldn't move. Couldn't breathe. Couldn't think.

*Then his hands were at Isaac's waist, pulling him close. He opened his
mouth and Isaac's tongue moved against his.*

"Isaac," he gasped against Isaac's lips. *"You don't... you don't have
to—"*

"But I want you," Isaac groaned softly. *"I... I can't fucking* explain *it.
I know it's wrong, and I know I shouldn't, but... I..."* Isaac's *hands knotted in
Gavin's hair.* "If you want me, too, then... please. Please.*"

Gavin sighed and surrendered.

*Isaac's hands went to the hem of Gavin's shirt and pulled it up over his
head. Isaac moved his hands to Gavin's chest, sliding up to his neck, tangling
in his hair, moving down to his shoulders, moving down further to his waist.
Gavin clutched at Isaac, his scars rough under his hands. Gavin's body ached
in all the places where he hurt Isaac: where he carved into him, beat him, broke*

him open, seared him. He ached where he shot Isaac and hadn't even known it. How much pain have I caused that I still don't know about?

Isaac moaned as Gavin opened his mouth to him, his hands moving up to cup Gavin's face, pulling Gavin's lips hard against his. Isaac crawled on top of Gavin and straddled his hips where he sat against the headboard. Gavin whimpered as Isaac pressed against where he was hardening against his pajama pants.

"How can you want me, after what you did to me?" Isaac gasped against Gavin's mouth, and kissed his way along Gavin's jaw to his ear.

Gavin trembled. "How can I not *want you? If I had known... I'm so sorry, Isaac, I'm so fucking* stupid. *I should have known after that very first phone call."*

Isaac pulled away, his gaze burning on Gavin's face. "What?"

Gavin licked his lips. "The... the phone call. I knew that... that you were strong, and brave, and I knew I found someone good, *someone I might not be able to break this time..." Gavin swallowed hard. "...as soon as you offered yourself up in Sam's place. I knew you were..." Gavin whimpered at the smoldering look Isaac gave him, at the fingers tightening in his hair. "I knew you were..." Gavin closed his eyes and pulled Isaac's forehead down against his. "I knew I wanted you to be mine. I just didn't know... that I wanted you like* that. *I thought I just wanted to, to* hurt *you, to watch your pain, but..." Gavin pulled Isaac back, his gaze moving over Isaac's face, resting at last on his lips. "I didn't know I wanted to have* you.*"*

Isaac smiled and pulled Gavin's mouth against his again.

Isaac moved back and palmed the throbbing heat between Gavin's legs. Gavin gasped and bucked into Isaac's hand, his mouth falling open. Isaac grinned. "You want me?"

"You know I do," Gavin rasped, tilting his head back.

"Hm." Isaac took Gavin's wrist in his hand and pulled it out to the corner of the bed, pinning it against the mattress. Gavin was too busy opening his mouth to Isaac's kiss to notice the winding of rope around his wrist until it tightened. Gavin's eyes widened as he stared at the rope tying him to the bed. He snapped his gaze back to Isaac. Isaac was smiling.

"Do you trust me?" Isaac said softly.

"Yes," Gavin whispered.

Isaac took Gavin's other wrist and pulled it to the other corner of the bed. This time Gavin watched as Isaac wound the rope around his wrist and tied it. He trembled with want. Isaac's mouth returned to his and Gavin sank deep into the kiss, his eyes fluttering closed.

Isaac pulled back. Gavin opened his eyes to see Isaac smiling wickedly. His stomach dropped.

Isaac moved his weight off Gavin. He grabbed Gavin's hips and jerked him down away from the headboard. Gavin cried out in surprise as Isaac dragged him flat on his back, his arms stretched above him, tied to the bed, vulnerable and exposed. His heart beat in his chest.

Isaac dragged his mouth from Gavin's throat down his chest, across his abdomen, biting Gavin's side and then sucking gently on the red mark he'd made. Gavin's chest heaved and he squeezed his eyes shut. Isaac kissed his way from Gavin's side, back across his abdomen, to Gavin's hip. Gavin dragged in a gasp as Isaac ran his tongue along the waistband of Gavin's pajama pants.

"Can I—"

"Yes," Gavin wheezed. Isaac smiled and pulled Gavin's pajama pants down around his hips. Gavin shivered as his cock sprang free. Isaac pulled Gavin's pants the rest of the way off his legs. His hands returned to Gavin's waist.

"I wonder what you would have done to me, if you'd realized how you felt from the start," Isaac murmured. "What you would have made me do."

"I wouldn't have hurt you," Gavin said weakly. "I... I couldn't."

"Hm." Isaac hummed low in his throat. "Maybe makes me wish you had known." He pressed his lips against Gavin's hip, inches from his cock. Gavin shuddered and bucked his hips up. "I wouldn't be so fucking broken," Isaac whispered. He wrapped his hand around Gavin's cock.

Gavin whimpered, his mouth falling open. "You're not broken, Isaac."

"You don't know that," Isaac said softly. He wouldn't meet Gavin's eyes.

"I do." Isaac looked up at him. "I do. You're not broken. You're not. You're... you're beautiful."

Isaac's hand pumped Gavin's cock. Gavin bit down hard on his lips to keep from moaning at the touch. "I wish I hadn't hurt you. But... I never broke you. You've never been broken, Isaac." Gavin wished he could reach out and touch Isaac's face, wished Isaac would turn his cheek in to Gavin's palm.

"I'm scarred forever," Isaac said softly, sadly.

"But not broken," Gavin breathed.

Isaac looked deep into Gavin's eyes. Gavin's mouth went dry, and his hips pushed up into Isaac's hand unconsciously. The corners of Isaac's mouth pulled up.

"Makes me wish you had known," Isaac murmured, "Because I would have liked to love you like this." He pressed his lips against the tip of Gavin's cock. Gavin gasped, every nerve in his body a live wire.

Isaac opened his lips and took Gavin's length slowly into his mouth.

Gavin shuddered and cried out softly, his vision momentarily going white. He whined high in his throat as Isaac took more and more of him, sliding his tongue down Gavin's cock, until Gavin felt himself press against the back of Isaac's throat.

Isaac pulled back a few inches, and Gavin shivered at the feeling of Isaac's mouth around him. Then Isaac began to move.

Gavin whimpered as Isaac fucked Gavin softly with his mouth, the tips of his fingers pressing into Gavin's skin. Gavin strained against the rope tying him to the bed, longing to run his fingers through Isaac's hair, to cup the back of his neck, to guide him along his length.

"I—" Gavin's voice faltered. He tried again. "Isaac..." He licked his lips. "Isaac, fuck..."

Isaac pulled back until his mouth hovered a few inches above Gavin's cock. "I will in a minute," he said softly, and put his mouth on Gavin again.

Gavin's hips bucked. The heat was already coiling in Gavin's pelvis, centered on where Isaac was putting his mouth. "Isaac... Jesus Christ... let me..."

Isaac reached up with one hand and put his thumb gently against Gavin's lips. Gavin opened his mouth and Isaac slid his thumb in, resting against Gavin's tongue, before pressing down. Gavin moaned as Isaac pushed his thumb further into his mouth.

He could feel his climax building already, stirring in his body, drawn out by Isaac's heat, by the swirl of Isaac's tongue against his cock, by the fact that he was so fucking deep that he could feel himself push a little into Isaac's throat. He pulled harder against the ropes, a thin sheen of sweat breaking out over his skin. Pleasure coiled tighter and tighter at the base of his cock.

Gavin closed his mouth around Isaac's thumb and sucked gently, his tongue pressing against the salt of Isaac's skin. Isaac pulled away from Gavin's cock and looked up at him. Gavin whimpered as Isaac pulled his hand away from Gavin's mouth.

"Do you want me to take you?" Isaac said softly.

Gavin moaned. He wanted Isaac to take him, wanted Isaac to finish him with his mouth, wanted to take Isaac into his mouth, wanted Isaac in every way there was to have him. He pulled against the ropes, his hips bucking towards Isaac again, desperate. "Yes," he whispered.

Isaac grinned and sat up. Gavin whined softly as his cock throbbed with the orgasm that was so close. If only Isaac would put his mouth on him again, if he would only let him finish...

Isaac reached over Gavin to the nightstand. Gavin followed his hand with his gaze, and his eyes widened when he saw what Isaac was reaching for: a bottle of lube.

Gavin spread his legs and planted his heels against the bed, trembling. His eyes rolled back as Isaac ran his fingers down Gavin's stomach, trailing down to his hip, while his other hand went between Gavin's legs. Gavin's toes curled as Isaac's slicked fingers circled Gavin's entrance. Isaac's lips pulled into a smile, and he pressed a finger into Gavin.

He trembled as Isaac pressed deeper, easing him open. Isaac leaned over Gavin and caught his moan with an open-mouthed kiss.

Gavin's hands squeezed into fists as he opened his legs wider to Isaac, opened his mouth to him. He sighed as Isaac's tongue moved against his lower lip. He relaxed around Isaac's finger. Isaac smiled against his lips and added another.

Isaac's other hand went back behind Gavin's neck, tilting his head back, making a fist in his hair. Gavin's mouth fell open in a groan as Isaac turned his head to the side and kissed down his neck, nibbling and sucking as *he went. Isaac drew his tongue down Gavin's collarbone as he added a third finger.*

Gavin's cock pressed against Isaac's arm as Isaac worked his fingers into Gavin, preparing him. Gavin moved his hips against Isaac, chasing the friction, silently begging for release. Isaac bit down hard on Gavin's chest just below his collarbone, over his scar. Gavin clenched his jaw to keep from crying out.

"Isaac, please," he rasped.

Isaac removed his fingers from inside Gavin and stood. He pulled his pants off around his hips and down his legs with a grin. Gavin's heart pounded in his chest as Isaac crawled on top of him and reached for the nightstand again. This time Gavin didn't follow his hand, but kept his gaze fixed on Isaac's face. His eyes widened as Isaac returned with what he was looking for and tore open the packet.

"Isaac," Gavin pleaded.

Isaac stopped halfway through rolling on the condom. He met Gavin's eyes, his hands moving slowly against his own cock. "Yeah?"

Gavin licked his lips. "Will you just... kiss me, please. I have to know this is real. I have to know you want this, too."

Isaac's gaze softened. He finished rolling on the condom and leaned forward, bracing himself on either side of Gavin's head. He pressed his lips softly against Gavin's.

Gavin moaned at the kiss, slow, stoking the fire in him, bringing him even closer to his climax. He quivered and opened his mouth to Isaac.

Isaac pulled back. Gavin made a strangled sound in his throat and leaned forward, trying to chase the kiss. His wrists pulled against the ropes, his hands nearly going numb. Isaac knelt between Gavin's knees, slicking up his cock and staring down at Gavin with a wicked grin.

Gavin panted, his eyes moving to Isaac's cock, and back to his face.

Isaac lifted an eyebrow, smiling wider. "What do you want?" he said softly.

Gavin's chest heaved with frantic need. "Fuck me," he whispered. "Please."

Isaac leaned over Gavin, pressing his cock against Gavin's stomach. Gavin whimpered. "Or what?" Isaac said with a grin. "You'll chain me up? Cut my clothes off? Beat me until I can't stand up?"

Gavin strained against the ropes, his eyes flicking to Isaac's lips. "Please," he managed.

Isaac hummed low in his throat. "Looks like the tables have turned, Stormbeck," he said softly. He held his lips to Gavin's ear. Goosebumps erupted over Gavin's skin as Isaac's breath tickled his neck. "You can have me," Isaac whispered.

Isaac lifted Gavin's hips up and lined himself up with Gavin's ass. He covered Gavin's mouth with his, his tongue moving against Gavin's lips. Isaac eased himself against Gavin and pushed himself in.

Gavin gasped as Isaac filled him up. Isaac's hand moved to Gavin's cock, pumping slowly, easing Gavin into the sensation of being so filled, so deliciously, perfectly taken. Claimed, not in the way he claimed Isaac before, but in an entirely new way. Gavin met Isaac's eyes, and something in him gave way. Gavin knew he wanted to be Isaac's for the rest of the night. For the rest of his life.

Isaac gently eased himself partway out of Gavin, and then back in, his hands going to Gavin's face. Isaac sucked on Gavin's lower lip and Gavin groaned. Gavin pushed his legs further apart, trying to take more of Isaac in. Trying to be his, completely. He relaxed against the pull of the rope and surrendered back onto the mattress, letting Isaac have every part of him. His body, Isaac's. His mind, Isaac's. His soul, Isaac's. Everything he was, everything he could be, he handed over to Isaac in that moment, lost in their kiss, filled up, tied down, taken.

Isaac thought Gavin had broken him. He thought Gavin had taken away everything he was, had claimed it for himself. But Gavin knew that wasn't true. Gavin knew now that Isaac had never surrendered anything of himself, had never lost any of himself to Gavin's torture. Gavin, though, had lost everything. Lost everything, and given it to Isaac, freely. Not at the point of a knife, but in the warmth of their bodies together, the heat of their skin and the friction of Isaac's body on his, the fullness inside him, the taste of Isaac on his lips.

Isaac picked up the pace, working his hips against Gavin's, hitting that spot in Gavin that made his entire body tremble with pleasure, reaching down with one hand to stroke Gavin's cock. Gavin's climax built in him, swelled, filled up his body with humming ecstasy, as Isaac moaned against his mouth, sweat shining on his skin. Isaac quivered against Gavin, his other hand tightening on his jaw. Isaac sped up against Gavin, whimpering and groaning as Gavin's voice rose, as he shuddered around Isaac, as he pulled so hard against the rope his wrists felt raw.

When Isaac built enough pleasure in Gavin's body he thought he would shake apart with it, as Isaac shuddered and cried out against Gavin's skin, Gavin threw his head back and came hard. Isaac collapsed on Gavin's chest, his mouth pressing against Gavin's shoulder, as Gavin came all over his stomach. Isaac whimpered, his hands moving to Gavin's face, to his hair, to his neck, pressing kisses against his jaw, trembling in the glow of his own climax. Their sweat dried on each other's skin. Gavin met Isaac's eyes and smiled.

Gavin jerked awake.

His sheets were soaked in a cold sweat. His pajama pants were sticky and wet. His heart beat so hard he could hear it in his ears.

What the fuck? What the fuck?

Chapter 40

Gavin's eyes stretched wide as they darted around his dark room. He panted, his hands twisting in the sheets. *No, no, no, no,* no.

That dream had to be some sick joke his mind was playing on him. *Isaac?* No way. No fucking way. He couldn't feel that way about Isaac, he *couldn't have feelings for Isaac.* Not after what Gavin did to him. Not after Gavin nearly destroyed him.

Isaac carries scars on his body because of me. Isaac has broken down, lost control, because of me. Isaac has nightmares still because of me. *I can't feel that way for him. What the fuck is* wrong *with me?*

He buried his face in his hands, his skin damp with sweat.

How could he *not* have feelings for Isaac? Torturing Sam had been, ultimately, a strategic move to gain knowledge about the people who'd been sabotaging his operations. But with Isaac… something had always been there, something Gavin didn't know how to explain. There'd been something about Isaac that Gavin wanted since that very first phone call. From that very first moment Isaac said, *"Take me,"* Gavin knew Isaac was special.

But not like *this.*

And yet… his body still sang with pleasure, his skin warm and tight. His heart *ached.*

How could he not have *known?* How could he have been so fucking *stupid?* How could he not have known, just from how Sam described him? Gavin knew going in that Isaac was brave. That Isaac was devoted. That Isaac loved his family so much he was willing to die screaming for them.

How had he not known when Isaac held Gavin's own knife to his throat? How had he not known when Isaac let himself be cut, just so the northerners would know how *broken* Gavin was? How had he not known, when Isaac stood in the doorway with a gun pointed at his chest, another gun in

Gavin's mouth, and demanded Gavin's life be spared? How had he not known, when Isaac was *worried* about him?

How could he not have known when he had Isaac on his knees in front of him, dripping wet from the drowning?

"Fuck you."

"Should you be so lucky."

Gavin flushed red. How could he have forgotten shooting Isaac, but remember *that?* Some things about those few days before his concussion were fuzzy, but *that* he could remember clear as day.

Gavin pressed his face into his hands. So what if he had known? So what if he knew from the very beginning? He wouldn't have… would never have *raped* Isaac, even then. He couldn't do that to anyone. And he couldn't have taken Isaac as a lover. Not after what he did to Sam.

I destroyed any chance I had with him before I even met him.

It could never have been any different. There was no world where Gavin could have broken Sam and still had Isaac. He cursed himself, cursed his life, cursed his fucked-up fucking brain for *wanting* to make people hurt. As good as that felt, as good as hurting people had made him feel for his whole life, it didn't come close to the unbearable pleasure he'd felt just *dreaming* about Isaac's touch. Dreaming about his lips, his body, his…

Gavin groaned and cut that thought off with a ferocity that made him shudder.

I can never have that with him. I'll never have him in my bed. I've done too much to him and his family. He could never love me like that.

And if he *could?* How would Sam feel? Gavin had tentatively thought of them as a friend a while back, but last month… he'd thrown them into a flashback of him torturing them. As kind and forgiving as Sam was, Gavin couldn't imagine them being alright with Isaac sleeping with the man that tortured them both.

And Vera… Gavin shuddered to think of what Vera would do to him if she found out he'd even *thought* about Isaac that way.

But there was nothing else his mind could think of. Nothing but Isaac in Gavin's bed.

The dream was starting to fade, the wisps of memory and feeling swept out of his brain like leaves in the breeze. He shivered and tried desperately to grab onto the feeling of Isaac's lips on his, his hands, how his scars felt under Gavin's fingertips. He clung to the feeling of the rope around his wrists, tying him down as Isaac fucked him.

He *loved* Isaac. He couldn't hide that from himself now.

For a dizzying moment, Gavin considered just how big of a dumbass he had to be to miss that for so long.

He'd always felt this way about Isaac. It had always been there. *Always.* Since that first phone call, it had been there.

I've always wanted him. I just didn't know why. Didn't know how.
How am I this fucking stupid?

How could he not know himself this much?

Still, he clung to the fading touches. He clung to the heat. He clung to how it all felt: Isaac's mouth, Isaac's hands, Isaac's cock.

Isaac had *taken him,* and all Gavin wanted was to feel it again.

Gavin had never had sex like that. He'd had good sex, with good partners. It never interested him as much as torture, but… he was different now. It wasn't just that he couldn't hurt people anymore, that he didn't want to… It was that he wanted *Isaac,* in every way there was to have him. Gavin would go to his knees for Isaac, on his back, would press Isaac into the mattress and fuck him until he was screaming Gavin's name if that's what Isaac wanted. Gavin would do anything for Isaac. He'd risk himself. He'd sacrifice himself. He'd spend his life by Isaac's side, as a friend. As whatever Isaac would let him be. He knew he couldn't be Isaac's lover, but he could be Isaac's friend. Isaac was so good, so strong, and so brave, that it *hurt.* Gavin could hurt if it meant being with Isaac. He could put away his pain, his longing.

A shudder rolled over Gavin, and for a moment he thought the longing would crush him.

How had it come to *this?* Gavin saw the inexorable chain of his actions leading him here, and he didn't know how it could have ended any differently. There was no way Gavin could have *not* loved Isaac. There was no way Gavin could have seen who Isaac was, his strength, his courage, how he held on through everything Gavin did to him, and wouldn't break, and *still* wouldn't break... There was no way Gavin could have seen that and not loved Isaac. There was no way Gavin could have seen Isaac's brokenness now, his vulnerability, and not wanted to comfort him. There was no way Gavin could see how protective Isaac had been of even *him,* and not wanted more. There was no way he could have thrown his arms around Isaac, and felt Isaac put his arms around him, and not have *ached* to feel that again.

It was as inevitable as the tide, and just as powerful, sweeping Gavin out to sea, drowning him. Gavin couldn't breathe.

He wound his arms around his chest and squeezed, whimpering in the dark. "I want Isaac," he whispered aloud. A wave of fear and warmth washed over him.

"I want Isaac."

"I love Isaac."

He squeezed his eyes shut against the burn of tears. The loneliness that had crushed him since he left home rose to a crescendo. He sobbed, muffling the sound with his hand.

"N-no," he whimpered. "I love Isaac."

Isaac didn't love him back. Isaac never *would*. Gavin knew he had to stay with the family for the rest of his life if he wanted to live. He was a fugitive from the people he had thought were his family, and a monster to everyone in the north. He could never leave this family. He never *wanted* to.

He could never get away from this feeling. He could never get away from Isaac.

He didn't want to. Now that this happened, now that he *knew,* he realized nothing could tear him from Isaac's side. It wasn't just his fear of death that kept him here with them anymore. More and more, the devotion and love the team shared tethered him here with them. Loving Isaac was just the seal. The final nail in his coffin.

Loving Isaac would undo him.

The vast expanse of his life stretched out in front of him, years and years if he was lucky. To Gavin it felt like a barren wasteland, trapped in a world of fear, of running, of never quite being accepted and trusted. It felt like being constantly on the outside. Not syndicate, but not civilian, either. Not northerner. Gavin was *nothing,* now.

A thrill went through Gavin's spine. *I'll never be able to keep this secret. Not for my whole life. Why not tell him? What's the worst that could happen?*

He'd kill me, that's the worst that could happen.

But maybe Isaac wouldn't. Isaac very nearly took a bullet for Gavin, after all. Isaac saved him.

He didn't know I loved him then. Maybe he would've let them blow my head off if he knew.

Gavin shivered as anguish wracked his chest. *I can't go my whole life loving him without telling him. I can't. It'll tear me apart.* Now that he knew, there was no way he could hide it. This was the truest thing he'd ever known.

I know myself enough to know that I can't hide this.

Isaac's going to find out.

Gavin folded forward and pressed his face against his knees. If Isaac was going to find out, Gavin was going to be the one to tell him. There was no way he was letting it run away from him. He shuddered to think of Gray finding out and telling Isaac, or Sam.

Or Vera.

Gavin *definitely* didn't want that.

But how to phrase it?

"Hey, I know I tortured your sibling, tortured your family, tortured you, planned to take your best friend and her girlfriend to my house to torture them together and (apparently, unknowingly,) put her back with her rapist, sicced my mother on you all, nearly got you killed several times because of my fucking Stormbeck name, *but now I love you and want you and never want to leave your side."*

"I made a mistake, I'm sorry I'm so fucking broken, I'm sorry I'm so fucking evil that I enjoyed your pain, but that's been taken from me, and now all that's left is a desire to be loved."

"I single-handedly nearly destroyed everything you love, but now I want you so badly I feel it like a physical pain."

Gavin whimpered, tugging at his hair as he forced his face harder against his knees. *I broke Isaac. I can't fucking deny that anymore, either.* That was the core of Gavin's pain. *It took a massive concussion to shake me loose in my own head, and then a bullet to the chest and the sight of my father being slaughtered to finally destroy the thing that made me evil.*

He shook his head.

No. It didn't make me evil. I took it and made it mine.

But that's gone. What's left?

Love for Isaac. Love for Sam, and Gray, and Finn. Love for Vera and Ellis. Love for Tori, although she'd been so distant she was almost a stranger. Love for Edrissa. *That's* what was left. That's who he was. That's what he wanted to fill him up now where the broken, shattered shell of his sadism, his evil, still scraped at the raw insides of his mind. Now that Vera and Isaac had broken him open and all the hate and pain had slithered out, he wanted to be filled with that kind of love.

He wanted to be filled with Isaac.

Gavin blushed in the dark and heaved a broken half-laugh, half-sob. *Fuck.*

He had to tell Isaac. Tomorrow. The team was already planning on leaving within the next two days, and this was *not* something Gavin wanted coming out on the road. He wanted to give Isaac the option to leave him behind. He couldn't be near Isaac, completely compromised, without Isaac even *knowing.* It put the whole team at risk. It wasn't fair to Isaac, to be trapped with Gavin on the road, learning about this for the first time. No, he had to tell Isaac before they left.

He'd suffer the consequences. If Isaac wanted him dead after that, Gavin would try to run. He would understand, but he'd still try to run. Maybe it was possible to live elsewhere. Maybe he really could find a place where nobody had ever heard of the Stormbeck name. He couldn't just stand and let Isaac kill him.

If Isaac wanted to leave him behind, he'd accept that too. A tendril of hope curled in his chest that maybe *Gray* would let him stay with them. Gray wouldn't be able to protect him from people who wanted to kill him, he knew that. But if he could stay with Gray, maybe he could learn to be a good person from them.

The tears in Gavin's eyes soaked into the comforter.

If Isaac still agreed to take Gavin south, use him for information, Gavin would make peace with that. He would go with Isaac, help him take down the syndicates. If he could be with Isaac, not in his bed but with him nevertheless, he could live with that. He would ache with longing every day, but he could do it. Knowing that Isaac knew the truth could be enough.

But if Isaac reciprocated his feelings? If Isaac wanted him?

Gavin ground his fists into his temples. There was no use thinking about that. Isaac didn't love him back, never would. Going down that train of thought would only hurt. It would only drive him crazy.

He curled up on his side under the blankets, shivering, forcing down his sobs. He pressed his face into his hands and cried himself to sleep.

Chapter 41

Vera woke slowly, the last few tendrils of sleep creeping out of her mind as her eyes fluttered open. She lay still for a while, listening to Tori's soft, even breathing next to her. She turned her head to look at Tori. The bedroom was dimly lit by the rising sunlight filtering through the curtains. The sun had risen earlier and earlier as summer approached, and Gray said soon it would rise as early as six in the morning. *Better than the ten hours of sunlight we had during the winter,* Vera thought distantly as she gazed at Tori.

Tori's face was relaxed, her eyes closed and her mouth just slightly open. She was curled on her side, her hand lying on the pillow next to her. She looked so peaceful. Vera's chest ached as she reached out and gently tucked a stray curl behind Tori's ear.

Tori stirred, her eyes opening halfway and closing again. She cuddled closer to Vera and sighed.

"Morning," Vera whispered. She cupped Tori's face and stroked her cheek with her thumb.

"Morning," Tori mumbled, and rested her forehead gently against Vera's. She smiled sleepily and pulled Vera close.

Vera pressed a kiss to Tori's lips and wound her arms around her. Unease throbbed in the back of Vera's mind with thoughts of leaving, and danger, and death. Vera swallowed and pushed the feeling down. She drew in a deep breath and settled in Tori's arms.

"I'm gonna miss beds," Tori murmured, and laughed softly. "Beds are fucking awesome."

Vera smiled. Her eyebrows pulled together, and she squeezed Tori tight. "Yeah, they are fucking awesome. But at least we won't be camping out of our cars in the *cold* again." She kissed Tori's forehead. "That was *miserable.*"

"Mm-hm." Tori nuzzled into Vera's neck.

Vera's fingers trailed up and down Tori's arm. Tori shivered slightly at the touch and cuddled even closer to Vera's side. *I could lay with her like this all morning,* Vera thought. *For the rest of the day. For the rest of the year.* It hurt to think about Tori being on a mission with her, right in the middle of danger. Vera knew Tori could take care of herself. *But I left her alone and Gavin shot Gray and took her and what if that happens again and what if I fail her again and—*

Tori's stomach grumbled. Vera shook off the threads of thought that clung to her. She smiled at Tori. "You want to go get some coffee?" she whispered.

Tori shook her head and pressed her lips to Vera's neck. "Uh-uh," she sighed. "I wanna stay in bed with you."

Vera laughed softly. "I was thinking the same thing. What if I bring you some?"

"Mmm," Tori murmured. "That sounds really, really, really nice." She yawned. Her breath tickled Vera's neck.

"Okay," Vera said, and smoothed Tori's hair away from her face. "Two coffees, coming right up. And then I intend to cuddle the ever-loving shit out of you until you get tired of me."

"Impossible," Tori sighed. Her eyes fluttered closed.

Vera pushed the covers back and sat up, groaning as she did. She rolled her neck and stretched out her back. Sleeping on a bed after so long on the run gave her some relief from the constant ache in her back.

Sleeping on a cement floor for three months will do that.

She pushed herself to her feet and stretched her arms over her head. She looked back down at Tori. Tori was already asleep again.

Vera smiled as she left the room and padded out into the hall. She smelled coffee already brewing. Her stomach growled. She walked into the kitchen to find Gray seated at the counter, sipping from their favorite mug. She smiled at them and crossed to the coffee pot.

"Morning, Gray," she said softly as she took down two mugs. "Is this the Gavin special?"

Gray chuckled. "No," they said, their mouth turning into a theatrical frown. "We don't get blessed with that today. He's still asleep."

"Lazy-ass," Vera said, her lips curving up slightly. She poured Tori and herself a cup and added a little milk to Tori's. She picked up the cups and turned to leave.

"A moment?" Gray said quietly, their tone sad and strained.

Vera turned slowly. "Y-yeah?" She swallowed hard.

Gray offered a shadow of a smile. "It's... not anything bad." Vera's shoulders relaxed slightly. "I just wanted to ask... what do you think is going to happen to the team once you leave, and I stay behind?"

Vera's eyes fell shut. She drew in a deep breath. "Ah."

"It needs to be talked about," Gray said softly. Vera looked up and met their gaze.

"I... I know that," Vera said thickly. She put the steaming cups of coffee back on the counter. Vera's stomach growled again. She felt the pull back to her room, to her warm bed, to Tori. She forced a tight smile. "I was planning on just calling you for any and all tactical decisions, at any time." She pressed her lips together and willed the tears in her eyes not to run down her cheeks. "Wasn't that your plan?"

Gray laughed softly and leaned back in their chair. "Now that's a solution I hadn't thought of," they said, their smile a little wider.

"Gray..." Vera bit her lip. "It's... something I've been doing my best to not think about."

Gray looked at her sadly. "Well..." They shook their head. "...you leave in a few days. It's something we have to think about now."

Vera hung her head. "Isaac would be a good choice," she said softly. "Or Tori. Tori knows so much about the operations both up here and down south. She would be—"

"I was thinking you," Gray said evenly. They held her gaze.

Vera's stomach dropped. "...you what now?"

Gray's lips quirked up. "I was thinking you. Why not? You're strong, capable, intelligent, and you have a working knowledge of tactics in a lot of different scenarios. You're a fighter. You already protect them. Why not you?"

Gray's praise moved over Vera's skin like flames. "Um..."

Gray tilted their head. "Why not you?"

"Uh…" Vera held out her hands. "All of it? I don't want the responsibility. And the pressure. I know jack shit about the syndicates compared to you, Gray. How am I supposed to lead them when I have that gap in my knowledge? Why not Isaac? Why not Tori?"

"I don't have anything against either of them leading the team," Gray said softly. "But I wanted to come to *you* first."

Vera shook her head. "Ask Isaac," she said, her voice edging towards desperation. "Ask… fuck, *any* of the others. I don't want it. Please."

"Vera…" Gray huffed out a breath. "You're a natural leader. The team already looks to you. I want them to feel safe when you head south."

"There is no 'safe', Gray," Vera said softly. "You know that."

Gray pressed their lips together. "I know. But I think you would give them the best shot."

Vera held Gray's gaze for a long moment. "Ask Isaac," she said, trying to keep the tremor out of her voice. "If he doesn't want it, then…" She ran a hand through her hair and sighed. "…then we can talk again. But ask Isaac. I don't want this."

Gray stared at her for a moment, their gaze moving over her face. They sat back. "Alright," they murmured. "I'll ask Isaac."

"Thank you," Vera breathed. She turned to take the coffees.

"Just so you know," Gray said, and Vera paused. "Whoever leads them south, I know they'll be in good hands. You're both strong and capable. I wouldn't want to be with anyone else."

Tears threatened in Vera's eyes. "Thanks, Gray," she rasped. She turned and left the kitchen.

Her mind whirled as she walked down the hall back to her room. She held the cups of coffee so tightly in her hands that her knuckles went white. She made it to her room and nudged the door closed behind her. She went to the bed and sat down beside Tori.

"Tori," Vera whispered. Tori groaned and rolled over. Her face lit up when she saw the coffee.

"Mmm," Tori sighed. "Thank you." She pushed herself up against the headboard and took the cup, gratitude shining in her eyes. Her face fell as she looked at Vera. "What's going on?"

Vera shrugged jerkily. "Just… talking with Gray."

"Oh." Tori took a sip. "About what?"

"Um…" Vera's throat bobbed. She was suddenly gripped with worry that Tori might be *upset* at Gray's offer. Tori had known Gray for over fifteen years. Maybe Tori should lead the team. Maybe she was meant for it. "About… um… things once we go south. Who's going to… um… be in charge."

"Oh," Tori said with a light chuckle. "I hope my name wasn't thrown into that hat. I'd rather stay here than do that."

Vera's mouth twisted in a wry smile. "It was," she said softly.

Tori rolled her eyes. "Well, no thanks. Better you than me." She grinned at Vera.

Vera smiled widely at Tori and leaned forward to press a kiss to her lips. "I told them to ask Isaac," she said.

"Mm," Tori agreed, nodding. "That's a good idea."

"He'd be good," Vera said, and sipped her coffee. It was cooler than she liked. "But right now…" She set her cup on the nightstand. "…I just want…" She brought her hands to Tori's face and kissed her softly.

"I haven't even finished my coffee," Tori said, meeting Vera's kiss with a smile. She turned and set her mug on her nightstand.

"Then maybe I can't wait that long," Vera murmured. She straddled Tori's hips and tangled her hands in Tori's hair.

"I would say some terrible line about you taking charge," Tori said, laughing. "But that just seems… ugh."

"Just kissing for right now," Vera whispered as she ran her lips down Tori's neck.

Tori shivered. "J-just kissing," she gasped out. She wound her arms around Vera's waist. "Sounds good."

Chapter 42

Isaac lounged on his bed, drifting in and out of consciousness. He wasn't tired enough to take a nap, but he didn't feel like doing anything else. He stared at the ceiling, his eyes moving slowly over the swirl of the drywall, finding patterns, and daydreaming.

He'd never been so well-rested that he wouldn't just pass out as soon as he got horizontal. He couldn't remember the last time he felt safe enough to sleep late and to nap whenever he wanted. The team had planning to do, but they still had *time*. Vera and Gray were discussing strategy in the living room with the sort of heavy sadness that came with knowing Gray wouldn't be coming with them. It was a conversation that Isaac knew he should be a part of, but he couldn't force himself to get out of bed and join them. He just wanted to *rest*. In a few days, their lives would be nothing but adrenaline and sleep deprivation again. For just this moment, he wanted peace. For just this moment, he wanted to rest. His eyes fluttered closed.

"Hey, you have a minute?"

Isaac jumped slightly, despite the gentle tone in Gray's voice. He groaned and pushed himself upright, planting his feet flat on the floor. "Yeah. Sorry. Do you need to talk strategy, or…?"

"No. I wanted to get outside, and I wanted to talk to you. Walk with me?"

Isaac nodded as he stood and reached for his jacket. "Yeah. Sure thing."

As he passed through the living room and paused to pull on his shoes, Vera smiled at him. He smiled back, his heart clenching, unsettled by the sadness behind her eyes. He swallowed and followed Gray out the door into the crisp afternoon air.

Winter was long since over. The sun was melting the hard, snowy ground into mud. The birds had returned from the south. The buds on the trees, the glimmer of the sun on the clouds, the purple flowers that pushed their heads up through the wet snow, were all beautiful. Already, homesickness cut his heart with shards sharp as glass. He pushed the feeling down and glanced at Gray.

"Gray?" Isaac said, his voice breaking. "What's, um… what's up?"

Gray smiled sadly. "We have a lot to talk about. I wanted to talk to you before I let the others know."

Isaac felt a prickle of sweat under his jacket. "Gray… *what is it?*"

Gray sighed. "I'm sorry. I'm being unnecessarily cryptic. I just…" They cleared their throat. "It's very hard for me to think about it myself." They looked up at the sky, and Isaac saw tears glittering in their eyes. "Ah. You know I can't go south with you."

Isaac's breath rushed out of him. "I… I know. Because of…" He glanced at Gray's chest.

"Not just because of that. Isaac…" Gray exhaled sharply in something that resembled a bitter laugh. "I'm fifty-three years old. I've been in this fight for… oh. Almost twenty years." They chuckled weakly. "I've been trying to outrun time all those years. Trying to outrun injuries and sickness. And death. Gavin very nearly killed me last year. If I was a few years older, he might have."

"No way," Isaac said brokenly, holding back tears. "Finn woulda patched you up. You would've been just fine."

Gray smiled. "I'm sure they would appreciate hearing that. And it's not that I don't have faith in them. Honestly, quite a few of us would be dead if it wasn't for them. But the fact is…" They ran their hand through their short, graying hair. "I'm slowing down. I can hardly keep up with the rest of you most of the time. I'm pretty sure I have arthritis in my knees. And… I have a feeling my breathing is going to be harder for the rest of my life. The doctors had to take a piece of my lung. That'll never fix itself. That'll never grow back. My place isn't on the front lines anymore."

"But you lead us," Isaac said, his voice small. "You make the decisions. You know the most about strategy. You know the syndicates inside and out. Gray, you… your decisions have kept us safe for as long as I've known you."

Gray bit their lip and walked in silence for a while. After several minutes they said, "I question so many decisions I've made."

"We all do that." Isaac swallowed the lump rising in his throat. His chest felt tight. His eyes burned. "Gray, p-please…"

293

Gray stopped and looked at Isaac square on. "Isaac... I'm sorry. It's not that I'm a liability to the team if I can't keep up. But I'd put myself in danger. I'd put *you* at risk. My body can't keep doing this forever."

A shuddering sob rolled over Isaac. Tears spilled over his cheeks. "Gray, no... *fuck*... G-Gray, please, I..." Isaac tried to swallow around the burning lump in his throat. "Gray, please don't... *leave*..." He covered his mouth with his hands.

"Oh," Gray whispered. They pulled Isaac into their arms.

Isaac unraveled in Gray's embrace, great, heaving sobs crashing through him. He clutched at Gray, digging his fingers into their back, latching onto their shirt. Gray swayed slowly as Isaac wept into their shoulder.

"It's okay," Gray murmured. "You're alright, Isaac."

"But I'm gonna miss you so *much*," Isaac sobbed.

"I know. I'm still gonna be around. I'll be up north, and you can still stay with me and recoup between missions."

"But it won't be the same. You... you won't be..."

Gray smoothed their fingers through Isaac's hair and laughed softly. "Now Isaac, don't say I won't be part of the family or my feelings will be hurt."

"*No,*" Isaac wailed. "No, you, you will be, you always will, you'll be in the family, but you won't be, be *here*. Gray, please, I've lost so many people, *please,* I can't lose you too."

"You're not losing me, Isaac," Gray soothed. "I'm not leaving you. Okay?" Gray took Isaac's chin in their hand and looked earnestly into Isaac's eyes. *"I'm not leaving you."*

Isaac shook his head against Gray's hand. "Gray, no, please no, don't do this."

"Isaac," Gray murmured, pitching their voice low. "Listen to me. Breathe in."

Isaac obeyed. He took in a deep breath, his gaze fixed on Gray's face.

"Good. Let it out."

Isaac let the breath go, trembling as it went.

"Okay. Now listen to me. *I am not leaving you.*"

Isaac bit his lip and nodded. "I'm s-sorry, I—"

"I know you have a lot of, ah, history around being abandoned, Isaac. Especially for… for people telling you that you're less than they demanded."

"But if I hadn't… If I killed Gavin, if I'd kept you *safe,* you wouldn't've been shot. You'd still be healthy. I c-can't stop, stop fucking *blaming myself…*"

"…and it feels like I'm leaving you for failing me."

Isaac looked at the ground. Gray ducked into Isaac's sight again. "Right?" Isaac sniffed and nodded.

Gray's hands rested on Isaac's shoulders. "Let's get a few things straight here. First, I am not leaving you. I'm retiring from the team because of my health, and so that you all can have somewhere safe to rest when you come north. With someone who knows you and understands. Okay?" Isaac nodded. "Okay. Second, you did not *fail me.* If anything, I've failed *you.* I failed to protect Sam, and I failed to prevent Gavin from taking you. The plan I helped make and was responsible for executing nearly got *all* of us killed. We only escaped because of you and Vera. And all that time, I…" Their hands tightened on Isaac's shoulders. "I had no idea you were still hurting this much."

Isaac stared at the ground. "I didn't want anyone to know."

Gray sighed. "Yes, I know. It was my responsibility to teach you that you can lean on people. I should have seen how deep your wounds go and helped you with them."

"That's not your job," Isaac mumbled.

Gray laughed. "No, but it is my calling. I used to be a counselor, remember?"

Isaac smiled slightly. "Yeah. I remember. But the rest… that wasn't your responsibility. *I* made the decision to go to Gavin. And I'm the one who left Sam vulnerable. You're the one who brought us to Tori, who had that connection that started this entire operation. You're the one who's been finding the rescues we saved last year. And more than that. You've gotten the family through the past seven years. You've done… *so much,* Gray. No one could ever replace you."

Gray's mouth twisted into a wry smile. "That's interesting. Because I was hoping you'd be the one to replace me."

Isaac's mouth dropped open.

Gray's smile grew wider. "What? What makes you less qualified than anyone else?"

"Um… because I'm a fucking mess?" Isaac scrubbed his face on his t-shirt.

Gray snorted. "We all are. Including me."

"No, you're… you're fine! But… Gavin still puts me on edge, I have flashbacks all the time, I can't go a fucking *week* without crying over something that happened fifteen years ago—"

"All of which you are *healing from.* And something tells me you'll be able to take care of Gavin, too."

"I can't control Gavin. I have *no fucking clue* how we're going to handle him once we go south."

Gray tilted their head. "He trusts you now."

Isaac scoffed. "He *trusts me?*"

"Yes." Gray cocked an eyebrow at Isaac. Isaac's expression softened.

Gray smiled ruefully. "You threw yourself in front of a loaded gun for him yesterday. You saved his life. Before this, he respected you. Now… now, he'll follow you."

"No way." Isaac shook his head. "No way. There's no way I ask him to fight with us against his *mother.*"

"I think you'd be surprised what he would be willing to do for someone who cares about whether he lives or dies. Makes him feel safe. Protects him. You do all of that for him, Isaac."

"That doesn't mean he'd fight his family for me. Family issues run deep. There's probably an entire iceberg of issues there that we don't know about."

Gray nodded. "All of which, I think, will just push him closer to your side."

"It's not something I'm willing to bet the family on," Isaac said darkly.

"That's fair." Gray tilted their head. "Unfortunately for us, we're stuck with him. Fortunately, he's proven very cooperative."

Isaac couldn't bring himself to make a snide remark about that. *I think he really does want to be a part of this family.*

Isaac raised his gaze to Gray's. "Why not Vera?"

Gray laughed. "I talked to her about it. She didn't want it."

"Neither do I!" Isaac cried.

Gray ruefully pressed their lips together. "I don't suppose I could ask you to share it?"

"Yes." Isaac nodded. "Yes. Please. I don't... I don't want this. I don't want the... the responsibility."

"You take responsibility for them every day," Gray said, laughing gently and shaking their head.

"This is... is different."

"Hm." Gray squeezed Isaac's shoulder. "Even so, I think you both could lead very well together. You already work so well as a team. Always have."

"Always will," Isaac said with a smile.

Gray nodded and smiled warmly. "I'm glad to know they'll be taken care of. This family is everything to me. I can't think of a better two people to take care of them."

Isaac blushed and looked at the ground. The praise made him feel shivery and warm. "I'll keep them safe."

Gray clicked their tongue. "No one can promise that. But I know you'll do your best, and your best has always, always been enough, Isaac."

Isaac's eyes welled with tears again. Gray turned the corner and kept walking. Isaac walked silently beside them for a long time before they turned back to walk to the house.

Chapter 43

Isaac rubbed the back of his neck as he left Gray in the living room, and made his way down the hall to his room. His mind was still reeling from his talk with Gray. He'd known it was coming; the doctor told Gray months ago that they would have to retire from the life they'd been living. Isaac had known it was coming. He'd *known*.

Gray was... family. They were the closest thing to a true, loving parent Isaac had since his father died. They were the core of the team, the first one to fight the syndicates. They'd picked up the others, one by one, over the years: first Ellis, then Vera, then himself, then Finn, then Sam. And Tori and Edrissa, now too. The family *was* Gray. And now they were leaving.

Isaac's chest ached with an ancient wound. *They're leaving me.* He pressed his hand to his chest. *They're leaving me because I failed.* He blew out a slow breath and shook his head. *They're not leaving me. They're keeping themself safe. And they'll always be there for me. They just won't be on the road.* He gritted his teeth and walked down the dark hall.

"Isaac..."

He paused as he passed Gavin's room. Isaac hadn't seen Gavin all day, now that he thought about it. He peered through Gavin's doorway. Gavin sat on the bed, his spine bent, his hands squeezed together in front of him so hard his knuckles were white.

"Whoa..." Isaac stood in the doorway, his eyebrows pulled together, his arms crossed over his chest.

"Um..." Gavin's eyes were wide as he looked up at Isaac. "I..."

Isaac took a slow step into the room, letting his hands fall open to the side. "Jesus, Gavin. Are you okay?" Isaac bit his lip as he searched Gavin's face. "Nightmares again?"

"What? Oh. N-no." Gavin shook his head, glancing at the floor.

"Okay..." Isaac leaned back against the wall. "Then what?" He pitched his voice lower. "Look, after yesterday I would understand—"

"It's not that," Gavin said quickly. "It's, um, it's not that."

Isaac tilted his head. "What is it? Gavin, I…" Isaac wet his lips. "I don't know how to help you if you won't talk to me."

"Okay." Gavin nodded and swallowed hard. He stood slowly from the bed, wrapping his arms around himself. He looked so fucking *small.*

"Gavin…" Isaac took a small step forward and hesitated. He took a step back. "This is really weird, but you can… um… you can talk to me? I know it's not…" Isaac shrugged, frustrated. He didn't know what he was saying. "I don't know…"

"I ha-have something I need to tell you," Gavin said quietly, shaking like a leaf.

Terror shot through Isaac's mind. *"I've been watching you for my mother all this time." "I've betrayed you." "I've sold you out." "I'm not who you thought I was turning into."* His hands shook before his eyes focused again and he saw Gavin standing in front of him. Looking up at him with something in his eyes that Isaac had seen flashes of before, but never like this. Gavin was staring at Isaac with something that looked like…

Isaac wasn't sure what it looked like, but it made his throat go hot and tight. "Okay," Isaac said quietly.

"Um…" Gavin took another step closer. He was halfway across the room now. "I…"

Isaac leaned forward. Gavin's voice was too low to hear. "Gavin, you're, um… you're scaring me."

"I'm sorry," Gavin whispered miserably. Another step closer. "Um…"

Isaac's shivered. He pressed himself back against the wall, his chest fluttering with something uncomfortable and raw. But Gavin wasn't torturing him any longer. He was standing in front of Isaac with an almost painful vulnerability. Gavin slowly raised his gaze to Isaac's, anguish twisting his features.

"Gavin, please… just talk to me."

"I…" Gavin glanced at Isaac's mouth. He closed the distance between them and pressed a kiss to Isaac's lips.

Isaac's mind went completely blank. Gavin's lips were warm, and a fire burned through Isaac, starting where Gavin's mouth was on him and sweeping everywhere else. He made a low moan in the back of his throat. His knees suddenly weren't up to the task of holding him upright. He hadn't been touched like this, hadn't been *kissed,* in over a year. Isaac had been too terrified to be with anyone. He'd been too busy unraveling, or healing, or protecting, or running missions to even have time to *think* about this. He hadn't wanted to open himself up to another person's hands, another person's lips, another person's body when he was so damaged. *Who could want me when I'm like this?*

Gavin's breath shivered on Isaac's lips as Gavin opened his mouth to Isaac's, placing his hands gently on either side of Isaac's face. He pressed Isaac back against the wall. Isaac was lost; lost in the touch, lost in the warmth of another person against him, lost in another person *wanting* him. He hadn't realized how much he missed being touched, being *wanted,* until this moment.

This wasn't just any person, though.

This was *Gavin.*

Isaac's stomach dropped, and a wave of horror hit him like a thunderclap.

He pulled his fist back and smashed it against Gavin's jaw with a *crack.*

Gavin's head snapped to the side and he crumpled to the floor. He stumbled back to his feet, nearly falling over again, staggering away from Isaac. He put his hand to his cheek, already red from the blow. He put his other hand out in front of him as if to ward Isaac off or pull him closer. Gavin's eyes filled with tears.

Isaac stood half-slumped against the wall, trembling and breathing hard, his hand pressed to his lips. He felt the ghost of Gavin's mouth still on him. Isaac steadied himself on the wall. He felt hollow, shattered, like everything he knew had been knocked out of him.

"Did you...?" Isaac rasped. "Did you... the whole time...?"

"No," Gavin sobbed, his eyes desperate. Apologetic. Agonized. "No. I had no idea. I'm sorry, I'm so *sorry...*"

"How... *what?*"

"I'm sorry," Gavin whispered. "I swear I didn't know."

"When...?"

"Um…" Gavin's throat bobbed as he swallowed. "In the past few… um… months…"

Isaac's eyes went wide. "You… felt about *me*…?"

Gavin whimpered. "When I… h-had you… I knew you were, um, good, I knew you were strong and I wanted to b-be a part of that…"

Isaac could hear his pulse in his ears, could feel his heart hammering in his chest. "You… you *tortured me* and you felt—"

"No," Gavin whispered. He cleared his throat. "No. I f-felt… *something*, I just didn't—"

Isaac's head spun. "And now you feel…?"

"I…" Gavin's hands dropped, and he wrapped his arms around his chest. "I… I'm so *sorry*…"

"What do you feel?" The words left Isaac's throat in a sort of strangled gasp.

"I…" Gavin buried his face in his hands. "I… f-feel… for you. I… I didn't want to. I didn't think I would… I swear to god, I didn't come find you because I wanted to—" Gavin heaved a trembling sob and stared at Isaac. "I just… I couldn't help it. The last three months, being with you… seeing how you, um, how you are with your family… and… um…" The tears in Gavin's eyes spilled over and he swiped them away. "You… s-saved me, when I thought you were going to, um, let me die…"

Isaac gasped in a breath.

"Isaac…" Gavin took another step back. "I didn't want you to, to take me on the road without… knowing. I wanted to be, um… honest. But I understand if you don't want me to be on the road with you. I understand. I understand if you want to leave me here. Or… um…" He shivered. "…or kill me. Okay? I, um, I get it. I f-fucked up. I'm so sorry. I'm sorry I tortured Sam, I'm sorry I tortured you, I'm sorry I tortured all of you. Not just because it ruined, um, this. I'm sorry. I'm *so sorry*. I know I can never fix it but I just wanted you to know."

Isaac couldn't breathe. There was a question burrowing up through his chest, into his throat, clenching his jaw. *How could he…?*

"How could you want me, after what you've done?"

Gavin recoiled, the pain in his eyes tightening even more.

"Isaac," Gavin breathed. "How could I... *not?*"

Isaac could barely think past the roaring in his ears. "What do you mean?"

"Isaac, you..." Gavin's voice choked off with a whimper. "You're so good. You're so strong, Isaac, you're *so* fucking strong. I... I know you said I broke you, and I get it now. I understand why you say that. But... I watched you survive something that should have killed you. I watched you... kill and fight and *bleed* for your family. Over these past few months... I've watched you care for them. I've watched you... um..." Gavin's gaze dropped to the floor. "I've watched you *heal.*"

"From what *you did.*" Isaac gripped the doorframe, terrified he would fall if he let go.

"I know." Gavin looked like he was being torn apart by Isaac's words. "I'm not asking you to forgive me. I'm not asking if you want me, too. I just... I couldn't keep this hidden. I wanted you to know what you were bringing with you." Gavin ducked his head. "If you still want to bring me."

"You have valuable intel," Isaac said robotically. His tongue felt stuck to the roof of his mouth.

"I'll tell you anything you want to know." Gavin's voice was pleading.

"I..." Isaac felt the emptiness welling up inside him, the bone-deep desire to be touched, held, kissed, fucked. He was starving for it. Thirsting like a man in the desert. The quiet need he always held in his body had been dragged to the surface, and he was burning with it.

But with *Gavin?*

"I..." Isaac tried again. "Gavin, you don't... I w-want... but..."

"I know," Gavin said softly.

"You *hurt me,*" Isaac whispered.

Gavin swallowed hard. "I know I did."

"I... c-can't..."

Gavin's eyes slowly went wide, fixed on Isaac's face. "I'm not asking you to."

I can't... Isaac shuddered. He couldn't follow that path in his mind.

I can't take him with us now. Not now that I know this.

How would I explain that to the others?

302

How do I tell them Gavin Stormbeck is…?

Isaac's mouth went dry. "Do you love me?" he croaked.

Gavin went still, his hands tightening into fists. Bracing for something. He wet his lips. "Yes."

All of the air rushed out of Isaac's lungs. *"Fuck."*

"I'm sorry," Gavin whispered.

"W-we…" Isaac tried to swallow. "We need to be able to trust you. *I* need to be able to trust you. And now…"

"I know," Gavin whimpered.

Isaac leaned against the wall, his heart beating in his chest, his lungs burning, his hands shaking. "We need you."

Gavin's eyes went wide. "I'll help you. I'll give you all the information I have."

Isaac's lips trembled. "Would you help us fight your mother?"

"She wants me dead," Gavin said through his teeth. "You don't. I don't think."

"But she's your *mother*."

Gavin took a deep breath. Held it. Let it out. Tears shone in his eyes. Slowly, he said, "She never loved me. I know that now. I want a real family. I want *this*. I want *y*—" Gavin's mouth snapped closed.

Isaac could barely get the words out. "And what if you… what if you can never have me?"

A deep sadness settled in Gavin's face. "I'm not asking to have you. All I'm asking for is…" Gavin looked around the room, then shrugged. "I don't know what I'm asking for. I guess I just wanted you to know the truth. And I wanted you to know before you committed to taking me south."

Isaac nodded slowly, his head spinning. "Okay," he murmured. "Okay." He lurched towards the door, his hand still clutching the doorframe.

"Isaac."

Isaac froze in the doorway. He slowly raised his eyes to look at Gavin.

Gavin bit his lip. "P-please don't…"

"Please don't what?"

Gavin drew in a deep breath. "If y-you're still taking me on the road, please don't tell Vera."

Isaac didn't have it in him to laugh. "We're taking you on the road," he said quietly. "We can't afford not to." He turned and fled the room.

Chapter 44

Isaac stumbled back to his bedroom and slammed the door shut. He staggered on shaking legs to his bed and sank into it, his hand pressed against his lips. *Gavin* was in love with *him?* What did that even mean?

How was that *possible?*

Isaac thought back, memories stabbing into his brain like shards of glass. Trying to find times when Gavin showed his hand. Trying to remember Gavin betraying his feelings.

Isaac's eyes went wide as he found the threads, the hints.

"Oh my god. I got Isaac Moore." A grin. "It is so great to meet you."

"Isaac, I am not doing mouth to mouth on you. Breathe, or you're going to die here on this table."

"I'm better at this and, let's be honest, you look so much better like this than you would doing what I'm doing."

"Much as I love a self-sacrificing idiot all tied up…"

And then…

"Fuck you."

"Should you be so lucky…" Gavin leaned in. Isaac was on his knees, *without his shirt, dripping wet, fighting Gavin like he knew Gavin wanted.*

Oh my god. How could I not have known?

How could Gavin *not have known? How could he not have known his own feelings?*

Isaac buried his face in his hands. *Gavin's a fucking idiot.*

Isaac trembled and wrapped his arms around himself. *What am I supposed to do with him now? I can't take him on the road. I can't have him around me, knowing he's… in* love *with me.* He stared blankly at the wall. *It's a huge liability.*

Isaac pushed out a slow breath. *Was* it a liability? Was having Gavin Stormbeck, syndicate son, traitor to his family, broken and twisted from what Isaac and Vera did to him… Was having him in love with Isaac such a bad thing? Gray said Gavin would follow Isaac. That he *trusted* him. Was having Gavin tied to his side by more than just fear really such a bad thing? If Isaac could depend on Gavin's devotion, would that be such a bad thing?

Isaac shuddered. *No.* Using Gavin's feelings for him was… was *wrong,* strange as that was. Gavin was healing, just as much as he was. Maybe more. Using Gavin's feelings for him would be just like what Gavin's mother had done: dangling him out into danger, putting him at risk, and depending on his loyalty to go through with it. It would just be one more person Gavin cared about using him for their own gain. As much as Gavin had hurt the family, Isaac couldn't do that to him. Not when Gavin was trying. Not when he was, against all odds, becoming a *good* person.

Now there's a sentence I never thought I'd say.

He couldn't tell the family, either. Gavin's fear of Vera was funny, and a little pathetic, but he had a point. Vera might actually kill him for that. Ellis would be next in line for that honor. And he couldn't tell Sam… How would they feel? How would they feel knowing the man that broke them both, very nearly *killed* them both, and more than once, now had feelings for Isaac? Was now in *love* with Isaac? They'd be horrified.

Could he even tell Gray? Of all people, they understood Gavin the best, Isaac thought. Of all people, Gray would know what to do. *How am I going to get by without their advice once we leave?*

Isaac felt the weight of their absence crushing him already. With him and Vera sharing the responsibility for the team now, these kinds of decisions would fall to them both. Maybe Vera *deserved* to know. Maybe Vera should have this information so she could make decisions knowing as much as possible.

But she might actually kill him. Isaac couldn't take that risk. He couldn't risk losing the biggest asset they had in this fight.

How was he supposed to move forward from here? How was he supposed to *face* Gavin again, knowing what he knew now?

How was he supposed to face Gavin again, knowing that Gavin kissed him, and that for a moment, Isaac kissed him back?

Isaac groaned and folded forward until his forehead pressed against his knees. *I kissed him back.*

It was nothing. It had to be nothing. Isaac had gone so long without being touched like that, kissed, but he was physically close with the family sometimes, holding Sam, being held by Vera, hugging Tori and Gray… He had that sort of contact. It wasn't like he was completely alone. Sometimes at night he ached for something more, someone to hold him and need him, kiss him, fuck him, but that was… that was fine. That was normal. That was life on the road, and he was used to it. What did it matter that he sometimes felt he would combust with jealousy at what Vera had with Tori, or Finn had with Ellis? It wasn't that he wanted that from his family, he just wanted what they had… together. He'd lived his whole life like that. This wasn't new.

But the feeling he'd gotten from the kiss? The fire, the heat, the moment where Isaac *wanted* so badly it physically hurt? *That* was new. And Isaac had no idea what to do with that. He *wanted*. He just didn't want that from Gavin.

How could he? Gavin had tortured him, forced him to his knees, cut into him, laid open his back with the whip. Gavin had choked Isaac until he thought he would die, over and over. Gavin had beaten Isaac until he could barely stand. Gavin had tortured Isaac's family in front of him, one by one. Gavin had nearly killed Sam. He'd held a gun to their head and demanded Isaac hurt them. He'd beaten Tori, for the crime of daring to be their friend. He'd nearly – so very nearly – taken Vera again, taken her back to the man who tortured her and raped her and *broke* her so hard that she forgot the man who'd tried to save her. Gavin nearly took her back to that man, to be tortured and raped again, over and over and *over*, right alongside her girlfriend. He'd done all those things. That would never go away. There was no way to undo that.

And yet… Gavin was *trying*. As bizarre as it felt to think it, Isaac truly believed Gavin felt *remorse* for what he'd done. Gavin knew, now, that it was wrong.

If I'd had his parents, would I have turned out the same way?

Isaac shuddered. There was no use going down that path. He knew how broken he had become, just with the parents he'd had. Just with run-of-the-mill misery and loss. *Abuse.* His mind still stuttered over that word, like it didn't belong to him. *Others have been through so much worse. What right do I have to call what I've been through abuse?*

If Isaac Moore had been raised by Gavin Stormbeck's parents... he could have turned out exactly the same as Gavin. How could Isaac not feel for Gavin, at least on some level? How could he not at least *appreciate* the effort Gavin was making to make amends, and repent? How could he not at least admit Gavin might deserve some sort of redemption?

But if Gavin could be redeemed... what justice was there? If people like Gavin could be forgiven of their crimes, what was the point of being good at all? Was everyone capable of redemption? Was Joseph Stormbeck?

No.

Isaac wasn't sure where the line was in his mind, or why, but he *knew* Joseph Stormbeck didn't deserve redemption.

He also understood, deep down, that Gavin Stormbeck *did.*

Where did that leave him, then?

Again, Isaac was flooded, nearly *leveled*, with the feeling of Gavin's lips on his. Of Gavin pushing him against the wall, touching him, their bodies flush with each other. Gavin, having to tilt his head up just slightly to kiss Isaac.

"Do you love me?"

"Yes."

Isaac's eyes filled with tears. *Why is it I want someone to love me so badly that I can feel it like poison in my veins, and the person who chooses me is* him?

He *hated* his body for betraying him. He *hated* himself for imagining, for a moment, how it would feel to have Gavin's warmth against him. How it would feel to have Gavin in his bed, to have Gavin's hands run over the scars he made. To have Gavin see him, every inch of him, every bit of damage done, every mark that showed the world that Isaac was broken, had been used, tortured, and to *love him anyway.* Gavin had broken him, destroyed him. And Gavin *loved him anyway.* Gavin had seen Isaac at the lowest he'd ever been, begging, torn open, drowned, bleeding. And Gavin still wanted him.

Shut up shut up shut UP!

What if Gavin wanted Isaac's torture again? What if all Gavin wanted from Isaac was his brokenness? What if Gavin planned to break him again, offer Isaac up to his mother so they could hurt him *together?* What if all Gavin wanted from Isaac was his blood, his pain?

No. Isaac knew that, at least. Isaac knew Gavin didn't want that anymore. Gavin said he loved Isaac for his strength. For his goodness, his devotion. And Isaac wasn't sure why, but he believed him.

Where did that leave them? Isaac would never *return* Gavin's feelings. *Couldn't.* He'd done too much. Even after months in this house with him, Isaac still jumped when Gavin came around a corner too fast. He still had nightmares about the five days he'd spent in Gavin's basement. He still shook sometimes, still felt like the room didn't have enough air and he couldn't breathe. He still ached, some days. His back, his hand, his shoulder. Phantom pains. Real aches when storms rolled in, or when he slept wrong. Sometimes he felt like the pain would never end. How could he fuck someone who did that to him? How could he *love* someone like that?

But what if I...?

Isaac groaned and flopped back on his bed. *How fucking desperate am I? That I'm fantasizing about the one person in the world who's hurt me the most, just because he kissed me?*

He wasn't fantasizing about that person. He was fantasizing about the person Gavin had become.

Gavin pushing him harder against the wall, opening his mouth against Isaac's. Gavin, pulling Isaac to the bed. Gavin, falling to the bed with Isaac on top of him, smiling, holding Isaac close. Gavin, letting Isaac be in control for once. Gavin being soft with him, cradling his face, touching Isaac's scars, kissing each one. Being wrapped in Gavin's arms, feeling *safe,* with Gavin trailing his fingers in gentle lines over Isaac's back. Gavin *holding* him, pressing soft kisses against his jaw, against his neck, against his lips. And Isaac, taking Gavin, against the wall, in bed, Isaac twisting his fingers through Gavin's hair as Gavin sucked Isaac's cock, making Isaac tremble with pleasure instead of agony. Gavin, mouth open against Isaac's skin, panting.

Jesus Christ. What the fuck is wrong *with me?*

It was one kiss. It was one kiss, for the first time in so long Isaac couldn't remember the last time. It was one kiss, with the man Isaac thought he hated most in this world. *I'm vulnerable because I'm lonely. I'm vulnerable because I'm hurting, and scared, and confused. He made me vulnerable.*

He didn't make me anything. I returned the kiss...

Isaac curled up on his side, hate and disgust for himself rankling in his stomach. He wasn't strong. Not if his loneliness and fear was rearing its head this strongly. *How can I lead them south with Vera if I'm this weak? If I'm this stupid?*

How am I supposed to face Gavin now? How am I supposed to go forward, now that I know what I know?

How am I supposed to be around Gavin, now that he knows I returned the kiss?

Chapter 45

The car was perfectly silent. Tori's hands were locked around the wheel, the road muddy now that spring was fully here. The ground was thawing, the trees were budding, and every single person in the car had a face like a storm cloud.

"Maybe… he won't be as bad this time?" Sam offered tentatively.

"He will be," Tori said, and clenched her jaw.

"Hopefully, he—"

"At least we don't have to deal with him for much longer," Ellis said snidely as they looked out the window.

"Yeah, I'd rather deal with Colleen Stormbeck," Finn said with a tight smile. The joke fell flat. They fell silent.

"This should be a straightforward conversation," Tori said as she pulled into the town center. "Just 'what are the most recent syndicate movements, what more do we need to know before we leave—'"

"'—how would you like my boot up your ass…?'" Ellis supplied.

Tori's lips quirked into a smile. "That too," she said softly.

"Seriously, how does a piece of shit like that become mayor to, like… the most important town in the region?"

"Probably the same way the syndicates take over an entire country," Finn said as they stared out the window.

Tori opened her mouth to speak, then closed it again. "Yeah," she said after a long moment. "Maybe."

Tori pulled the car into the main square and up to the town hall. She parked. The four of them got out.

Sam drew close to her side. "You don't think he… *took over* this town, do you?" Sam murmured. Tori looked at them and they stared back at her with wide eyes. "Do you think he…"

"I don't know," Tori said, and pulled them into a one-armed hug. "But that doesn't matter right now. Until we leave for Fort Meyers, we've got to work with him. What matters right now is Colleen." Sam looked at the ground and nodded.

They climbed the steps of the hall. Tori reached the door first and pulled it open for the others. They all muttered their thanks as they stepped inside. The atrium of the town hall was cool, and their steps echoed around the room. Tori took the stairs to their right, and the others followed behind.

"I wish Isaac had come," Sam said quietly.

"I know," Tori said over her shoulder. "Me too. I wish all of them came. But we've got so much to do before we leave tomorrow, we've got to split up."

"Then… then I wish at least Edrissa had come," Sam said, a little quieter.

A small smile pulled at Tori's lips. "She's not coming with us," Tori said softly. "She can stay home if she wants."

"But she just stays in her *room,*" Sam said, a hint of sadness in their voice.

Oh, honey. We'll be back soon enough.

Tori led them all down the hall. The wood-paneled walls and the dark green carpet made the hall look darker than Tori thought it should. Sam walked beside her, and Finn and Ellis walked together behind them, hand in hand. Tori reached the door with the brass plate stamped with *Daniel Schiester, Mayor* on the door. She glanced back at the others and knocked three times.

"Come in," the deep, even voice behind the door said. Tori turned the knob and pushed the door open. The room was lit only by the sun through the open window, the walls and carpet the same wood and deep green from the hallway. Pictures hung from the walls, pictures of families, young couples, and the occasional person standing alone. Everyone in the pictures had haunted eyes and frightened smiles.

Tori's eyes widened. *Refugees. They're all refugees.*

Daniel Schiester sat behind his desk, typing slowly at an ancient computer. He glanced up momentarily from his work. Tori could swear she saw the briefest flash of a smirk pull at his lips before he looked back at the screen. He typed for another moment, then settled back in his chair. The dark brown leather was faded, almost worn away along the arms. He raised his eyes to the group and tilted his head.

"What can I do for you?" he said with a smile.

"We wanted to get the latest update of syndicate movements before we leave tomorrow," Tori said. She found it surprisingly difficult to keep her voice even.

"And this errand took all four of you?" Daniel said, and raised an eyebrow.

"We like to travel in packs," Ellis said, their voice dripping sarcasm.

Tori closed her eyes. *Probably shouldn't have brought Ellis on this one.*

"And it's better if we don't leave anyone alone," Sam said beside her. Daniel's gaze flicked to them.

Tori froze. She glanced at Sam out of the corner of her eye. They were staring at Daniel, holding his gaze, their hands tightened oh-so-slightly at their sides. Tori pressed her lips together and swallowed weakly.

Daniel's smile fell slightly. "As I told you yesterday," he said, his voice dropping, "I had nothing to do with the attack on your syndicate prisoner. It is truly regrettable. I'm so glad no one was killed."

"You probably should be," Ellis said sharply.

Tori turned to them with a huff. "Ellis," she said evenly, "Do you want to wait outside?"

"Not particularly," they said, grimacing at Daniel.

"If I'd known this was going to turn into a rehash of yesterday's conversation, I might not have answered the door," Daniel said, false good nature in his voice. "I have work to do, if that's the plan."

"I told you, we're here for information," Tori said exasperatedly. "I apologize."

Daniel magnanimously bowed his head. "Of course. What can I tell you?"

"You said several weeks ago the rebels in Beringer had managed to take a bridge the syndicates were using to move their people in and out. Is that still—"

"No. Fallen to the Sawyers and Manors both. They decided to work together to take back the bridge. Now they're at each other's throats again. Destroyed a marketplace in their skirmishes."

Tori's stomach dropped. "Oh," she said softly. "Okay. Um... The eastern sector? Is that still—"

"Still vastly uncontrolled," Daniel said with a grin. "The power vacuum left by one Gavin Stormbeck has yet to be filled."

Tori's eyes went wide. "What? That's not something you've mentioned before."

"My information was wrong before," Daniel said, his smile never wavering. "It was my understanding his bafflingly unintelligent cousin had been awarded that territory. It appears that the area is being... *held*... for someone."

"Sucks for them," Finn said sardonically.

Daniel huffed out a laugh. "Ah," he said. "You still believe your young Stormbeck has renounced his claim on half the region."

"He *has*," Sam said, and took a step forward.

Daniel smiled. "Be that as it may," he said evenly, "It does bring into question certain other things. Such as." He fixed Tori with his gaze. "What do you plan to do with your captive when you return south?"

"Is that any of your business?" Ellis snapped. Tori fought the urge to suppress an eyeroll. *Ellis, I love you, but... Jesus...*

Daniel's smile widened. His eyes remained flat and cold. "It is my business if he escapes your custody and reclaims the region. Having things so unstable there has proven incredibly helpful. We're receiving refugees by the dozens every week. We've heard of fewer disappearances, fewer raids... If Gavin Stormbeck returns to his post—"

"He won't," Tori said. "I don't want to discuss this again."

"You haven't answered my question," Daniel said softly. "What. Is. Your. Plan?"

Tori clenched her teeth. "We're taking him with us."

Daniel's ice blue eyes bored into hers. His expression didn't change, but his lips twitched down slightly. "I see."

"We don't think it would be safe for him to stay here without protection," Tori said.

"Hm." Daniel nodded sagely. "Yes. I'm sure there are enough vehemently anti-syndicate people up here that protecting that boy from the consequences of his actions could become a full-time job."

Tori locked her jaw shut against her retort.

"Probably. Protecting him has been a full-time pain in my ass," Ellis snapped.

Tori sighed. "Ellis," she said softly. "Please."

"What?" Ellis's eyebrows pulled together, looking wounded. Tori raised an eyebrow at them. Ellis rolled their eyes and heaved a sigh. "Fine. Waiting outside." They turned on their heel and walked out.

"Why do you hate him so much?" Sam murmured. Tori's gaze snapped to them. They stood staring at Daniel.

Daniel snorted. "Why don't you?" he said with a wide grin.

Sam pressed their lips into a thin line.

Daniel looked at Tori. "Did you have any other questions? I'm happy to hear your frustrations. Part of my job." He raised one hand to gesture vaguely about the room. "But if you had nothing else…"

Tori bit her lip. "Not unless you have anything else to tell me," she said.

Daniel shook his head. "Unfortunately, no. I wish I did. But…" He leaned forward. "What are your plans if the Stormbeck boy proves to be less… reformed… than you thought?"

Tori held his gaze. He was always so *calm,* always so perfectly in control. It scratched at the back of Tori's mind. She pushed it down and wet her lips.

"We're taking him with us," she said quietly. "And we'll keep him in our custody. If he tries to betray us…" Tori pushed out a slow breath. "We'll kill him then."

Daniel chuckled. "Seems that you could skip a step there, if you're so inclined."

Tori shook her head. "We…" She cleared her throat. "We're not killing the only syndicate member on the planet who doesn't want us dead," she rasped. "I… *have* to believe we can make him better."

Something in Daniel's eyes tightened. "I wish I had your kind of faith," he said with a smile that didn't warm his steely-cold eyes. "And I wish you good luck in your travels."

"Thank you, Daniel," Tori said. She *almost* wished he would insist she call him 'mayor', just to watch and thoroughly enjoy Ellis tearing him a new asshole. She turned to go. The others followed behind.

Once they were down the stairs and out of hearing range, Tori said, "I don't know why you like antagonizing him like that." She threw a glare at Ellis, softened just a little by a smile. "He wants Gavin dead. It's so obvious it hurts. I'd think you'd at least be in the same *camp* as this guy, if not on his team."

Ellis pursed their lips. "Yeah, usually," they said curtly. "He's got some good points. But fact is he just fucking annoys me."

Tori laughed softly and glanced at Ellis, a broad smile chasing away her glare. She dipped her head, conceding. "Fair enough." She walked across the atrium and out into the afternoon sun. "Personally, I think it would be hilarious to see you and him in a cage match."

"Only if I get to use a folding chair to rearrange his stupid goddamned face," Ellis replied with a laugh. Sam followed quietly behind.

Once they got to the car, Tori looked at Sam. Their eyes were downcast, their mouth twisted.

"Sam?" Tori said and ducked into their line of sight. "You okay?"

"Yeah," Sam said quietly with a shrug. "I don't know. He just…" They pulled the car door open. "There's just something about him I don't like."

"Like the fact that he's an asshole?" Ellis snorted.

"Um…" Sam chewed their lips. "I don't know. He's just…" They raised their eyes to meet Tori's.

"I think I know what you mean," Tori said, and started the car. "He's just…"

"…an asshole," Ellis finished helpfully.

Tori smiled at them in the rearview mirror. "I'm so glad you came on this trip," she said, laughing. "You've been most instructive."

Ellis grinned back. "Damn right I am. I'm a fucking delight." They leaned forward in the seat. "Do you mind swinging by that sweet shop on the way back? I refuse to go the next few days without a single goddamned piece of candy."

Tori pulled away from the town hall. "Sure," she said. "Let's bring some for the others, too."

"Gavin's favorite is the lemon drops," Sam murmured. They looked out the window as Tori made a turn. A smile pulled at Tori's lips.

Chapter 46

Isaac scrubbed his face with his hands as he looked down at the map of the eastern sector spread over the kitchen island. Gray and Vera stood on either side, their eyes scanning it as they planned their attack. Isaac felt like he was going cross-eyed from the hours he'd spent poring over the hundreds of miles of road between here and Colleen's headquarters in Fort Meyers, the seat of the Stormbecks' power. As long as Colleen lived, she posed the greatest threat to the family.

"I think if we take 87 south, we could bypass the checkpoints in Brookdale and make it to her house in... two days? If we hurry?" Vera's brow furrowed as she followed the highway with her finger. "It would take us through Porter, but—"

"Daniel's people say the Wilsons have moved people into Porter," Gray said quietly, pinching the bridge of their nose. "There's no way we could get through there undetected."

"Maybe we forget about being undetected," Vera said, irritated. "Who gives a shit if we take down a few syndicate members? We've never been shy about doing that."

Gray drew in a deep breath. "The only advantage we have, the *only* advantage, is the element of surprise. We have to assume she knows we've reached the north, if she tracked us all the way to the turnpike. Where else would we be headed?"

"Kind of weird she hasn't sent her *army* up to grab us," Isaac interjected. "It's not like she doesn't have the people."

Vera bit her nail as her eyes moved over the map. "She might assume we have Gavin, too, if we're assuming she thinks we've made it north." Vera shrugged. "She might not be willing to fight us if she thinks we'll kill Stormbeck Junior. She might not want us to kill him."

"She does."

Vera, Gray, and Isaac jumped and looked to the doorway of the kitchen, where Gavin leaned against the wall. He met Isaac's gaze for a split second before looking down again, blushing. Isaac's cheeks blazed.

"I already told you, she, um." Gavin took a step closer to the map. "She wants you to kill me. She has this whole time. I *told* you. That's why I left."

"Gavin…" Vera's voice was heavy with skepticism. "I don't—"

"She wants you to kill me," Gavin said with finality.

Vera bit her lip. "Gavin…"

"I want you to think about who I am for a second," Gavin said, meeting Vera's eyes. "Remember who I… who I *was*. What I did. Some of that I got from my father."

Vera winced.

Gavin drew in a slow breath. "I got some of that from my mother, too. My mother wants me dead for getting my father killed. My father always wanted what she wanted. They understood each other. But me…" Gavin laughed bitterly. "I put a toe out of line. I wasn't her *son* anymore." Gavin's mouth twisted as his eyes filled with tears. Isaac's heart clenched. "I didn't want to torture people anymore. I didn't want that life. And with my mother there is no life but the life she lives. Okay?"

Vera pressed her lips together and nodded.

"Tell us more, Gavin," Gray said softly. Isaac met their eyes. They were probing for information about Colleen, yes. But Gray also cared. Gray wanted Gavin to heal, too.

Gavin walked to the kitchen island and glanced at the map. He wrapped his arms around his chest. "Um…" He sniffed. "My mom thinks… She thinks we own the world because we… I don't know, we *deserve* it or something. All the syndicates, but especially ours. It's like…" He shrugged. "It's like… she thinks it's our divine right. Like we were *born* to rule, or something. I was part of a, um…" He flushed and ducked his head. "A *bloodline,* fit to rule. My mom said a lot of crazy shit like that growing up. And then… I turned my back on it. I decided I didn't want that. And that was, um… unacceptable. I'm either with her, or against her. Now I guess that means I'm the enemy." Gavin ducked his head lower.

"But you found a new side," Vera said softly. She gasped and snapped her mouth closed.

Gavin swallowed. "Um. Y-yeah. I did." Gavin raised his eyes to Isaac, his mouth curving up momentarily into a smile.

Isaac's stomach dropped and he cleared his throat. "Gavin... how willing would you be to help us with our plans?"

Gavin's gaze moved slowly over the map. "I don't know the most recent movements. But I—"

"We'll tell you," Gray interrupted.

Gavin nodded, biting his lip, not taking his eyes off the map. He leaned in and put his finger on a small town a half-day south of Crayton. "Here. Bartram Springs. It's a city w-we—" He swallowed and raised his eyes apologetically to Gray. "Is it okay if I, um... if I talk about Stormbeck holdings like they're... like they're not mine? I don't..." Again, his eyes flicked to Isaac, and back to Gray. He wet his lips. "I don't want to talk like my family is still the, um... the Stormbecks."

"Who else would your family be?" Vera asked, a hard edge to her voice, but her gaze was soft as she looked across the island at Gavin.

Gavin blanched and fell a step back from the group. *"Oh, fuck,"* he breathed.

Vera leaned over the island, her expression darkening. The fear in her tense shoulders and fists fell behind a wall of rage. Isaac glanced quickly between them, as Vera's lip curled into a predatory snarl, and Gavin fell back another step, wide-eyed and shaking, looking for all the world like *prey.*

"Whoa, Vera... *hang on* a sec," Isaac said quietly, holding his hands out to her, giving himself space to lunge between them if need be. "Vera, wait—"

"What is he so afraid that he just gave away?" she hissed.

"Vera, *please,*" Gavin whimpered.

"I know for a fact that it's not whatever you're thinking of," Isaac said, his voice taking on a harder edge. "Vera, I need you to just listen for *five seconds* before you decide to kill him, okay?"

Vera's jaw clenched, but she tore her gaze away from Gavin to look at Isaac. "Explain to me why he looks like that."

320

"I knew you'd kill me," Gavin whispered.

"Gavin, shut *up*," Isaac ground out between his teeth.

"Isaac, what's going on?" Gray said gently. They reached a hand out to Vera and froze a few inches from her, like touching her would burn them.

"Um…" Isaac looked at Gavin where he stood cowering in the middle of the kitchen, with his eyes fixed on Vera like she would leap across the island and murder him right then and there. "He…" Isaac swallowed hard. *Might as well just get it out now and worry about the shitstorm later.* "Gavin wants to be part of *our* family."

Vera froze, her eyes darting between Gavin and Isaac. *"What?"* she breathed.

"I'm sorry," Gavin whimpered.

"For fuck's sake, Gavin, shut *up*," Isaac snapped.

"No, let him talk," Vera said, glaring at Gavin. "I wanna know why he reacted to spilling that like he'd just accidently mentioned he was planning on selling us out when we get south."

"No," Gavin gasped. "I wouldn't—" He trembled and stumbled another step back. His eyes darted between Isaac and Vera. "I'm s-sorry, Vera, I…" He flushed red and collapsed into himself, staring miserably at the floor. "I didn't want to tell you b-because… I…" He swallowed hard. "I'm *sorry*."

"Gavin," Gray said gently. "When Isaac says you want to be part of our family, what does that mean?"

"Um…" Gavin lifted his gaze to Gray, looking like a man clinging to a life raft in the middle of a stormy ocean. "I, um…" He squeezed his eyes shut and took a deep breath. "I, uh, didn't really know until… uh… yesterday… when the men…" Gavin shuddered and opened his eyes. "But spending all this time with you, you've all been so k-kind, and good, and, um…" He raised his gaze to Gray. "I want in. I want that. I want the, uh… the *love* you have. I've never seen that before. I didn't know people could… um… love each other like that. How you protect each other…" Tears stood in Gavin's eyes. "I want to feel that, too. There's something in me that's missing, and…" He looked to Vera. "I w-want something like what you have with Tori, or…" He gestured to Isaac and Vera both. "…what you have with each other, or, Isaac, what you have with Sam…" He turned to Gray, tears running down his cheeks. "I want

321

what you've given me. I want to be, um, safe. I want to be protected. And I want to protect you. I'll tell you everything I know about the syndicates. I'll do everything I can to get you through this."

Vera stared at Gavin, open-mouthed.

Gavin's gaze returned to Vera. "I'm learning. Please, I don't know… how to do this, exactly, but I want to be in your family. Please. Just… tell me how to do it. Please don't kill me. I… I'm *sorry*." He bit his lip, his throat bobbing as tears rolled down his cheeks.

Isaac's hands shook slightly. "Vera… I know it sounds fucking weird but—"

"Why didn't you say anything before?" Vera murmured, her eyes fixed on Gavin.

"Um…" Gavin looked helplessly at the others. "I th-thought you'd kill me for it. I wasn't trying to, to *keep* it from you, I swear…"

"Gavin," Vera said softly. "I'm not… why would I *kill you* for this?"

"Um…" Gavin's voice trailed off in the barest hint of a whimper.

Vera blushed and leaned back from the island. "Okay. No, that's fair actually. Um." She smoothed her hands through her hair, looking at Gray and Isaac in turn. "What do you… what do you think about this?"

"Um…" Isaac swallowed. "I think it's, um, fine." For a moment, Isaac felt the ghost of Gavin's lips on his. His cheeks burned and he stared at the map in front of him.

"Gray?" Vera said.

Isaac glanced up at them. They stared at Gavin with a slight, almost fond smile, their eyes blazing with something akin to triumph. "I think it's great," Gray said quietly.

Gavin bit his lip and stared tremulously at Vera. Her jaw worked as her gaze moved over the map, unfocused. Finally, she raised her eyes to look at Gavin. Her body no longer trembled with tension. Her shoulders relaxed and she held Gavin's gaze with sadness that made Isaac's bones ache.

"Gavin," Vera said, her tone even, "This is more than a family. We put ourselves in situations we might not walk away from, where we *have* to depend on the other person to keep us safe or pull us out. If you want in with us, *really* in, you have to know that that's what it'll be like. That's what we give each

322

other. If you want that from us, we *have* to know we can have that from you, too."

"I swear," Gavin whispered. "I… You've already risked so much for me. And after I—" Gavin sucked in a breath. "You risked yourselves coming north with me. And Isaac, you—" Gavin and Isaac both blushed, their eyes flicking to the floor in tandem. Isaac glanced at Gray, who watched them both intently. "Isaac, you had a fucking *gun* pointed at you yesterday, for me. When you could have l-let me die." Gavin swallowed hard. "I don't want to die. But I want to… to be in this family. I'd rather risk my life with you than have my own mother risk it. I'm sorry I kept this from you, Vera."

Vera's expression softened further. "I understand why you did."

Gavin shook his head and stared at the floor. "I know the others won't like it. I know that Tori—"

"Tori will come around," Vera said gently.

Gavin's head snapped up. "What?"

Vera smiled. "Tori will come around. Trust me."

"But—"

"She's been dealing with fucked-up people for a long time. She knows nobody is innocent. She's housed people before who've done terrible things to escape the syndicates."

"What I did was different," Gavin murmured.

"You're right. It was." Vera shrugged. "It was torture. It was evil. But—"

Gavin flinched. Vera looked up at him, pinned him down with her gaze. "But I know you've changed. I can see it. So, if you're serious… then yeah. We can do that."

Gavin's eyes went wide. "What… really?"

Vera glanced at Gray, as if for confirmation. Gray's gaze pierced Vera, then Isaac. "It's your decision," they said quietly. "It's your team now."

Isaac swallowed hard and met Vera's eyes. Isaac could read the look on her face, could read her better than anyone else in the world, except maybe Tori. *If he means it… if he really means that he wants to be in our family, to risk his life right alongside us…*

I trust him.

Vera's mouth hardened into a line, and he knew he was doing the same. They held each other's gaze for another moment. They both nodded.

"Okay," Vera said softly. "You're in the family."

Gavin let out a gusty breath and crumpled forward, his eyes swimming with tears. "Thank you," he huffed.

"We'll tell the others tonight. And we'll leave tomorrow." Vera straightened and turned her gaze back to the map. "Until then, we have to plan our trip south. You know your mo—" Vera pressed her lips together. "You know Colleen Stormbeck is our next target, right?"

Gavin nodded gravely. "Yeah," he whispered.

Vera sought out Gavin's gaze and held it. "If we don't have to kill her to do what we have to, we won't. We just want to cripple her operations. But you have to understand the threat she poses to the family. So, if she tries to carry out her threat, she dies. Do you understand that?"

Gavin's jaw worked and he tore his eyes away from Vera's gaze. "I understand," he said softly.

Vera drew in a deep breath. "Are you okay with that?"

Gavin bit his lip, his eyes falling closed. "I know she's my mom," he said, pronouncing each word carefully. "I know she's my f-family. But…" His eyes opened and fixed on Gray. "I'm remembering things. Things she used to say, things she used to do… I know she never loved me, okay? She only ever acted like it when I was being like my father. Like *her*. She didn't even know I never raped my playthings."

Vera flinched. Gavin looked at her, an apology heavy in his eyes.

"I'm sorry," he murmured. "But… they never knew I wasn't like them. If they did…" Gavin shuddered. "If we'd managed to get you and Tori back to the house, and I refused to rape you…" He nodded slowly. "I think my father would have killed me then."

Vera's mouth opened, then closed again. She closed her eyes and blew out a slow breath through her nose. When she spoke, her voice shook. "I know he would have."

"Okay." Gavin took a step closer to the map. "I want to help you. I'll tell you everything I know. Like I said, I don't know the most current movements. All my information is at least nine months old. But—"

"Anything you tell us will be helpful," Gray said, and placed a hand gently on Gavin's shoulder.

Isaac watched as Gavin relaxed into the touch, his eyes closing in a slow blink before he focused on the map again, studiously keeping his eyes away from Isaac.

I wonder if he'd ever been touched like that before he came to us. I wonder if he only ever touched people when he was hurting them.

Isaac's stomach bucked as he watched Gavin's eyes move over the map.

I wonder if we could teach him all the ways he can be loved.

Gavin drew his finger down a county road that cut through the far west of Stormbeck territory. "Once we get to Bartram Springs, we can take this road down. This line," Gavin said, his voice deeper, stronger, "Is right on the border of the Stormbeck and Anderson territories. We—" He cleared his throat. "The Stormbecks patrol this area sometimes, and so do the Andersons, but most of the time they stay away from each other. There isn't much in the area worth negotiating for. That's your best bet to get you here." He pointed to a city northwest of Colleen's headquarters. "Richfield. I know it's contested, but the Stormbecks will be too busy focusing on the dissenters to look for us."

Isaac and Vera shared a look.

"From Richfield, we can take the 25 to Broadmoore, as long as they haven't ID'ed the car. And from Broadmoore we can make it to Fort Meyers." His finger lingered on the dot marking the location of the town. "Where my mom lives," he murmured.

Isaac's heart pounded. *We've never had this much information before. This could change everything.*

"Thank you, Gavin," Gray said softly.

Gavin nodded stiffly. "Once C-Colleen's operations are crippled, the entire western sector will fall. They won't be able to rebuild. Everything goes through her along this route."

"This has been... more than helpful." Gray looked at Isaac and Vera.

Isaac nodded, stunned. "Th-thank you, Gavin," he murmured.

Gavin shyly raised his eyes to Isaac's, and Isaac held his gaze.

I trust him.

Chapter 47

The family gathered around the island, looking down at the map, now marked with their path south. Finn and Ellis stood together, their arms around each other's waists. Tori leaned gently against Vera, their hips touching. Sam stood beside Isaac, dwarfed by both his height and Gray's, on their other side. Edrissa stood slightly behind Gray, her eyes constantly moving between the others and Gavin. The pen Gavin used to mark the route was still held tight in his fist as he carefully looked at the others, some of them looking interested, some of them looking excited, some of them looking skeptical.

"You're sure this is the way to go?" Ellis said, doubt darkening their tone.

"Everything Gavin said checks out with what we've learned from Daniel Shit-ster," Vera said, her gaze moving over the map before she met Ellis's eyes. "This is a good route. It's a good plan."

Ellis's jaw worked, and their eyes flicked to Gavin. "You're absolutely sure this is the safest way?"

Gavin bit his lip. "I'm not *sure*," he said weakly. "I haven't been involved in Stormbeck operations since—" He glanced at Isaac, guilt curdling in his stomach. *I'll always mark my life like that. Life before Isaac, and life after.* He cleared his throat. "Um. After my head injury I never stepped back into my role in the eastern sector. I w-went…" He flushed red. "I went after you, and that obviously that didn't work out. So, all the information I have is from before I met you. From what I have, what I remember, this is the best way."

Ellis's mouth twisted. "Okay. What if it's not? We're planning for contingencies, right?"

"Of course we are," Vera said, a little annoyed. "It'll be tricky, though. Just because we have a syndicate son with us doesn't mean we have a free pass like we did with the bounty hunters. By now, Colleen will be after Gavin, too."

"We've talked to the contacts along the way," Isaac said. "They're making preparations. Getting cars ready in case ours gets ID'ed. Setting aside rations and bedding. We have no idea what we're going to deal with, here. We need all the help we can get."

"And everyone you've talked to is okay with that?" Tori said softly. "It's quite the risk, taking seven people."

"Seven?" Finn's eyebrows pulled together in confusion.

"I decided to come," Tori said, ducking her head. Vera pressed a kiss into her hair.

"When did that happen?" Ellis murmured.

"Um. Recently. I wasn't totally sure before today." Tori swallowed hard. "I know I planned on opening a safehouse up here. But I want to be a part of this mission. Colleen Stormbeck is responsible for so much suffering down south. I want to help solve the problem, then come back and open the safehouse."

Ellis glanced at Gavin. "Um… Gavin…"

"I'm on board with the plan, too." Gavin wouldn't meet anyone's eyes.

"There have been a lot of developments in the past two days," Gray said gently. "Since our timetable has been pushed up so quickly, we haven't had time to get everyone on the same page. You're leaving tomorrow. This is more than a conversation about your route south. This is a conversation about the makeup of the team."

"Okay…" Ellis said carefully. "What does that mean?"

"For starters, I won't be coming with you," Gray said, their voice breaking.

Gavin looked down at the floor.

"We knew that already," Finn said softly.

"I know. But…" When Gavin looked up, Gray had tears in their eyes. "It's been hard for me to accept. You're leaving tomorrow. This is the first time that has felt… *real* to me."

Tori drew close to Gray and wrapped her arm around their waist, tears shining on her cheeks. Gavin looked at Gray's chest, guilt crushing his own chest like he'd been shot again.

"With me staying here, Isaac and Vera will be leading the team together."

Sam grinned at Isaac, and he looked down at them with a tentative smile.

Ellis looked from Isaac to Vera. "Um… yeah. We kinda assumed."

Gray huffed out a laugh and wiped their face on their sleeve. "Well. Then I guess most of this meeting is redundant."

"S-so…" Finn swallowed hard and glanced at Gavin. "So, the plan is still to go after Colleen? And to… um…" They looked miserably at Isaac. "…neutralize her?"

"Yeah," Gavin murmured. "The plan is to go south and kill my mom."

"I just…" Finn licked their lips. "I just want to… *clarify*… that you're okay with us killing your family…"

"She's not my family anymore," Gavin said through clenched teeth, his eyes shining with tears.

"Oh," Sam said softly.

"Um, yeah, she is," Ellis said, staring Gavin down. "She's—"

"She's not my family anymore," Gavin said, his head snapping up, his eyes meeting Ellis's. "She's not. She wants me dead. She *never fucking loved me,* okay? She… she *used* me. She taught me to be like her, she and my dad. They used me to torture our dissenters. She was going to use me to capture you. She—" He forced down a sob. "I could have been someone different. I could have… started a different way. I could have had a different life. I know I'm responsible for what I did. I know that was my choice and I can never undo it. But she and my father *used me.* She's *not* my family anymore. And if she has to die for people to stop being tortured and killed by my family, that's…" His voice broke, his hands squeezed into a fist. The pen pressed into his palm. "That's something I can do. Something I can live with."

The distrust in Ellis's eyes faded as they stared at Gavin. They swallowed and looked to the others. "Um…" They shot an apologetic look at Gavin, and Gavin's head spun. *Even Ellis. Even Ellis can accept me, at least a little bit.*

"Um…" Isaac cleared his throat and looked at Ellis and Finn. "We're Gavin's family now."

328

Sam and Tori gasped. Edrissa's eyes went wide.

"Oh, for fuck's—" Ellis huffed out an incredulous breath and stepped back from the table. "Are you... *fucking*..."

Gavin could barely look at Finn, but he forced himself to. Finn tore their eyes from Ellis and met his gaze, their lips pressed together. They nodded slightly. Gavin's throat bobbed as he forced down his tears.

"Ellis," Isaac said gently, "He's been more than helpful. We probably wouldn't even make it to Fort Meyers without him. He's the one person who could make this happen. And he's... Ellis, come on, you have to see he's—"

"He's *what*?" Ellis snapped. "*Changed?* Are you fucking *nuts?* Letting him stay with us is one thing, letting him eat our food and put us at risk of being murdered by these fucking northerners is one thing, but... the *family?* Are you *insane?*"

"No," Isaac said, his voice dropping, ringing with authority. "But I am in charge of this decision. You don't have to love him like family. I'm not going to tell you that you have to *trust* him like family. But he has the protection of the family now. He's as much ours as anyone else in this kitchen."

"Vera—" Ellis looked helplessly at her. "Do you...? I mean..."

Darkness settled over Vera's face. "Ellis... do *not* try to play Isaac and I off each other. We came to this agreement together, or it wouldn't have happened. Gavin's in the family because he's helping us and because he's *different*. He's healing. We've all done terrible shit while we're healing." Vera raised an eyebrow, and Ellis quailed, biting their lip as pained guilt moved across their face.

What the hell is that all about?

Ellis looked at Finn, who wrapped their arm around Ellis's waist and pressed a kiss to the side of their head. Ellis squeezed their eyes shut, taking a slow breath in and out.

"Ellis," Isaac murmured. "I know—" He cut off with a choke. "I know it's hard. I know it fucking *hurts.*"

Gavin's gaze snapped to Isaac. *Accepting me hurts him?* He blinked back sudden tears.

"But I know he's different. Okay? I *know* he is. I wouldn't place my trust in *anyone* who was a risk to my family, and neither would Vera. Neither would Gray."

Ellis looked at Gray. "Gray, are you... are you on board with this?"

Gray leveled their gaze at Ellis. "Ellis—"

"I'm not questioning their authority," Ellis said in a rush. "I'm not. I'm just... please help me understand, I don't *get it.*"

Gavin fell back a step as Ellis's eyes filled with tears. Finn wrapped their arms tightly around them, pressing their face into Ellis's hair.

Before Gray could say anything, Sam stepped away from the island, carefully making their way around it until they stood in front of Gavin. Old shame burned in Gavin's chest. He had taken Sam, tortured them, broken them. Sam, who still chose to be kind after everything Gavin had done to them. Gavin had taken them, and ended in Isaac being broken, Gray being shot, Tori being beaten, everyone being so goddamned *hurt.* Because of *him,* because *he'd* gotten a taste for hurting people and he'd never pulled his head out of his ass long enough to figure out that that was a bad thing. His throat closed around the knot forming there, and he forced himself to meet Sam's eyes.

He wet his lips. "Sam... I'm so—"

"Do you want forgiveness?" Sam asked softly.

Gavin's stomach dropped. It took him a moment to speak. "I don't deserve it," he murmured. "I can't undo what I did. I regret it, every fucking day. I'm going to do everything I can to keep you safe."

Sam's mouth twisted. "In this family... what would your name be?"

Moore.

Dammit.

"Um..." Gavin cleared his throat. He looked at Gray, shivering as their gaze pierced into him. His mouth went dry and he swallowed hard. "Uriah."

Gray lurched forward, tears suddenly filling their eyes. *"Oh,"* they whispered.

"If that's okay," Gavin said quickly. "I'm sorry. I don't..." His hands trembled. *Why am I still holding this fucking pen?* "If you don't want me to that's... I'm sorry. I didn't mean—"

"It's fine," Gray rasped. They pressed their lips together. "Gavin Uriah." Their gaze turned to Ellis, who was crying quietly in Finn's arms. "Gavin is in the family," they said, speaking slowly, "Because he's healing from who he was. He's done terrible things, yes. He knows it. We all know it."

Gavin ducked his head. His mouth twisted.

"But he sees what he's done wrong. He's turned his back on who he was, at great personal cost." Gavin raised his head up, looking at Gray, then Ellis.

Ellis's forehead wrinkled. "What—"

"He lost everything, Ellis," Gray reminded them gently. "He lost his family, his home, his inheritance. Every person he's ever known is someone he can never see again."

"N-not everyone," Gavin muttered.

Gray's mouth closed slowly as they looked at Gavin. "Not everyone?"

"No," he said softly. "I have all of you."

Ellis pulled slightly out of Finn's grasp. "*Necessity* isn't—"

"Ellis," Gray said, soothingly. "I know this isn't easy. I know I can't just say, 'It'll all work out, you'll see!' because our lives depend on Gavin being who he says he is now. I know that. But fact is… we've depended on each other for a long time. We haven't always trusted each other. But we found a way to become a family and survive."

Ellis trembled. "That's fucking hard for me."

"We know it is," Vera said, looking at Ellis now with compassion. "It's hard for me, too."

Ellis turned their gaze to Vera, softening, for the first time, at the look on her face. "But you trust him," Ellis said softly, a question weaving through the words.

Gavin took a step back as Isaac and Vera both turned their gazes to him. He felt completely exposed. Vulnerable.

"Yes," they said together.

Ellis bit their lip, looking across the island from Vera and Isaac to Gavin. They squeezed Finn tighter. "Okay," they said finally. "I can try."

Gavin let out a breath and relaxed, just slightly.

"We're gonna kill you if you betray us, though," Ellis said.

Gavin rolled his eyes, unable to contain his frustration for a moment. "Yeah, I'm aware."

"Just making su—"

"I'd rather die than betray you anyway."

Gavin froze as the words left his mouth. He hadn't meant to say them. He hadn't meant to *think* them. They just came out of him, like the truth existed in the air around him and all he had to do was speak to make it real.

Everyone else froze too, all of them looking at him with varying degrees of surprise. He swallowed and looked at the floor.

"We don't ask that of anyone," Gray said softly.

Gavin looked at Isaac. *No, but it's been offered. His life, for Sam's. I don't know if I could do the same, but I'd rather die than see him hurt.* Isaac shifted uncomfortably under his gaze. Gavin swallowed. "I... I know." *God, I'm such a fucking idiot.*

Sam looked up at Gavin. "Um..." They watched him carefully, almost like they were watching *him* for signs of fear. "Do you want a hug?"

A strangled noise came from Gavin's throat, and he flushed with embarrassment. He glanced at Isaac, who stared at Sam with love and amazement and pride written all over his face. Gavin returned his gaze to Sam. "Um... y-yeah. That would be nice."

Sam carefully wrapped their arms around Gavin, pressing their cheek into the space between Gavin's collarbones. Gavin's heart pounded in his chest, anxious disbelief coursing through his blood. But underneath was *comfort*. He'd barely been touched since he'd run, and now Sam was pressed against his chest, their arms squeezing around his waist. Gavin's mind reeled at the idea that someone would touch him like this, make him feel so seen and held and *understood*... and that that person would be *Sam. Sam,* whom he'd beaten and cut and waterboarded, fucked with their mind until they were ready to kill Isaac. Sam, *Sam* was willing to be this kind to him.

His skin ached with the touch, and he just wanted more. He wanted more kindness. He wanted to be held and touched, casually, like he was family. *With them, maybe I can have that. With this family, maybe I can have touch that doesn't mean anything. Maybe I can have something that doesn't carry a threat, or a manipulation. Maybe I can have something good.*

He blinked, and realized he stood frozen, Sam still hugging him but looking up at him with concern in their dark eyes. Tears pricked Gavin's eyes and he wrapped his arms around them, too, squeezing his eyes shut, burying his face in their curls. Two tears ran down his cheeks.

"Okay, fine," Ellis murmured behind him.

Gavin lifted his head and let Sam go, turning slightly to look at Ellis. They stared at him with distrust twisting their mouth, but something softened in their eyes.

Ellis rolled their eyes up to the ceiling. "Fucking *fine*. Okay. Whatever. He's part of the family."

He couldn't help it, he couldn't fucking *help* it, but his gaze flicked to Isaac. A smile drifted across Isaac's face as he met Gavin's eyes for a moment, and then looked away. Out of the corner of his eye, Gavin saw Gray smile, too.